SCARLET MOON

SCARLET MOON

CHILDREN OF THE BLOOD MOON

———

BOOK ONE

S.D. GRIMM

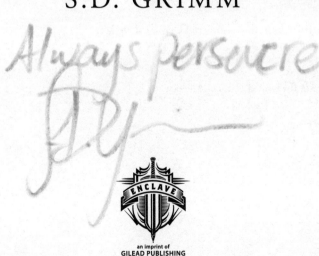

ENCLAVE

an imprint of
GILEAD PUBLISHING

Scarlet Moon by S.D. Grimm
Published by Enclave, an imprint of Gilead Publishing, Wheaton, IL 60187
www.enclavepublishing.com

ISBN: 978-1-68370-050-0 (print)
ISBN: 978-1-68370-051-7 (eBook)

Scarlet Moon
Copyright © 2016 by S.D. Grimm

Cover design by Kirk DouPonce of Dogearred Design
Interior design/typesetting by Beth Shagene
Edited by Ramona Richards

Printed in the United States of America

This book is dedicated to

My dad, N.O.F.,
who encouraged me to be a writer
because I wanted to be one.

And my mom,
who quite possibly loves each of my characters
as much as I do.

I love you both.

CHAPTER 1

SHADOWS OF MEN

Jayden tightened her grip on the dagger's hilt and focused on the apple instead of Geoffrey's head. Her sweat slicked the weapon's handle. Sunshine spilled through the tree branches and caused leaves to cast moving shadows on her target, which only played tricks on her eyes. The tattered edge of Geoffrey's tunic fluttered in the summer breeze, breaking her concentration. This was madness. What if she missed? The dagger tip quivered as a shiver raced through her body.

She swallowed, her throat dry. "I don't think I can do this."

"Concentrate, Jae. It's all muscle memory." Daniel's voice was steady, calming.

Fear still gripped her. Made her freeze. The only way she knew to overcome the fear was to let another emotion take over. She focused on one of her many Blood Moon talents: the ability to feel other people's emotions. Daniel was near enough that she could sense his feelings, so she made eye contact with him, and, like an open window ushers in a breeze, her brother's emotions swept over her, knocked on the door of her being, and begged to be let in.

She searched his most prominent feelings. As always, Daniel exuded confidence. Jayden reached with her talent for that feeling and latched on. Confidence seeped into her like rainfall on thirsty ground. Became hers.

Filled with her brother's calm strength, she turned her attention back to the apple on Geoffrey's head. Her muscles relaxed. The heavy weight on her chest lifted. She could breathe.

"Atta girl." Daniel's praise warmed her.

The confidence in her swelled, mirroring Daniel's. With renewed determination, she gripped the dagger's hilt. Aimed. Her gaze slipped, and she looked right into Geoffrey's eyes. His permanent smile never wavered even as he faced her, tied to the trunk of a slim apple tree to keep him from falling over or moving. Somehow he managed to keep the fruit on his head. Her heart pounded. Everything started to spin. Blood. She saw blood. Felt it between her fingers. She squeezed her eyes shut. It wasn't real.

"Jayden, stay with me. You have to get over this." Daniel's calm voice cut through the fear.

She clung to his emotions. He didn't know what she'd seen behind the smithy with their father, and she didn't want him to find out.

He leaned closer and whispered, "Come on. I've got two silver coins riding on this shot."

What? She tore her gaze from Geoffrey and the fear vanished. She glanced left where her other three brothers leaned against trees in the cool shade. "Who bet against me?"

Kyle rolled the piece of straw he was chewing to the corner of his mouth. "I did. You choke every time you have to throw a knife at something with . . . eyes." He motioned to Geoffrey. "It's a scarecrow, Jae. And you're hesitating like we're asking you to kill the neighbor's cat."

Luc and Nic chuckled. Their emotions flooded her and made her want to laugh, too. She turned off her talent so she wouldn't be burdened with more than she could handle. Like a candle being snuffed, their feelings left her.

Kyle pushed off the tree and walked toward the scarecrow. "You're too much of a healer to harm anything. Living or *otherwise*." He patted the scarecrow's shoulder. Then his expression grew serious. "But we won't always be there to protect you."

"He's right." Nic sheathed the knife he'd been sharpening. "In two weeks it'll just be you and Ryan. It's crazy really—you can some-how stick that knife into an apple core as it spins through the air, but asking you to take out a rabbit—"

"Enough." Daniel's strong voice quieted Nic. He gripped Jayden's shoulders and turned her back toward the tree and Geoffrey. "If it's a wolf after your sheep or a fox after your chickens, it won't stop until you take care of it. And with Ryan working at the smithy all day, well, Kyle's right—you've got learn to kill something. Something with eyes."

They were right. And lately the wolves had been braver.

"So . . ." Kyle plucked the apple off of Geoffrey's head, took a bite, and placed it back. "Prove me wrong. Hit the mark."

"You can do this, Jayden. Remember, the dagger is an extension of your hand." Daniel's smooth voice willed her to concentrate.

Focus.

Feel the weight of the dagger.

Let it become a part of her.

Geoffrey's eyes, two black circles, stared back at her. He wasn't alive, yet the thought of throwing a knife at him brought the fear. Why? It couldn't be his fear that flooded her—he wasn't real. It didn't make sense. She sighed. If only a storm were coming. Sensing one always calmed her.

"You won't miss if you just concentrate." Daniel squeezed her shoulder.

Kyle stuck out his hand and shot Jayden a devious grin. "You might as well pay up, Daniel. She doesn't have the guts."

Heat flared in her chest and she glared at Kyle. "No guts?"

His smile showed off his white teeth. "That's right. You're a—"

"Don't say it."

"—chicken. A gutless chicken."

She gripped the weapon tighter. Kyle certainly knew how to fan her temper. No guts? She had plenty of guts. "And I suppose every-one has forgotten who beat you in the sparring match every morning this week? Or who bested the champion swordsman yesterday? He was twice my size, and *I* delivered the fatal blow."

Nic's eyebrows shot up. "False fatal blow. It was a sporting match, Jayden."

"Yes." Daniel steered her to face Geoffrey. "Pretend this is a sparring match, sister. You know we Jorah boys and our sister, Hidden Dagger, never lose." He patted her shoulder. "This time, it's all up to you, and there's a lot of money at stake."

Sparring match. Her emotions never got in the way while she was sparring because she never meant real harm. The only time fear suffocated her was while hunting. And now with poor Geoff. She stared at the scarecrow and his stupid smile.

"If Geoffrey was alive, he'd be laughing at you." Kyle's voice taunted.

He was right. Jayden gripped her dagger tighter and glanced over her shoulder at Daniel's encouraging expression. Then she opened her talent. Confidence welled up inside Daniel and poured into her. Banished the fear. A smile tugged the corner of Jayden's mouth as she faced the lifeless scarecrow. Kyle had bet wrong.

She let the dagger fly. It sailed toward the tree, end over end, and pierced the apple's center. Then she reached up her sleeve and pulled out one of her knives. The worn handle felt familiar in her hands. She stepped forward two paces. Her eyes locked with Geoffrey's and then she let the knife fly. The scarecrow's head snapped back as the blade nailed him to the trunk. The handle quivered between its eyes.

Cheers struck up around her and her brothers' hands slapped her back. Jayden's heart beat fast. Had she really done that?

Kyle nudged her arm. "Now it's Geoffrey who has no guts. You burst his head open."

Hay spilled out from the hole her knife had made. It turned red. Blood oozed down the scarecrow's face. Gushed between her fingers, hot and sticky. She'd hurt him. Another person. Fear flooded her. No. She squeezed her eyes shut. This wasn't real. He *wasn't* alive.

Daniel patted her shoulder, and Nic and Luc appeared in front of her, clapping. She thought they were clapping, but their hands blurred. All of her brothers' voices slurred. She sank to her knees. Why was she so dizzy?

She was six again behind the smithy with her father. He'd just treated a sick horse and they were headed home.

A smile formed on his mouth. "You did wonderful today, calming that horse. I don't know anyone who can calm injured animals like you can."

As quickly as it had sprouted, her father's smile melted, and he pushed her behind him. He took three steps forward, blocking her view. She looked around his tall form and saw two young men. One lay on the ground, and the other held a knife. Blood dripped off its blade and fell onto the dirt.

The drip always echoed in her memory, like a heavy raindrop pelting dry soil.

Her father yelled something, and the young man dropped his knife and bolted. Then Jayden's father rushed to the young man on the ground. His side was sliced open, blood gushed from the deep wound.

Jayden pressed her hands to her mouth. Her stomach roiled.

Her father's face blocked her view. "I have to try and help him, Jayden. Can you be strong?"

She nodded.

Her father knelt next to the fallen man. "Jayden, come here."

She rushed to her father's side and looked into the man's eyes. They were wide, the whites around them clearly visible, like a frightened horse's.

Her father's hands engulfed hers. "Jayden, look at me."

She met his gaze, choked back tears, and opened her talent. Her father's emotions filled her. Calm. Peace. Confidence. These she grasped on to. They made her tears subside.

Her father's eyebrows pulled together, as if he was about to ask her a hard question. "He needs your help. Can you do this?"

She knelt near the injured man. "Yes."

"That's my girl. Now, press here. Hard as you can." He placed her hands on the wound. The man cried out. Jayden pulled back, but her father's hands, on top of hers, showed her what she needed to do, kept her steady. "You can do this."

She bit her lip and pushed. Warm liquid gushed through her fingers. Stained them red. So much red. Her stomach lurched. Fear started to push away the confidence she tried to hang on to—the injured man's fear. Jayden breathed in. Her father was talking to the young man, but she tuned it out. Instead, she stared at her father's calm features and embraced his emotions just like she did when she helped him tend an injured animal. She let her father's emotions fill her while she willed the young man to calm down. Beneath her hands, the young man relaxed.

Jayden's father pulled out his supplies, and then he cleaned the area and stitched the wound. At last, he moved her hands. "Thank you, Jayden. You did beautifully."

A sudden lightness flooded her. It matched her father's relief. She knelt back with her legs folded beneath her and noticed the blood-stained knife lying on the ground a few paces away. Dark liquid on the blade glistened in the setting sun's orange light. She picked it up.

Her ears tingled. That was a strange sensation. Then fear jolted her heart and leaked into her very being. She looked up. The man stared at her, terror clutching his heart, squeezing hers along with it. She realized her talent was latching onto his emotions and she turned it off. Still the man stared at the knife with his eyes wide. The skin behind her ears tingled again, and fear blossomed in her heart. It wasn't *her* fear—it was *his*. How was that possible?

The tingling sensation behind her ears intensified, and her talent began to open like a thief trying to pry open a locked door. No. She squeezed her eyes shut and pushed against the unwanted fear. She was losing control. Her heart thudded and her palms broke out in sweat. Everything in her willed the door of her talent to remain closed, but it opened, almost like the door handle slipped through her fingers. The man's fear burst into her, made her want to scream. How had someone else controlled her talent?

"Jayden! No!" Her father stole the weapon from her grasp, wrapped it in a cloth, and put it behind his bag. "Those are dangerous."

Her talent turned off like a door slamming shut. Her ears stopped tingling. She sat on the ground, dazed, while the blacksmith helped her father load the young man into the back of the wagon to take him to the town physician. Then her father returned to her.

While he washed off her hands with one of his clean cloths, his kind eyes searched her face. "You were brave today, daughter."

A smile warmed her for the first time since the man's fear had chilled her. "Thank you."

"You will make a fine wise woman." His eyes crinkled in the corners. "Many people would not be able to do what you did today."

She nodded. Tending a wounded human had been a little different than tending an injured animal, but she'd been able to calm him too. Until the knife.

A shudder rocked her body. "Why would someone hurt him, Father?"

He nodded toward the reddened cloth that held the knife inside. "Robbers. They carry weapons like that. They hurt people because of their greed. Blades can do more than harm, though. They can kill. You'll understand that after today, won't you?"

Yes. She understood. The blade had evoked fear in that man. He thought she was going to hurt him, and that was how afraid it had made him. She'd never hurt so much as a grasshopper.

Her father sighed and his shoulders sagged. "I'm sorry you had to witness that."

She touched his hand. "I'm not. I'm going to become a wise woman someday and tend to the sick."

A smile tugged her father's lips. But he stared at his empty hands. The blade had obviously scared him too. Why? Were they so powerful? Jayden straightened her back. Blades would not cripple her with fear. And she'd learn to defend herself if anyone ever came after her with one.

"You okay, Jayden?" Luc's voice brought her out of her memory.

She put on a smile and nodded. Sure, she could defend herself unless she meant to do harm. Then fear flooded her and she lost control of her talent. The only reason any of her hunts had been successful was because she'd channeled the calm emotions from her father or Daniel. What would happen when they weren't there?

Could Ryan's emotions steady her? Not if he wasn't there. Her brothers were right. She'd have to get over this—before the wedding. With the betrothal ceremony in two days, and the following twelve dedicated to every pre-wedding custom under the sun, that didn't leave much time.

"I want to try again."

Daniel squeezed her shoulder. "You did great, okay? We'll try again tomorrow. Right now we'd better head back before Mother and Father get home from town. I'll go ahead and hide our weapons." Daniel walked over to the tree, pulled Jayden's knife from Geoffrey's head and dagger from the apple, and cut the scarecrow's bindings. "Kyle, you might want stitch him up and get him back in the field."

"Why me?"

Nic gently smacked Kyle's arm. "Because you're the one that made her mad enough to kill him."

Jayden sighed as she sank to the ground with an apple tree at her back. The weight in her pocket tapped her leg, took her thoughts from one worry to another. She reached in and pulled out the small object that reminded her how her life was about to change.

The smooth stone, black and red like a smoldering ember, rested in her palm. She traced the surface with her finger, searching for rough spots—anything that could catch on Ryan's clothes or scrape his skin. Hard to believe he'd wear this stone close to his heart in just two days. Jayden breathed deep as jitters scurried through her chest—again.

Was she really ready for this? To leave her family?

Kyle joined her with his back against the same tree. He took another bite out of the apple she'd skewered. How he could eat the under-ripe, misshapen fruit she had no idea. But it wasn't like the apples would likely be any better this year. Better get used to it. All the crops seemed to be suffering from drought or pests. She'd even overheard Norm Grotter say he'd spotted a black leather vine choking the life out of a cherry tree with its poisonous sap. Then again, Norm knew how to tell a story. Why not embellish details with an extinct vine known for disappearing back into the ground after it killed a plant?

Kyle nodded toward the marriage stone in her hand. "Does it look different now than it did this morning?" His voice carried a teasing tone and he leaned closer. "Wait. I do see a spot that needs to be polished. Or is it sanded?"

She slipped the stone back into her pocket and smirked. "You might want to learn the difference. It'll be your turn in a year."

"Not necessarily. Daniel isn't married, and he's older than you." Kyle folded his arms behind his head like he had nothing to fear. Like no one was forcing him to leave his family too soon.

It was nothing against Ryan. He was her best friend, which was why her parents had picked him. And there was no denying that he was handsome with his storm cloud-gray eyes and wet-sand colored hair. He just . . . well, she wasn't ready to leave home. Her parents, her brothers—they were her home. And that was being taken from her.

Kyle cleared his throat, and Jayden shook free of her thoughts. Her brother stared at her through squinted eyes. "No snappy comeback? This marriage stuff must be getting to you."

"You could say that." She glanced at her lap and smoothed the green fabric of her riding dress.

"Here." Nic tossed the scarecrow at Kyle. Then he shot Kyle a funny look. "You two weren't having a brother-sister bonding moment, were you?"

Luc, who stood next to Nic with a book under his arm, chuckled. "Jayden was just explaining to Kyle that he was next in line to be married off."

"Really?" Nic's eyebrows shot up. "What makes you think I'm not better husband material? After all, Daniel is older than you and he's not married."

"That's because *Daniel* has been accepted to be a soldier. Kyle would never make the cut." Jayden shot her brother a smirk as she stood and dusted off her riding dress. She headed toward the house.

Kyle caught up with her, the others close behind. "Apparently overpolishing a marriage stone brings out her claws."

Nic laughed. "It's enough to drive anyone crazy, I'm sure. She's been fussing over that rock all week because *it's got to be perfect*." His voice held a high pitch, and he clasped his hands in front of him and batted his eyelashes.

Jayden rolled her eyes. "I don't talk like that."

Luc chuckled, but didn't look up from his open book. "I thought that *was* you."

Jayden breathed in, surprised at the tightening in her chest. She would miss them so much. Even their teasing. Especially their teasing.

They reached the edge of the farm in time to see Mother and Father at the barn unhitching the horses from the wagon. Jayden stroked the smaller of the two cart horses, Aureolin—the palomino—and the horse nudged her. Daniel exited the house and Jayden breathed a sigh. That meant he'd already hidden the weapons. Father didn't even know they owned weapons.

Jayden's mother saw them coming up the path from the orchard. Her green eyes brightened as she smiled. "You kids go get ready for supper. I trust you put the pot of stew on?"

"Yes." Jayden hugged her mother and breathed in the aroma of fresh bread along with her usual scent of jasmine. They'd lingered at the baker's no doubt. The baker's daughter loved to gossip. She'd cornered Jayden just last week, talking about some terrible destruction in Salea.

"Good." Her mother squeezed back. Her eyes sparkled. "Now get washed up. You're all filthy."

As they entered the house, the scent of chicken stew with dumplings welcomed them. Jayden walked into the main room and checked on the pot. The vegetables were a bit thin and probably bitter, but the seasonings would help. When she turned around, she noticed all four of her brothers clustered behind her.

She eyed each of their stoic faces. "What's going on?"

Daniel was leaning against the archway that separated the main room from the kitchen. His lips sprouted into a half-smile as he pushed himself off the doorframe and strode into the room. He stopped in front of her.

"Here." He held out a black leather cord in the palm of his hand. The intricate braid made it look like a rope of reptile skin. "I know you wanted Ryan to have this one for the marriage stone."

Jayden stared at the gift. Her mouth dropped open and tears stung her eyes. She blinked them back, unwilling to cry in front of her brothers. "It was so expensive! How did you—"

"It's from all of us." Kyle was the first one to hug her. "It won't be the same around here without you."

Luc embraced her next. "She'll be right down the road."

Nic's arms wrapped around her. "That's why she's crying."

She shoved him lightly, but there was no denying the tears now.

"You're welcome." Daniel put the cord in her hands and pulled her close.

Maybe she could persuade her parents to let her wait a year.

Daniel's arms tightened around her and his body stiffened. Something was wrong.

"What is it?" Jayden wiggled out of his tight grip and followed his gaze to the window.

Her question died in the air as she saw what headed up the walkway.

A long line of torches snaked up the winding path toward their house. There must have been two dozen at least. They bobbed in the air, as if disembodied hands held them. As the torches filtered up the curved path, Jayden saw the truth. People, nearly invisible except when the firelight backlit them, carried the torches.

Invisible people? That only meant one thing: the Feravolk and their magical cloaks.

Jayden sucked in a breath. What did they want?

The person in front lowered his hood and his face came into clear view. Jayden struggled to see the outline of his body beneath the camouflage, but she could just make it out.

"Get in the kitchen." Their mother's harsh whisper cut through the silence as she weaved her way around her children.

Jayden hadn't even noticed her mother had come in.

Strong fingers curled around her arm and Daniel pushed her farther into the house.

A knock echoed into the room.

Jayden's mother rushed to the door. "Who's there?"

"Open up in the name of the Feravolk." The voice on the other side boomed.

Her mother turned toward her children, her eyes wide. "Luc, your father's still in the barn. Go out back and get him."

"Mother—"

"*Go.*"

Luc dropped his shoulders and headed out the back. Jayden's remaining brothers clustered in front of her so she could no longer see the front door.

A loud crack filled the room and the door rattled. The pounding continued.

"What do you want?" her mother shouted.

For a moment, the pounding stopped. "Your neighbors tell me you have a Child of the Blood Moon." The harsh voice leaked through the door.

Jayden's heart stalled. Who would betray them like that? And why did the Feravolk want the Children?

Daniel glanced over his shoulder, and his worried eyes met hers. "Maybe you should run."

She gripped his shirtsleeve. "No."

His sleeve slipped through her fingers as he raced forward to help his mother brace the door.

Kyle swallowed. "Run, Jae!"

She opened her talent and her brother's emotions swirled into her. Fear. Sorrow. Regret. Love. The strongest was love. "Kyle, you can't—"

Nic gripped her arm. "The barn is burning!"

Jayden turned. Luc had left the back door open. Flames shot out from the top of the barn and lit the night sky. Ice trickled through her veins.

"Jayden." Her mother's hand touched her cheek and pulled her out of her panic. She handed Jayden a packed satchel. "I need you to run."

Jayden's eyes trailed from the burden in her hands to her mother's face. "What is this? What's going on?"

Another sharp crack echoed through the house and the door splintered. Daniel stood in front of everyone, his sword in hand. He must have opened the secret board in their floor and pulled out the swords because all of her brothers were armed now.

Daniel glanced over his shoulder. "Run, Jayden. Please."

No! This was madness. This was why she'd learned to fight. She dropped the satchel and pulled up the floorboard. Her knives were nestled in the secret cubby. She pulled two out and strapped them to her arms.

The door clattered against the floor. Shadows of men poured over the threshold. Jayden's throat tightened. She pulled out her knives. Her mother stood next to Daniel, holding daggers behind her back. Daggers? Where did she get those?

The Feravolk all unsheathed swords. "Hand over your Child and we won't harm you."

"Give me the code," her mother said.

Code? Jayden's heart jumped.

The cloaked man sneered. "It seems I've found the right house." His eyes scanned the room and locked on Jayden. "It's you, isn't it?"

A shiver raced through her body. How did he know? Her birthmark was covered.

His lips spread into a wicked smile. "Give yourself up and we won't harm your family."

Jayden lowered her weapons. "Do you promise?"

"No!" Her mother brought the daggers out from behind her back and lurched toward the man.

The blade cut into the man's side under his torch-bearing arm. Blood stained his clothes. The torch dropped and the rug caught fire. Sword ready, the man lunged at her. Daniel's blade blocked the man's blow.

This couldn't be happening. Jayden glared at the man who attacked her mother and clutched the knife hilt. The skin behind her ears prickled. No. She couldn't lose control now.

Too late. His foremost emotion slammed into her, but it wasn't fear. It was anger. It burned in Jayden's heart. She gasped and focused on Daniel instead. His confidence wavered, but he was trying hard to hang on to it. There was no time to think. Jayden embraced her brother's ability to remain calm and focused on her enemy. He would not hurt her family. She whipped her hand back then forward. Her knife cut through the air and sunk into the Feravolk man's side. He fell to his knees.

"Run, sister!" Kyle smacked the satchel against Jayden's chest, then he raced forward to join the fray.

There were at least twenty Feravolk. Her family needed her help. If she gave herself up, would the Feravolk stop the fighting?

Kyle's scream resounded off the walls. Jayden's knees weakened as she watched a bloodied sword protrude from her brother's back. He slid off the blade and fell to the ground.

"No!" Jayden raced toward him only to slam into something hard.

Jayden's mother's face filled her view. She pushed Jayden toward the back door. "Get a horse and run! Run, Jayden! *You* have to survive."

Go alone? Where? And how? How was she supposed to survive without them?

A blade slashed open Nic's throat. He spun and crumpled to the ground.

No! Jayden's senses returned to her and she screamed. Hot tears filled her eyes. She fought to reach her brothers. How did her mother get so strong? Jayden got one more pleading look into her mother's eyes before the door slammed in front of her. Tears streamed down her face while she pounded her fists against the door and begged her mother to open it.

Daniel cried out and her mother's sobs rang in her ears, then silence. Jayden sank to the ground and leaned against the door. Why didn't they let her help?

"Find the girl!" A gruff voice she recognized as one of the Feravolk spoke.

They were coming for her. Heart pounding, Jayden cleared her eyes. She turned around. Flames ate at the barn. Horses were scattered out in the meadow. No sign of her brother or father.

Soft steps sounded against the soil. Jayden gripped her knife and turned. Aureolin, the horse she loved, nuzzled her. Who had bridled her? Stashing her weapon away, Jayden grabbed the reins, then mounted the horse and steered her toward the barn.

A tremor rocked through the ground and Aureolin stumbled. Jayden urged the horse forward, but she reared up, and Jayden gripped tight so she wouldn't fall off.

Aureolin's hooves thudded against the earth. Jayden regained her balance. "What's wrong, girl?" She scanned the way ahead to the barn. It was clear. What had Aureolin so spooked? Jayden urged her forward again, but Aureolin wouldn't move. Jayden opened her talent. Fear coursed through the horse. "It's okay." She tried to calm Aureolin, but her own hands shook.

Jayden glanced over her shoulder. The Feravolk rounded the side of the house. Her heart sped. They couldn't catch her. She wouldn't let them. They were on foot. With Aureolin she had a chance to get away. But she wouldn't go without Luc and Father. She rocked forward and squeezed her legs to get Aureolin moving, but the horse danced sideways. What was her problem?

The ground quaked. Sparks flooded the night sky as the barn collapsed.

CHAPTER 2

STONE WOLF

Two weeks earlier

Ethan slammed his opponent's arm against the wooden tabletop, and the eight men gathered around the table burst into cheers and groans. Gold and silver coins clattered across the wood. Some landed in drops of ale that had sloshed over drunk men's mugs or had spilled down their beards.

While bickering consumed the other eight men, Ethan swept his hand across the smooth pine and scooped up his winnings. Mostly gold coins tonight. He left one on the table for the serving girl. The rest clinked in his drawstring pouch. Breath tinged with alcohol warmed the side of his face.

"You don't look that strong, kid." A callused hand clapped Ethan's shoulder and squeezed just hard enough to be uncomfortable.

The man's nostrils flared, and Ethan figured he'd overstayed his welcome. That was a shame, since the tavern was just starting to get crowded.

The scent of lamb stew wafted out from the kitchen, and he hadn't eaten yet. Not that lamb made his mouth water. One of the tavern owner's daughters tilted her candle and lit the chandeliers. *Must be dusk.*

Ethan shot the man his best smile and shrugged.

The man glowered and a snarl showed off broken teeth. "I want a chance to win my gold back."

Ethan beckoned the man closer and motioned toward a man across the table whose nose looked to have been broken several times. "He's not as strong as he looks."

Hoping for a quick exit, Ethan scooted his chair back, but it shrieked against the wooden floor.

The guy with broken teeth slammed a meaty fist on the table in front of Ethan. "You're not going anywhere yet."

Every gaze at the table fell on Ethan. Message received. Chest heaving, he gripped the sides of his chair and scanned for an escape. A barmaid approached and stole the attention of every burly man at the table. How she could stand their groping eyes, he had no idea, but she gave him the chance he needed.

Ethan slid off his chair and headed toward the Blind Pig's back exit. With one last look over his shoulder, he placed his hand on the wooden door and pushed.

"Let me go, please." A panicked female voice cut through all the other tavern noise.

Ethan turned toward the plea.

A young barmaid tried to retract her trapped arm, but the man wouldn't let go. "Aw, c'mon, missy. Just one little peck."

Dirty pig. Ethan let the door shut, balled his hands into fists, and glanced at the table he'd just left. The beefy ringleader pointed to Ethan's empty chair and scanned the room.

Great. His presence was already missed. If he didn't get out now—

"Just let me go." The barmaid strained to free her arm.

Enough. This girl needed help. In four strides Ethan stood next to her. He glared at the red-faced man who held her shirtsleeve. "She told you to let go."

"Oh, so what are you? Her knight? I'm just asking the lady a question."

Ethan grabbed the man's wrist and squeezed. Red's eyes widened as his hand turned dark pink, then purple. He dropped the woman's arm. Ethan kept hold of Red's wrist while he leaned in. "And she gave you an answer."

A soft hand touched Ethan's shoulder. "Looks like you've attracted some attention."

Great. Ethan eyed the barmaid. "Really big guy with a temper?"

She nodded, and her lips curved deviously. "Allow me to return the favor?"

Her tray flew at the table. Dishes of steaming soup clattered all over the table. Chairs slid backward and toppled over as Red and his friends jumped from their seats to avoid a scalding.

Ethan shot her a smile. "Thanks."

Amid the ruckus, he darted through the crowd and headed once more toward the back door. A quick glance over his shoulder told him no one had spotted him. He pushed the door open. Cool evening air met him. The din muffled as the door swung shut. He shook his head and chuckled as he descended the steps. His coin bag jingled as it slapped against his thigh. A good night for winnings.

"Going somewhere with my gold?"

Ethan halted. A familiar heat fanned across his chest—his Blood Moon talent warning him that someone meant to do him harm—but he didn't need the warning. That voice was memorable enough. He never should have challenged a man with that kind of temper in a strength match.

Drunk or not, muscular men tended to overestimate their prowess, but at half the man's thickness Ethan should have lost. This guy's pride was oozing blood, and Ethan was the blade in his side. Already gawkers had stopped to watch the show outside of the Blind Pig tavern. Ethan pivoted to face his opponent and his lungs deflated.

Six men—every one of them ox-huge and flexing massive muscles. Great.

He squared his shoulders and let his arms fall to his sides. His right hand twitched ever so slightly, itching to grab at his sword. The sword that wasn't there.

He bent his knees and held up his hands, ready to strike.

The shortest man had to be a head taller than Ethan, and this not-so-shorty snorted like an ox too. "He thinks he can take us."

Six rumbles of laughter filled the air.

Broken Teeth pounded a finger in Ethan's chest. "We don't like to be cheated."

With his hands out in front of him, Ethan backed away from the angry pack closer to the alley through which he planned to escape. "I won the money fairly."

"Fairly? Where's your birthmark, boy?"

"You think I'm a Child?"

The man ground his fist into his palm. "I know it."

Another of the six advanced. "He's stalling because his strength won't help him here."

It wouldn't. Not against six at once. But he had other Blood Moon talents to help with that—speed for one, and his ability to perceive when someone threatened him. Warmth spread across his chest again—as if he needed the reminder. He filled his lungs and summoned his speed.

All six advanced toward him. He spun away from Shorty and planted his heel in Broken Teeth's gut, but someone else's arm wrapped around his neck. They weren't going to make this easy. He sunk his teeth into that man's bicep and stomped on his foot.

The man howled and let him go. Ethan whirled toward him and punched him. Hot blood sprayed over Ethan's fist, and the man backed away with his hands over his bleeding nose.

Four beefy hands grabbed Ethan's shoulders and threw him backward. Dust clouded around him as he landed on the gravel. Grit crunched between his teeth. Now they were just making him mad.

It was his money. So what if he used his talent of strength to get it? He hadn't lied or anything. They never asked, so why tell? He lashed his leg out and kicked the closest attacker, who thudded to the dirt next to him.

Hands dragged Ethan to his feet. He dug his heels into the ground and almost had one arm free when Bloody Nose showed up in front of him.

One more twist. He got an arm free and blocked Bloody Nose's blow with his forearm.

Someone yanked him off balance and he crashed into his captor's sweaty, smelly chest. Strong hands locked around his ankles and wrists. They lifted, swung him toward the sky, and let go. Ethan curled into a tight ball to brace himself for the landing.

Cold water enveloped him. He surfaced, sputtered, and grabbed the sides of the trough in which he sat.

Broken Teeth leaned over him. "Thirsty?"

Ethan swore. Bubbles danced before his eyes as he fought to remain calm. They let him up just in time. He gasped for air. Heavy hands pressed his head and shoulders under the water again. He was losing his fight.

C'mon, Ethan. You're stronger than this. Faster.

He shot his feet into the edge of the trough, braced himself with his legs, and leaned his back against the rear of the trough until his head resurfaced.

The men pushed. He strained. A steady *clap, clap, clap* interrupted the sound of sloshing water.

"Well done, gentlemen. Now, how would he fare one on one?"

A woman?

One of the ox-men tightened his grip on Ethan's arm. "He stole—"

"Save it." Her voice drew closer.

Broken Teeth ripped the collar of Ethan's shirt open and revealed a raised patch of pink skin that resembled the moon in all its glorious detail.

"He's got the birthmark. He cheated." Broken Teeth flexed a muscle as if that was enough proof that Ethan could never have beaten him. He pointed a finger in Ethan's face. "You don't arm wrestle for money if you're gifted with great strength."

"Why not?"

The woman came into view, but she wore a black leather mask. Her wavy, blonde hair was pulled into a long ponytail, and she wore a leather jerkin and slacks with leather padding over her thighs. Two daggers hung from a belt strapped around her waist.

She crossed her arms. "I bear the birthmark too. Not all of us are *blessed* with gifts."

One of the men laughed. "Where's your birthmark, lady?"

The woman tilted her head. "Wouldn't it be nice if we could all hide our marks with a shirt?"

Broken Teeth chuckled and released Ethan's collar. "So, what do you wish? To fight with the thief because you two share a birthday? Will you better his odds?"

"No." She turned to Ethan and stared at him with dark blue eyes. "I wish a turn to fight him for money. First to draw blood wins."

Ethan hefted himself out of the trough and landed with a squelch on the wet ground. "I don't fight women."

"They call me Swallow."

"I don't care."

"I want to fight the famous Stone Wolf."

A hushed murmur swept through the gathered crowd. Ethan's shoulders drooped. He'd wanted to keep that a secret today. There were at least ten faces he knew, and that was easily a quarter of the crowd. Now he'd have to find a new place to arm wrestle if he needed more money in a pinch. Perhaps he should have traveled farther from home. Or not messed with ox-huge men.

There was always denial. Ethan crossed his arms, squishing water from his clothes. "I'm not him."

"Yes, he is. I recognize him from the picture at the Winking Fox," a girl said from the crowd. Within moments the whole dusty street buzzed with energy.

The six laughed. Bloody Nose slapped his leg. "Stone Wolf rescued by a woman."

"Give me a sword, and we'll see how you laugh then." Ethan leaned toward them. They shrank back. Ah, the power of a name.

Swallow stepped closer to him. "What do you say, Stone Wolf? I hear you never turn down a fight."

"I have no sword."

A weapon thumped on the ground at his feet. Ethan looked up to see Max, the smithy, give him a wink. Whose sword had Max been delivering?

Max rubbed his hands together. "It's worth more if Stone Wolf uses it."

Swallow's eyes practically sparkled. Ethan shook his head. He wanted out of this. "Hand-to-hand combat. No weapons. Pin me to the ground for five seconds and you win. Unless I pin you for ten first."

"No weapons?" Swallow dropped her daggers. "I like this. Something new. Now, if I win, you give me the gold you took from these men."

"And if I win?"

"You keep your gold."

"If I walk away, I keep my gold."

"True. Then what would you ask of me?"

"You remove your mask."

Her eyes widened, but she nodded once. "Done."

A wave of murmurs swelled through the crowd.

Ethan bent his knees. "Your move."

Swallow kicked at him, harder than Ethan expected. Ethan blocked her hits, but wouldn't strike her.

"Fight back," she said.

He swung at her, and she blocked his blow with substantial strength. Good. A surge of pride swept through him that she should be so talented. Why? What sort of kinship did he feel from a woman who wanted to fight him?

She kicked his ribs. He stymied her punch and curled his fingers around her wrist, then spun around her. He twisted her arm behind her back and pushed her to the ground.

Something popped. She grunted. He'd snapped her shoulder out of place.

Ethan loosened his grip. How could he have been so careless?

She wrenched her arm free and pushed up. Ethan fell to the side and she rolled atop him. Swallow sat on his chest and pinned his biceps to the ground.

He scanned her arm up and down while the crowd counted. She

seemed unharmed, but he had felt something pop—he'd twisted too hard. Why wasn't she in agony?

Groans and cheers split the crowd. Money exchanged hands. Swallow released him and stood, her hand extended down to help him up.

He took it and slid his hand up her arm. "I hurt you. I didn't mean to."

"Too much of a gentleman. I'm not hurt." Swallow shook her head, and those same smile lines creased the corners of her eyes. She rolled her shoulders. "See? Fine."

"I thought I—"

"Is that why you lessened your grip? You wanted me to win, so you only blocked my blows? I'm no match for Stone Wolf."

He couldn't help but smile. "You're quite good."

"For a woman."

"For anyone."

From behind her mask, her blue eyes searched his face. "I'll take the compliment."

Ethan reached into his pocket, pulled out the soggy bag of gold, and dangled it between them by its string.

Swallow laughed. "Keep it. I didn't exactly earn it."

"What's your name?"

"I told you. Swallow."

"Your real name?"

"Perhaps we'll meet again." She winked at him, picked up her daggers, and whisked away.

Ethan watched her until the familiar flame of heat danced across his chest. Danger. The six were coming after him again? Men like them never quit. Ethan picked up the sword at his feet and faced them.

They wielded staffs and daggers. Bloody Nose had managed to get his meaty hands on an axe. Before they even started toward him, Ethan lunged at Broken Teeth and hacked his staff in two, then smacked the hilt of his sword against the Broken Teeth's head. The man fell to the ground unconscious.

Ethan leveled his gaze at the others. They all charged him at once. Ethan nicked Shorty's cheek and disarmed him in his moment of shock, then backed Bloody Nose into the wall of the tavern with his sword a hair away from piercing the man's stomach. "I could kill him now."

The other three stopped. "You *are* Stone Wolf."

Ethan nodded.

"Maybe next time you want to arm wrestle you'll ask your opponent if he *or she* has any special talents first." Swallow's wind-chime voice came from beside him.

Surprised, Ethan glanced at her. She leaned against the tavern as if she'd never left. Maybe she hadn't.

Ethan pulled his blade away from Bloody Nose's stomach. The man stumbled away, and his friends staggered after him. Cowards.

Ethan turned to Swallow. "You ever take off the mask?"

"Sure."

He leaned next to her and waited, but she didn't remove it. He cocked an eyebrow.

She giggled. "Not today."

A man ran toward the tavern, his face ashen and eyes wide.

Ethan pushed off the building and watched him.

The man stood in the road and cupped his hands around his mouth. "If you have Blood Moon Children, hide them. They're being hunted."

Townspeople around him stopped and stared. The man turned toward a woman who had bread under one arm and a child clinging to the other.

"Spread the word." He stepped near her, but she shrank away. "You know me, Penelope. I'm not crazy." He reached a shaky hand for her arm, but she steered her child away and quickened her pace.

"Penelope," he called. "Your son could be in danger."

If Penelope knew the guy, she wasn't letting on. Enough. Ethan dropped the borrowed sword and headed over to the stranger with Swallow on his heels. "Who's hunting them?"

The man turned. "Cloques."

"You mean Feravolk?"

The man's lip curled. "Call 'em what you like, they're hunting Children."

"That can't be right. Feravolk are peaceful, they—"

"Peaceful? You weren't around for the wars, boy. They burned Primo and they're in Balta now, headed this way."

Balta? Ethan sucked in a breath. If they found Tessa . . . Why couldn't he breathe? "What do they want with the Children?"

"I don't know."

Ethan clutched the man's elbow. "Listen, spreading rumors isn't—"

"It's no rumor. I've just come from Primo. I saw them dressed like shadows in their camouflage cloaks. Common people don't have magic like that. What more proof do you need?" The man's eyes widened. "Please. My son was born that day. I must go warn my family."

Ethan released him and looked at Swallow. Her face might be hidden, but her eyes had widened. He touched her arm and she jumped. "I'd get out of Salea if I were you."

He turned the other way and ran.

"Wait!" she called after him.

He fought the urge to stop.

"Stone Wolf, you're running the wrong way."

He slowed, and she caught up with him.

Her dark blue eyes met his. "You're headed to Balta."

"I know."

"You—" She stared at him for precious seconds. "Let me come with you."

"No." It came out harsher than he'd intended. "You don't need to get hurt on account of me."

"I wouldn't. It's my choice."

"You—you don't know me."

"You're right. I thought Stone Wolf was an orphan."

Ethan's breath hitched. "I am."

"Then you're far nobler than I thought."

"No. They're like family."

She touched his arm. Her hands were warm. "Then I'll come with you."

"I can hide my birthmark. You—they'll take off your mask." He stepped back and her fingers slid off his arm. It was too late—his talent had latched on to her. Why?

"I can't explain this, but I feel like I'm supposed to go with you." She shook her head. "You don't feel it, do you?"

Oh, he did. Accompanied by an overwhelming desire to protect her. That was his burden, or one of his talents. An unrelenting need to protect—well, typically family, loved ones. That was why he found it so strange that Swallow stoked his protective instinct to blazing. He didn't even know her, yet he wanted—no needed—to protect her.

That was how his talent worked. If she was in danger, he'd have no choice but to protect her, no matter the cost. If she came along, and he had more than one person to protect in Balta, it would stretch him too thin. That could get her killed, him killed, Tessa killed. He pinched the bridge of his nose.

Stronger than his urge to let her follow was his need to keep her safe. If he made Swallow get out of here now, he was protecting her. Still, he couldn't expect her to understand his dilemma. "Go home, Swallow."

"Please. I'll be more help where you're going."

"No. You'll be in the way."

Her eyelids fluttered and she stared at him, silent. She stepped away from him. "I think I understand." She nodded once before she turned and fled.

Ethan watched her disappear behind the bakery and hoped he'd done the right thing.

CHAPTER 3

RELUCTANT TRUST

Ethan's heart thudded as his heels dug into the gritty road. His legs pumped harder and he tried to ignore the persistent burn in his muscles. Balta lay ahead only a few miles, but already a thick stream of black smoke poured into the sky from Primo—Balta's twin—the other tiny town on the outskirts of Salea. For now, Balta lacked a matching dark cloud, but that didn't guarantee Tessa's safety.

People headed toward him, fleeing the towns.

Don't look at anyone.

The way his protective talent had latched onto Swallow scared him. He couldn't let it happen again. The problem was, he didn't know what had prompted it.

The people ahead neared him at an alarming speed. As Ethan carved his way through the masses, he smelled the odor of soot from their clothes. Most of them had to be from Primo. If they were from Balta, he could be too late.

He searched with his talent—nothing. He was too far away to tell if Tessa was in danger.

C'mon, Ethan! Run! He urged his burning legs forward. What good was a talent for speed if he was too late?

A man on the path stopped in front of him and held out his hands. Ethan slammed into him. The ground smacked against Ethan's back and knocked the air from his lungs.

The man helped him up. Ethan bent over to catch his breath.

"Sorry. I had to stop you. You're going the wrong way."

"Thank you, sir." Ethan tried to slip from the man's grasp, but the man wouldn't release his shirt. Ethan tugged again. "Sir—"

"You don't want to go that way. Trust me, Stone Wolf."

The burn pulsed across his chest like an unwelcome reminder: Danger, not for him this time but for Tessa. His stomach hardened. "I have to go."

"It's too dangerous. They took my son. He shares your birthmark."

This man knew him? No. He recognized Stone Wolf. "You're from Primo?"

"Balta. They've already destroyed Primo. You're not safe."

"I have . . . family in Balta."

Wind gusted between them, and the heavy stench of smoke stifled Ethan's breathing. He peered over his shoulder. Balta's west side burned. The Feravolk were there.

He pulled, but the man wouldn't loosen his grip. Ethan grasped the man's fist and stared into the stranger's kind eyes. "It's a risk I'll have to take."

The man released Ethan's shirt. "The Creator keep you safe."

"Thank you."

He drew closer to Balta. Screams sounded up ahead. Men in camouflaged cloaks secured the path. Feravolk.

Ethan headed east toward the trees. The Winking Fox Inn sat on the east side, close to the forest. The sun sank lower, vanishing beyond the horizon. He didn't slow until he reached the town's wall. With a running start, he leapt and clambered to the top.

He scrambled across the surface of the crumbling stone and hid in a crevice by the nearest obelisk. From his perch he had a clear view of the inn. The plaque with a picture of a winking fox swayed in the wind. The place appeared unharmed. The scent of smoke didn't ride on the wind here. Yet.

He checked his surroundings before he dropped to the ground. After he donned a calm exterior, he crossed over to the back door and dusted the loose gravel from his clothes.

A low growl rumbled behind him. His stomach twisted. He

turned around slowly. A wolfish, rust-colored dog approached him with his head low.

"Scout?" Ethan whispered.

The dog's posture loosened, and he whimpered as he wriggled close. Ethan patted his head. "Good boy. You stay here."

When Ethan opened the kitchen door, the faint scent of chicken soup greeted him, but he stepped into darkness. An empty kitchen at this hour? Dread carved a pit in his stomach. The threat he felt for Tessa remained distant. It hadn't occurred to him that she might not be here.

"Tess?"

Nothing.

"Martha?"

Still no answer. Ethan crept to the other side of the kitchen and opened the door to the dining hall. It was empty, too.

"Martha? Tess?"

His voice bounced off the walls. The faint throb of heat pulsed in his chest. Danger moved closer. He raced up the stairs. The creaking echoed louder with no typical tavern noise to swallow it. He needed his sword from his room—and his bow. He'd feel better armed.

Ethan pushed his key into the keyhole and twisted. The door pulled from his grip and flew open in front of him. Moonlight betrayed a flash of steel in the dark room.

Pulse racing, he jumped back.

"Ethan?" A portly woman stood in the doorway.

His lungs deflated. "Snare me, Martha."

"Watch your language, young man." She grabbed his wrist and pulled him into the room, then shut the door behind them. "You gave me quite a start."

He gave *her* a start? "Is that my sword?"

Martha winced and relinquished the weapon. "Tessa and I thought we'd be safer in here. And we hoped to intercept you if you came back before . . ."

"Mother just wanted to use your sword I think." Tessa stepped out of the shadows and threw her arms around him. She placed her chin on his shoulder. "You had me worried."

"You're the one in trouble. We have to get you out of here. Now."

Tessa stepped back. "How do you figure *I'm* the one in trouble? You have the birthmark too."

Ethan sighed. He couldn't tell her that he'd used his talent to gain that information. He attached his quiver to his belt and grabbed his bow, then rummaged through his drawer. He stuffed an extra shirt into a satchel.

"Get your things. We're getting out of here." He pulled a knife from beneath his pillow and tucked it in his satchel as well.

"Mother?" Tessa's voice was soft.

Ethan turned when Martha didn't respond to her daughter. Martha stood in place with her arms folded. A tear, visible in the moonlight, glistened on her cheek.

Ethan walked to her. "Martha?"

"I'll slow you two down."

"We're not leaving you," he and Tessa said together.

"They won't be looking for me."

Tessa turned to Ethan. "She's right."

Ethan threw his hands in the air. "What? How could—"

"They won't hurt me." Martha touched his arm. "And no one in town would mention that I have a daughter the right age."

"Martha, you don't know what people will do when it comes to saving their own children."

She put her other hand on Tessa's shoulder. "You two run. I'm doing this to keep you safe."

"Martha, I—"

"No, Ethan. I hoped you'd come back so I wouldn't have to take Tessa into the woods alone. I can take care of myself here. Go."

In the pit of Ethan's stomach, urgency fought with decency.

Martha stroked her daughter's hair. "You'll only have to stay away for a time."

Another tingle of heat spiked across Ethan's chest. He raced to the window and peered outside.

Torches approached. Men on horseback flooded the street out front. They knew a Child of the Blood Moon lived here. Someone had talked.

Ethan dug his fingernails into his palms. His talent's unrelenting need to keep her safe at all costs—even his own life—poured into him.

Tessa's hand touched his shoulder. He turned to her and braced himself against the window frame so she couldn't see out. "Do you trust me?"

"Of course, Ethan. You're like a brother."

"Good. Stay here." He turned to Martha. "You'll do as I say?"

She nodded.

"Come with me." He strode to the door, opened it and motioned for Martha to head out.

Tessa grabbed his arm before he could follow. "What are you doing?"

Looking her in the eye seemed impossible. "Keeping you safe."

"Ethan, if you put yourself in danger for me—"

His eyes met hers. "What? Only you can do that?"

"That was different."

"No. It wasn't."

For the second time that day, reluctance kept his shirt in someone else's fist.

"Tessa, let me do this."

Downstairs something heavy pounded against the door. "In the name of the Feravolk, open up."

Tessa's brown eyes widened. She rushed to the window and peered out, then turned back to Ethan, horror on her face. "Ethan, don't do this. We can get out."

"Just trust me. And stay quiet." He closed the door, and twisted the key, locking her inside. Then he pressed his room key into Martha's palm.

Her eyes grew wide. "What are you—"

"Whatever you do, don't admit to having a daughter."

"Ethan—"

A sharp knock interrupted her. "Give up your Child and no harm will come to you." The voice outside held a mocking tone. "Or don't. Either way, I'll get what I came for."

A heavy thump rattled the door.

Whatever they were using as a battering ram would work soon. Ethan's pulse throbbed in every vein.

Martha grabbed Ethan's arms so hard he stumbled. Her eyes pleaded. "You can't give yourself to them. They'll kill you."

Didn't he know it. "This is for Tessa."

"You owe her nothing. She helped you freely."

"I'm doing the same."

The ram jolted the door again. A hinge clattered to the floor.

Martha dropped her hold. "Go through the kitchen, it's—"

A loud crack interrupted her. Wood splintered.

"Get behind me." Ethan's fingers curled around his sword hilt.

He slid his sword from its sheath and held the blade in front of him. He breathed deep and focused on the comfortable pull of his talents. Strength and speed were his best allies now, and his throbbing desire to protect Tessa.

Another boom shook the inn. The door gave and crashed down. The scent of fire wafted in.

Boots crunched the broken wood as Feravolk walked in. Their cloaks changed from the dusky gray of the outside sky to the warm orange of the inn's wooden walls. It was a good thing they carried torches or Ethan might have missed some of them.

Then, it might have been better if he hadn't seen all of them. After the fifth man entered, they clearly outnumbered him. When the twelfth strode over the broken door, Ethan's sword was little more than decoration.

"Didn't you see the sign out front?" Martha's voice rang out strong behind him. "We're not open to scum."

The man in front lowered his hood, revealing a curved scar under his left eye. "I'll burn the sign, wench."

Ethan's blood boiled.

"You'll do no such thing. This is my property and I don't appreciate—"

With a gloved hand, Scarface pulled his cloak aside, showing off the sword on his belt. "Your neighbors pointed us in this direction. Do you believe it? People here are quite accommodating."

His smile made Ethan's stomach churn.

"My request is simple. Hand over your Child and I call off my torch bearers. Don't, and I'll burn down your beautiful property—sign included—and get what I came for anyway."

"I don't have a Child."

The man chuckled and stared at Martha. "Why do they all lie?"

Ethan could only imagine the stubborn innkeeper was glaring back. He shifted his weight, not lowering his weapon. There was no telling what these other Feravolk hid under their cloaks. As a breeze tickled their garments, he almost made out the outline of a weapon or two—maybe. It could just be that stupid camouflage playing tricks.

Still the glaring match continued.

Silence ate at Ethan's patience.

"You seem like a resourceful woman. Call off your watch hound," Scarface motioned toward Ethan, "and hand over your Child."

"I have no Child."

One of the men moved a torch dangerously close to the drapery.

Ethan sheathed his sword. "You'll spare my mother and her property if I give myself up?"

The torch stilled.

Scarface cocked his head and smiled. "Mother? I can't say that surprised me."

"Ethan, please." Martha's hand gripped his shoulder.

"Mother, if this man burns the inn, you'll starve."

Tears glistened in her eyes. "Why are you doing this?"

"I told you not to lie to me." Scarface's boots tapped on the floor as he drew closer.

That was close enough. Ethan squared his shoulders and faced the man. "Let her go."

"Then prove you're a Child and surrender."

He dropped his sword and then pulled the right side of his collar over, all the while keeping his stare on Scarface.

A grin deepened the curve of Scarface's blemish. "See? If he can be reasonable, so can I." He turned to his men. "Call the soldiers off. We have what we came for." Then he faced Ethan again. "Bind his hands."

The moon was full tonight. A warm summer breeze rippled Ethan's shirt. The sweet scent of peaches from Martha's fruit tree wafted in with the wind and mingled with the faint smell of smoke. The destruction hadn't made it this far into the town, yet no crickets chirped and the frogs in the nearby pond were quiet. Strange.

The Feravolk gripped Ethan's elbow and pushed him toward the covered wagon. "Move, boy."

The mint leaves this guy chewed didn't exactly mask the scent of alcohol. The thought of hooking a leg behind Minty's ankle and buckling his knee tempted Ethan. That would be tricky with his hands bound. Even if he could bring Minty down, he still had the others to worry about.

Not good odds. Impossible really. His quiet surrender kept Tessa and Martha safe anyway. No sense jeopardizing that.

Without a word, Ethan boarded the wagon. Fifteen soot-stained faces stared back at him, most of them familiar.

One girl gasped. "Stone Wolf?"

A hopeful glint flashed in her eyes. Why? Why did they get like that? He wasn't a hero. Far from it.

The prisoners knelt with their hands bound behind their backs. One Blood Moon birthmark—a perfect replica of Ethan's—peeked out from beneath a young man's shirt sleeve.

Ethan clenched his jaw. What did the Feravolk want with the Children anyway? His mind reeled as he tried to recall any detail about the Feravolk that might tell him what they wanted.

All Children were said to be of the Feravolk bloodline. So what?

Were they trying to build up their numbers? Make a bigger army so they could defeat the queen? It would never work. The only ones with the power to defeat the queen and her magic were the deliverers.

Of course. They were searching for the deliverers.

The eighteenth anniversary of the Blood Moon was months away. The day the deliverers were supposed to be able to obtain their power. But why would Feravolk hurt their own? Unless they weren't Feravolk at all.

Wait. There were no frogs making noise. No animals at all. Feravolk attracted animals. Who were these men?

Minty squeezed the pressure point near Ethan's elbow tighter. "I said, sit." He pushed Ethan toward the others.

Ethan faced Minty and pointed his chin toward the other prisoners. "You don't need them. You want your deliverer? You've got him. Let the others go."

"Excuse me?" Minty's forehead crinkled. "Deliverer?"

That clinched it. Ethan took a step back. "You aren't true Feravolk."

Minty cocked his head. "Didn't you see my fancy cloak?"

Ethan retreated farther, baiting Minty to follow. "Where are your animals?"

The man's lip curled and he advanced. Before his foot hit the ground, Ethan hooked his ankle behind Minty's right heel. Minty's left knee slammed onto the wagon's floor, and Ethan bashed his knee into Minty's face. The man rolled to his side, knocked out.

Ethan scanned the prisoner's stunned faces. "We don't have much time here."

The girl who'd recognized him as Stone Wolf wore a smile so big he thought she might try to hug him if her hands weren't bound. They weren't out of this yet.

His knees hit the floor in a thud and he leaned near Minty's body. Blindly, he searched for the man's belt knife with his fingers.

"A little to your left." One of the girls directed him.

Ethan's hand grazed the stiff leather sheath. He found the hilt and pulled. His thumb slid along the edge and pain pricked him.

Well, that was the sharp side, and it was plenty sharp. He flipped the knife in his hands and set the blade on the rope. Blood slicked the handle. He tightened his grip and sawed at his bindings.

The sound of boots scuffing against the wagon's stairs broke the silence.

Ethan's breathing came out shaky. His heart hammered. The ropes loosened.

The footsteps ceased.

Fire fanned over his chest. The chuckle that filled the wagon belonged to Scarface.

Ethan stood and met his enemy's gaze. Scarface nodded toward Minty. "He'll likely want payback for that."

Ethan sawed the knife still against his bindings. He needed a little more time. "Why pretend to be Feravolk?"

"Most people around here call us Cloques. You're not a local?" Scarface glanced at the ground and lost his smile.

He tilted his head to the side like a bird of prey eyeing a meal. Then he walked forward. One step. Two steps.

Ethan shuffled back. He was almost free of his ropes. He didn't have much room if Scarface was going to keep advancing.

Three steps.

Scarface stopped and pointed to the floor. "Sloppy."

Ethan looked down. Four drops of blood, wet and shiny. Heat exploded in his chest. He strained against the loose bindings. If he could just get one hand free. Scarface bashed Ethan's temple with a club, and Ethan blacked out before he hit the floor.

○

Ethan's eyes opened.

Greens and browns blurred together. Where was he? He blinked. Still blurry, but clearer. He shook his head. That was a mistake. Pain throbbed behind his eyes. He tried to lean forward, but something stopped him. Rope?

He sucked in a breath as his memory rushed back to him.

Rough bark dug into his back. His tailbone was definitely asleep.

His shoulders ached and his throat was dry. How long had he been knocked out?

He tried to struggle free, but the ropes holding his hands to the tree didn't budge any more than what they'd coiled around his chest and arms.

"Nice to see you're awake."

The strong scent of peppermint made Ethan's stomach churn. "Where am I?"

Minty's face blocked his line of sight, and Ethan could see him clearly. At least his vision was coming back.

Minty held out his hands and looked up at the towering trees. "The Forest of Legends."

Where? Blood pumped through Ethan's veins twice as fast. It was five days from Salea to the edge of the Forest of Legends. There was no way he'd been knocked out for that long. He'd—Ethan swallowed thick spit—he'd been drugged.

A deep chuckle pierced his thoughts. "The drug dissolves in wine really fast. Don't worry, there's no permanent damage." Minty thrust a waterskin to Ethan's lips. "Care for a drink?"

Ethan turned away.

Minty chuckled.

The sound of boots thudding against the ground drew closer. A face Ethan remembered from the Winking Fox crowded his line of sight.

The white, crescent-moon scar beneath the man's eye lifted as he smiled. "So, what's this I hear about you being a deliverer?"

Ethan remained silent.

Scarface lifted a rope. He tied it around Ethan's neck and cinched the knot. "You'll give me my answers."

Rope dug into Ethan's skin. His insides chilled like a winter's morning. When he swallowed, the rope's prickly strands rubbed against his neck.

Scarface handed Minty the end of the rope. "Unbind him, but leave his hands tied. We'll show him how Feravolk get answers."

"You asked where we kept our animals." Minty held up his end of the rope. "I keep my dogs on a leash."

The bindings around Ethan's chest and arms loosened, but his hands were still connected behind his back. Didn't matter, he still had his legs. There were seven of them, though. He breathed deep and relaxed his knees. He had desperation on his side. That had to count for something. And it's not like they were going to kill him. Well, not if he could make them believe he was a deliverer.

Pressure slammed into the back of Ethan's neck and he rocked forward.

"Let's play a little game." Peppermint spit landed on Ethan's cheek.

The rope jerked him again. Someone kicked him forward. His teeth rattled as his chin collided with the hard ground. Blood trickled from his tongue.

Minty chuckled. "The rules are simple. All you have to do is stand up, and the beating stops."

Ethan's talent warned him with a burning wave. Flat on his belly, he rolled to his side and tried to rise. Pain coursed through his side as a boot crashed into him. His body slammed against a tree. He gasped for air. Dirt flew into his lungs and choked him.

"I said, get up."

Another boot rammed into him. Then another.

Ethan curled up, trying to protect his ribs from the barrage of kicks. Muffled laughter echoed in his ears. Pain shot through him. A flash of white light flooded his vision. His whole left side throbbed. Every muscle strained to protect his injured side. He had to get up.

Blood pounded in his ears, drowning out the shouts and jeers and orders to stand. But something pierced through it all like a whisper.

Ethan, Ethan, Ethan, Ethan, Ethan.

A thousand voices staggered, calling his name.

A gust of wind whipped through the trees, louder this time.

Stand up.

Rocks and dirt pelted against Ethan's face, but the kicking stilled. He opened his eyes.

They were still there, only their legs were suspended. In slow motion their kicks reached for his battered body.

Wind pushed into him hard, and helped him to his knees. How easily he stood. How quickly the wind died down. His enemies' legs all sped at once, but each kick missed him. They all stared at him with gaping mouths and bulging eyes.

Whatever had helped him stunned him just as much.

A hand thudded against Ethan's back and he gasped at the stabbing ache in his ribs.

Scarface's fingers curled around the back of Ethan's neck and dug in. "Took you long enough. Now, tell me about the deliverers, or you get to play another round, *dog*."

A shudder rippled through Ethan's body.

CHAPTER 4

NOT ALONE

Logan stepped through the thick brush beneath the towering trees of the Forest of Legends. One hand pushed against the hilt of his sword to keep its tip from getting caught in the underbrush. His traveling companion, Westwind, scanned the surroundings up ahead. Large trees gave way to larger ones that towered above them like giants. When the wind touched them, they groaned like men. He knew now why the Forest of Legends was devoid of humans.

Westwind walked farther ahead and motioned for Logan to quicken his pace. They reached an area where the dense brush didn't overpopulate the ground anymore. Instead, massive trees, thicker around than a grizzly bear, littered the forest floor like a battlefield of moss-covered corpses.

Logan followed his companion through the maze of fallen logs. Westwind proved to be a good guide. He listened to the forest and stepped, light-footed, through the brush. Logan tried his best to be as soundless. Their mission depended on secrecy.

Up ahead, Westwind froze. He looked over his shoulder at Logan and motioned north. Logan trusted Westwind's ears better than his own. He stopped to listen. Something rustled in the underbrush. A twig snapped. The birds overhead quieted.

Logan crouched behind a downed tree. Hidden, he readied his bow and nocked an arrow. Westwind hunkered behind the base of a tree, poised to fight. Logan's ears picked up the thumping sound of more than one person. He waited. Five men came into view. Four of them bore the sigil of the queen on their leather jerkins. The fifth walked between them, hands bound behind his back, a blood-soaked rope around his neck. One of the soldiers held the other end of the leash.

A fire raged in Logan's chest. So the queen's men were still playing the same games. The old scar at his throat tingled. He had a mind to let his arrow fly, but these men seemed familiar with their surroundings, and he had to keep his presence secret. If there were more soldiers, killing these men would only arouse suspicion. He needed to find the Whisperer soon. It seemed as though Queen Idla might already be looking.

One man yanked the rope leash. The young man flew forward at the jolt and landed on the ground. He cried out in pain. A soldier kicked the young man's side. Logan gritted his teeth as the others joined the torture.

Heat, from Westwind's anger, rippled across their shared bond.

"We can't." Logan spoke to his friend through the bond. *"Staying a step ahead of Idla is our only advantage."*

Westwind glanced over his shoulder and his amber eyes met Logan's. Westwind's snarl revealed strong fangs. *"No one would find a wolf in the woods suspicious. I can scare them."*

"Westwind—"

Before Logan could stop him, a growl thundered from Westwind's chest and he stalked closer. There was no stopping the stubborn wolf once he'd made up his mind. Logan readied his arrow should his friend need help.

Ruddy-brown fur blurred as Westwind's lithe body sailed out of the brush. He landed in close to the men and lowered his head. His snarl stopped them enough for the poor kid to scramble to his feet. The soldiers drew swords. Logan's heart thumped in his chest, but Westwind backed away, bristling.

One solider kept his sword trained at Westwind and motioned for the others to run. "It smells blood! Get the prisoner out of here."

The growl in Westwind's chest rumbled and the final soldier

backed away a few more paces then turned and ran after the others. When they were gone from view, Westwind loped to where Logan hid.

One side of his whiskered lip lifted. *"I'm not really an expert on human behavior, but it seems to me they were in a hurry to get somewhere."*

Logan chuckled. "You certainly set fire to their boots."

Westwind's chuckle rumbled in his chest. *"I saw the whites of their eyes."*

"You know, for not being an expert on human behavior, you have mastered the art of inflection." Logan lifted his eyebrow and glanced at Westwind askance as he replaced his arrow.

"We're going after them?"

Logan clenched his jaw. "Remember our purpose here, Westwind. Alistair sent us to find the Whisperer—not to attract attention. There are too many soldiers. If one were to get away and alert Idla to our presence—"

"He's a pup, Logan." Westwind's expressive eyes rounded.

Logan smiled. "I think the term you're looking for is 'kid.' And I said we weren't going after the soldiers, but I intend to save the kid. As soon as it's dark, we'll move."

"Good. For a moment I almost believed your duty to follow orders had gotten the better of your judgment. You had me worried."

"Worried, Westwind?" Logan chuckled. "And that earlier display of compassion? Human emotion looks good on you, friend."

Teeth nipped his wrist in response.

He shoved the wolf's face.

Westwind sat. *"Do you think Balton is with them?"*

Logan's blood burned and he realized he'd touched the familiar scar on his chest. "If he is, we will be going after those soldiers— orders or not."

CHAPTER 5

SECRET EXIT

A studded, black glove reached for Jayden's elbow.

If the Feravolk caught her, everything her family fought for would be lost. Her heartbeat exploded like a thousand frightened doves taking flight, but she didn't spur her horse forward. Instead, her right hand reached up her left sleeve. She curled her fingers around the familiar handle and pulled her last knife free. Weapon ready, she turned her attention to the gloved man.

His eyes opened wide.

A shiver prickled the skin behind Jayden's ears, and fear flooded her. His fear. She tried to turn her talent off, but she couldn't. Her own fear joined his and terror suffocated her as those wide eyes pleaded. Except fear wasn't his only emotion.

Anger also pulsed through him. Clawed at his insides like a burning flame. She gripped the hilt of her dagger tighter and clung to that emotion. Her family was dead because of this man. This Feravolk. A murderer who had to be stopped. His fear would not cripple her. A new fire fueled Jayden—white-hot anger.

Her blade slid across the enemy's neck. Red trailed over his skin and he fell to the ground with his lifeless eyes open. Immediately, everything she'd felt from him winked out.

Firelight reflected in the dead man's pupils. What had she done? Her pulse thundered, drowning out the cries of the townsfolk. Bile burned her throat. Stickiness coated the reins and covered her hands.

Blood. She'd just killed a man. Killed . . . A lump rose in her throat. As in *gone.*

Like her family.

Jayden clawed at her ears. The prickling sensation had stopped the moment her enemy's head hit the ground, but her skin still crawled, reminding her of the man's anger. She'd embraced it. Her stomach roiled. Weren't her Blood Moon talents supposed to be considered gifts? Reading people's emotions was no gift—not if she couldn't control it.

The stench of burning pitch made Jayden's stomach lurch. The thick air choked her. Sweat dripped down her back and her hair clung to her neck. She tore her eyes from the dead Feravolk's face.

Every thatched roof blazed, lighting up the dark night. Townspeople encircled the well like a human spider web. Water sloshed as they passed buckets to burning homes and barns. Their efforts did little against the destruction.

The Feravolk had left no structure unharmed. They wouldn't stop until they got the Children, and she hadn't surrendered. All of this destruction was her fault. Her family's deaths were her fault. She urged Aureolin toward the barn. This time the horse complied.

She dismounted and raced toward the barn. Heat scorched her skin. Burning wood piled high. Black smoke tainted the dusky sky. "Luc!" She screamed so her throat ached. "Father!" Sobs shook her chest. She screamed their names over and over. But no one answered.

Embers popped and flames roared. Ash floated up to the sky.

There was no way to help them. They were gone. Forever. Her mother's last words rang clear in her head: *"You have to survive."*

Without them? How? Her throat burned as she screamed for her brother and father again. Then she ran toward the flames.

A strong grip stopped her. "Jayden."

She whirled around, fist ready, but Ryan caught her punch. "We have to get out of here. More are coming."

She fought his grip. "Luc is in there!"

He pulled her away from the scorching heat. She pounded her fist against his chest, his arm. "Let me go!"

He pulled her close, hugged her tight. "I'm sorry. I'm so sorry, Jayden."

Her knees weakened and she fell into his embrace. They were gone. Sobs wracked her.

"Listen to me." He gripped her upper arms tight and pushed her back to look into her eyes. "They're looking for you. We have to go. Now."

She wiped her eyes and nodded. Her mother had told her to survive. That's what she had to do. She breathed deep and expelled a shaking breath. She scanned the pandemonium. "Aureolin!"

Across the meadow, the yellow horse came galloping. Jayden gripped Ryan's hand. "She can carry us both."

His eyes grew wide and he pushed her down. Her hands slid across grass and dirt, spreading a burn over her palms. Arrows zipped above her. One slammed into Ryan's chest. He staggered backward and she screamed. A second hit his leg.

"Ryan!"

He got up to his knees. Gray eyes met hers and he waved her on. "Go."

Aureolin stood near now, shielding them from the direction the arrows had come. She nudged Jayden's shoulder. There was little time. Jayden gripped the horse's reins and scrambled up. She held her hand out to Ryan. "Not without you."

The arrow shaft in his chest was too close to his lung, and another shaft had embedded in his left thigh. Her throat tightened and her fingers tingled. So much blood already stained his shirt.

She gripped the shaft sticking out of Ryan's chest in her reddened fingers. Her eyes met his and he nodded once. She broke it. He cried out. Then she pulled the one in his leg. The arrow came free, but the arrowhead hadn't. Jayden gasped. If he didn't get help soon, he'd die too.

She'd be alone.

Movement to the north caught her eye. She searched for its source. Flames licked the sides of the barn. Mothers rushed their children into wagons. Animals ran loose. But the movement she'd seen was slow, calculating, stalking. Her hands shook.

Seven cloaked forms, dark against the flames behind them, headed straight toward her. If she didn't get Ryan out of there, the Feravolk would take them both into the depths of the forest.

Despite the heat, a chill rushed through Jayden's core. She'd never make it out of the city. Her family had died in vain. The Feravolk would take her.

Ryan's eyes were glued to the approaching enemy, too.

Jayden wrapped a trembling arm around his back. "Let's get out of here."

Ryan's eyes squeezed shut, and a cry escaped his throat, but he stood. His weight pulled at her while she guided him the few steps to Aureolin. He steadied himself against the horse.

Jayden locked her reddened fingers together to give him a leg up. Knifeless fingers. She didn't even remember dropping the weapon. Now she had no defense.

She shook the thought away. "Hurry."

Groaning, he hoisted himself onto Aureolin's back, and Jayden mounted the horse in front of him, careful not to bump what was left of the broken arrow shaft in his chest.

Forms, like shadows of men, drew closer.

A shudder rippled through Jayden's body. She'd never make it past the Feravolk. She would be trapped. Wait. Her heartbeat fluttered. The secret exit.

Ryan curled his arms around her waist in a weak grip. "We won't make it past the city gates."

Jayden rammed her heels into Aureolin's sides and steered her galloping horse toward the crumbled opening in the city wall. "I'm not headed to the city gates."

"Jayden, she won't make that jump."

"Hold on."

They neared the stone wall. Rock had toppled from rock as moss and storms and age had worn away the mortar. Jayden kept Aureolin in line with the familiar dip in the crumbled stone.

The fire's blazing heat ebbed away as they headed closer to the exit.

Hoofbeats thundered against the grass and soil. The horse kept her speed. If Aureolin balked, there would be no time to restart, and then the Feravolk would be close enough to see them leave. It had to be now. This jump.

Aureolin's weight shifted. Her head lowered and her neck stretched out. Tension built up in all her muscles, energy waited like a coiled spring.

Jayden leaned with her. C'mon, Aureolin. You can do this.

Wind fluttered Jayden's long hair as they sailed over the collapsed stone and landed on the other side with a jolt.

Ryan's head hit her shoulder. He squeezed her waist and cried out.

She touched the arm he'd wrapped around her. "I'm sorry."

"Been practicing I see." He chuckled then groaned, but he hadn't lifted his head from her shoulder.

How weak was he?

"Can you get this horse to quit bouncing? It's killing me." His smile was evident in his voice.

"Cracking jokes? Really?" She shook her head, but his sorry sense of humor comforted her a little. At least he tried to act normal.

Normal. That was gone.

Ryan's weight pulled her off balance. She struggled to compensate so they wouldn't fall off the horse. His grip weakened.

"Ryan? Ryan!"

"No need to yell. My ear's right by your head." The words dragged out of his mouth slow and sleepy.

She exhaled, her breath shaking.

The thumping of hooves sounded behind them. Her heart hammered against her ribs as the Feravolk poured over the collapsed wall.

They'd found her.

Stomach pressed into a tight ball, Jayden forced the fear away. Which way should she go? Hadn't the baker's daughter mentioned that the Feravolk had attacked Salea? Her breath caught. She could head west to Westhollow, or south toward Erivale—no, that was too close. Jayden turned Aureolin west.

A gust of cool wind twisted loose strands of her hair as if asking her to turn around. Jayden glanced over her shoulder. Towering trees shifted in the wind. Their creaking sounded like giants singing. The Forest of Legends. It was said the trees' trunks were bigger around than a dragon's middle. A man could chop at one of the massive trees for a day and not fell it. Only a fool would go in there. Even the Feravolk had abandoned this forest long ago.

Jayden shivered. She turned Aureolin and urged her toward its dark arbor. So she was a fool, a desperate fool.

Ryan lifted his head. "You can't go in there."

"They'd be stupid to follow us, wouldn't they?"

What was she doing? Ryan needed a doctor. She didn't know enough to take care of his wounds. But cities weren't safe. The Feravolk would be searching for Children of the Blood Moon every-where. If she could hide her talents and her birthmark, no one ever had to know she was one of them.

Ryan had no special talents—he was odd that way—but his birthmark was on his chest. He could hide it too . . . curse that wretched, wretched moon. Whoever tended to his wounds would see it. They'd be identified wherever they went. Hunted.

An arrow zipped by Jayden's ear. She thumped her heels into Aureolin's sides.

The horse galloped over the threshold of the Forest of Legends and everything quieted. Darkness grew deeper and a chill sur-rounded them. Moss-covered trunks towered above her so high it dizzied her to look up. Thick branches blocked out the moon.

Fog surrounded them and cast a blue haze over the whole place. Ferns covered much of the ground—ferns large enough to hide a full-grown gryphon. Jayden hugged Ryan's arm.

She risked a glance behind. No one. When she was certain she'd lost the Feravolk, she'd take care of Ryan herself—if only she'd packed her medical supplies. Maybe there was something in the satchel her mother had given her.

He gripped her tighter, shaking. "It burns."

"Hush. What burns?"

"Everything."

She reached over her shoulder and touched his cheek. Sweat covered his face. His skin was so hot.

"You have a fever."

"My blood is *boiling*."

Low tree branches seemed to reach toward him.

Jayden maneuvered Aureolin as far from their towering forms as she could. "Please try to be quiet."

His breath heated her hair. "Leave me."

What? Her fingers squeezed the reins. "No."

"I'm just . . . slowing you down." He slurred like he'd had too much ale.

"You're being foolish."

His hand cupped her knee. "I won't . . . make it."

"Don't talk like that."

Tears pricked the corners of her eyes. Maybe she was the foolish one. The stiff, wet fabric that clung to her back wasn't drenched in sweat. It was blood. Too much blood.

He pressed against her and stifled most of another groan.

The lump in Jayden's throat choked her. "I'm not leaving you."

"Of course not," he whispered. "I always liked that about you. Your perseverance."

"Don't you dare say good-bye to me. I just lost my whole family. I can't lose you too."

A rough thumb brushed her cheek. "I'm sorry."

His weight shifted.

Aureolin faltered.

He was letting himself fall.

Jayden grabbed his arms, unwilling to let go. He had no strength to fight against her. She pulled him back and stopped the horse.

"Don't leave me alone. Not here." She tore the hem of her riding dress and ripped a long strip from the bottom and tied the cloth around both their waists.

Ryan's bloodied hand closed around her wrist. "What are you doing?"

"Now, if you think about dismounting in the middle of a ride, you'll take me down with you." Tears streamed down her face, but she refused to acknowledge them.

"If I black out, I'll take you down with me."

"I don't care."

"Jayden, you can't—" He buckled over and his scream echoed through the trees.

When he was quiet again, she gripped his hands in hers. "Just a little farther, okay?"

He exhaled a shaky breath. "Okay."

All of his weight slumped against her. "Ryan?"

He didn't respond.

She touched the side of his neck. A faint pulse thumped against her trembling finger. *Thank the Creator.*

He'd make it. He had to make it. He was all she had left.

CHAPTER 6

SIMILAR SCARS

Ethan's eyes shot open. Something rough and warm clasped his mouth. A hand. His pulse quickened. Another of Minty's late night torture sessions? But he didn't smell peppermint. He thrashed his head trying to loosen the grip. A face he didn't recognize blocked his view.

"Quiet. Okay?" the stranger whispered.

Ethan nodded, staring. This man wore a cloak, too, but it was different somehow. If his captors' cloaks made their bodies seem like shadows, this man was even more invisible, like a hazy ripple.

Ethan blinked and let his eyes refocus. "Who are you?"

"Name's Logan." He held up his hand and a knife blade glinted.

Ethan flinched against his bindings.

Logan's hand stilled. "Don't worry, kid. I'll get you out of here. Starting with this leash."

The leash off? Sounded great. Except that after seven days of torture, the skin beneath it had been rubbed raw and healed so many times that the stupid rope was a part of him now. Still, he nodded. No one would ever leash him again.

A form ghosted behind the stranger and disappeared.

Ethan sucked in a breath. What was going on? He scanned for more movement. Nothing. Wait. Two yellow, gleaming eyes appeared over the stranger's shoulder. A tremor rocked his body. A wolf.

A smile grew on Logan's face and he pointed a thumb over his shoulder. "Don't let Westwind scare you. He's the one who found you."

The wolf huh? Probably because he smelled like blood. Didn't wolves attack sick and injured prey? Great.

Logan's knife blade pressed against the leash's knot.

The steady sawing seemed loud enough to wake Ethan's captors. Each tug sent a twinge through him. Just the thought of that rope peeling away from his raw skin made his stomach twist.

"Ethan?"

Something, like a grip around his heart, pulled at him, begged him to listen. Faint heat burned in his chest. A threat? For whom? Ethan didn't know anyone out here. How could he feel threats for people he didn't know? He only got warnings for people his talent bound him to protect.

"Hurry. Please hurry."

Something about the weird pull was so familiar. And strong. It was someone he'd protected before. Okay, as soon as he got free, he'd check it out.

The sawing stopped. At last the knot unraveled.

Logan winced. "This is going to hurt, kid."

He gritted his teeth. "Just rip it off."

Logan's eye met his. "You'll keep quiet?"

Ethan clenched his jaw as hard as he could and nodded. Pain seared his skin. He squeezed his eyes shut and held his breath, willing the intensity to die down. At last he breathed in. The blood-blackened rope sat mangled on the ground. At least he was rid of it. And the feeling of utter helplessness tied to it. Anyone who tried to leash him again would have to kill him first.

"They've got enough rope on you to keep a moose tied down, kid."

The tug against his bindings grated against his cracked ribs as Logan cut the rope.

The knife stilled. Ethan realized his eyes were closed when he opened them to see what was wrong.

Logan just stared at him, eyebrows pinched together. "How bad are you?"

"Worse if you don't get me out."

Taut rope loosened and fell away from Ethan's body. Freedom was so close. Just his hands remained tied together. The knife sawed through bindings with little trouble. Ethan rolled his aching shoulders back into place. It was the ache in his side that wouldn't ease. Thankfully, he healed fast. Unfortunately, not fast enough.

Logan handed Ethan his sword, quiver, and satchel. "Follow Westwind north. I'll make a false trail and join you at the river."

Nice or not, he wasn't about to follow Toothy the Wolf any deeper into this creepy forest. "Thank you, but really, I—"

"Go."

Teeth clamped down on Ethan's breeches. He looked down at the massive animal and decided those yellow eyes were actually persuasive.

"All right, I'll follow you."

Westwind loped away from the camp.

Ethan followed. Every step shot pain through his side.

The wolf stopped. His whole body stiffened, and he crouched low.

Ethan froze. Great. Now that the man was gone, this animal was going to attack him. But Westwind's eyes weren't fixed on Ethan. It was something behind him. His heart pounded. Slowly he turned. He didn't see anything. Westwind's deep growl sent a shiver through his body.

Ethan stood motionless, waiting. The growling stopped. Teeth clipped his hand gently. Ethan turned to Westwind, who loped away again.

Morning light began to appear over the horizon by the time they made it to the river. Westwind finally stopped.

Grateful for a chance to sit, Ethan sank to the ground. He hadn't intended on waiting around for this Logan fellow, but after seven days of the kicking game, his whole body ached.

Westwind sat across from him, watching with those golden eyes. He cocked his head.

"Are you making sure I stay put or something?"

The wolf opened his mouth and stretched his lips to reveal all his teeth in what looked like a smile, then he nodded.

Great.

Westwind's mouth closed. He rose, slowly, facing left. A low growl rumbled.

"Westwind, he's a friend." Logan's voice came from behind the tall reeds.

Friend? Ethan rose to his feet, his sword hand ready. A rust-colored farm dog raced toward him. Scout?

Ethan tried to stop his dog from jumping on him, and the quick movement shot pain through his side anyway. He didn't need this Logan fellow knowing, so he knelt near his dog.

"Easy, boy." Ethan pushed his dog off of him and scratched that perpetually itchy spot on Scout's neck. "Where'd he come from?"

Logan sighed. "He found me."

"Well, thanks for the rescue."

Logan nodded.

Curiosity nagged Ethan. "Those men weren't Feravolk, were they?"

"No."

"Who were they?"

Logan lowered to the ground. "Queen Idla's soldiers."

Idla? Why did *she* want the Children? "How do you figure? I thought the deliverers were supposed to defeat the queen."

Logan tilted his chin and Ethan got a good look at the scar around the man's neck. "They still torture the same." Then he pulled something out of his pocket and handed it to Ethan.

It was a letter, opened, but the wax seal—a muzzled dragon—was the queen's. Ethan opened the letter. The fancy calligraphy read:

Next stop, Tareal.

That's where the soldiers had just gone. "So she's just going to kidnap all the Children? It doesn't make sense."

Logan scratched his head. "I know. We're trying to stop her."

"She's already got you beat."

Logan cocked an eyebrow.

Ethan shook his head. "Don't you see? Feravolk are supposed to care for Soleden. Since the Blood Moon, Idla has managed to send all Feravolk into hiding. The land yields less fruit with every year she gains power. More towns fall under her oppression. More people turn poor. And now *Cloques* run into towns, burning people's homes and demanding the Children be turned over. Royal Army or not, the people see what they want to see. Idla has the Feravolk pegged as the enemy. She has you beaten."

Logan just stared at him through squinted eyes. "Cloques?"

"Common people call Feravolk Cl—"

"I know. You're saying people dressed as Cloques burned your town?" Logan growled in a way unnatural to any human.

"You're saying you didn't know?"

"I knew she'd burned towns, but our wolf scouts didn't say anything about us being impersonated. Did you overhear anything? Do you know where they'll strike next? Did they just take you?"

"They took fifteen others. Since I told them they weren't true Feravolk, I got special treatment." Ethan handed the letter back. "They just hit Tareal yesterday."

Westwind growled.

Logan looked over his shoulder at Westwind who shook his head.

Shook his head? A wolf? Wait. "Are you talking to him?"

Logan smiled. "You seem to know a lot about Feravolk. You didn't know we bond to animals?"

"Ethan . . . hurry." The strange pull tugged against him again and his knees buckled. He sat down and shook his head, trying to clear it. Still it nagged. Ethan felt for it and tugged back. The resistance told him where his protection was needed. It seemed to want him to go toward . . . Tareal?

Logan crouched close. "You okay, kid?"

"Ethan. My name is Ethan. And I'm fine. I should really get going." Standing, he dusted himself off. "Thanks for the rescue."

"Do you have any food? Coin?" Logan dug in his sack and pulled out some dried meat and cheese. "Here."

Ethan stared at the food and willed his stomach not to growl. He just didn't feel right taking from this man's meager rations.

Logan thrust his hand closer. "When's the last time you ate, kid?"

Hunger won. Ethan accepted the gift. "Thank you. Why did you rescue me?"

"Because you needed it."

A debt then. "If you're headed to Tareal to figure out what Idla's after, I can go with you."

"I'm not."

"Then where are you headed?"

Logan rubbed his palm over his face. "My tribe sent me to . . . I have to take care of something important before I follow these—these *Cloques*."

"What could be more important than stopping the queen?"

"I agree with you, kid. I can't disobey orders."

Orders, huh? Clearly there was much about the Feravolk Ethan didn't understand. That nagging pull gripped him again. It was like a string in his heart that tugged him. If he was going to Tareal anyway, maybe he could repay his debt too. "I can check out Tareal for you."

Logan's eyes popped open wide. "What?"

"Do you believe in following your Destiny Path?"

Logan chuckled. "No."

"Well, I do. It was no accident that you rescued me. We can't let Idla kill every Child in Soleden. I'll head to Tareal and find out what I can about where they're going next, and why the queen wants the Children."

"I can't ask you to do that, kid."

"You didn't."

CHAPTER 7

WHISPERS IN THE WIND

Logan's legs burned from fatigue. He and Westwind continued their search for the Whisperer even as the stars started to dim.

The riverbank was close. Westwind crouched at the edge and lapped up water.

Logan joined his friend. Frustration grabbed a hold of him, and he fought the urge to toss a rock. He wiped a hand over his face and sat near the water's edge.

He didn't want this. He wanted to be helping his people. Instead he was searching for some elusive Whisperer. The queen had plotted to destroy all the Feravolk, and all Alistair and the Feravolk Council could think to do was send him off to find the Whisperer so she could tell him where the deliverers were in hiding before it was too late. And for what? To fulfill some prophecy?

The real way to save his people and all of Soleden was to draw his sword and march against the queen. Once communication between Feravolk and the animals and trees was cut off, the land would die. It was already starting. Trees produced less fruit. Crops died off. Magical creatures that were once legend were said to be returning. The prison that held the Mistress of Shadows was breaking.

Logan caught himself fingering his marriage stone and winced as he let go of it. He had to stop doing that. It only reminded him of Rebekah; she was the reason he was so deep in this mess to begin with. He picked up a rock and threw it. It sailed into the calm water, and the river swallowed it without a splash.

Westwind settled next to him. *"You could cook a rabbit with that heat."*

"Heat?"

"I think the forest is getting to you."

Logan looked at the wolf, but Westwind's amber gaze was serious. "Getting to me?"

Westwind sniffed the air. *"It's getting to me. This place is . . . too quiet for one thing. But there's something else that makes my fur stand on end."*

"What is it?"

"It's different. The trees, the brook, and the ground even, everything is . . . breathing." Westwind's eyes searched Logan. *"You feel it?"*

Logan lay back in the soft soil. He closed his eyes and let his other senses take over. Westwind always told Logan he relied too much on what he saw and not enough on what he heard, smelled, touched, or even tasted.

He dug his fingers into the soil. Felt for the tiny tremors of life. A rabbit thumped against the ground nearby. Deer raced through the trees. The rippling brook bubbled in his ears. Wind caressed his face. The trees above him creaked, groaning, humming, singing. It was different, all of it.

Westwind was right. Something about the sounds, the movement of the air, the moaning of the trees seemed peculiar. Breathing. Beating.

"My senses aren't as developed as yours, Westwind."

"But you feel it?"

"Yes. Perhaps it is the heart of the forest."

"The heart?"

"My father told me every forest has a heart and the Feravolk can feel it. It's what keeps a forest alive. If the heart is killed, the forest will die."

"I understand this."

The sky turned from black to gray, and the moon lost its luster as the sun pushed it closer to the horizon.

Westwind's eyes widened and his ears twitched. The rest of his body became rigid. *"Did you hear that?"*

Logan strained his ears, but he didn't need to listen hard at all. The sound grew.

Logan, Logan, Logan, Logan, Logan.

It echoed through the trees, as quiet as a padded footfall at first, but grew to a deafening thunder in his ears. It came again. His name flitted through the trees as if passed between them on the breezes. A hundred whispers resounded, and his name filled the air as a gust rippled through the trees, overlapping his name so he couldn't find the direction of the speakers, then dying with the wind.

Bristling, Westwind looked up at the treetops. *"The forest is speaking my name."*

"Your name? I hear my own."

The surrounding voices subsided. Westwind's gaze turned to Logan, but the wolf didn't move his head, just his eyes. *"Should we answer?"*

"I'm here," Logan whispered, the ghost of his courage fleshing out.

"Finally we meet." A voice, distinctly feminine, spoke.

Westwind lowered his head and crouched low, ready to spring. *"That wasn't the forest."*

Logan grabbed his bow and faced the direction of the voice, arrow already nocked.

"Am I such a threat to you?" The female spoke again.

"Show yourself." Logan still scanned for movement. He sniffed the air. Listened for rustling. Anything that would pinpoint her location.

The tall grass on the opposite side of the creek moved, and she stepped out from behind it. Her hands didn't rise in surrender. She clasped them in front of her and walked into view. Her blue eyes were bold and her wrinkled face serene. Her white hair was pulled back in a loose bun. She was an old woman, yet neither Logan nor Westwind lowered any guard.

"One of the true Feravolk in flesh and blood, here in the Forest of Legends. It has been a long time." A hint of a smile touched her face.

Long, long time. Long time. Long, long time.

Another breeze echoed through the trees in those hundreds of whispers, but no longer deafening. This time they sounded sad.

Logan lowered his weapon. "You're the—"

She interrupted him with a wave of her hand. "I am whom you seek. Come. We shall talk where it is safe. Your wolf friend is welcome if he minds my chickens."

"She is the Whisperer?" Westwind turned to Logan. *"And she has chickens?"* His tongue wet his nose.

Logan splashed through the creek, mindful of the slick rocks of the riverbed. When they reached the other side, Westwind shook excess water from his coat and headed to the tall grass after the Whisperer. He nosed the air before following her scent until they came to a meadow.

A hut sat in the center of the clearing. Smoke rose from the chimney. Behind the cottage goats and sheep grazed and chickens pecked at the ground. The sun awakened the littering of birds surrounding the house. Flowers adorned the sides of the home and embellished the paths in the yard.

"Chickens, huh? I can smell chicken, and it's roasting on a spit." Drool hung in the corner of Westwind's mouth.

"Come in." The woman stepped on to her porch and waved for the two of them to follow.

They approached the hut and stepped inside. Logan made no move to venture farther into the house than a few steps. He scanned the whole area. Beside him Westwind's nose worked the room from where he stood.

The Whisperer tilted her head as she eyed Logan. "You like my home?"

He stepped farther into the house. "Yes, I just expected the Wh—er—you would live in something more . . . portable."

A smile grew across her face that reminded Logan of a flower blooming.

"It is safe to talk here." She turned her attention to Westwind. "Your wolf friend smiles, does he?" The blooming grin sprouted on her face again. "You two must have been together awhile."

"We have."

"So, what brings you to my doorstep Logan Laugnahagn of the wolves, from the tribe Moon Over Water, descendant of the tribe of the Forest of Legends?"

Logan straightened at this strange greeting from a stranger. "I don't recall meeting you before."

"Of course, you don't. You were naked as a newborn rabbit and slippery as a fish when I gave you your first bath and blessing and handed you to your mother." She paused and looked at him. A sad smile filled her countenance. "You look very much like your father. He had the same chin, same strong arms, and able hands. The same dark, wavy hair. But your eyes, warm sky blue, like your mother's." The corners of her eyes crinkled even deeper. "My name is Anna, Whisperer of the Forest of Legends. Welcome to my home."

"Thank you."

"Come. Sit." Anna ventured into her sitting room. "I have something for you."

"You knew I was coming?"

A smile spread her lips as she placed two velvet cases on the table. The large, oblong one rolled open to reveal two short swords and eight daggers—four the right size for throwing, and four that were almost as long as the short swords. Slim swords, meant for feminine hands. "These are the deliverers' weapons."

Logan swallowed, his throat tightening.

She opened the second velvet bag and spilled the contents on the table. Eight wooden tokens. "The deliverers will be drawn to you, Logan. You are their protector."

He backed away from her. "I am no protector."

"You can deny it, but the Creator chooses whom he chooses."

Logan shook his head. "I might have been chosen, but I transferred my right. My council will decide who the new protectors are. My only order now is to take the deliverers safely to my camp. Can you help me or not?"

"Oh, I can help you. But you may not like what I have to say."

CHAPTER 8

BROKEN PROMISES

Jayden pulled on Aureolin's reins and the horse stopped. Moonlight filtered through the trees. Not a single shadowed form had danced in the corner of her eye since they entered the Forest of Legends. If the Feravolk were near, they were being too quiet about it.

"You're stopping?" Ryan's voice rasped against his throat. "Thank the Creator. All that bouncing."

Honestly, how he could still be joking around was incredible. She turned her head to look at him. A smile grew on his pale—so very pale—face.

Her own smile faded. "I need to look at you. It can't wait another moment."

"Aw, Jayden. I love looking at you too."

"Funny." She released Aureolin's reins and untied the piece of her dress she'd looped around their waists.

He let go of her, and she swung her leg over and slid off the horse, careful not to bump that ever present arrow.

Blood covered the front of his shirt. Her throat tightened.

Ryan wavered without her to support him on the animal. "It's really a shame about tomorrow."

What was he talking about?

"Oh, Jayden, don't tell me you forgot about tomorrow? That hurts."

His mock-wounded look made her smile. Leave it to Ryan to take her mind off of all things urgent.

She held out her hands to help him. "The betrothal ceremony? Yes, it is a shame we'll miss it."

He moved and inhaled sharply, wincing. "Can't I just sit here a moment longer?"

Jayden took his hand in hers. If she didn't stop the bleeding there would be no tomorrow for him. "I'm afraid not."

"That bad, huh?" This time his smile twisted with regret.

She couldn't let him give up. "Well, you're still trying to be funny, so maybe it's not."

He swayed on Aureolin's back. "At least I got you out of there."

"Don't. You'll be fine. You know what a great doctor I am. Now, let's—" she broke off before her voice faltered.

"I got you this beautiful stone and everything. It's nearly black. My mother—"

"Ryan, please."

His eyes bored into hers, pleading. "My mother said black wasn't a good color to choose for a marriage stone. If you look close, you can tell it's really a mix of grays—like storm clouds. Kinsey said it was perfect for you."

Of course it was. Her chin trembled. The stone she'd picked for him was still in her pocket.

Her hand brushed against the charm on the necklace she wore. A small, wooden, white horse—it had been her mother's. At least she had something to remember her by. Jayden blinked and a warm tear slid down her cheek. She wiped it away and hoped Ryan hadn't seen.

He put his arms on her shoulders and swung his good leg over Aureolin's back. He slid off the horse and Jayden steadied him while he sat with his back to a tree.

She grabbed the satchel her mother had given her. "I'm sorry about the ceremony, but I've got a good excuse for missing it."

"Really?"

"I'm taking care of a stubborn patient."

"Right. Wise woman in training misses her own betrothal

ceremony because—" He curled forward, squeezed his stomach, and held in a scream.

Jayden gripped his hand and pressed her face into the base of his neck until it ended, but he went limp in her arms.

"Ryan? Ryan!"

His chest still rose and fell.

She laid him down, then picked up the satchel and looked inside. Her stomach tightened and she sobbed. Her mother had packed her provisions and her father had bridled Aureolin. What had they known?

All they'd told her to do was run.

Why? She balled her hands into fists. Her parents could think of nothing but saving her.

Now she had nothing.

She cleared her eyes and dug past the food, change of clothes, and scratchy woolen blanket. A knife? That she stashed up her sleeve before she resumed her search for medical supplies, her father's ointments, anything.

Jayden's hand brushed against a piece of paper. She lifted it from the sack and held it up in the moonlight. Her name was on the front written in her mother's hand, but age had yellowed the parchment. She stuffed it in her boot and refocused on her search. The medical supplies were there. She exhaled trapped air and dared hope they'd be enough.

Now she needed water. She walked toward the bank, then filled the waterskin from her satchel. What had spurred her mother to pack supplies? And daggers? Since when did her peace-loving mother own a pair of daggers? Before the door had slammed shut, Jayden had read her mother's emotions—hope and regret, sadness and pain. Then she sacrificed herself for Jayden's escape. What had her mother been hiding?

Jayden crouched next to Ryan and shook the thoughts away. It wouldn't change anything. Her family was dead. Gone. And her home destroyed. Moving forward was her only choice.

But moving forward terrified her.

Ryan's shallow breaths quickened. He was getting worse. She laid him down and poured water over his wound. He stirred, but didn't wake. More tears threatened to flow. She breathed deep and peace blanketed her.

With steady hands, she thrust the knife through his shirt and ripped.

The arrow angled into him—too near his lung. Feravolk used barbed arrows. She'd have to dig the arrowhead out, but if she dug too far, or pressed the arrowhead in farther, she might kill him.

Creator in heaven, Ryan was going to die, too.

There had to be something she could do for him. She shifted her attention to the gaping wound in his leg. The embedded arrowhead was close to the surface. She cut his trousers and poured water over the wound.

He trembled and moaned about the fire in his veins. Fire in his heart.

The knife sunk in next to the arrowhead and found the bottom. Maneuvering the tip beneath the end, she pushed against the knife's hilt. The arrowhead lifted enough for her to extract it. Ryan only flinched. Didn't even scream. His eyes remained closed. Tears blurred her vision as she cleaned and stitched his wound.

He couldn't die. This was all her fault. The Feravolk wanted her. If she had just done as they asked and gone with them, they would have left her family alone.

She smoothed Ryan's hair and bent over to kiss his forehead. Hot. Far too hot. "You keep fighting. You hear me? I'm going to get you help."

She tucked the blanket around him. Under her hands, he trembled. Where would she find this help? Cities were no longer safe, and no one lived in the Forest of Legends. A memory of the trees reaching out for Ryan as he cried out chilled her to the core. If anyone lived here, did she really want their help?

○

Jayden slapped her legs against Aureolin's sides, pushing the horse to go faster. The maze of trees distorted her sense of direction. The farther she went, the harder it would be to remember how to get back to Ryan. She kept the river in her view so she could find her way back. Under the gray light of approaching dawn, she scanned the woods for any sign of life, but of course there was nothing. No one lived in the Forest of Legends.

A wispy gray cloud rose from the trees to the north. Jayden sucked in a breath. Her hands trembled. Smoke—chimney smoke. And the faint scent of cooking chicken. She pressed her palm to her mouth and a shaky laugh escaped her throat. Could someone really live here?

Jayden steered Aureolin toward the smoke, her eyes on the cloud. It hovered over the trees just past the stream. She was almost there.

Aureolin snorted and her nostrils flared. Her hooves dug into the ground and the horse skidded to a halt.

"Not now. Let's go, Aureolin." Jayden squeezed her horse's sides.

Aureolin pawed at the water and danced away from the edge.

Jayden's stomach clenched. She was losing precious time, but Aureolin wasn't going anywhere, and Jayden couldn't calm her now, not with her own emotions being so volatile. She steered Aureolin to a tree and knotted the reins to a low branch, then she raced across the stream alone.

Cool water splashed against her legs, and twice she almost slipped on the smooth stones. She scrambled up the bank. A well-worn path disappeared into the tall grass in front of her.

Jayden charged down the trail as fast as she could. Her lungs began to burn, but the path took her deeper into the reeds. Marshy ground squished beneath her boots.

The scent of cooked chicken grew stronger. Jayden cupped her hands to her mouth. "Help me! Please, help!"

"Oh, I'll help you, missy." The voice was strong, deep, and cold.

A chill spread through Jayden's veins. Breath emptied from her lungs.

Reeds snapped behind her. Rustling accompanied the sound of bows creaking. Tremors skittered through Jayden's muscles. Before she turned, she knew what she'd find. Men in camouflaged cloaks that made them look like faint shadows of men. She slipped her hand up her sleeve, clutched her knife—her only knife—and turned.

Seven faces sneered at her. Seven arrows pointed in her direction.

Her fingers squeezed the knife handle tighter. The skin behind her ears prickled and pleasure shot through her. Not hers. That emotion belonged to these men. Her heart beat faster. She would not let that emotion overtake her. She tried to focus on being calm.

"We have to bring you back alive, but a little blood loss won't kill you. Unless you intend to come peacefully this time."

Her heart pounded. Even if she got one good throw away, she'd be left with six attackers and no weapons. Her foot inched closer to the tree line on her left. Too far for her to run, but still she'd try. After all, they said they wouldn't kill her.

A heavy chuckle broke the silence. "You really mean to run?"

Jayden held up the knife. "You killed my family."

The man shrugged. "They were in the way."

The pleasure welled up inside her. Made her want to fight back. Anger joined it. Like a mad rage. This man was crazy.

Jayden gripped her knife and bent her knees. "What do you want with me?"

"We want the Children of the Blood Moon."

"Why?"

"I'm not here to answer your questions."

All seven glided closer. Their cloaks hid their movement. Shadows rippled as the material fluttered in the wind.

An arrow shot into the ground near Jayden's left foot. She sucked in a breath. Her body shook as she stared at the man who had spoken. Hatred and anger shot through him and slammed into Jayden. She sucked in a breath, trying to push those emotions away.

A wicked smile spread his lips. "I'm here to collect."

A collector, huh? Jayden smiled back as his rage fueled her. Melted her fear. Enabled her to focus. "Not this time."

Embracing the collector's emotions, Jayden stood tall, breathed deep, and relaxed her shoulders. The knife handle became a part of her hand. An extension. Muscle memory kicked in and the knife sailed true. The blade sunk deep into the Feravolk's chest, and the armed man on the collector's right fell. His bow slid out of his limp arms.

Jayden blinked. Her heart jolted. A shudder rushed through her. What had she done? She was becoming a monster.

The collector sneered. "Bold move. Bold and stupid. Take her."

A scream lodged in Jayden's throat and she turned to run. An arrow zipped past her—from the trees? She glanced back to watch one of the Feravolk fall. Another cried out, an arrow shaft in his chest. What was going on?

Brittle reeds clawed against her dress and she toppled over. Another cry pierced the night. Jayden scrambled to rise. The dried cattails cracked. Fingers gripped her wrist and yanked her hair. Someone threw her backward and pinned her down. Her arm was trapped in a strong hold.

Flat on her back, she reached for anything she could use as a weapon. Panic clutched her chest. Cold fingers grabbed her other hand and she caught her attacker's eyes—the man who had come to collect her. Persistent jerk. And heavy too.

Jayden pushed against his weight, but he wouldn't budge. So this was it. Ryan would die. She'd be taken. Tears dripped into her ears, and the skin behind them prickled. He thought this was funny, did he? Her legs flailed, but still she couldn't knock him off.

He held a rock above her head. "You squirm too much."

The rock crashed down. Pain shot through her head and darkness overtook her thoughts.

CHAPTER 9

SHRED OF HOPE

Ryan lay on the cool, mossy ground and replayed his last moments with Jayden. Over and over he felt her tears drip on his face, listened to Aureolin's hooves carry her away. If something happened to her out there, it was on him—his fault. He shifted and pain stabbed his chest. He breathed through his teeth.

Dawn's light pierced through the branches above. Everything blurred. Fire shot through his blood again, and he bit down on his shirtsleeve.

Knife my bloody, bloody heart. Why hadn't he bled out by now? White light shot through his vision as the pain hit him again. Then the burning. His blood was on fire.

This was the end. Jayden wouldn't find anyone, and he'd leave her alone and unprotected. And his sisters—he'd promised to go back for them. If only there was some way to keep them safe after he was gone. He needed . . . Ethan.

Hope spread through him. Ethan always knew when Ryan or his sisters were in trouble. Picturing his brother's face, Ryan reached out just like he had when they were kids and he was in trouble. Ethan had always heard then. Creator willing, he'd hear now.

Ethan? If you can hear me, I need you, brother. The girls are in trouble, and I'm—I'm not going to be able to protect them anymore. And Jayden, she's—well, I love her and I need you to protect her, too.

Please, brother. Take care of her for me. Take care of all of them. And hurry. Please hurry.

Something warm trickled down the side of his cheek. A tear? When was the last time he'd cried? Fire pulsed through him. He leaned over and retched. Blood wet the ground beside him. He closed his eyes and something soft brushed his face. It felt strangely like his mother's hand.

"Don't worry. The transformation won't last forever."

That voice wasn't familiar. "What?"

The pain ebbed away from him. He no longer lay shivering on the ground. He stood in a wood filled so densely with light that only the few trees closest to him weren't washed out by the blinding white. The calming scent of lavender and a soft hum surrounded him.

"Who—who's there?"

A white beast stepped in front of the trees. Its eyes, yellow like the harvest moon, locked onto him. A mountain lion of sorts, only all white.

He squared his shoulders. "What do you want?"

The fire bit from the inside. All of his limbs burned. He fell to his knees and curled his arms around his stomach. A roar pierced the air. Ryan bent over and threw up. Blood splashed rich and red against the white ground, staining it with speckles, and a scarlet puddle spread at Ryan's knees. It ended just as fast and the pain subsided again.

"Don't worry. The transformation won't last forever."

Ryan wiped his mouth with his sleeve, trailing crimson on his shirt. "So you said. What does it mean?" The lion's paws were stained red. "Did I do that?"

"It's all part of the transformation. You will become like me soon enough."

"Like you?" Ryan tried to move away, but he faltered.

The harsh ground smacked his back. He tried to sit up, but the beast placed its bloodied paws on his chest. Its claws extended and pressed into his skin. "S-stop. Please."

"I cannot. I'm inside you."

Inside? The fire. It had to be the fire. It was the only explanation.

Another roar filled the silence. It cut off as if strangled, and Ryan choked on blood. Swiveling his head, he vomited it on the ground. It flowed away from him like a red river. Was that roar coming from him? He looked back at the beast. Its legs were half scarlet now.

"What are you?"

The beast lay on his chest. Its purr vibrated his whole being. Its claws kneaded his skin. He wanted to cry out, but he couldn't breathe. He sucked in air, trying to get enough, but his chest wouldn't lift. It was too heavy. So heavy.

The purr turned into a chuckle. *That's right. Let me finish my work.*

Fire shot through him again. Ryan tried to scream, but the roar drowned it out. Those yellow-moon eyes watched him as if it pleased the creature to see him writhe. Its legs were all crimson now. *That's right. Let me finish.*

He didn't like whatever this creature was doing to him. He gathered the blood pooled in his mouth and spat at the beast. "No."

It lunged at his face. Ryan turned his head, helpless under the massive paws. Breath like burnt lavender heated his face.

"What are you?"

Nothing but silence. The heaviness of the beast still pinned him to the ground. He opened his eyes and the white was gone. Complete darkness covered him. All he could see was two yellow-beacon eyes staring at him.

"You ask 'what' when you should ask 'who.'" The beast growled and all the pain washed over him again. He choked on a scream.

There was no way he'd give that beast any recognition. "*What* is killing me?"

A ray of light pierced the darkness.

Ryan caught a glimpse of the creature on his chest. It was no longer a white lion, but a black one with massive wings. Paws pressed harder into his chest as it leaned closer and bared its long, white fangs. *"This is killing you. Venom from a black lion. But I am no black lion. They are my soldiers, sent to find the one who will make the perfect vessel. I think I've found my vessel. Now, let me transform you."*

The black lion melted back into the white lion, but the eyes—the eyes were the same no matter what color the fur was—they were evil. "N-never."

Ryan, Ryan, Ryan, Ryan, Ryan.

Hundreds of far off whispers called to him.

The lion hissed. Did it fear the whispers?

Ryan clung to a shred of hope. "I'm h-here."

The whispers struck up again, this time as one.

Hold on.

CHAPTER 10

CAT OR MOUSE

Rebekah stood in front of the massive window in her room and took in the magnificent view. The distant fields radiated summertime green, and the gardens just under her window were in full bloom.

Not far from the edge of the gardens, her son Connor sparred with his instructor again. It was an escape for him, much like walking the paths of the garden was to her. They didn't afford her the same sense of security and relief as towering trees in her forest home, but she was allowed among the gardens alone, so she made due.

A harsh rap sounded from the door. Rebekah already knew who waited on the other side—Idla and her entourage. When the door opened, Rebekah still stared out the window at first, then turned to face the queen and bowed.

"Rebekah, I have a request of you."

Rebekah stilled a shiver as she turned her attention back to Connor sparring below. Not another request from the queen. Another *task* for Idla to prove how she controlled Rebekah like a horse with a gag bit.

Rebekah would play the part. She had to. But at times she wasn't so sure the part wasn't playing her instead.

Idla had long since removed torture from Rebekah's routine, but the thought of disobeying the queen brought the stench of sweat and blood to Rebekah's nostrils and the sound of a cracking whip to her ears.

The only thing that kept her heart willing to beat was Connor. She had to do what she could to protect Connor. To keep him from becoming corrupt.

"I need you to locate the other three deliverers."

Rebekah closed her eyes. The deliverers. Idla often spoke about how they were her path to ultimate power. Rebekah composed herself before she faced the queen again.

"You would recognize them, correct?" Idla smiled and glanced to her left. Belladonna stood there, hand on her hip. She wore nothing but black. Black pants, black shirt, black boots, and black leather overlays. It went well with her dark eyes and black hair.

Rebekah had learned not to lie around Belladonna years ago; she was a healer who could sense lies. "Yes, I believe I may be able to, but I couldn't guarantee—"

"Of course not." Idla used her sweet tone. Rebekah hated it when the queen tried to be something she wasn't. "Come. I have several possible deliverers downstairs right now that I need you to look at."

Rebekah followed the queen out into the hall. As they made their way to the throne room, they passed the chambers of the queen's son Franco. Idla sent her trusted advisor Oswell to knock on Franco's door.

The prince opened the door and leaned on the frame with a lazy smile on his face. His tunic wasn't tucked in, and his dark hair disheveled. Rebekah's heart broke. Franco had defiled another young woman.

She peered over his shoulder to see the small form of a serving girl bundled in the prince's silk sheets. Her red-rimmed eyes glistened with tears, and yet she sat compliant. They always seemed so compliant. What kind of magic did he use on them? Rebekah's fists trembled, but she dared not insult the prince.

His hand slid from the doorframe and he pulled the door shut, locking the girl inside. He shot Rebekah a crooked smile as he sauntered past, but there was no mistaking the glare in those hard, blue eyes—just like Idla's.

Rebekah stilled the horror in her heart when she entered the throne room. At least forty young men and women lined up before her, all wearing expressions of shock and fear. Idla stood with Franco on one side and Oswell on the other. The healer, Belladonna, stood nearby as well. Her sneer said she was probably waiting for Rebekah to make a mistake and lie.

"They were kidnapped by the Feravolk, but our men rescued them." A deep voice resonated behind her.

Rebekah recognized the voice of General Balton. She turned toward him and his slick smile. Though handsome with greedy brown eyes, grizzled hair, and stubble, he was more well-known for his violent temper. Rebekah knew scores of serving girls who had left his chambers with purple marks on their skin.

He liked to whisper compliments in Rebekah's ear when he got the chance, and he always stood too close to her. Much, much too close. She shuddered.

"Thank you, General," Idla said. "Oswell, see to it that these Children get something to eat."

Rebekah's stomach twisted. Last month Idla had asked how Feravolk created their magical camouflage cloaks. Now Rebekah knew why. Idla was kidnapping Children of the Blood Moon under the guise of Rebekah's people—a desperate, but effective practice.

Franco grabbed Rebekah's arm. He smiled just like his mother. "Do you see any of the deliverers?"

Rebekah straightened her spine and scanned the group. "I do not."

Franco looked to Belladonna, who gave a slight nod, then turned back to Rebekah. His hot breath caressed her ear. "How can you be so sure?"

Her eyes lingered on a couple of girls with dark hair and soft, blue eyes like Logan's, but neither of them were her daughter. She felt no pull of protection for any of them—a secret she wanted to keep. She kept her voice a whisper. "I was bonded to a wolf. I know the scents of my children and those of my best friends."

Franco cocked an eyebrow and grinned. "Your sense of smell is your guide?"

She leaned toward his ear and whispered, "You smell like your mother—and of a man I know. A man who isn't the deceased king."

Franco's eyes widened, and his face darkened. He steeled himself quickly. "That's enough."

He squeezed her arm tight enough to produce a bruise. At least he'd caught her meaning, and he'd harbor no more doubt about her sense of smell. Neither would Belladonna.

The healer stalked off behind the prince. Idla glared at Rebekah from across the room. They wouldn't discuss it now, but it would come later. She'd kept Idla's secret without her knowledge for this long.

Rebekah shivered at the thought of entering the torture chamber, at her recollection of its scent of sweat and feces and blood.

The hair on her arms prickled and she turned to see Felix Balton striding closer. His slick smile slithered across his lips—only ever his lips. Never his eyes.

She pictured Logan and the way his eyes crinkled in the corners when he laughed. How she missed his laugh. He didn't smell like steel and sword oil. That scent belonged to Balton.

"You are looking magnificent today, as usual," Balton said.

She bowed her head. "Thank you."

"Your son is talented. I keep trying to convince Idla to let me make him a lieutenant in my army. She is reluctant."

"I don't know her motives, Felix, but Connor wants to join your army. I think it is why he practices in your presence so often."

"He has done a good job of getting my attention. He wields weapons some of my men will not touch."

"He prefers the quarterstaff. He says there's something light and freeing about the way smooth wood fits in his hands." Rebekah smiled and immediately regretted it. Felix's return leer made her back up a pace. He matched her step, then encroached even more.

"He is skilled, but I disagree. There is nothing like wrapping your fingers around cold steel to jolt you into battle."

"It has been said you can tell a lot about a man by his choice of weapon."

"And what of your husband? What did he use?"

Felix swept a strand of her hair away from Rebekah's face and she caught her breath.

"A sword." She dropped her eyes from his. "He said those who fight by the sword should feel the blade."

Idla's summons echoed through the hall. Rebekah turned away from General Balton, for once thankful Idla had called her.

Back in her room Rebekah found herself alone with Idla, Belladonna, and Oswell. She sunk into her chair, but the scent of daffodils, though faint, permeated the dark corner behind the drapes. That meant Idla had also brought the assassin sisters, Thea and Kara. Those two scared her more than the queen.

Idla motioned for Oswell to pour tea. "I am disappointed in the replica cloaks you had made for me."

Rebekah's heart skidded through a beat. Disappointed? That word sent dread through her core. She could almost taste the tang of fresh blood in her mouth.

"Thea," Idla called. One of the sisters strode out of the shadows—Thea, the one with corn silk hair and dark blue eyes. She was the more petite of the two sisters. Though it was easy to tell them apart—Kara kept her reddish-blonde hair shoulder length and her eyes bore more green than blue—they moved the same. Spoke the same. There was one subtle style difference Rebekah had come to notice. Thea liked to strike like a mountain lion—from behind. Kara wanted her prey to know who was killing them.

Thea slid out of a Feravolk cloak, and dropped it in front of Rebekah. "This cloak is the real thing. Our crude ones pale in comparison."

"Where did you get that?" Rebekah whispered.

"Relax. I didn't get to kill anyone for it." Thea picked up the cloak and dangled it in front of Rebekah. "I found it at a merchant shop in Nivek."

Rebekah knew relief filled her face, but her eyes darted to Idla. "I told you. You cannot make the true cloaks anymore."

Idla's blue eyes narrowed. "Why not?"

"You need unicorn-tail hair. Unicorns are extinct."

"Are they?" The other sister stepped out of the shadows. Where one was, the other was never far. Kara might not seem as dangerous as her sister, but that was only because she liked to let her prey know she was going to strike. "I think they're still alive."

"Well, good luck finding one, Kara." Rebekah glared at her. It was bold, but she didn't want either of the sisters to know how much she feared them.

"I can't. They make themselves invisible." Kara cocked an eyebrow.

"We will continue using the spelled horse-tail hair until we can get a unicorn." Idla rose. With a wave of her hand she dismissed everyone, then stepped closer to Rebekah. "It is time your boy learned to work for me."

"He wants to join Balton's army." Rebekah tried to hide her quaking voice. Her sole purpose hinged on protecting her son, and she couldn't do that if Idla no longer found her useful. But Idla would never gain Connor's trust if she hurt Rebekah, and Connor had a temper that rivaled a rabid wolf's.

"You know I cannot let him."

"I do not. Just because you don't want to risk sending him to war doesn't mean you have to stop him from joining the army."

"After all these years, your tongue is still sharp. I heard about what you said to Franco."

"It is a secret I have kept."

"Because you have no proof."

"Because I have no desire to tell it."

Idla pressed her lips into a firm line. "Still, Connor will give his queen allegiance. I will take his allegiance, and with it his right to one of the four thrones. I will do the same with all of the deliverers when the time is right. And you will help me to find them."

Idla knew far too much about the prophecies.

Rebekah bowed her head. "Of course."

"Good. Take care that Connor sees you in no danger. I'd hate for him to give his life for yours when you're trying so hard to protect him." Idla turned and her cloak whisked around behind her as she left the room. All the others followed her.

Rebekah sat at the table, numb. If Connor would give his life without hesitation for her, then she needed to change her strategy. She needed to leave. But how?

Her wolf-keen ears picked up a sound. She focused on the dark corner of the room. "I hear you there."

Nothing but the scent of daffodil. "Thea."

The assassin stepped forward.

The woman dressed in form-fitting clothes. Leather overlays protected her thighs, arms, and abdomen. Her boots were quiet, and her movements were always deliberate. Calculating. Movements of an assassin.

"I know what you're thinking." Thea slid into the seat across the table from Rebekah and locked eyes with her.

Rebekah let a small smile tug her lips and Thea's blue eyes lit up for it. The sisters loved to play games. But their games resembled something like cat and mouse. They were never the mice.

"Do you?" Rebekah folded her arms.

"Yes. And I think I can help you."

"I would not take help from you, Thea."

"Don't be so sure."

"You are the queen's assassin."

"Even Idla isn't sure who I work for."

Hope dared to rise, but to trust Thea made her instinct for fear rise too. "Why would you tell me that?"

"Because you wouldn't tell her. I know your loyalty lies elsewhere."

She did? Rebekah's heart sped. "And where does yours lie?"

"With my sister." Thea smiled.

"And how could you be of help to me?"

"I can break the trace spell."

Rebekah's hope lifted again. Dangerously high. She didn't want to trust in hope. It had let her down for too long. "How? You don't wield magic."

"No, but I am an assassin. Lifting traces is part of my line of work." She cocked an eyebrow and grinned like a cat who'd cornered a mouse. "I can also give you a poison to knock out your guard without killing him. Since you're so . . . averse to bloodshed."

"What would you ask in return?"

"You tell me where your Feravolk camp is."

Rebekah shook her head. "I could never do that."

"You could, and you asked what I wanted in return, so you're halfway there. I'll give you time to think if you need it."

"I don't need time to think. I wouldn't share it with you. Even so, the camp moves often."

Thea leaned closer, interest plain on her face. "Oh?"

"They are very careful."

"Well, that information is worth a little something." She placed a small bag on the table and pushed it toward Rebekah. "But your bonded wolf would be able to tell you where they are."

"Aurora is no longer bonded to me."

Thea tilted her head. "Really?"

Rebekah eyed the bag. "What is that?"

"Tangle flower seed. It's already crushed to powder form. One dab in the bloodstream can put a grown man out for hours. It works if you ingest some too." Thea left without a sound.

Rebekah sat there and stared at the small bag on the table. When she heard soft footfalls outside her door, she pocketed Thea's gift and stood.

The knock told her who it was. "Come in, Connor."

The door opened and Connor slipped inside. He was sweaty from sparring, and smiling from it too.

Rebekah crinkled her nose, but smiled at her son. "I think you should bathe. You smell like a musty wolf."

"Thanks." He rolled his eyes and unlaced his shirt. He grabbed an apple from the fresh fruit bowl next to the tea tray. Between bites he asked, "Idla visited?"

Rebekah nodded as she walked over to her dresser.

"What did she want?"

Rebekah sighed. "More of the same."

"I heard she's been burning towns in the name of the Feravolk."

Rebekah turned toward her son and growled. That wolfish habit had not left her. "*Burning*? Not merely kidnapping then? I should have known it would be worse."

She turned back to her dresser and lifted the small bag of tangle flower seed from her pocket and placed it inside.

Connor leaned toward her. "What is that?"

"It's nothing."

"Nothing?" Connor neared the dresser. "What kind of nothing, Mother, and why are you afraid?"

"I am not . . . afraid."

"Do you forget I can smell fear?"

Rebekah turned to face her son. He looked nothing like her. He was tall, a trait she didn't give him. His eyes weren't the deep brown of hers or the light blue of Logan's. They were amber. Even his hair held no hint of her gold. It was a rich brown like wet tree bark.

She lowered her head from his probing gaze. "I'm afraid you are becoming too protective of me."

"Of course I'm protective of you. You're my mother."

"Connor, it's my job to protect you, not the other way around." She had no trouble meeting his eyes now.

"I am to protect you, too."

"No. You are not a protector. I am. And I won't have you endanger your life for me. The game I play here is mine alone."

"I am capable of stealth like the sisters."

"But not capable of lies. Belladonna will see right through them. We need to leave."

"The trace? How will you get past it?" He looked at the drawer where she had placed her mysterious bag. His mouth opened and he clamped it shut.

Rebekah sighed. "I do not wish you to know what is in the bag."

Connor set his jaw. He was stubborn, but smart. "Who gave it to you?"

"Connor—"

"Kara? Thea?"

She turned away from his prying eyes. Holding her emotions from him—the only person she could trust—was not easy.

"No." He must have seen it in her face, or smelled her fear. "You cannot trust them."

"And I don't." She met his gaze. "I trust my instincts."

Connor sighed, but he seemed to accept this response. "When do we leave?"

CHAPTER 11

UNWANTED WEAPONS

Jayden's eyes opened. No cloaked man pinned her to the ground or held a rock over her head. Instead, she stared at a ceiling with thick wooden beams. Low voices whispered nearby, but she didn't see anyone. Sunlight spilled in through the window above the couch where she lay. Where was she?

Slowly, she sat up. Her head throbbed, and she ran her fingers over a tender lump above her temple. She had to get out of here.

The couch creaked under her. The voices stopped. Jayden froze and held her breath. The whispering started again.

Okay, leaving wouldn't be easy. Carefully, she moved the blanket aside. What was she wearing? Her pants, her shirt, and her favorite green, divided riding dress, but they were clean. No trace of blood. Someone had cleaned her clothes and dressed her? And her wounds. Shiny ointment coated every scratch on her hands and arms. Ryan's stone had even been put back in her pocket. Still, she had to get out of there.

It would be nice if she could find her boots before bolting. She scanned the room. To her left was a massive stone fireplace. The scent of chicken stew bubbled from the pot over the flames. So this was the cabin she'd tried to get to. Did that mean the Feravolk didn't have her? Maybe whoever lived here could help Ryan.

Across from the couch were two rocking chairs with high, curved backs and carved designs etched into the wood. Someone had taken great care in crafting them. Between them was a table with legs that resembled a lion's, complete with paws.

On the table were weapons—two swords, four long daggers and four assassin daggers. Her heart sped. Before she blacked out someone had shot arrows at her enemy, and that someone had good aim. Maybe whoever lived here was just as dangerous.

Next to the basket of yarn and knitting needles sat her satchel and boots. Jayden dashed over to them.

The murmurs quieted.

An icy chill pricked Jayden's skin and she looked to her right. On the other side of the room's archway was another room. A small, wrinkled, white-haired woman sat at a table with a middle-aged man who could have been her grandson. He had dark hair and kind, blue eyes—not unlike the old woman's. Jayden swallowed. Maybe they were just helping her.

"You're awake." The woman stood and walked toward her. "I washed your clothes."

"How long have I been here?"

"A couple of hours. Please, eat something. You look famished." The woman wrapped a comforting arm around Jayden's shoulders. "I'm Anna. What's your name, dear one?"

Hours? Ryan could still be alive, if she hurried. "Jayden. I'm—I can't stay. My friend, he—he's dying."

Anna's mouth dropped open.

A chair slid across the floor and the man stood. "Where's your friend?"

Heaviness, like a sack of flour, dropped into Jayden's stomach. He wore the cloak and carried a sword. He was one of the Feravolk.

Jayden snatched two daggers from the table, one in each fist. One assassin dagger and one long one. This way she could throw one and use the other like a sword. The hilts pressed against her palms as if made for her hands. Blue light blazed from the sapphire stones in the daggers' hilts. The light, like a fine mist, wrapped around her wrists and faded away, as if her skin absorbed it. She froze, but wouldn't let go of her only means of salvation.

There was no way to reach the door without walking past the man. Shielding the old woman, Jayden faced her enemy. "What do you want with me?"

The Feravolk man released his sword, and it clanked at his feet. He raised his hands, palms up. "I'm not going to hurt you."

He was calm, he felt . . . sorry for her? That familiar iron grip of fear clutched her chest. She tightened her hold on the weapon. If she let him know she was scared, he'd . . . who knew what he'd do to her?

She motioned the dagger toward the door, but her eyes never left his. "I know what you are. Out, or I will kill you." She hoped he wouldn't hear the tremor in her voice.

The man walked toward the door. She shifted with him, watchful of his every move.

He stopped in the doorway. "Jayden?"

Her heart fluttered to a faster beat. He'd heard her name? What if he told others about her? Would they come for her? "I could kill you now."

"Let's just stop and think this through." He took a step toward her.

He'd kill her. Her heart jumped like one of the frightened rabbits her brothers had made her hunt, and she froze. The man took another step toward her, his hands out as if trying to keep her calm. Calm. She reached out with her talent. His emotions leaked into her—calmness, like Daniel. She grasped that feeling and slung the dagger at him.

Anna screamed.

The weapon sailed true, right for the man's chest. He dropped his shoulder and leaned back. The blade grazed the skin between his ribs and pinned his shirt to the wall. He froze, his blue eyes locked on her.

Still clutching the other dagger, she faced him.

A loud crack and clattering came from the beyond the door. A huge wolf barreled into the room, fangs exposed.

It bounded between Jayden and the Feravolk, its amber eyes fixed on her. Every fur on its body bristled and its growl resounded in the floorboards, vibrating in Jayden's legs. A shiver ratcheted through her, so even the dagger tip trembled.

"She's one of them, Westwind," the man said.

He could talk to it? Jayden's chest shook as she breathed. "Don't speak."

"Please." Anna positioned herself between Westwind and Jayden's dagger.

Jayden lowered the weapon, but only for a moment. "You're with him?"

"We aren't armed." Anna took a step closer.

The door was her only way out. Speed was another one of her talents, but to what extent? She'd never been able to outrun an animal before, and she'd have to get past them. Those amber eyes still burned holes in her face. She was trapped.

"What is going on here, Child?" Anna's voice reached through her clouded thoughts.

Jayden registered the small tug against the dagger, and she relinquished the weapon. *I'm sorry, Ryan.* She sank to the floor and buried her face in her hands.

"Dear one," the old woman whispered in her ear. Soft hands touched her shoulders.

Dear one? "Aren't you going to kill me?"

"*Kill* you?" Logan's voice came out so harsh that Jayden flinched. "I *rescued* you from those men."

He had? She peered between her fingers and saw him pull the dagger from the wall, releasing his shirt. He winced, then wiped the blood from the blade on his sleeve. Creator in heaven, she'd tried to kill him and he'd been helping her? She *was* a monster.

"You're okay now." He knelt next to her. Westwind followed like a guard dog. A very large, scary guard dog.

Jayden couldn't control her shaking. "You fought your own?"

Logan's eyes narrowed. "They *aren't* my own."

Jayden shrank back. "I'm sorry. I thought—well, the Feravolk attacked our village last night. You dress like them."

"No. *They* dress like *me*." Logan's deep voice bordered on a growl.

"You're not a Feravolk?"

Logan stood and ran his hand through his hair. A spot of blood from his side dripped onto the floor. "I am. They aren't."

He really expected her to believe that? Then she glanced at the wolf and her insides squeezed. Had the men who attacked her village brought animals? Maybe this Logan was telling the truth.

"Tell me, Jayden, when these . . . Feravolk . . . attacked your village, what did they say?"

"They demanded every Child born the night of the Blood Moon. When no one came forward, they started burning things and killing people."

"They were after her." Anna smoothed Jayden's hair.

Jayden stood. "Not just me. All the Children are in danger."

Logan clenched his jaw. "The Feravolk wouldn't lead an attack."

"They wore cloaks like yours."

"Rebekah doesn't keep secrets well."

The animal-like way Logan growled Rebekah's name had Jayden reaching for her weapons. "Who's Rebekah?"

"Never mind. The Feravolk sent me to find the deliverers and protect them. We are *not* behind those attacks."

Another rumble rose in Westwind's throat. Jayden's eyes darted to the wolf, but he wasn't growling at her.

Anna squeezed Jayden's arm. "It has begun, Logan. The deliverers need their protector, and they need him now."

What? Jayden backed away from both of them. "Deliverer? I'm not your deliverer. I—what's going on here?"

Warmth pressed against her leg and stiff, thick fur brushed her hand. Jayden gasped and looked down at the wolf. His amber eyes locked on her face, but they were soft this time. She searched his emotions with her talent. The wolf expressed much more than any other animal she'd ever used her talent on. She looked into his eyes and noticed how expressive they were. The worry she felt in him shone there, too.

Worry for her? She swallowed. What had her parents kept from her?

"He doesn't let people pet him." Logan smiled. "He must really like you."

"Even after I tried to kill you?"

"You said you were sorry."

"Did you see the daggers glow when you picked them up?" Anna asked.

Jayden nodded, her hand resting on Westwind's side.

"Here." Anna handed Jayden the last two blue-stoned daggers from the table. "All four daggers were made by my late husband."

At the woman's nod, Jayden accepted the other two daggers. Again, the sapphire jewels glowed at her touch. The light wrapped around her, and she tried to drop the weapons, but they remained in her hands until the blue aura died away. Then they clattered against the floor.

Jayden stepped away from them. "I don't want to take—"

"They're yours. They've marked you as one of the deliverers."

Jayden stared at the old woman. What had she done? "Marked? What do you mean?"

Anna's blue eyes were kind, but her gaze grew intense, like one of the wise women in Jayden's town. "Didn't you feel them connect to you? That's because a Wielder made them for the deliverers the night they were born. The sapphires would only glow when the owner of these weapons bonds to them." Anna picked them up and handed them back to Jayden. "They'll listen to you like no other weapon can—almost like they'll know what you want from them before you do." The woman put her hand over Jayden's. "They'll also help you control your talent."

Jayden pulled away from the old woman. Magical daggers? This was some trick. "No, I'm—you have the wrong girl."

Anna's brows furrowed. "They don't make mistakes. You are one of the deliverers."

Jayden's eyes darted between Logan and Anna. Wielder? Her heart sank. That would make Anna a Whisperer. What had her mother told her about Whisperers? They were good healers. Good with plants. Wise women took everything they knew about medicine from the ancient Whisperers. Anna might be able to save Ryan. Maybe if she just played their game for a little while. Let them think she was their precious deliverer. "My friend. He's dying."

Westwind whined softly at her side.

"Where is he?" Logan asked.

Everything in her screamed for her to run from him. He was one of the Feravolk and they killed her family, but his eyes were gentle and kind.

Logan frowned. "The Royal Army burned your village, not the Feravolk. I'll prove it to you. First, let me help your friend."

Ryan needed help if . . . if he was still alive. As soon as he was better, they would run away from this Feravolk man, but for now there were no other options.

Jayden slipped her shoes on, then she sheathed her new daggers and strapped the long ones to her belt. The small ones she tucked in her boots. Maybe these weapons would work like she needed. Keep her focused. Make it so the fear didn't cripple her and others couldn't open her talent. Likely that was too much to ask. "I'm going with you. You won't find him without me."

She looked into Logan's eyes. Jayden's heart tripped on a beat as all the memories of Feravolk rushed back to her. Trusting this Logan was another of her desperate and foolish decisions.

CHAPTER 12

MIRACLE BLOOD

If the boy was dying, Logan had no time to argue. He motioned for Jayden to lead. Westwind stepped out at her heels.

"Just over that ridge. I left my horse when she acted like the stream was going to swallow her whole."

They entered the place where Logan and Westwind had met Anna. Tied to a tree near the water's edge stood a palomino mare. Her eyes widened at the sight of Westwind.

"Relax, pony. Horsemeat's too tough for me anyway." Westwind chuckled.

His throaty, barking laugh did nothing to calm the horse's nerves, but Jayden stroked the mare's nose and spoke to her softly until the horse relaxed.

"We'll need her to bring Ryan back." Jayden grabbed the horse's reins. "Her name is Aureolin."

She said no more as she led them through the trees.

The woods thickened as they stepped onto hillier terrain. Logan listened for anything different, unnatural. Westwind's ears flattened. He heard it first, but Logan caught it too—the groaning and labored breathing of someone in trouble.

They approached a dip in the forest floor. Halfway down the hill, hidden between two close trees, Logan spotted the form of a young man. They rushed to him.

A boy no older than Jayden lay on the ground, covered with a blanket.

Westwind chuffed. *"He smells dead."*

Logan glanced at Westwind. *"Let's hope he's got enough time left."*

A broken arrow shaft protruded from the young man's chest. Sweat beaded on his forehead, and he breathed irregular breaths. Logan threw back the blanket and his insides froze. Ryan's shirt was only green along the bottom edges. Everywhere else it was wet and red.

Jayden grabbed his hand. "Ryan, I brought some . . . friends to help you."

This kid had little time left, if any. "How long has he been like this?"

"Since last night." Her voice shook.

Dried blood covering his ripped pant leg showed where a wound had already been bandaged.

"You did this?" Logan asked Jayden. "He's lucky to have had you there."

She tried to smile, but the corners of her mouth fought back.

Logan surveyed Ryan's chest. He poured water over the area and rinsed away layers of blood. The kid's pink birthmark sat to the right of the arrow.

It was buried deep in his chest. Logan gritted his teeth. He caught a whiff of the decaying smell Westwind had wrinkled his nose toward. They would lose him soon if they didn't hurry.

Jayden's fingers curled around his wrist. Her blue eyes penetrated him. "You tell me straight. I want no secrets. Can you help him?"

"Aren't Whisperers known for their healing abilities?" Westwind asked.

"Our best option is to take him to Anna's. Help me get him on Aureolin."

Together they positioned Ryan on the horse and tied him to her. Jayden stumbled often as they walked back to the Whisperer's house.

Poor girl was probably exhausted.

"Honestly, Jayden, your friend is very strong."

"Unbelievably," Westwind said.

By the time they made it back to Anna's, the sun dipped closer toward the horizon. This time they were able to coax Aureolin across the creek.

Anna came out to meet them. Her trees must have told her they were close. She helped them inside, where cloths, ointments, and a bowl of clean water waited on her sturdy, oak table. Logan placed Ryan's body on the table where Anna directed.

Anna looked Ryan over, her face serene. "Help me get this shirt off him."

Logan cut the bloody garment and peeled it over Ryan's limp arms. It didn't look good. Anna moved Logan out of the way and slipped her hand into a jar of thick, yellow paste, which she smoothed around where the arrow embedded in his skin.

"What's that?" Jayden's voice trembled.

Anna looked at the poor girl. "Don't worry, Jayden. I have a lot of experience tending to injuries. This will numb the area so it won't hurt as badly when I dig the arrowhead out."

Jayden nodded, but her eyes didn't leave Ryan's still form on the table.

Anna motioned to Logan. "Why don't the three of you sit outside? I'll tell you when I need you."

Logan and Westwind escorted Jayden outside. She curled up with Westwind's haunches as a pillow, and he let her.

Logan raised his eyebrows. *"You going soft?"*

The left side of Westwind's whiskered lip lifted and revealed a white fang. *"You know, taking care of the deliverers might not be as bad as we assumed."*

"We aren't taking care of them. All we have to do is get them back to Moon Over Water."

"Anna still calls you a protector. That means—"

"She's wrong. I gave up that right when I let Alistair handle it."

Anna emerged in the doorway, holding a candle. Westwind nudged his nose on Jayden's neck and she woke. When she noticed Anna, she bolted upright.

"This wound is going to be beyond my power to heal alone, but there is hope. I may be able to keep him stable until you can get me what I need."

"What do you need?" Logan rose to his feet.

"I have removed the arrow, but it was covered in a poison created by venom and dark magic. I need something to counteract it. I'll keep the wound open so I can extract all the poison, but I will need you to hurry."

"We'll hurry," Jayden answered before Logan could open his mouth.

"*We'll* hurry." Logan pointed to himself and Westwind. "You stay and help Anna."

Anna put a hand on Jayden's shoulder. "Actually, I have to agree with Jayden. You will need all the eyes you can get. The plant I need you to bring back is scarce. Also, you know the deliverers subconsciously want to be near their protectors."

"I did *not* know." Logan made sure Anna saw him narrow his eyes. He wished she wouldn't call him protector in front of Jayden. She might start to believe it.

"Now, this is what you'll need to bring me." Anna walked down the steps and onto the grass. She set the candle down and blew into her palm. As her breath waved the tops of the long grass, a small green sprout grew from among the blades.

The leaves of this new plant unfurled and lengthened. It resembled a tiny fern, though the limbs weren't as stiff and the leaves were thin and bristly. There were so many on each stem it looked almost fuzzy.

Jayden stared with eyes wide. "Why can't you just make your own?"

Anna picked the plant, and it turned to grass. "A Whisperer cannot grow something without the right seeds, but I can give the illusion of something that isn't."

She bent down and grew another spurious specimen. This time she unearthed the soft soil around it, and handed it to Logan. It retained its exotic shape.

"I only need one." Anna looked Logan in the eyes. "Come in. I'll show you where you need to go. Do you still have the map I gave you?"

They followed Anna inside and Logan produced the map from his sack.

"Jayden?" Ryan whispered.

She ran to him. "How are you?"

A weak smile formed on his face. "Much better."

"You sound better." Jayden's voice held some relief.

Logan stood behind Jayden. "You look better too." In truth, the kid looked weak and pale.

Anna fluffed the pillows in her sitting room. "Will you move him to the couch?"

Logan and Jayden got Ryan to his feet and supported him the short distance to the couch. Once they helped him lie down, Anna placed a wet cloth over the gaping hole in his chest.

Ryan winced, then focused on Logan. "I guess I should thank you. For saving my life."

Logan nodded toward Jayden. "That was her doing. I just helped."

Westwind walked over.

"Whoa." Ryan's interjection wasn't loud, but the shock in his voice was evident when Westwind stuck his massive head near his face. "Is that a wolf?"

"His name's Westwind. He's my friend."

"They're going to help me find the plant," Jayden said.

Ryan smiled. "Good. She needs all the help she can get. This girl finds trouble."

Logan couldn't help but chuckle. "We'll keep her safe. You just get better, kid."

"Yes, sir."

Jayden smiled, even though her lips still quivered.

"What, I survive an arrow in my chest, and I can't even get a real smile?"

Jayden knelt next him and took his hand in hers. "Ryan—"

"Stop worrying. The worst is over for me."

"You could get sick."

"I never get sick, Jayden. Remember when I cut my leg?"

"You mean impaled?"

Anna approached and put her hand on Ryan's forehead. She handed him a cup. "Drink this."

He sniffed it.

"It'll help with the pain." Anna smiled. Then she patted Jayden's shoulder. "Be sure he drinks all of it."

Logan followed Anna to the other room and pulled out the map she'd given him. "That kid going to make it?"

Anna stared at him for an uncomfortable moment. "Not without the plant. If you hurry he has a good chance." She paused and glanced in Ryan's direction. "He is a Child. I don't know what is keeping him alive."

"What do you think is keeping alive?"

Anna shook her head. "His blood runs hotter. I believe it will help him fight the infection."

"But not without the plant?"

For the first time since meeting her, even after she'd told him about his supposed destiny with the deliverers and listened to him deny that he'd take part in any of it, Logan watched the Whisperer's eyebrows pull together in worry.

"You are here now." Anna pointed. "I need you to make this journey to this valley between the mountains and back. The whole trip should take no more than seven full days." Her fingers traced the path. Westwind placed his forepaws on the table to see the course. "I need you to make it in less time."

"The Valley of the Hidden Ones? Legend has it more than unicorns dwell there."

Anna nodded. "Some *darker* creatures."

Logan's eyes wandered to the young woman in the other room sitting beside her dying friend. "You still think it's a good idea for me to bring her?"

"She won't stay here, not if you leave."

Westwind tilted his head. *This trail will take us right through the Royal Army's camp. We'll have to be careful or someone may notice us.*

"All right. It looks like we've got a journey ahead of us. When do we leave?"

"As soon as possible. I can pack you some food, water, and supplies. If I were you, I'd leave the horse. They tend to attract unwanted predators."

"We'll be back soon enough anyway."

"I pray you will." Anna shuffled over to the bookshelf flanking her fireplace and returned with a wooden dagger. She pressed the hilt into Logan's palm.

Was this some strange Whisperer ritual he knew nothing about? "Anna—"

"Should you meet a darker creature, drive that into its heart."

CHAPTER 13

TANGIBLE PROOF

Tareal smoldered. Acrid smoke clouded the whole city.

Scout followed Ethan through the unguarded city gates. There was nothing left to guard.

He turned around at the entrance of the city to stare at the woods—again. He willed himself to remember the fallen log, the patch of moss, the exact location where he'd stashed his sword, bow, and arrows. He hadn't wanted to bring them into the city.

The less attention he could bring to himself, the better. He excelled at not being seen if he didn't want to be, but a sword and full quiver at his hip would attract attention no matter how well he hid in the shadows.

His stomach growled. That wouldn't help either.

"First order of business, get some food and water." Ethan patted the golden-orange dog's big, silly head, then sighed. All he had was a sack full of apples. Those wouldn't last long, now that cities were no longer safe.

He covered his nose with his hand. The stink of blood and vomit and death hung in the air. He hitched his sack higher on his back and walked down an alley. Less death met him there, but the face of hunger stared at him: a young girl, her blue eyes hopeless.

Ethan took a step back from her. *Don't get attached.*

She was so young to be on her own—seven maybe. Ethan tossed

her an apple, and she looked as if she would spring up and hug him. He put his hands out in front of himself to stop her.

She frowned and dropped back against the wall, biting her lip. Ethan turned away. It was a selfish move, he knew, but if he got too close, he might want to protect her—if his protective talent latched on to her. Well, he couldn't afford to protect anyone right now.

He could hardly take care of himself. Even with his ability to heal quickly, every movement still hurt. If it weren't for that pull leading him here, he would have stayed curled up in the Forest of Legends until he was mended, even if took days.

Scout nudged Ethan's hand. The dog's deer-like ears splayed from the sides of his head and Ethan scratched behind one of them. "Let's go."

A soft whimper slowed his steps for a heartbeat. With his protective instinct latching onto Swallow so readily, it scared him to look any more helpless kids in the eye. He fought the urge to turn around and lost.

Creator help him. There were *two* hungry girls sharing the apple. How had he missed the other one? That stupid pull started to flare in his chest. He had to get away from them or he'd bring them under his wing for sure.

Ethan grabbed all but two apples from his bag. He left them on the ground and rushed out of the alley without looking back. Clear of the innocent-eyed beggars, he strayed farther into the city. Destruction this severe left desperation in its wake.

Ethan stopped in front of a fire-stained building. The door hung crooked, dangling from one hinge. His hand hovered over his knife. The plan was easy—just walk in, see if there was anything worth stealing, and walk out.

He peered inside and the faint aroma of leather reminded him of his father's shop. Ethan slipped past the teetering door with Scout close. Perhaps he could find another quiver to replace his worn one. The rip down its side grew daily, and he couldn't afford to lose any arrows.

The place had already been looted. Bare shelves and hooks

adorned the walls and goods littered the floor. One quiver, hanging on a hook in the wall, caught his eye. Ethan ran his fingers along the smooth leather and fingered the design. A moon. How appropriate. And no wonder it was left. The quality rivaled his father's ability. Ethan's throat tightened.

He draped the strap over his shoulder. There was no coin in his pocket for such a gift, but he'd make up for it, someday.

He stepped back out into the stink of death. Every other shop on the street looked as bad as this one. Scout stuck closer than ever. "We'll have to keep to the forest now, boy. Cities are no longer safe for us."

The sound of hooves along cobblestones turned Ethan's head. A carriage rode down the city center flanked by four rows of soldiers on each side, in front and in back. Shields and flags displayed the red and yellow crest of the muzzled dragon.

The queen's carriage.

Maybe it would be easier to find out what Idla wanted with the Children than he'd thought. Ethan slid into the shadows and counted on his Blood Moon talent of remaining hidden to shield him. It would only work so long as he didn't move. Scout drifted behind him and they watched.

Evil herself, the queen stepped out of the carriage and stood on the stair. Her soldiers clustered close. People started coming out of the shadows and inched closer to the procession, but Ethan stayed put. He had no desire to get any closer to that witch.

The queen raised her hand. "Good people of Tareal, news of the Feravolk's destruction has reached the palace."

I'll bet it has.

"Rest assured. The palace will help you rebuild your city."

Did he hear her right?

"We will also find and punish those responsible for ruining your lives and taking your children—the Feravolk."

Cheers started quietly, but began to resound off of the refuse and debris. Ethan had to get to Nivek. The queen couldn't already have sent soldiers to the city he was raised in. It was too far from here.

There were enough people in Nivek still friendly to the Feravolk. People still aware of the teachings of the prophecies and the promise of the deliverers. Teachings and prophecies that this queen had tried to banish from schools. Yes, Nivek was his hope.

"I have a gift for you." The queen turned and nodded toward one of her soldiers. He opened the carriage door and people who all appeared his age spilled out. Children of the Blood Moon, no doubt. Idla had played her cards well.

A growl rose in Ethan's throat. She would be the undoing of everything Soleden held dear. Freedom would no longer be accessible. Her will would be law.

Mothers and fathers rushed forward as the Children thundered out of the carriage. Cries of reunion filled the air.

Ethan's fingernails dug into his palms.

"My men rescued these young ones from the Feravolk. We killed all those in sight, save one." The queen motioned to her right and grinned. "This man is one of the Feravolk. One of the ones that destroyed your city. He admits to having done so."

Ethan's attention drifted past the reuniting families. A new carriage entered the city—an iron cage—also guarded, though not as heavily. He squinted to try and get a better look at the man huddled inside. Older, middle-aged, thin. He wore a cloak like Logan's.

Shouts and jeers began. People raced close to the carriage and threw stones. Soldiers parted to let the people closer. The carriage rocked. Stones clinked off metal. The man huddled in the center of his torture chamber, pleading.

"Back away. I will show you what your queen does to traitors against the crown."

The townspeople made a wide circle around the cage.

Idla extended her arm and pointed at the prisoner. "You betrayed me. Death is your punishment."

The air tingled. A flash of lightning shot from Idla's fingers into the prisoner's chest. Thunder cracked, drowning out the man's scream.

Ethan turned away from the charred body. That man was

probably no guiltier than any of the townspeople. Yet he had given tangible proof that the Feravolk were the enemy. The air cooled and sprinkles of rain—healing rain that the parched land needed—fell from the sky. Cries of happiness and praise for the queen resounded. Of course she'd bring rain after she destroyed the city.

"Dear people! Help me fight these Feravolk. Join my army so we will be rid of these traitors!"

Ethan could bear the cheers no longer. He turned to leave and heat exploded in his chest. Before he could find the source of the threat, a hand gripped his shoulder.

"What's the matter, boy? Don't you want to give praise where it's due?"

The scent of peppermint swirled around him. He trembled as he faced Minty.

"Dogs shouldn't chew through their leashes and run. It earns them a beating."

CHAPTER 14

GUARD DOG
IN THE WOODS

Logan paced in front of Anna's house until the door creaked open and Anna stepped onto the porch.

"I've packed you some food and a few extra waterskins. And two more bedrolls—one for Jayden and an extra. It gets chilly in the mountains at night." She paused, searching Logan's face. "You will be a good protector." She nodded once before she turned to go back into her house. "I'll get Jayden."

Logan kicked a rock. He wasn't a protector. He picked up another rock and threw it. It didn't make him feel any better.

Something like a deep breath sounded in his thoughts. Westwind had been about to say something and changed his mind.

Logan didn't look at Westwind. *"What?"*

"You rethinking this protector thing?"

He shot Westwind a glare. *"No."*

"All right."

"What does that mean?"

Westwind shrugged. *"Nothing."*

"You know I can't do it."

"Can't?" Westwind's return glance held a hint of challenge.

Logan laced his fingers together behind his head. *"I'm no deserter."*

"I didn't say you were."

"I will be on the frontlines when the battle horn sounds."

"I believe you."

"I will get to the deliverers if it kills me."

"I know."

"It's one thing I'm not embracing. One thing. I have a right."

"A right?"

Logan made hard eye contact with Westwind. *"A reason."*

"Many."

There were others better suited for the task. Better able to face the queen and her spies—Bekah. No, *Rebekah*. She was no longer his Bekah. If Logan faced her, he wasn't sure he'd be able to put a knife in her heart. After all, that heart had belonged to him before she gave allegiance to the queen. No one could ever know he still harbored love for the woman who betrayed his people.

"Still," Westwind watched him, *"no one ever said destiny was kind."*

The door squeaked open again and Anna waved them in. Logan nodded at the Whisperer before she disappeared back into her house. He and Westwind followed.

Jayden tearfully hugged Ryan. The kid winced, but didn't let Jayden see.

Logan gave them a moment alone. He picked up his belongings.

Anna handed him a rolled-up bag that held the Wielder-crafted weapons made to identify the deliverers—minus Jayden's set of four daggers—and a small drawstring pouch holding the strange tokens she'd told him about earlier. "You may need these."

Logan set down the two bags. "I'll be back soon enough. And lighter travel is faster travel."

He shoved the map book she'd given him in his satchel.

Jayden joined him, tears wiped away. She grabbed her small pack.

"Don't worry. He's in good hands." Anna smoothed Jayden's hair, then her eyes met Logan's. He didn't have to be bonded to the Whisperer to sense the urgency in her stare.

"May the Creator's wings speed your travel."

The moon hung high above the trees, a sliver of silver light. Logan had no trouble seeing in the dark, but he didn't want to take for granted what Jayden could distinguish, so he kept his pace slower until she seemed adjusted.

"I'm not your deliverer." Jayden's quiet voice broke the silence.

Logan sighed. "The daggers revealed—"

"The daggers are wrong."

"And yet you use them."

She whipped her head around and stared directly in the eyes. "My village was just burned by Feravolk." She held up her hand at his protest. "Or so they claim. And you question my acceptance of new weapons?"

No use fighting with her now. She wasn't going anywhere, at least not until her friend got better—or died. "I'm sorry."

She dropped her head and her dark hair fell around her face. She sniffed.

How was he going to handle a young woman and her emotions? "Are you okay?"

"I'm fine." Jayden tucked her hair behind her ears, but she still stared at the ground. "Are all Children of the Blood Moon called deliverers?"

"Only four."

"Four? Four in thousands? So you could be wrong."

"I'm not."

"Listen, Logan, I appreciate your honesty. I really do. The thing is I'm not who you're looking for."

"Have you not heard the prophecy? It states: The moon shall rise red and call the births of the deliverers, and when they come of age, they shall deliver us. There shall be four in all: two sets of twins each consisting of a boy and a girl. Only two sets of twins consisting of a boy and a girl shall be born the night of the Blood Moon."

Jayden rolled her eyes. "I know. I've heard this bedtime story: A sorceress will come with power to destroy all the Creator has built. She'll break the land and the people's hearts and bring death to those who'd oppose her. But hope will be found when the deliverers rise through fire, through ash, and heal the heart of the land." She paused and shook her head. "It sounds pretty, but it doesn't make a lot of sense. And I didn't rise through fire and—" She stopped. After a few deep breaths, she turned her back on him and kept walking, but her words cut through the night loud and clear. "I'm not your deliverer."

Logan quickened his pace to catch up with her. "You have a twin brother. I have not seen him since the night the two of you were born, and I carried *you* to the wet nurse that took you to live with the Jorah family."

Jayden stopped walking. "The Jorahs?" She twirled a strand of dark hair in her fingers. So like her birth mother.

"Yes. So, you can argue against your destiny all you want, but I'm telling you, I haven't made a mistake. I'd recognize your face anywhere." He saw it in his nightmares often enough.

"The Jorahs were killed last night, by the false Feravolk. They died protecting me."

Of course. What a fool he'd been for not thinking of that. "They were good people."

"Yes. But they kept secrets from me. I don't tolerate secrets, *Protector*."

Protector. Of course she would have picked up on that little detail. "It was for your safety."

"And what of theirs?"

Logan bowed his head and ground his teeth.

She pointed a finger at him and stepped closer. "If I agree to play this allotted part—be this deliverer—I need something in return."

She was a fiery little thing. "What, Jayden?"

Her arm fell. She stood straight. Tears coated her eyes. "No secrets about this. I've got to know all the stakes. You tell me straight."

Westwind cocked his head. *"You going to tell her you're not her protector?"*

"You think she's ready to hear that? She'll take off and we'll have to track her down."

"Maybe not. She's desperate to help her friend."

"Let me handle this." He looked at Jayden. "All right. No secrets. You ask, I'll answer you. Straight."

"Good." She nodded once and resumed walking, but she tripped on a tree root and stumbled. She righted herself and kept walking as if nothing had happened.

Logan shook his head and followed her. "I'm sorry about the Jorahs. It's the queen's doing."

"Then maybe I want to make that wretched woman rue the day I was born."

"Oh, she already does."

"We've been noticed." Westwind's ear twitched toward the sound he'd picked up.

Logan stopped walking and listened. *"I don't hear anything. Wait."*

Faint laughter.

He found a place where brush grew around a downed tree and led them behind its cover and stopped.

Jayden's eyes fixed on him, but she made no sound.

Logan kept his voice low. "There's a camp here. The Royal Army—the ones who pose as my people. *Our* people. They may be aware of our presence. If I can set a false trail, I may be able to get them away from us. You wait here with Westwind. I'll be fast."

"I could help." Jayden pulled a dagger from her boot and smiled.

"I believe you could, but I'm fast."

"I'm fast."

"You're staying."

Her hands went to her hips, but they didn't stick. "I—"

"You will not approach the Royal Army while I'm trying to keep you *away* from the queen."

Jayden's eyes bored into his. "Until I face her?"

Guilt stabbed his stomach. Had the prophecies said anything about the deliverers surviving their attempt to rescue the Feravolk?

"All right," Jayden said. "This time."

Westwind chuffed. *"So I'm babysitting now?"*

"It's hardly babysitting, Westwind. It's guarding. You're like a guard do—"

Westwind growled.

CHAPTER 15

KEEP FIGHTING

Ryan stared up at the ceiling from where he lay on Anna's couch. Candlelight danced in a soft yellow orb across the beams above him. He focused on its mercurial movement as Anna peeled the blood-soaked cloth off the gaping wound on his chest.

As soon as she uncovered it, she paused. Not a breath left her lungs for five full heartbeats. That bad, huh? He glanced at the wound. It was hard to see from this angle, but the edges of the hole—which seemed to have grown—were no longer angry red and raw. Now the skin looked almost gray. Dead.

He was dying.

Anna touched his forehead. "You're still hot." She applied more of the ointment. It stung like ice. A more bearable pain than the burning.

He breathed deep. "It's getting worse."

"That's to be expected." Warm, yellow light cast moving shadows on her face and deepened the worry lines on her brow.

"I'm going to die, aren't I?"

She touched his hand. "I'm doing everything I can, but it's not for me to know. You are a fighter. Don't give up hope." Her palm was cool against his forehead.

He didn't plan to give up, but right now even the thought of staying awake seemed difficult.

"Rest is the best thing for you, Ryan," she said. Then she blew out the light. "I'll be close."

She shuffled across the floor, and then the steady creaking of her rocking chair eased the feeling of darkness pressing against him from all sides. He closed his eyes. The comforting creak reminded him of the rusty hinge on his family's back door at home. The sound lulled him to sleep.

The sun sank near the horizon as Ryan made his way up the familiar dirt path that led from the forge to his house. Jayden's marriage stone sat in his pocket and slapped against his thigh with every movement. Finally finished. At least something had gone right today.

Ryan opened the back door to his home. It creaked, announcing his entrance. The scent of chicken and carrots met him as did his sister's devious smirk. Ryan sighed. Apparently Chloe had heard what happened at the smithy.

Kinsey glanced up from the pair of trousers she was patching. Her smile was warm at least.

He set the bag of lentils Mrs. Calloway had used to pay for her horse's re-shoeing on top of the potato basket in the corner of the kitchen and rolled his sore shoulder.

From behind, Chloe looked so much like his mother that he could almost pretend it was. All three of his sisters had inherited her red hair and green eyes. He had not.

Chloe added a chopped carrot to the stew and then motioned to the bag with her cutting knife. "The widow? You shouldn't let her pay you in food. She has three mouths to feed plus her own."

And none of them old enough to do much work. "I gave her most of it back, but she insisted."

"Well, that's kind of her. I'll soak them and we can have them tomorrow."

Chloe moved to the table and pulled out the bread knife. "Father said you had a hard day?" She eyed him over the loaf of bread she'd started cutting, and her green eyes seemed to glitter with mischief. "Don't tell me. William's horse?"

"Oh, Ryan." Kinsey's shoulders drooped. "Father has warned you about that horse before."

"Someone has to shoe that horse."

"But it spooks so easily. It's not safe."

"It's not like they can afford another." He crossed his arms. "Did Father say I couldn't handle him?"

"Not exactly." Chloe's smirk returned. "But I recall something about you landing in a pile of manure."

Kinsey hid a smile and mouthed, "Sorry."

Okay, that part had been a little funny.

He snatched a slice of bread, dodging Chloe's attempt to slap his hand. Her green eyes squeezed like tart limes, but a smile played on her face. "Ryan Granden."

He bit into the slice. Still warm.

Chloe placed her hands on her hips. "Next time William's horse needs shoes, let me know."

"So you can be there to watch me—"

"So I can hold the horse for you."

He stared at his sister, certain his eyes looked like a bullfrog's.

She rolled her eyes. "We both know William is too frail to control the horse, and that's the problem. Not you. No matter what Father says."

Ryan blinked. "That would be nice. Thank you."

She laughed. "Don't let this go to your head. I'm the oldest. It's still my job to keep you humble." She winked. "Now, Kinsey, I need water. Will you go to the well? And, Ryan, have you seen Wren?"

His heart skipped a beat. Not again. "I . . . saw her on my way home. I thought she'd be on her way soon. I'll go get her." Ryan shoved the rest of his stolen bread into his mouth.

Chloe whispered, "You're a terrible liar."

He chuckled and headed out the back door, Kinsey right behind him.

She picked up the empty bucket. "Wren?"

"Not a word to Father."

"I wouldn't dare." She shot him a smile.

He stopped in front of her and stuck his hand in his pocket. "You're the only one who will appreciate this, since Father doesn't approve, and Chloe only approves of what he approves of."

Kinsey whirled to face him, her eyes sparkling. "You finished Jayden's marriage stone?" She wiggled her fingers. "Let me see!"

He fished the stone from his pocket and handed it over. Her mouth dropped open as she turned it over, inspecting it from every angle, feeling the smooth surface. "Oh, Ryan, It's perfect." Her green eyes glittered as she grinned. "She'll love it."

"You think?" He rocked back on his heels.

"I know it. Look how these pretty gray swirls have come through as you polished it." She handed back. "Mother would have liked it."

"Even though she told me no black stones?"

Kinsey's smile turned sad and she touched Ryan's arm. "She'd understand how perfect it is."

"You're probably right." He placed the stone back in his pocket and headed to find his youngest sister.

"Ryan." Kinsey snagged hold of his shirtsleeve. "Are you okay? I heard you almost got trampled." Her round green eyes searched his face.

"I'm fine." Aside from the fact that he couldn't understand what had come over his father. "Father says not to help them anymore."

Kinsey stepped back. "That's not like him."

"You're telling me."

"He's been acting strange lately. I'll see what I can find out."

"Thanks. You better get to the well before dark."

She picked up the bucket. "And good luck with Wren."

He chuckled.

Dusk would be settling soon, so Ryan picked up his pace and headed right for the alley behind town hall. The streets were nearly empty. A few people who lived right in town were heading back from the well or the butcher's shop, and Ryan tipped his head toward those who looked his way. Truthfully, he didn't want anyone to remember he'd been here.

"Let me go, you little maggot!" A shout came from behind town hall's outbuilding, and Ryan raced into the alley.

He caught sight of a red-haired girl straddled on top of another kid whose legs thrashed against the dusty ground. Wren was bending the other kid's arm at a very unnatural angle.

"Whoa, whoa." Ryan grabbed hold of his sister. About five other kids caught sight of him and scattered.

Ryan tugged his sister's waist. "Let go of him, Wren."

She released the kid's arm, and Ryan picked her up.

Her arms swung at the empty air. "He attacked her!" Wren screeched.

Ryan recognized the other kid as one they all called Peter the Beater.

Peter scrambled to his feet. "Your sister's crazy." Dust covered his clothes and he picked up his hat, slapping it against his leg. Blood dripped out of his nose, and he smeared it over his lip with the back of his hand. "She needs a thrashing."

Ryan leveled a look at the kid. "She's not crazy, and if I catch you after her again, I'll have a nice long talk with your papa." He flexed his arm for good measure.

That widened Peter's eyes nicely, and he raced off.

Ryan set Wren down and crouched in front of her. He moved her hair so he could see her freckled face. "Again?" He gingerly touched the red, swollen skin by her left eye and winced. "He got you pretty good, huh?"

"No." She pushed Ryan's hand away.

He cocked an eyebrow and her shoulders sagged.

She looked down and drew a line in the dirt with her shoe. "He deserved it."

"People don't deserve that kind of beating, Wren. You've got to tell me what this is about."

She glared at him. "I heal fast enough. Father won't find out."

"Okay, but *I* need to know."

Clara, the smallest Calloway, stepped out from behind an empty barrel, leaning on her little wooden crutch. Her brown eyes, already huge, widened. "Don't be mad at her. She was protecting me."

Of course she was. He looked at Wren. "Is this true?"

"Clara brings bread here twice a week. Peter's always waiting for her. He won't let her pass until she has to walk home in the dark." Wren's little body went rigid and her hands fisted. "He pushed her down!"

Ryan noticed blood seeping through the knees of Clara's pants and his heart squeezed.

Clara fidgeted her fingers. "I can't stand up real good. Wren helps me get home sometimes."

He looked back and forth between the two girls. "For heaven's sake, Wren. Why don't you ask me to help you?"

She smiled bright, showing off her missing tooth. "You could show Peter really good."

"Apparently you still have a lesson to learn." He stood. "Come on. Let's walk Clara home. It's going to get dark soon."

Clara bit her lip.

"You want a lift?" Ryan smiled and her eyes glittered as she nodded.

He picked her up and set her on his shoulders. She was so light.

When they reached her home, he set her down at her front door. "Now, if anyone gives you trouble, you tell them the blacksmith's son protects you. Can you do that?"

"Oh yes. Thank you!" Even with her limp there was a bounce to her step as she headed inside.

Ryan rolled his sore shoulder. Then he turned to Wren. "Your eye looks better."

She crossed her arms and jutted out her chin. "I heal fast."

"Must be a Granden thing." He tousled her red hair.

She looked at the ground as they walked out of the Calloways' property. "You're mad at me."

"No. I'm disappointed that you thought you should fight someone."

She kicked a loose stone. "He took a swing at me first."

"And that makes it right?"

"No, but I had to do something. Never let people take advantage of the poor or weak because they're poor and weak. That's what you said today in the smithy when Father was yelling at you about William's horse. I heard you."

A pang squeezed his heart, but he couldn't deny the surge of pride. "I did, but—"

"I wasn't picking a fight, I swear." She looked up at him and grabbed his hand. "I'm only standing up for those who can't stand up for themselves. Just like you. Just like . . . like Father used to."

Ryan glanced at the ground. "I think Father still does, Wren. I think maybe he's just lost his way a bit."

"Because of Mother."

He breathed deep. "It's been hard on all of us." He smiled at her. "But we manage."

"Because we're Grandens."

"That's right."

She raced him to the top of the hill. They would make it home before dark, barely. Hopefully Chloe would be easy on Wren today.

"What's that?" Wren pointed and Ryan looked down the hill. Torches seemed to walk the paths of the city, splitting into lines like ants marching to find food. A line of disembodied torches headed right for his house.

Without missing a beat, he picked up his sister and ran home. The back door screamed as he burst through it.

"There you are!" His father's eyes were wild. "Ryan, you have to get out of here."

"What? No. I—I'm—"

"Kinsey, get Ryan's bow and arrows."

Kinsey ran to his room. Then his father picked up the basket of potatoes beside the fireplace. Behind it a sword sat propped against the wall. Ryan blinked. His father owned a sword?

Kinsey returned with his bow. She pressed it into his hand.

"Girls, you hide in the cellar. Ryan, you go to Jayden's house. The two of you need to get out of here."

He clutched his weapon and stared at Chloe, then turned back to his father. "I can't just leave y—"

"Listen to me." His father grabbed his shoulders. "Your sisters will meet you at the battered oak by morning. I promise. Come back for them and take them to safety." He squeezed Ryan's shoulders. "You always protect those in need, son. I'm proud of the man you've become."

Ryan's arms started shaking. Why did he feel dizzy? Why did it sound like his father was saying good-bye?

Father's hand pressed against his back, leading him to the door. "Get your sisters to the cellar and go rescue Jayden. They're here for the Children."

The front door burst open and Kinsey screamed.

Ryan herded his sisters out the back door. They ran out behind him and his father swung his sword at an intruder.

Ryan turned. Three men in Feravolk cloaks headed his way. He readied three arrows. Shot one. Two. Three.

Men fell.

Men. Not deer. What was he doing?

"Ryan, run!" Kinsey's scream cut off as Chloe shut the cellar door behind them and locked it.

His father stood surrounded my three men. Four more men lay motionless and bloody on the ground.

Metal shrieked against metal.

He should go like his father said, but he couldn't leave him alone. Couldn't pick up his iron feet. This was his family. Ryan raised his bow. Steadied his shaking hands. Breathed out. All the sounds around him muted.

He shot. One.

Two.

Three.

There were too many coming through the door. One man made eye contact with Ryan. "Do you have the birthmark?"

"Go, son!" His father's voice rang out.

His father's sword punctured another man. But there were too many. A sword stabbed through Ryan's father.

"Father!" His scream reached his ears and seemed to bring back every other sound in the room.

Father fell. His mouth formed the words, "Go, my son," but no sound came out. Only blood.

Blood.

Ryan raised his bow and an arrow and shot. The arrow imbedded in his father's killer's shoulder. He fell to his knees. Another man stepped over Ryan's father.

Father just lay there. Wouldn't even blink. Ryan shot again, hitting the other man in the chest. Then he ran.

He ran toward Jayden's house. Fire flickered from thatched roofs everywhere. The torches spreading deeper into town. Screams pierced the darkness.

His blood burned.

He fell to his knees. No, this wasn't how it happened. He'd made it to Jayden. Jayden was safe. He'd fulfilled his promise.

Smoke consumed him. He looked up, trying to find an escape.

A lion's head, white and soot-stained, punctured the cloud and roared as if in pain.

Let me complete the transformation.

"Never!"

○

"Ryan. Ryan?"

He sucked in a breath and opened his eyes. The kind-faced Whisperer hovered over him, a concerned look in her eyes.

"It's a dream," she said.

And some of it had been. But some was so real.

"Here." She pressed a drink to his lips and he swallowed.

As the pillow consumed his head and the candlelight disappeared through the slit in his eyes, he remembered what he was supposed to be doing: going back for his sisters.

If he didn't find them, who would?

CHAPTER 16

UNWRITTEN DESTINY

Jayden sat alone as she waited for Logan to return. Well, truthfully, she wasn't alone. The wolf stayed with her.

He paced from one edge of the small clearing behind the thicket of dead branches to the other. The fluid movement of his trot and graceful rock of his shoulders made him appear so majestic. Beautiful. Wolves were feared by townsfolk. Her family feared them. The horses feared them. Yet this one had been left to protect her.

Westwind's sleek body made another pass in front of her.

Jayden watched the wolf. "Can you understand me?"

His pacing stopped. A greenish gleam flickered in his eyes as he nodded.

"You're quite dangerous, aren't you?"

Westwind sat. An amused smile seemed to form on his face.

"You can talk to Logan?"

The wolf nodded again.

"This far away?"

A soft bark of a laugh rumbled in his chest.

Jayden smiled. She recalled the deep emotions she'd felt in him earlier. "Don't laugh. This is all very new to me. I've never seen a wolf that traveled with a man before. But I know why you travel with Logan."

Westwind tilted his head.

"He treats you like an equal instead of a pet."

The wolf squinted, a look intensely human.

"I understand. You don't belong to him any more than he belongs to you."

Westwind chuffed, but he nodded once.

She tore her eyes from him and pulled out one of her daggers. The blue stones didn't glow at her touch anymore. Must have been part of the bonding.

Such a beautiful weapon. All four of them had fit in her palms like they were made for her. Her fingers glided across the etching. The design might be muted in the moonlight, but she saw it clearly in her head. A lightning bolt.

The two assassin daggers even felt the perfect weight for throwing. It was like she'd practiced with them all her life. And the two long ones were so light, but nearly as long as her brothers' short swords. Whoever made these made them for her. The picture carved in the blade made that much clear. And would they really help her control her talent, make it so the emotions of others didn't fuel her actions? Was that too much to hope for? Even if they didn't, she had to make sure this Logan fellow didn't figure out she had reservations about using them against living things.

A rolled-up parchment on the ground caught her eye. The note she'd stuffed in her boot. It must've fallen out when she removed the dagger. Jayden reached for her mother's last message.

Breathing deep, she unfurled the roll.

Dearest Jayden,

You came to us the night of the Blood Moon, but not as our own flesh and blood. We loved you no differently than your brothers, and we love you still, but we knew this day would come, when the Feravolk would take you home. We let you go because of our love for you, just as we took you in.

We will see you again, but, for now, your world is changing. We raised you to accept change when it comes from noble and just causes. We raised you to be strong in adversity. And we raised you to know right from wrong. Above all, we raised you to love. Trust these things now.

Don't worry. Logan Laugnahagn is our friend. Trust him.
He knows where your destiny lies. I hope you understand.
The Creator's blessings, our cherished daughter.

Love,
Mother and Father

Jayden's chest tightened. Logan? Could it be this Logan? No. But he had called her a deliverer. Claimed to know her parents. It hurt to breathe. No, this wasn't real. She couldn't be adopted.

She turned the letter over and ran her fingers along the name on the front between the creases. It was hers.

But Feravolk were the enemy. Surely her parents wouldn't ask her to trust them now. Not after what they had done. She wouldn't help them. They'd betrayed and killed her parents.

Not once had her parents mentioned a man named Logan, so how much could they possibly trust him now, after all these years? Well, they hadn't mentioned she was adopted either. Not that it mattered, right? They loved her as their own.

It *did* matter. It was a secret worth telling her now, a secret worth her family's sacrifice. She wanted to ball up the paper, scream that they'd lied. She wanted to hate everyone who had kept secrets from her. If her stupid destiny was only important enough to mention now, then it wasn't that important.

Jayden rested her head in her hands. The trees around her swayed in a gust of wind. The wolf padded closer.

The letter, Logan knowing the name of her family, the daggers glowing, and the lightning bolt all pointed directly at her. Perhaps she *was* their stupid deliverer. Or maybe Logan had been wrong when he found her.

Anger joined sorrow as tears trickled down her cheeks.

Should she have known the only blue-eyed daughter in a house of green-eyed boys was adopted? Yes. She should have seen, should have known. There was no one to be angry with but herself. She'd killed everyone she loved except Ryan, and he was dying too. The Feravolk were after her and he just got in the way. Everyone she loved got in the way. They were all killed because of her.

Love made people take risks they shouldn't. Now she was alone and empty. Broken. Weak. If anyone else she loved died for her, she wouldn't survive. It had to stop. No one else could love her enough to die for her. She wouldn't let her feelings get the better of her ever again. Even if that meant she had to stop caring—stop loving. Or at least pretend. A tear trickled down her cheek. She wiped it away.

If she was supposed to defeat some sorceress queen, she'd have to be strong. Emotions had always had a hold on her. Not anymore. Love would never make her weak again. She pulled Ryan's marriage stone from her pocket and hurled it into the woods.

Westwind stared at her.

"What? It was just some rock."

He tilted his head.

"I kept it because it meant something to me. Now it's just a future I can't have." Every word pulled at the ache in her throat.

The fur between Westwind's ears wrinkled.

Yes. Wolves were dangerous, but for some reason Jayden wanted to trust this one.

Logan returned. Westwind sat with his back to the man, but didn't seem surprised by Logan's entrance into their thicket.

She tore her gaze away from Westwind's glowing stare. "Well?"

"I got some of the soldiers to follow me, and I lost them at the river. We'll have to fly to make sure they don't catch us."

Westwind's head perked up. Logan froze.

Jayden stepped closer to him. "Is something wrong?"

"Logan?" A hushed voice caught Jayden's attention. "It's Ethan."

Logan's fingers curled around her wrist. She glanced at his hand, then his face. He mouthed the words, "Stay here."

"Who's Ethan?" she whispered.

"A boy I rescued."

"A boy? Out here, alone? You should go to him."

Westwind lowered his head and a growl rumbled in his throat.

Logan shook his head. "Leave the dog alone, will you?"

The wolf yawned, exposing huge prongs of teeth.

A large farm dog stepped into view, and a young man followed a few steps behind.

Logan had called *him* a boy? He certainly wasn't a boy. Not at all. He was no younger than she. Did Logan think of her as just a girl?

The limited light of predawn made Ethan's eyes appear nearly black. His hair too. Jayden let her gaze stray from his face. A thick, deep gash encircled his neck. Blood spots covered his shirt. His wrists looked as if they'd been chewed by rope.

Why had someone done that to him? Unless he was a criminal. Jayden shrank away from him.

Logan didn't. He walked over to Ethan and grabbed his elbow. "How did you find me?"

Ethan nodded toward the dog. "Scout did."

Logan turned to the dog who wagged his tail in response. "I should have guessed."

Ethan looked over his shoulder. "I'm being tracked."

Westwind and Scout simultaneously perked their heads up, ears swiveling.

Logan swore. "How many? How far?"

"Up that ridge. I don't know how many."

"We'll run."

"You don't have time."

Logan nodded toward Ethan's sword. "You any good?"

"Compared to some." Ethan gripped the weapon's hilt in his right hand.

Logan motioned toward her. "We protect Jayden with our lives."

"Yes, sir."

Criminal or not, if Logan trusted Ethan, Jayden would tolerate him—for now. She slid her long daggers from their sheaths, and a sense of confidence washed over her, as if she were channeling Daniel's emotions. Maybe they were magical after all.

She clutched the hilts tighter. "No one dies for me today."

CHAPTER 17

WORTH KEEPING

Silence thickened. The stink of sweat and alcohol rode on the wind. The soldiers were close. Logan glanced at the kids behind him. Ethan's eyes widened, Jayden's narrowed.

Westwind bristled. *"They're here."*

Logan hoped for less than four men.

Six emerged from the trees.

He advanced to Ethan's side, cutting off the soldiers from Jayden. He rubbed his chest, the ridges of the familiar scar palpable through his shirt, and scanned the faces of his enemy out of habit. Balton wasn't among them. No revenge tonight.

"Thought you could outrun me, dog?" A soldier motioned to Ethan and grinned. Green—likely from chewing too many peppermint leaves—tinted his teeth.

"What's this? Another Child of the Blood Moon?" A thick, muscular man pointed his sword in Jayden's direction. "Show us your birthmark, girlie."

Westwind's ensuing growl backed them up a pace or two.

One of the soldiers stared at Westwind, then pointed at Logan. "He's a Feravolk."

Another soldier drew his sword. "That means he doesn't get out of here alive."

Ethan raised his sword.

"You don't stand a chance." The soldier with the green teeth sneered.

"I was thinking the same about you." Ethan shot him a challenging grin.

Logan prayed the kid could back that up. The queen's soldiers may not all fight like Balton, but they didn't lack skill.

"Look, little girlie's going to play too." The muscular man chuckled, and the others joined him.

Logan lunged forward. The clash of metal resounded as his sword met two others at once. Through their bond he felt Westwind throw his weight onto a soldier and then rip open the man's throat.

Logan kicked one of his attackers into a tree. The man's head slammed against the trunk and he fell. Westwind darted over and finished him off while Logan turned his attention to the next soldier.

He dodged a blade coming for his head. Logan's sword took the full weight of the next blow, and a shock rippled through his muscles. Logan hacked at his opponent and the soldier stepped backward.

The soldier's eyes widened, but he blocked Logan's swings. Logan ducked another swing at his head. As he rose, he thrust his blade into the man's stomach. It punctured the soldier's leather jerkin and dug into his flesh. Logan yanked it out and brilliant red dripped down to the ground.

Logan scanned for Jayden and relief filled his chest. She stood over a dead soldier and wiped blood from her clothes. She was all right. After a quick survey of the surrounding trees, Logan saw no new soldiers approaching. Scout and Westwind both licked bloody muzzles. The remaining clash of steel came from Ethan and the final living soldier.

Ethan's talent exceeded the other man's by far. He disarmed the soldier, who dropped to his knees. Ethan aimed a blow at the soldier's neck.

Logan held up his hand. "Ethan, wait. He might have answers for us."

Ethan's sword stopped mid-swing, and he turned his head toward Logan.

The soldier rocked backward, planted his hand on the ground, and swung his leg up. His heel hit Ethan on the left side of his chest. While Ethan doubled over and crumpled to the ground, the soldier scooped up his fallen sword.

Logan ran toward them, but a dagger embedded in the soldier's back before he could intervene. The soldier's sword clanked to the ground, and his body tumbled down beside it.

Logan expelled a nervous breath, then he turned to Jayden. How many battles had she seen?

Jayden breathed. "Sorry. I thought he was going to kill Ethan."

With a grimace, Ethan sat up. "He was. Thanks."

"You did the right thing." Logan touched Jayden's shoulder. They both walked over to Ethan.

"So long, Minty." Ethan wiped his sword on the dead man's shirt, then he turned to Jayden. "Well, Jayden. I can officially say it's nice to meet you."

"Nice to meet you too." Jayden smiled, then cocked an eyebrow at Logan. She whispered, "I thought you said you rescued a *boy*."

Ethan turned his head away with a smile. From his spot on the ground, he retrieved Jayden's dagger from the dead soldier, cleaned the blade and handed it to her, hilt first. "You're pretty good with that."

Jayden smiled. "My brothers taught me well. You weren't so bad yourself." She extended a hand to help him up.

Ethan shied away. "I can get myself up."

"Did he hurt you?" Jayden knelt next to him and reached her hand toward his chest.

He backed away.

"It's okay. You were hurt already. Weren't you?" She touched one of the old blood stains on his shirt. Early morning light revealed where new blood seeped through.

Logan crouched next to both of them. "How bad are you, kid?"

The response he got was a guarded glance.

Jayden pressed her hand against Ethan's side. The sound that came out of him was almost a whimper.

Her eyes widened. "Who did this to you?"

"Those soldiers."

"Ethan, I think your ribs are broken."

He eyed her. "You don't have to tell me."

"Why didn't you say anything?"

"Like what? I wasn't just going to sit this one out."

"You still should have told us."

"I don't see what good it would have done. They already knew."

Jayden folded her arms. "Exactly."

Logan frowned. Would the two of them get along?

Ethan clenched his jaw. "Sorry."

Jayden's gaze softened. "I just meant we could have protected you more."

"That"—he pointed a finger at her—"is precisely what I was avoiding."

She regarded him for a moment while Logan leaned to help Ethan to his feet despite his protest. "Westwind, you take Scout and find us a place to set up camp. Somewhere out of the way. You kids go with them. I'll make a different trail."

Westwind sat. *"Excuse me? Take the dog?"*

"Westwind, what's—"

"Why don't you ask the dog what's wrong? You bonded to it."

"No, no, no, I—"

"The dog's thoughts are in my head." Westwind stood, his eyes locked with Logan. The fur along his back stood straight up and he bared his teeth.

Scout shot between Westwind and Logan.

"Whoa, Scout." Ethan lunged toward his dog, but Logan put out his hand to stop the kid.

A second growl struck up in Westwind's gullet, and he lowered his head. *"Out of the way, mutt."*

"Please, don't hurt him," Scout said.

Westwind snorted. Then he shook his whole body, draining the tension from his stance. *"Satisfied? Why would he want to protect you except that he's bonded to you?"*

Scout looked up at Logan, his brown eyes round. *"Is it true?"*

Westwind chuffed. *"Of course, it's true. Now, are you on our side or not?"*

"Do you think you two can get along?" Logan smiled at Westwind who shot him a dagger-glare.

Scout bristled. *"If he does not fight me or my human, I will not fight him."*

"I'm not going to hurt you, dog." Westwind sat. *"And I won't fight your human. I helped rescue him."*

"Then I thank you. You are the nicest wolf I have met."

Westwind approached Scout and dwarfed him. *"Just keep your thoughts to yourself."* Scout's tail drooped and Westwind sighed. *"Unless it's necessary."*

Scout wagged his tail.

Jayden's eyes were wide. "Are they okay?"

Logan chuckled. "They sorted it out."

Ethan patted his leg and his dog wiggled over to him. "Look, if Scout's going to cause trouble, we can leave."

"You're not going anywhere like that, kid." Logan gently took hold of Jayden's arm. He motioned toward Ethan and kept his voice low. "You take care of him once you get to camp, okay?"

"Okay."

"And make sure he doesn't run off."

Jayden's expression was tight, but at least she nodded. Maybe he should've asked Ethan to make sure Jayden didn't run off. Not that it mattered. If she did, he'd be able to find her. A strange pull in his chest seemed to hone in on her presence. Still, it didn't hurt to be careful.

"Westwind, keep an eye on her, will you?"

"The rabbit ready to bolt? If you don't gain her trust soon, I'll be tracking her down."

CHAPTER 18

TASTE OF POWER

Rebekah lay on her bed in the quiet darkness. No moonlight tonight. The gentle patter of rain splashed against the stone sill and made it more difficult to hear, but she'd heard anyway.

Soft breaths.

Quiet padding on the floor.

Someone was in her room.

She lay still and breathed deep to create the illusion that she was sleeping. Though she was no longer bonded to her wolf, Aurora, she still picked up the softest of noises, and her eyes adjusted to the dark.

The faint scent of daffodils wafted in with the damp air. Daffodils were a telltale sign of Thea's presence. Rebekah slid her hand beneath her pillow and curled her fingers around the hilt of her knife.

"I'm not here to kill you." Thea's voice broke the silence.

Rebekah sat up, her back against the wall and the knife in her lap. She scanned the room. There, by the wardrobe across from the foot of Rebekah's bed, a shadowy form moved.

"Then why are you here?" Rebekah kept her voice hard.

Thea moved closer, and the edge of Rebekah's bed dipped as she slid onto the mattress. "Have you given any more thought to my proposal?"

The request that she tell this assassin where to find Logan and her Feravolk camp of Moon Over Water? "I gave you my answer."

"Aren't you interested in leaving the palace?"

"You don't need to sneak into my room at night to—What did you do to my guards?"

"Relax. It's just tangle flower seed. They'll wake by morning, and neither will say a word since they both fell asleep. I thought a demonstration might help you change your mind."

Rebekah leaned closer to the assassin. "Why are you here?"

"To talk about Connor."

Rebekah's heart trembled. "What of him?"

"Idla is working for the Mistress of Shadows. She has a seeing stone. Did you know?"

Rebekah remained silent. She knew Idla had ties with the dark stones of the Mistress, but the fact that the sorceress had contacted Idla was news. It shouldn't be. The Mistress made the stones after all. She probably kept one when the Creator banished her into her prison. "Idla kidnapped my son and me because of the prophecies. I know she wishes to free the Mistress."

"The power Idla has now was given to her by the Mistress. The secret spell book Idla keeps hidden in her potions room is the source of all her power. It's the Mistress's book. But if Idla were to obtain the deliverers' power for herself, she would no longer need spells. She'd be powerful without them. All she needs are the deliverers. She already has Connor."

Idla would never have Connor's loyalty, but it wasn't a comment Rebekah was willing to make to Thea. Who knew how many sides this assassin was playing?

Thea tilted her head. "According to prophecy, Connor and the other three deliverers *are* the key to unlocking the power of Soleden's four thrones. There is a way to transfer the power. In order for the transfer to work, each deliverer must give Idla fealty willingly, without force."

"I know the prophecies, Thea."

"Of course you do. I'm just concerned that you won't make your escape from the palace like you need to. The deliverers are being drawn to their parents. That means you. Do you want them to be drawn here?"

Rebekah pressed her palm against her chest. The marriage stone beneath her clothes gave her comfort. She was technically a protector, being the mother of two deliverers. But where in the prophecies had it stated that the deliverers would be drawn to her?

That must have been Idla's plan all along. She knew the deliverers could defeat her, which meant she wasn't trying to kill them yet. But she'd have a plan in place. Rebekah needed to find out what that was.

"You didn't know?" Thea's voice broke her thoughts. She sounded smug.

Rebekah looked at Thea's face. Darkness made it impossible to read her expression. Thea and Kara were both Children; yet, they seemed to harbor no loyalty for the Feravolk or the Children. Not until this moment anyway. Connor's words still rang true. She could not trust either of them. But she could possibly use them. "Who do you work for?"

"I have my own mission."

"Why is finding my camp such an important part?"

"You wouldn't understand."

"Try me, Thea."

She shook her head and stood up. "Don't let Idla use her trap to bait the deliverers here."

"The deliverers will have to face her to defeat her."

"The deliverers have to claim the Creator's power before anyone else gets it. If they face Idla first, they could lose."

"That's what has you afraid? They could also win."

Thea placed her hand on her hip. "So that is your plan? Hide in the shadows? Protect your son until you can kill Idla? You think you're playing the game to win, Rebekah, but you're actually playing to survive. Time to decide which is more important."

CHAPTER 19

A NEW SWORD

"So, where are you from?" Jayden asked as she and Ethan followed Westwind and Scout through the trees.

"Salea."

"Oh." Hadn't Salea been hit hard by the so-called Feravolk not long before they came to her home city of Tareal? "I'm sorry."

"For what?" Ethan laughed. "You don't like Saleans?"

She looked at him askance. "The ones I've met have been okay."

"I'm more than okay."

He leaned in and bent a branch for her to walk past. She wouldn't admit it to him, but she liked the way he smiled. It was a confident smile, but also soft and warm. Boyish—that's what it was. Strange smile for a criminal.

She recalled his talent with a sword. Sweet smile or not, Ethan was dangerous. Still, something in her heart wanted to trust him. She shook her head. That had to be sleep deprivation talking. Best to bury thoughts like that.

Maybe she should find out a little more about this Ethan. "So, what made you prisoner to the queen?"

He lost his smile. "I surrendered when they came to our town looking for Children."

"A talented swordsman like you? Are you sure they didn't over-whelm you with numbers?"

His return chuckle sounded sad. He stared at the ground and kicked a rock as he walked along.

Jayden gaped. He really had surrendered. "Why?"

His jaw tightened.

Vivid memories stung her—the fire, the screaming, her dead brothers. She regretted pushing him. "I'm sorry, I—"

Ethan's brown eyes met hers. "If you knew you could save everyone you loved, wouldn't you do whatever it took?"

Her lungs seemed to constrict. She could have saved her family, perhaps her whole village. She should have surrendered. "Did you? Save them?"

"For now."

She would never make that mistake again. "All right."

He kicked the rock aside and looked at her. "All right what?"

"You're more than okay."

A lopsided smile spread across his face, and Jayden couldn't help but smile back. Her cheeks flushed. He didn't think she was flirting, did he? An uncomfortable knot formed in her stomach and she glanced away. There was no reason to overanalyze.

Westwind stopped ahead of them in a secluded clearing. Large trees encircled the whole area and the river flowed just down the descending embankment.

"It's perfect." Jayden acknowledged the wolf.

His lips pulled back in what looked like a grin, and he lay down and stretched.

"You." Jayden glanced at Ethan and pointed to a tree in front of her. "Sit right here. Let me get some clean water and—"

"Oh no. No, no, no, no." Ethan shook his head. "I can take care of myself."

"Logan's orders." She hoped those words and her cocked eyebrow would persuade him. If it didn't, she had plenty of tricks. She'd learned a few things from tending to all those brothers and the other boys that helped on her father's farm. They were always managing to get into one scrape or another. "My father was an animal doctor."

"Oh, thanks."

She displayed one of those stares every mother knows how to use. "Don't make me force you."

He crossed his arms and widened his stance. "Right."

Jayden pursed her lips, then headed toward the stream and filled her waterskin. When she returned, she placed her pack on the ground and began digging through it, aware of Ethan's eyes on her.

She gave him her most compassionate smile. "I'll be gentle."

Ethan's arms fell to his sides. "That's not what I'm worried about."

"Really?" Jayden raised an eyebrow, then smiled to herself as he dropped his shoulders and walked over.

Westwind chuckled.

Jayden pointed her finger at him. "I said *animal* doctor."

The wolf snorted.

Ethan stood in front of Jayden, with his back to the tree. "This where you want me?"

"That'll do. Now sit."

Ethan steadied his hand against the tree and carefully lowered himself to the ground.

"You'll be fine, huh?" Jayden let a little sympathy leak into her smile.

She reached to unlace the top of his shirt and caught sight of his Blood Moon birthmark. The replica of the moon was on the right side of his chest halfway between his sternum and shoulder—just like Ryan's, only on the opposite side. Strange that it should be such an exact mirror image. Usually that type of thing was seen in twins.

"I can untie my own shirt." His voice jumped a few octaves.

Jayden shook her head to clear her thoughts. "All right then, but hurry."

He attempted to lift it over his head and stopped.

Jayden pulled out a dagger. "I'll cut it off."

He put out a hand to stop her. "I don't have another shirt."

Jayden laughed. "Then let me help you."

He sighed, but conceded.

She made sure to be careful, but hurting him was unavoidable. She tossed the shirt to the side. Her hand went to her mouth.

Cuts and bruises covered his chest and back. His whole left side was purple, green, and yellow.

"Who'd you cross for this kind of torture?"

Ethan frowned. "The Royal Army didn't like that I figured out they were impersonating the Feravolk."

So what Logan had said was true. "Why didn't they kill you?"

Ethan's intense stare met her eyes. "I'd like to know that too."

She picked up her clean cloth and wetted it, then spread ointment on it. One of her father's recipes. She silently thanked him for teaching her to make it. "This will sting."

Ethan just watched her as if he'd had someone tend to his wounds before. "So how many brothers do you have?"

Jayden took his arm and prepared to answer the question. Ethan flinched when her disinfecting solution hit him, but he relaxed quickly.

"I had four."

His eyes met hers. "Had?"

Painful memories pulled forward in her thoughts. Westwind came to sit by her. She drew comfort from the warmth against her leg.

"It was a few days ago when the false Feravolk came through Tareal."

"Oh. I am so sorry."

She kept her eyes lowered. Her loss was still too raw for her to accept his condolences with the intimacy of direct eye contact.

"It's okay. I got out with . . . a friend of mine. Logan and I are on our way to the Valley of the Hidden Ones to find a plant with special qualities to help him get better." She didn't want to say too much about the Whisperer or the poison.

"Valley of the Hidden Ones, huh? Plant must be important if you're willing to go there. It's not exactly . . . safe."

"If it saves my friend, I'd risk anything."

His eyes searched her face. "Good thing I'm going to help you, then."

"Really?" For some reason a huge grin broke out across her face and stuck there. If that wasn't bad enough, heat filled her cheeks.

"If Logan lets me, I'll stick around." He assured her with a lop-sided smile.

She tore her eyes from his face. A pang hit her heart when she realized how much she liked making him smile. By today she was supposed to be betrothed to Ryan. His pale form on Anna's couch invaded her thoughts again. Breathing deep, she focused on Ethan's injuries.

The cut she'd cleaned wouldn't need stitching, but she noticed a large reddish gash nestled just under his ribs on his right side. She reached to check it and Ethan's strong grip closed around her wrist. She froze.

"It's old." He released her.

She leaned toward it anyway. It had healed at least, but wasn't old.

"There's another one here." He touched his back and Jayden saw a similar scar. He didn't elaborate, so she left it alone, and resumed tending his wounds in silence.

She let her eyes flicker to his again. "I'll have to bind your ribs. Put your arms on my shoulders. You can squeeze if you need to." She wrapped the first cloth around him and pulled carefully. Ethan gripped her shoulders. She tied it off, applied some glue to the ends, and brushed it down with her fingers.

"Two more." She grabbed the next cloth.

His eyes shut and he went rigid. His fingers dug into her shoulders as she pulled. She had bound a number of ribs in her time helping her father, but no one had ever gripped as hard as Ethan.

She tied the last strip, and he finally released her. "Better?"

"Yes. Thank you." He eased himself back to rest on the tree behind him.

Jayden rolled her shoulders as she waited for his breathing to even out.

Ethan's eyes grew round. "Did I hurt you?"

"No, but you're pretty strong." She smiled. "Now scoot this way a little so I can have a look at your neck."

"You're thorough, aren't you?"

"It's not my fault you got yourself beat to a pulp."

He smiled that bashful, boyish grin and her stomach turned sour. What was wrong with her? She loved Ryan. Right?

She scooted behind Ethan. At least she couldn't see his smile from back here. He leaned his head forward and she dabbed the cloth on his neck. He flinched at the contact.

"This is deep, Ethan."

He didn't respond.

Someone hurt him because he'd saved those he loved—something she hadn't done. Something others had done for her. Something others were going to continue to do for her now that she was some stupid deliverer.

Snare deliverers.

Her family's death, Ryan's delicate life hinging on her journey—it was all too much to bear. A tear broke free.

"Jayden?" Ethan turned to face her. "Hey, what's wrong?"

She squeezed her eyes shut and the rest of the collecting tears trickled down her cheeks. "It's nothing."

"Nothing?"

She nodded.

"You just lost your family. That's hardly nothing."

"You saved yours."

Ethan winced. "Jayden, there's nothing wrong with letting people who love you protect you."

"No? Try being the only one who survives."

He flinched. "I'm sure that hurts."

She could have sworn she sensed sadness roll off of him, but she hadn't used her talent to feel his emotions, so she must have imagined it. Wishing she'd been nicer, she reached out to touch his arm.

Ethan looked at her hand, then her face. "It isn't your fault. Do you hear me? Your family would have protected you no matter what."

That was the problem. No one seemed to understand. That was *why* it was her fault.

"Hey." Ethan put a finger under her chin and lifted her head closer to his. "I'm going to protect you, too."

No, no, no. No more people getting hurt for her. "Great. Another man to take care of."

He smiled. "You won't even know I'm here. Unless you need my sword."

"I can look after myself." Jayden tapped a dagger hilt.

"So I've seen. Still, a pretty girl like you is bound to attract unwanted attention."

"Oh?"

"The day will come that you'll be glad for a shadow like me." His cocky smirk unnerved her a tiny bit—mostly because she liked it.

"Well." She turned away as a bit of heat hit her cheeks. "I better finish this before Logan gets back and wonders what I've been doing."

A gentle grip closed around her arm as she moved to get behind him once more. His eyes latched onto hers. "You don't have to."

"Logan's orders." Her gaze lingered on his for a heartbeat.

A very long heartbeat.

CHAPTER 20

HIDDEN WEAKNESS

S cout stood and rushed toward the bushes.

Jayden straightened. "What is it, boy?"

Logan walked into camp moments later. She breathed a sigh of relief, and the dog greeted him with a wagging tail. Westwind emitted a low groan.

Logan nodded toward Ethan. "Will he be all right?"

"He'll be fine when I'm done with him."

A wry smile spread across Ethan's face. "I'm fine now."

"You look better," Logan said, then he turned his attention to Jayden. "*You* look hungry."

Famished was more like it. She caught the smooth, round apple Logan tossed to her. "How did you find fruit that looks so normal?"

He looked up at the trees. "It's the Forest of Legends, where all things begin. The sorceress's power hasn't reached here yet. When it does . . . This place guards an evil you can't even comprehend. Like nothing that's been here in thousands of years. If Idla kills off my people, the Forest of Legends will die. For now," he nodded toward the fruit in her hand and half smiled, "there is still hope."

She brought the apple to her lips. A sweet-tart scent permeated the skin. She wasted no time biting into it. Cool, tangy liquid trickled over her tongue.

Logan glanced up at the sun, already up and climbing higher. "You think you can go a few more hours?"

Jayden tucked the last of her supplies in her bag. "I'm ready, but I don't know about—"

"Let's go." Ethan stood. "I'm itching to get as far away from here as possible."

"Good." Logan gave him an apple too.

"Are you still headed to Nivek?" Ethan asked.

Logan rubbed the stubble on his chin. "Yes, though not right away. We have something more urgent to take care of first."

"How urgent? I've news from Tareal."

"News?" Jayden whirled to face him. "Is anyone alive?"

Ethan's brown eyes softened. "Some people are."

Jayden bowed her head. Her heart hurt. Her home, everything she'd known, gone. "It's bad?"

"Very. The queen showed up while I was there. She had a prisoner with her. A man who claimed to be one of the Feravolk. She killed him publicly and asked for volunteers for her cause. By the time she declares war on the Feravolk, they'll be unable to stop her."

A growl rose in Logan's throat. "By the Blood Moon."

Jayden backed away from him and bumped into Ethan. He placed a hand on her shoulder and squeezed. The contact stirred something in her, made her feel protected. She leaned closer to him.

Ethan continued, "If we can reach Nivek before she extends her kidnappings and burnings to the north—"

Logan put up his hand. "I'll send word to my camp now."

"How?" Ethan asked.

"Wolves. They'll take the message home. I'll have Westwind pass it along. In the meantime, we'll need any information we can get about where the queen plans to strike next, and when. Idla won't get away with this."

If the queen had truly killed her parents, then the queen would die for it. Jayden crossed her arms. "No, she won't."

Logan nodded once. "You won't be alone."

Yes, she would. Love would not make her weak again—she'd have to ditch Logan before she started getting too attached. He was already beginning to remind her of an older Daniel.

"Wait." Ethan's hands gripped her shoulders and he turned her to face him. His eyes squinted and searched her face. "You're one of the deliverers?"

She was playing that part for now. "Yes."

Logan let out a frustrated sigh. "Don't go telling people that."

Ethan stepped closer to Logan. "You're a protector?"

Logan hesitated. "Kid, how are you coming to these conclusions?"

"I learned about the prophecies in school."

"Right."

Ethan's intense stare latched on to her. Then his emotions hit her—worry so strong, it ached. Jayden's knees weakened and her fingers clutched the white horse charm at her throat. Why? And why was she feeling his emotions? She looked away from him.

Logan stared at Ethan for a long moment. "All right, we've got a message to spread and a kid to cure, Westwind."

Westwind dashed off. Scout raced after, his tail wagging.

"Let's go." Jayden slung her sack over her shoulders and bit deeply into her apple.

○

Jayden tried to keep the pace as Logan led them closer to the Valley of the Hidden Ones. The sun neared the western horizon with every step. They were still in the Forest of Legends, but they had traveled north, nearing the green, rolling mountains in the distance.

"What's in the Valley?" Ethan's voice came from behind her.

"The Whisperer sent us to find a special plant. It will extract the poison in Jayden's friend's blood." Logan pulled out the plant Anna had made and showed it to Ethan. "Memorize it. This one is taking up valuable space."

Jayden put her hand to her mouth. It had wilted already.

Ethan came up beside her and inspected the plant. "I've never seen anything like it."

"You will very soon." Logan pulled the soil from around the plant's roots and it turned to grass, which he tossed aside.

Jayden looked back at the withered grass and hoped the real plant they were after was hardier.

"Do you know anything about the Valley of the Hidden Ones?" Ethan asked.

Logan looked over his shoulder. "Not much. Care to share?"

"Sure." Ethan cleared his throat. "Despite what you may believe, unicorns are dangerous. They know when something new enters their home and they protect it fiercely from anything . . . impure. Also, unicorns aren't the only dangerous animals there."

"What other dangerous animals?" Logan asked.

"Black lions for one thing."

"Black lions don't exist," Jayden hoped aloud.

Logan sighed. "From what I've heard recently, I wouldn't be surprised if they do. What do you know about them?"

"They're bigger than any natural lion. They have massive, furry wings. They love unicorn blood, which is why they stalk the perimeter of the Valley of the Hidden Ones."

Jayden bit her lip.

Ethan nudged her shoulder and when she turned to him, that boyish smile filled his face. "They only hunt at night. Everything about them is meant to lure you—from their lavender scent and velvety soft fur to their soothing purr. If that doesn't work, they sneak up on you."

He grabbed her elbow and Jayden jumped at the contact.

He chuckled. "You won't even know they're coming. They hardly make a sound, and under the cover of darkness the only thing visible is their glowing, yellow eyes."

Jayden tripped. Ethan steadied her with another touch to her elbow. She scowled and stole her arm back, then stormed ahead of him.

Such a boy, trying to scare her like one of her brothers. It had worked, though. The thought of a black lion had her trembling. She ignored the soft chuckle behind her.

"Do they have any weaknesses?" Logan asked.

Jayden sucked in a breath.

"If they do, they weren't important to the bedtime story I grew up with."

"Well, let's hope we figure out what their weakness is *before* we meet one." Logan set a faster pace.

Jayden hugged her stomach. She did not want to meet one.

Rocks littered the ground more profusely as their walk turned into a steady climb. How long had they been walking?

Jayden stumbled over a stone, the second time she'd tripped in the last ten paces, and barely regained her balance. Exhaustion set in, but she desperately wanted to keep that a secret.

Stupid rocks. Another tripped her, but a soft grip on her elbow steadied her. She looked over her shoulder and met Ethan's smile. He let go of her. "Thank you."

She stepped up her pace only to trip again. Ethan's presence was unmistakable against her arm. The scent of pine and snow and a hint of leather enveloped her, and another soft touch steadied her.

"Careful," he whispered.

Did he have to walk so close? Did he have to make her feel so safe? Try as she might to stay away, she kept gravitating near him.

Logan stopped. Finally. "This place will do. Don't you think?"

Jayden looked around. She had no idea where she was, or how to get back to Ryan. Ethan was entirely too distracting.

No, she was tired. Tomorrow she'd be refreshed, better able to keep track of where she was going instead of following two strangers into the heart of the unknown.

"Looks secluded." Ethan's pine and leather scent blended in perfect harmony around her.

The trees were closer together and the rocks larger. The mountain was visible ahead of them, silhouetted by the setting sun. It was beautiful.

Logan set down his pack. "You two can set up camp and gather some wood. Westwind and I will bring back some food."

As if called, Westwind and Scout peered through the trees.

Logan stared at Westwind. "He says the message has been sent. My camp will be aware of how the Royal Army is impersonating our people within a few days. Wolves are fast." Logan glanced at the rust-colored farm dog. "No, Scout. You stay here and listen for me. You can warn me if danger approaches."

Scout lay down and rested his head on his paws.

"You kids may want to wash tonight. We'll leave at first light." Logan bent down and fondled the dog's big ears before he swept his cloak around him and disappeared into the woods, Westwind beside him.

Ethan began collecting wood and Jayden helped him. She avoided his eyes. And his shoulders. And decided she needed to get away from him altogether. Something about being tired made her stare at him.

She cleared her throat. "I think I'll go down to the river."

"Just don't go far."

Scout walked to Jayden's side.

"Good idea." Ethan nodded to his dog, then looked at Jayden. "Still, don't go too far."

She rolled her eyes. "I got it, Protector."

The sun's warm residue lingered in the darkening sky, and the clear river cooled her skin when she dipped her hand in. She undressed and stepped into the water, so refreshing after a day of hiking. She washed, scrubbed her teeth, and thanked Anna for the jasmine soap.

The less men thought about women doing things like sweating, the better. Jayden's mother had taught her that. Growing up in a house full of boys, she needed something that set her apart. She could be tough *and* feminine her mother always said.

Jayden closed her eyes for a moment and envisioned her mother's face. Then her father's. Then each of her brothers' in turn. She let fond memories mingle with the aching hole in her heart.

Why had they kept secrets from her? They shouldn't have. She knew what they would say. It was for her protection. Jayden squeezed her eyes shut, as tears trickled down her face.

Her fist hit the water. Snare secrets. Oh, and snare tears. They made her feel anything but strong. And she needed to be strong. She was supposed to defeat a sorceress.

Still feeling the ache of loss, she stepped out of the water and dressed. She picked up one of her new daggers and unsheathed it. The hilt fit comfortably in her palm. It had obeyed her so flawlessly when she fought. Just like the Whisperer had said. And with these weapons, she'd been calm—as if she were at a sparring match. Her enemies hadn't been able to force her talent open. The fear hadn't controlled her like before. Perhaps these daggers really were made for her. She thanked her brothers for training her to use them.

When she returned to the camp, Ethan headed out, which left her with Logan and a pile of skinned rabbits. Westwind licked his blood-stained muzzle, and Logan placed firewood together. He lit his creation after a few clashes with his flint and steel.

Jayden stayed five paces from him and opened her Blood Moon-given talent for feeling emotions. As the door opened, Logan's mood slowly filled her. Peace ebbed from him as he watched the orange tongue peek through the wood. He breathed on the flames to stimulate their strength. Yes, something about Logan seemed peaceful, with a hint of mourning.

He picked up the rabbits on a spit and placed it over the flames. Then he placed his flint and steel into a small bag tied to one of the two cords that hung around his neck. She caught a glimpse of the marriage stone tied to the other cord he wore, and also an awful scar on his neck, not unlike Ethan's. Who was this Logan anyway?

"Logan?" Jayden bit her lip and turned her gaze to the dancing flames in front of her. "Did you know my birth parents well?"

The spit stopped turning. Deep sorrow flooded him.

She'd done enough prying and closed off the connection. Logan's emotions were his own now. "You don't have to tell me."

He gazed at her with those piercing blue eyes and inhaled. "They were like family to me."

A lump rose in Jayden's throat. "So you feel obligated to protect me?"

He just stared at her.

Hadn't she just decided she never wanted the burden of love to protect her ever again? "You shouldn't. You don't know me."

Logan nodded. "Fair enough. Your father was kind enough to bring Westwind and me to his Feravolk camp. I was about your age. His wolf found me."

Jayden sat near him. "My *birth* father was bonded to wolves?"

Logan smiled. "So was your mother."

"So will I bond to wolves?"

"It doesn't work that way. You inherit the ability to bond, but children don't always bond to the same animals as their parents."

"I wonder what I will bond to."

"Me too." Logan's eyes crinkled at the corners, but his stare seemed directed at the orange flames.

Jayden crept closer, settling next to him. "Wait. You were bonded to Westwind when you were my age?"

"Yes. Bonding gives Westwind the ability to understand humans, but he also has a longer life, a moral sense of right and wrong, the ability to discern intentions, things like that."

"And a sense of humor." Jayden smiled at Westwind. "How many animals can you bond to?"

Logan paused. "It seems typically one, but I am bonded to two wolves, Westwind here, and his mate, Aurora."

Jayden looked at Westwind. "Aurora. I'd like to meet her."

Westwind's tail rose.

"He says you'll like her." Logan winked.

"What's she like?"

Logan's eyebrows shot up. "Westwind says she's a lot like you. That's a tremendous compliment."

"I can't wait then."

Logan bowed his head. "And now I'm bonded to Scout."

"Is that why Westwind is angry with you?"

He shot a meaningful glance at Westwind. "The others can sense the dissention."

Westwind chuffed.

Jayden laughed. "What did he say?"

"It wasn't very nice. He'll get over it. I didn't intend to bond with Scout. The dog reached out to me without knowing what he was doing."

Westwind approached and put his huge head on Logan's knee, but Logan didn't pet him. "I never thought I'd bond to a dog either."

Westwind seemed, for the moment, like a tame animal.

Logan checked the rabbits. As he placed the spit aside to cool, he sighed. "Your mother, Loralye, died protecting you. . . . Your father, Nathaniel, died protecting me. I am sorry."

Jayden sucked in a breath. She put her hand on his arm and then looked back at the fire. "Don't apologize for that. Thank you for telling me. And for being honest."

She folded her hands on her lap. Now she was supposed to face Queen Idla, who had almost destroyed a whole race of people? A lump rose in her throat. "Logan, what kind of magic is the queen capable of?"

His eyes met hers with an intensity that unnerved her. "They say she can control the weather. Some say she prevents the crops from growing. She's killing the Feravolk. The prison I told you about is real. As it cracks, evil breaks through. Things like black lions and—"

"Black leather vines?"

Logan nodded. "The land is dying." He poked the fire with a stick, sending embers into the air.

"But aren't those rumors?" Why was her throat so thick?

"I've seen her kill the very grass she walked on. And I've seen her disappear into a funnel cloud." His cheek twitched and he dragged the charred end of the stick across the ground. "The wars of the Blood Moon were fought during storms. Surely you know this?"

Jayden nodded.

"That's because Idla's weapon of choice is a bolt of lightning."

Goose bumps skittered over Jayden's skin, starting with her scalp. How would she defeat a woman who wielded that much power?

Movement in the trees distracted her. It was just Ethan returning. He smiled. Not the smile. That stupid, wonderful smile. Why did it melt her fear?

Logan removed a cooked rabbit from the spit and passed the rest to Jayden and Ethan. They ate in silence. The hot meat warmed her stomach. She was so hungry, even the charred parts tasted good.

After eating, Jayden pulled out her bag and motioned for Ethan to remove his shirt. He sat still while she applied her special ointment, flinched when she dabbed some on his neck, and squeezed her shoulders gently while she bound his ribs. His dark eyes met hers.

A feeling washed over her. Gratitude? But not from her. From Ethan? Jayden shook her head.

She looked at Logan to make sure she'd succeeded in turning off her talent. No emotions from him. She glanced back at Ethan. Nothing. Good.

"Thanks." Ethan grabbed his shirt and pulled it over his head before he settled next to the fire a little too close to her.

She didn't move away. Instead she watched the orange glow flirt across his arm as he poked the fire with a stick. The stick stilled. Her gaze wandered up to his face and she caught those dark eyes peering at her.

Heavens—she felt like a cat caught with her paws in the milk jug. At least Ryan wasn't here to witness her blatant staring. She tucked her knees to her chest and wrapped her arms around her legs. No more looking into his eyes. They tempted feelings she was trying to banish.

"You think the black lions are this far from the mountain?" Ethan asked.

Jayden shot him a glare, but he was watching Logan.

"I think it's wise to assume." Logan picked up his waterskin and headed toward the river.

Jayden went right back to staring at Ethan. At the two moles on his right cheek. His eyes flicked in her direction and his lips curved slightly. Heat hit her cheeks and she stared at her hands.

He eased back against a tree and let his head lay against the trunk. "Sorry, I didn't mean to scare you."

"I'm not scared."

He eyed her and laughed. "My mistake."

Her face burned. Could she control nothing around him? "I mean, I'm worried. About that . . . and other things."

His smile faded. "About your friend?"

"Yes."

"I'm sure we'll get him the plant in time."

She tried to ignore the flip of her heart. "I'm sure we will." She cheated a glance at Ethan. "You think those black lions will sneak up on us?"

Ethan shot her a grin. "Not without me knowing first."

"Oh really? Your hearing is that good?"

He stared at her a moment, those brown eyes intense. Then his boyish smile returned. "It's excellent."

"Well, hopefully we won't have to test it."

The fire began to dwindle. Ethan picked up another piece of wood and bent toward the flames. He stopped short, a grimace crossed his face.

Jayden leaned over to take the wood from him. "Here, let me—"

"I got it. Thanks." He smiled softly.

Not just cocky, but stubborn too. She shook her head while he breathed new life into the flames. "Ethan?"

"Yes."

"Who did you save? In Salea, I mean."

He leaned back against the tree again. "A friend."

Not family then? "A very good friend?"

Ethan chuckled. "What's a bad friend, Jayden?"

She smiled and ventured to look at him. His eyes were already on her.

"I just mean—well, you could have died."

Ethan's eyebrows pinched together. "They weren't exactly killing us."

"You didn't know that."

"True. But some people are worth dying for."

"Very good friends?"

"*Especially* very good friends." He smiled a new smile—a sad smile. Jayden loved it just as much as the boyish one. It was just as intimate.

CHAPTER 21

DARK BLOOD

A harsh hiss echoed through the densely wooded forest, and Ryan spun around to face the source of the noise. Nothing.

Dark trees covered in crimson moss towered above him. They seemed to grow out of a thick fog. The air carried a metallic tang that tasted like blood. He tried to squeeze his eyes closed and make it all disappear. It didn't.

It wasn't real. It couldn't be. He was caught in another fever dream. If he concentrated hard enough, perhaps he could get free of it.

The trees seemed to shatter where they stood. The ground rocked back and forth, and he stumbled.

Splitting pain shot through Ryan's chest as though his veins caught fire. He fell to his knees. Blood poured out of his chest.

This wasn't real.

The hiss echoed again and two yellow-moon eyes peered at him through the trees. Purring vibrated through the ground and into Ryan's very core. *Let me finish the transformation.*

Ryan pressed his hands over his ears. "Get out of my head."

A lion, white as a summer cloud and as tall as Ryan stepped into view. Its legs were red. Its tail swished back and forth as it stalked closer. Circled him. *Don't try to make me leave. You're not strong enough.*

He wished he had a hammer or a sword, something he could

swing at the beast and put an end to these dreams. He just had to remind himself that these were fever dreams, nothing else.

Jayden had brought him to the old woman's house. He squeezed his eyes closed as if he could sear the memory to his brain like a brand.

Losing his mind right now would not be good. "You're not real."

"Is this real?"

The lithe body of the lion sailed toward him. Heavy paws slammed into his chest and knocked him to the ground. The weight against him crushed him.

"Stay with me, Child."

That voice was different. The same voice that had told him to hold on when Jayden left to find help. The Whisperer. He was with a Whisperer. He tried to cling to that reality.

Arrows piercing his chest and leg—that had been real.

Pulling Jayden away from her burning barn—that had been real.

His father dying to save him—that had been real.

So real.

The weight on Ryan's chest seemed to lessen. He sucked in a breath and opened his eyes to darkness. But he was in the Whisperer's home.

The couch was lumpy. The blanket scratched against his skin. It was too dark now to stare at the heavy wooden beams that made up the ceiling or count the rings on the ruddy wooden logs flanking the stone fireplace.

There were seventy-four rings. Occasionally seventy-three or seventy-six, and seventy-nine that one time the wave of pain through his blood was so bad he'd thrown up red all over Anna's soft blanket.

The scratchy blanket distracted him better anyway.

Another shot of pain shook him from the inside out, and he desperately searched the dark room for something to steal his focus. He fingered the knitted blanket and started counting ridges in the fabric.

"Let the transformation take place."

Thirteen. Fourteen. Fifteen.

"Stop trying to fight me."

Six—teen. Did it have to hurt so bloody much?

The hiss deafened him. Tried to gain a hold on his attention, but he hung on to the reality. The scratchy blanket. The lumpy couch. Anna's soft humming. Humming.

She was here?

Twenty-three. Twenty-four.

Everything burned.

Thirty-something.

No, think of the scratchy bl—he screamed.

"Hush, Child." Gnarled fingers pressed against his forehead. His cheek. They felt nothing like his mother's, and that comforted him, because the white lion in his head had used his mother's touch—his own mother—to try and hold his thoughts. Anna's hands grounded him in this time, this reality.

Whatever had control of his mind wanted him to fall under. If he went under again, he might never come out.

His screams still rang in his ears, but his blood stopped shooting fire through his insides. Just a gentle simmer now. He could breathe again. For the moment.

Anna lit a candle and the soft yellow glow bathed her wrinkled face. "I'm sorry there's not more I can do for you."

He smiled. "Oh, you've done plenty. Putting up with such a lazy guest must be terrible." He spoke in gasps as if he'd just run down a bolting horse. He leaned back into the soft pillow, only just aware that every muscle in his body had been completely tensed.

"Get some rest," Anna said.

That's all he'd been doing. But he was supposed to be doing something else. Something important. A spark of fire ignited in his shoulder and his thigh. No. Not again. It was like an explosion of sparks, not one of the good kind like lighting bonfires or fanning the forge. He bit down on the scratchy blanket and held in a scream.

He was vaguely aware of Anna's hands on his head, supporting his back. "Let it out, dear one."

Dear one. Such a sweet old woman. Nothing like Old Mara, wise woman extraordinaire from Tareal, who took care of his sisters when they'd gotten the murmur fever. Poor girls had to endure with Mara's constant *tsk*-ing every time they shivered uncontrollably or threw up.

"It's okay. Let it out."

Ryan screamed.

The fire seemed to rip through his throat. He half-expected to catch the blanket on fire. But the only red to come out of him was more blood.

Over.

It was over.

Sweat dripped off the tip of his nose. Into the pool of red he'd just thrown up all over the scratchy blanket. "I'm sorry. I'm—"

"No. No sorrys for that." She helped him lie back, and he realized how exhausted he was.

So this was what it was like to be sick. He never wanted to be sick again.

Anna scooped up the blanket, folding unstained portions over the blood. She held a candlewick up to the material until it caught fire.

"I fear I'm just going to do it again." He offered a rueful smile.

Her eyes, glittering with wisdom, regarded him. "I fear so too." She touched his knee and wrinkles creased her face—an intricate pattern created from each time she'd ever felt that same emotion.

"I was bringing you this." She placed the bowl in his lap and chuckled. "I'm little late, I guess."

He laughed too. A harsh, raw sound.

"I have something else for you. I'll be right back."

Ryan shivered, unable to control his muscles. Whatever had infiltrated his blood was very unwelcome.

"Here you are." Anna lifted the bowl and placed another blanket over him. This one smelled of woods and fire and the faint aroma of tobacco. That reminded him of home. Anna didn't seem the type to smoke. Then again, the couch he lay on sat across from two rocking chairs.

Two.

Anna hadn't always been alone.

"I'm not a very good guest, soiling all your blankets. Dirtying your dishes." He smiled.

"Drink this." She held a hand behind his head and pressed a cup to his lips. It smelled of honey and lemon. If she was anything like his mother, those two ingredients were hiding something else in the drink. Bitter things.

He didn't drink.

Anna chuckled. It sounded so young. Like a glimpse into her past—maybe as a mother. "You won't taste the tangle flower, and it won't hurt you. It'll let you sleep."

"W-without dreams?"

Her hand cupped his cheek. "For your sake, I hope so." The way her eyes scanned his face made his stomach squeeze. She was looking at him, but it was like she was observing him even though he was right there.

"I'm getting worse."

She sighed and her eyes softened as she nudged the drink closer to him again.

He felt as though he was supposed to remember something. The thought kept slipping away from him like a dream in the corner of his mind. The more he tried to remember, the harder it was to see. He couldn't shake the feeling that it was important. He pushed the drink away and remembered. "My sisters."

"Hush." She pressed her crooked fingers up to his forehead.

"No, I was supposed to go back for them." Why was talking exhausting? "I have to go back for my sisters . . ." His father hadn't made it. His sisters were alone. He placed his hands on the couch and pushed himself up. Pain shot through his shoulder and his leg. Ate deep into his muscles.

The room spun and he dry heaved.

Anna's hand pressed against his back as he doubled over. "You can't go after your sisters. The poultice I'm using on you is slowing the poison from spreading, but it's also keeping your body from healing."

That was a problem. He was used to healing fast. Not healing at all was going to be a different story. He looked into Anna's eyes. "What will this poison do to me?"

Her hand slipped from his back and she sat back on the sofa. Her blue eyes peered deep into him now, almost as if she could see the poison in his blood. "It's attacking your heart. Not just your physical heart. Your metaphysical heart."

As in who he was? "Can I stop it?"

"You're fighting it the best you can. The dreams, that's the poison attacking your mind. You fight it. I can see it on your face when you sleep. I can hear it in your screams. Keep fighting. That's your job right now."

"But my sisters need me. They could—" He started to stand and found himself weaker than expected.

Anna steadied him. "If you fall on the floor, I'll be unable to lift you back onto my sofa."

Good point. He sat back down, but blood dripped out of the hole in his chest and hit the floor.

Dark blood.

Not quite black. Not even the gross dried brownish color. Dark red. Almost as if someone had added a swirl of black paint to the mix. Ryan reached out to wipe it up, but Anna's gnarled fingers curled around his wrist with the strength of someone who had been startled past surprise and right into fear.

"Don't touch," she whispered.

Ryan retracted his hand as far as her tight grip would allow and looked into her face. She stared at the blood. What was she looking at?

It moved.

The black swirl in the center of the drop seemed to be attacking the red.

Then there was no grip on his arm.

Anna wiped up the spot with her apron and then tossed it into the fireplace with the burning blanket. "I can use the trees to lure your sisters here. Tell me, what are their names?" She didn't look at him when she spoke.

Ryan inhaled a shuddering breath. Maybe he could help them after all. "Chloe, Kinsey, and Wren."

She faced him now, the apron burning behind her, and nodded. "The trees are looking."

Ryan swung his legs onto the couch and laid his head back to keep from dripping any more blood onto her floor. Or anything. He'd thought she was throwing the wetted rags she was using to clean his wounds into the fire because they were stained with too much blood to wash clean again. But one drop? On a whole apron? And she'd burned it.

He swallowed. "That's inside me? What's it doing?"

"Killing you."

That much he knew. What he wanted was specific answers.

She stared at him for a long time while Ryan tried to think of a way to lighten the situation. Nothing came to mind. Besides, Anna already knew the truth. She wouldn't be affected by his death terribly. There was no use hiding here. He needed to know what was inside him.

She sat near his legs on the couch and folded her hands in her lap. "Something is keeping you alive. This venom would have killed most people by now. Your blood is putting up a good fight. It should be black by now, but it's not. I told Logan to hurry, I told him you had seven days, but in reality I thought you only had three. We are on day four, and your blood is still fighting." She touched his arm with a cool hand. "Your skin is like fire. Fire is the only thing I know that will kill the poison. Whatever you're doing—"

"I'm not doing anything."

She regarded him. "Well, don't stop whatever it is. It's keeping you alive."

The transformation. Was he being kept alive so that he could transform into whatever that beast was? No. That was nothing but a fever dream. "I feel weak. All the time."

She nodded. "I know. You look pale. Gaunt." She touched his cheek and her eyes softened. "Fight it."

It would be a whole lot easier if he knew what it was. "Yes, ma'am."

Her sigh was heavy. "Creator willing, they'll return soon." Her eyes met his. "If the venom gets a hold of your heart, you'll never be the same."

"What do you mean?"

She breathed deep and stared at the rocking chair across from her. No, she seemed to be staring into a memory. "I'm a thousand years old, Ryan, and I remember a great may things. Many of my memories have been passed along to the trees, because it's a lot for an old woman to remember." She giggled and patted his knee.

Was this the strange start to a story he'd never heard? Surely she couldn't mean she'd been alive for a thousand years.

She looked at him with those eyes focused on the memory, and he saw a purple flame flutter through her pupil. There, then gone. As if he'd imagined it. Perhaps he had.

She continued, "Something happened to me over nine hundred years ago that I remember as clearly as yesterday's memories: Two black lions attacked my camp and they bit seven soldiers before we killed them. Seven."

He didn't interrupt to ask what a black lion was. He was pretty sure the fever dream had already showed him one.

"The poison that runs through your veins is from the venom of one of those dark beasts. We had a healer with us, but a healer can only heal one person with the venom. The poison would knock her out. She did know how to make a cure, and she taught me, but in three hours it took, four of the soldiers died. She treated one with her powers, and it put her and the soldier to sleep for a week. I treated two with the poultice and it put them to sleep for a week. I guarded the bodies in the black lion territory, but more healers came to guide us into the safety of the valley.

"Though I had used the poultice on two of the soldiers, the healers instructed me that it was indeed too late for one of them. My dearest friend. Her heart had been tainted."

Ryan's insides tightened.

"I asked what that meant, and they told me some of the venom reached the soldier's heart before I could extract it all. This I knew.

When the healing was taking place, I could feel it, strangely enough. I knew her heart had been compromised. I just didn't know what that meant. They told me to kill her."

"What?" Ryan gripped the blanket in his hands.

Anna touched his fist and her eyes grew gentle, glistening with unshed tears. "I didn't kill her. I couldn't. But when she woke from the sleeping state, the venom had spread into so much of her heart that she became a monster. The venom had claimed her, made her something else—a killer. Her heart had turned to coal. Dark and incapable of loving. She killed one of the other soldiers and tried to kill the healers, but they are fierce warriors and eventually they stopped her. Killed her.

"The damage she'd done was my fault. They warned me and I didn't heed. If I had done what they asked, she wouldn't have come back a monster. I could have prevented so much loss."

Ryan breathed deep and watched a tear drip over Anna's eyelid. "Are you going to kill me?"

Her blue eyes, darker in the candlelight, met his. "When I heal you, I'll feel whether or not the taint has reached your heart."

It wasn't an answer. Her words felt like a choice. He stared at the fireplace, where the apron was nothing but smoldering embers. "I don't want to hurt my friends. I don't want to hurt anyone."

"I know, Child." She gripped his hand in hers. "If you're a danger, I'll be sure to tell you."

"Logan will—"

"He won't let you harm anyone."

CHAPTER 22

STICKS AND STONES

The mountain seemed closer all the time, but mountains had a way of doing that. Logan turned to make sure Ethan and Jayden were keeping up with him. Jayden already seemed exhausted. Logan wasn't sure how much she'd slept. Her screams had pierced the night more than once. Thankfully, Ethan had been able to nudge her from her nightmares.

Jayden closed her eyes and breathed in. "A storm is coming."

The clouds were placid. The sky above boasted a rich blue color, not like that of a flimsy, cool day, but deep and bright. No clouds touched the sun. It didn't look like a storm loomed anywhere near them.

Logan felt for Westwind. *"You sense a storm?"*

"I would tell you if I did," Westwind said.

Logan's thoughts must've interrupted his hunt.

"I would say it's still half a day away." Jayden still wore that dreamy smile. "It might not be good to be too high up. It will be a strong storm, but it won't last too long."

Logan stared at her with one eyebrow raised.

She opened her eyes and saw his expression. She bit her bottom lip. "You don't believe me?"

Westwind's senses were a good indicator, but to predict a storm with such detail was unheard of. Still, a small voice echoed in the back of Logan's mind, something Anna had said when she told him about the deliverers: *She'll be your friend in water and storm.* "I do believe you."

Her smile held a hint of challenge. "Good, because I'm rarely wrong about these things."

"I'll have Westwind and Scout find shelter with cover."

As they walked in silence, old memories infiltrated Logan's thoughts. Jayden brought those memories to the surface, this he knew, which was why he wanted to hand over his protector duty as soon as he could. She would be fine with whomever the council had chosen to protect her.

Safer too. There was no way he could face Rebekah. And if the deliverers had to defeat the queen, facing Rebekah was inevitable. Jayden would understand.

A lump rose in his throat. Nathaniel's dying request had been that Logan protect his children. Logan wiped his palm over his face. It was his fault Nathaniel was dead. Everything was his fault, all because he'd failed to see that his wife was rubbing shoulders with the queen.

Was he being too selfish in refusing to face his wife? Was it his destiny? If it was, he was doomed to fail.

Snare destinies. Snare protectors. Snare love.

"Logan." Westwind appeared from the brush ahead.

"Yes?"

Westwind lifted his head. *"You're doing it again. It wasn't your fault."*

"You don't know that. If I had seen through Rebekah—"

"You can't play Creator, Logan. You have to play with the sticks you've been given, the stones you've been dealt. And you have to stop trying to change something that cannot be altered. If you reconsider this protector thing, you aren't alone. The pack may have lost a few, but the rest of us will help."

It was true. He'd lost Loralye and Nathaniel, but he still had Westwind, Aurora, Gavin . . . and Melanie. Though sometimes Melanie's presence seemed more of a curse than a blessing.

Logan thought he'd try and lighten the mood a bit. "Tell me, who trained the two of you?"

"Like I said before, my brothers. We fought for sport." Jayden shot Logan an impish grin and sent a small dagger hurtling toward a tree about ten paces away. It stuck out of the center of a knot on the trunk. Logan raised an eyebrow.

"Impressive." Ethan eyed her. "Who trained your brothers?"

Jayden pursed her lips. "My uncle Perceval. He was a general in the Royal Army before the queen took the throne."

"You mean One Eye?" Logan was just as surprised to hear what Jayden said as he was to hear Ethan echoing the name "One Eye." "He trained you too, kid?"

Ethan nodded.

Jayden's lips curved up in the corners. "I know the kind of people he helps, you know. People bent on revenge."

Ethan studied the ground.

Logan chuckled. "One Eye taught me how to fight, but in so doing, he also taught me that revenge isn't worth living for, but other things are. That's the short of it anyway."

Jayden hurtled another small dagger at the tree. It stuck near her first one. "He always spoke of the boys he'd helped to become men. I had no idea I'd been traveling with two of them."

Westwind chuckled. *"Sounds like a lot of coincidence to me."*

Scout tilted his head. *"Dogs don't believe in coincidence."*

"Neither do wolves." Logan winked.

Westwind grinned at Scout, who wagged his tail.

Jayden retrieved the daggers and handed them to Ethan. A challenging smirk sprouted on her face.

Logan groaned and set a faster pace. "Let's get moving. We've got a lot of ground to cover."

That had them scurrying away from one another and putting away their knives and silly smiles.

"You're opposed to this love story?" Westwind's thoughts broke in.

Logan didn't even look at the wolf. *"What about Ryan? She loves him, and when he's healed, this love story will be over. I can't let Ethan get his heart torn up or we'll lose him. And right now, I need him."*

"He'll stick around for her, Logan."

Logan shot Westwind a glare. *"Young love never works out."*

Westwind's eyes softened, but he said nothing.

"Will we meet your wife, Logan?"

Jayden's question made his heart trip a nervous beat. He glanced back at her.

Her eyes grew round. "Sorry. I just thought since you wear a cord . . . Well, I assumed it was a marriage cord."

A pang clutched Logan's heart. "I am married. Her name is Rebekah. Creator willing, you will not meet her."

"I—I'm sorry, I didn't—"

"I wear it because of my children." He lifted the marriage cord over his head and handed it to her. Its absence was palpable against his chest.

A wolf head, howling at the moon, was carved into the black rock, revealing the golden hue underneath. He extended it to Jayden, who took it with caution.

"It's beautiful." She flinched as if she wasn't sure she should have said so.

"It is."

"Will we meet your children?"

He sighed. It was time. He'd promised not to keep secrets from her after all.

"The four deliverers were born the night of the Blood Moon in my camp. I was there." He paused. "It was as bloody as the stories claim. All of the women went into labor at once. The screams were unbearable. My men and I were supposed to be searching for the deliverers. I found the first set of twins because I wasn't where I was supposed to be. I was in my tent with my wife, holding her hand, as the first was born—the boy. His cry was the most beautiful sound I had ever heard.

"You can't imagine what it feels like: a piece of happiness in the middle of war, and then the deepest surge of dread. I feared for my son, but that fear grew when we found out there was another. I prayed it wouldn't be a girl. It was. I remembered thinking she was the most beautiful thing I had ever seen, but the burden of what we faced surrounded her birth. No joy. Only sorrow.

"We had to hide them, or the queen would have found them. She sent an army into my camp that night in search of the deliverers. I was going to find my men and leave one of my children with my wife for the time being. I didn't want either of us to be caught with both of the babies.

"I had letters in my tent, drafted in preparation for that night. I took one of the letters and my daughter and left, reassuring my wife I'd be back for our son. No sooner had I handed my daughter to the wet nurse who would take her to the southern town of Meese did I hear one of my men calling my name. It was Nathaniel. He had found the other twins the same way I'd found mine. I instructed him to take his boy to the wet nurse waiting to take him to Nivek. Then I took you, Jayden, to the wet nurse that would take you to your temporary home in Tareal. My son was to go to Salea, but he never made it.

"I went back to the tent and my wife was gone, as was my son. Instead I faced Queen Idla herself. I could smell the wickedness in her, like blood left in the air too long. The stories are true; she is as beautiful as she is powerful. I threw my dagger at her, but her magic kept my weapon from reaching her body. It fell to the ground at her feet.

"'Missing someone?' she asked me, 'I want you to know you shouldn't be surprised. Your wife has entered my carriage with your son willingly.'

"She held up a mirror. In it I saw Rebekah cooing a crying baby, telling him it would be all right, everything would be all right, that they were safe. Finally safe. I watched her board the queen's carriage of her own volition. No knife pressed against her back. No one threatened to take the child from her. No one even escorted her there. She knew exactly where the carriage would be.

"I watched the soldiers step out of the way to let her pass onto it. I saw them bow and call her Mistress Rebekah. When the man inside the carriage gave her water, I heard her say, 'Thank you, Oswell' though he hadn't introduced himself to her. And I heard Oswell say, 'The queen is pleased that you have chosen to join us.' Rebekah looked back at him, clutching our son close to her, and she said to him, 'Of course. You expected me to deny Her Majesty's generous offer?'

"'Where is the other baby?' Oswell asked her. Rebekah looked into his eyes and said . . .'" Logan breathed deep, relaxing the tightening in his throat. "She said, 'Don't worry. Logan has my daughter. I'm sure Idla will find them.'

"I told Idla she was lying. She replied simply, 'You know as well as I do that one cannot spell a mirror to lie. Mirrors show only what they see.'

"I called for men to join me in the tent, but Idla threw a vial of something on the ground and a violet funnel cloud formed. It touched nothing but the queen—swallowed her whole—then vanished." Logan looked at Jayden. "That night Nathaniel died saving me. I didn't dare go to my daughter, or you, or your brother, fearing the queen would have spies watching me. You had to remain safe, you understand?"

"Of course, I understand." Jayden placed a hand on his arm and returned the marriage stone. "You did the right thing. I am sorry it cost you so much."

Logan's fingers tightened around the stone. "*Cost* me? I live. Others paid a price I would have paid for them."

"So, where do we go next, Protector?" Ethan asked.

Protector. Everyone needed to stop calling him that. Logan placed the cord back over his head. The stone once again swayed against his chest. "After we return to Anna's, our next task will be to find my daughter and Jayden's twin brother. When Nathaniel died, I remained the only one who knew the locations of the deliverers. Before I left my camp, I shared my secret with the one man I trust my life with—Gavin. But I will share the secret with the two of you."

Ethan halted. "You can trust me, Logan, but why risk it?"

Logan stopped and faced them. He breathed deep. "Will you continue if I fail?"

Ethan stared at him. Then the kid clutched his right fist to his chest, just over his heart. A pledge. "Creator willing, you will not fail, Logan. Even so, I swear I will not fail you."

"I accept your pledge." Logan pulled out a knife and slit his palm.

He passed the same knife to Ethan, who repeated the gesture. They locked their hands together in a shake. Their mingled blood squeezed out and dripped to the ground.

CHAPTER 23

THE WAY
A STORM FEELS

Jayden stared at the drops of blood on the ground. Why would they vow to protect her?

Logan, she understood. Two of the deliverers were his own children, so of course he'd want to protect them, but Jayden couldn't fathom Ethan's commitment. Didn't he understand he could die? Didn't he know the finality of an oath scar? There was no backing out. If he tried to, the scar would throb, make him sick. In some cases, he'd be driven to death or insanity. At least those were the stories her parents had told her. Father even had a story about a man who'd cut off his own hand to stop the scar from killing him after he'd abandoned an oath.

Logan sheathed his knife and started walking.

Jayden released her lip from between her teeth and tasted the metallic tang on her tongue. She shuddered. She might be the one everyone else was protecting, but it didn't mean she couldn't protect them back. Yes, she needed to protect the Feravolk—she wouldn't let evil win. No more innocent blood on her hands.

Ethan came up beside her. "Hey, you okay?"

"Of course." She picked up her rooted feet to follow Logan, who was already a dozen paces away.

"Hmm."

She whirled to face Ethan, who still stood where she'd left him, watching her through squinted eyes. Jayden crossed her arms. "What?"

"I just . . . don't believe you." He shrugged. "But keep your secrets. You're entitled to them."

"I—I'm not—"

He chuckled. "You think I'm that thick? I have three sisters—well, four."

"You don't even know how many sisters you have? Now who's lying?"

"I've lived with more than one family."

"Oh."

Ethan motioned up ahead where Logan had gone. "He's getting away."

"Ethan, I . . ."

"You don't have to tell me a thing."

Her feet stayed planted. Secrets had gotten her family killed, and now she was keeping them. No. *Love* had gotten them killed.

Ethan stepped closer to her and put a finger under her chin, nudging her to look at him. "Jayden?"

"We better get moving. If my friend dies, it's on my hands." She pulled her chin from his warm hand and marched after Logan.

Ethan caught her arm. "Jayden, it's not your fault."

She faced him and planted a finger in his chest. "Were you there, Ethan?"

Brown eyes stared back at her, wide.

"When my friend got hurt, were you there?"

He closed his eyes and shook his head. "No."

"Then don't tell me it wasn't my fault." She turned away from him and ran to catch up to Logan.

He glanced over his shoulder at her. "Westwind found a spot partway up the mountain. The hike in should take us about three hours. Will that be enough time?"

Jayden took a deep breath. Of all her Blood Moon talents, feeling for a storm was her favorite. They always calmed her. Heavens knew she needed that now.

She stopped and closed her eyes. The air around her hinted at what would come like the mist before a waterfall. Wind kissed her face with the clean scent of gathering clouds. This storm would be a friendly downpour, rather than a violent tempest or a flashy chorus of wind and thunder. A drenching storm. Her favorite kind to wash her hair in.

She opened her eyes to find Logan staring at her. "It will be enough time."

Logan nodded. "It will make it harder for us to hear approaching danger tonight. Scout and Westwind will stay up with you and Ethan during your watches."

As they followed Scout's wagging tail, trees engulfed the path. A sense of joy welled in Jayden's heart that she should be so trusted. Being the only daughter in a house with four brothers, her opinion was not highly regarded—well, anywhere.

Their hike took a steeper incline and Jayden's legs burned from the climb. Dense patches of rock infiltrated their path more often, and the air thinned. The slender trees that peppered the cliffs hardly resembled their stocky cousins below. Jayden slowed her pace to look around. And to catch her breath, but no one else needed to know that. "It's so pretty here."

The scent of snow-covered pine enveloped her. Pine and a hint of leather.

"You think so?" The closeness of Ethan's voice startled her.

"I do."

"Wait until we get higher."

Contentment and a bit of excitement washed over Jayden, but they weren't her feelings. They had to be Ethan's.

So strange. His emotions slammed into her without warning or invitation. Yet they didn't make her ears tingle. It wasn't as if he were forcing her talent open. It was as if his emotions belonged, were a part of her. She shook her head. That was absurd. Ryan's emotions had always come to her so naturally, she never even had to look at him to get her talent to focus on him. But she did have to wonder what he was feeling. Still, Ryan's emotions didn't drench her when she simply glanced at him. She resolved to be very careful about looking at Ethan—or wondering what he felt.

"Have you been here?" she asked.

"No. I just love being on the mountains."

What was the source of his sudden nostalgia? "I don't recall mountains in Salea."

"Nivek, where I'm from, is in the mountains."

"I've never been."

That familiar smile, Jayden's favorite, grew on Ethan's face. "You'd like it."

"So why did you leave if you liked it so much?"

His brown eyes met hers tentatively. She felt the sorrow that welled up in him, followed by a burst of anger. Familiar, white-hot anger. "Revenge."

Yes, she needed to figure out how to turn off her talent with him.

The inclines steepened, and the sun baked her clothes as they climbed. The steady thunder of rushing water revealed that the river still surged near.

Logan stopped ahead of them and waited until they caught up. Jayden hoped she wasn't slowing them down. She was giving the climb all she had. Ethan stuck close to her, but she imagined it was out of duty more than his inability to keep Logan's pace. Or was it because of his ribs? He sometimes held a protective arm over them.

"Westwind can sense your storm, Jayden," Logan said. "He is impressed with your ability."

She tried to catch her breath. "Thank you, Westwind."

"We should be at the camp spot soon." Logan led them higher.

The climb grew harsher still, but the looming clouds above reminded them of the urgency that kept their pace quick. Colder winds and darker skies enveloped the ground behind them. A breeze tickled Jayden's skin, a welcome and exciting chill that sent a tingle through her whole body.

Ahead, Scout danced around and Westwind reappeared from

behind a tree outcropping on the rocky hillside. They followed the canines into the small mass of trees and unloaded their packs.

Jayden breathed in the sweet scent of approaching rain. Storms were like a dance partner—they shook her to the bone and caressed her face all at once. She couldn't wait.

The sky above darkened. The winds brushed at them through their loose shelter of trees and swirled Jayden's hair around her shoulders.

The treetops swayed. Lightning spread above them and illuminated the clouds with warped fingers. The rustling of leaves drowned out every other sound until thunder rumbled in the distance. Clouds billowed and crashed into one another as they sped past, visual messengers of the wind's power. Lightning preceded the booms by a dozen beats, and Jayden's heart raced as the thunder caught up.

The air grew thick. Colder. Thunder cracked. The sky ripped. Thousands of cooling beads descended from the heavens in a chorus of splashes. Rain fell in a crescendo to the storm's climax. The lightning married the thunder's crashing. Rumbles shook the core of the forest. Flashes of lightning pulsed above them, accompanied by the resounding drumfire of the heavens—a passionate heartbeat.

The heart of the storm never stayed long. Even storms succumb to the wind's majesty. Once the portentous element had passed, Jayden rose and headed into the clearing. The rain continued, a steady pitter-pat on the forest floor.

Ethan released his hold on Scout's neck and stood. "Jayden, where are you going?"

Of course he had no idea of her love affair with storms. Her family understood her desire to wander out into the rain, to watch the lightning, let the raindrops fall on her face, her hair. "To have a look around."

Logan watched her with pensive eyes. "Is it safe to fill the waterskins?"

Jayden smiled. It seemed Logan would accept her, storm fetish and all. But even as she nodded, the weight of the storm lifted off of the trees around her. The sky began to lighten. Westwind rose and shook himself off.

"You aren't going alone." Ethan grabbed the waterskins and followed her as she headed toward the near river.

She smirked. "I guess not."

Ethan caught up to her. "You really like storms?"

"I love them. You don't?"

Ethan found a safe place to stand on the riverbank. "They're not my favorite thing in the world."

"How sad."

"Sad? Why sad?" Ethan bent over and put one of the waterskins into the water.

"I just couldn't imagine not liking storms."

"Well, you can like them all you want."

"Yes, but I hoped you would like them too." She bit her lip. Why should it bother her that Ethan didn't like storms?

That irresistible soft smile grew on his face. "Well, I'll try, but don't count on it."

Her eyes caught his and his emotions drenched her like the steady rain that had passed over them. Sadness—just a profound sadness. And yet he smiled?

Stupid talent. It was so strangely intimate. She would be more than happy to turn this unwanted connection off. If only she could figure out why his emotions poured into her uninvited. "Why don't you like storms?"

Ethan turned back to his task. "I need a reason?"

"No, but you have one, don't you?"

That did it.

Ethan stopped moving for a beat, then he turned toward her. "I do."

Jayden might as well have been looking at a stone. But sorrow welled up in him—sadness so thick, Jayden longed to hug him.

She stilled herself from giving anything away. "Maybe I can change your mind about them."

His guarded expression softened. "I guess if it's that important, you can try."

Jayden stared. Fear joined the sorrow in Ethan's emotions. She changed the subject. "Brace yourself. The storm isn't over."

"Thanks for the warning, but I didn't say I was *afraid* of storms."

"No, you're right." You didn't say anything.

They walked back to camp. Jayden marveled at the fire. Despite the wetness of the available wood, Logan had started one. He passed around some bread, cheese, and dried meat.

Ethan spread out his bedroll. "I can take first watch."

Logan laid down on his. Propping his head on one hand, he fingered his sharpening stone with the other.

Jayden gathered her supplies and beckoned Ethan over to have the cloth around his ribs retied. He rolled his eyes, but complied. "They're already much better."

Jayden took his hand in hers and inspected the rope burns on his wrist. The batch of ointment her mother had packed for her must have been particularly potent. Ethan was right—his wounds did look better.

"They are." She looked at his neck. She'd never seen anyone heal so fast. "How do you feel?"

"Right as rain."

She shot him a smile. "Of course you do."

When Jayden finished, Ethan left to find a tree to lean against and she settled on her bedroll and brushed her hair. As she inhaled the sweet, stormy air, she knew she wouldn't be able to sleep. Not with the next storm so close.

She sat up and faced Westwind's glowing eyes. "Do you mind if we volunteer first watch?"

The wolf cocked his head.

"I'm not sure what that means, Westwind, but watching a lightning storm is my favorite way to spend the evening. I'll stay awake for it, my watch or not."

Westwind chuffed.

Jayden smiled and slipped off her bedroll. She walked over to Ethan, and Westwind followed. Ethan sat with his back against the trunk of a tall pine. Scout raised his head and thumped his tail as she approached.

Jayden reached down and scratched behind his ears. "I can take first watch if you want. I want to see the rest of the storm ride out."

Ethan stared at her for what seemed an eternity before he sighed. "I'll watch the storm with you then."

Jayden's eyes widened. "You will?"

"I'm not fond of sleeping during storms."

Jayden settled next to Scout, who whined and earned a stifling look from Ethan. Scout slipped away from him and settled near Jayden's feet. She twirled her finger in the dog's fur and folded her other arm around her shins.

Maybe Ethan had nightmares like her. Already he'd woken her from several because she'd screamed in her sleep. Hopefully night screams didn't attract black lions.

Placing her chin on her knees, she looked at the side of Ethan's face. His short, dark hair curved where it rested against his neck. That terrible gash sat just underneath.

"Nightmares?" she asked him. "Afraid you'll attract unwanted attention?"

He glanced at her out of the corner of his eye. "Hey, don't worry about the screaming. It's not like you mean for it to happen."

So quick to comfort, or so quick to redirect?

Teasing seemed like a good way to entice conversation from him. She nudged his arm with her elbow. "So you're not a screamer?"

He smiled a little and bowed his head. "With the unknown dangers around here, it's best to be careful."

Lightning lit up the cloud cover above them in a flash of white. Jayden couldn't help but look up. She repeated his words, "Well, don't worry about the screaming. It's not like you mean for it to happen."

He stared at his hands. "Right."

A wave of sadness rolled off of him and crashed into her. Heavens, she wanted to touch him. "What is it?"

He looked at her.

She leaned closer. "You can trust me, you know."

His intense eyes searched her face. Then he focused on the ground. "My parents were murdered during a storm."

"Oh, Ethan." She stared at him, though his gaze never left the ground. "You saw it happen, didn't you?"

"I was nine." His voice remained eerily calm. "Whenever lightning strikes, I see my father and mother on the ground with their throats covered in blood. I've learned to ignore it. When my eyes are closed, I can't—I—I can't get away from it."

Jayden gripped his hand and squeezed. "Dreams about real things aren't exactly just dreams. Are they?"

He looked up at her. "No."

"I am so sorry. And I am sorry to have made you share that."

"You didn't make me share it." He squeezed back.

"You were so young. Where did you go?"

"My friend's family took me in. They had a son and three daughters of their own, and still they took me in. That's how I got three of my four sisters, and my only brother." He bowed his head and shook it. "I couldn't stay forever. I was too . . . I needed to heal without causing them grief."

The hurt she had expected to see in his eyes wasn't there. Ethan's face remained placid, but emotion leaked from him even so—pain, sorrow, anger, and a touch of gratitude.

"Well, maybe if you aren't alone tonight—I mean, maybe if I sit with you—I can scare the nightmares away."

The feeling of gratitude exploded. "You don't have to—"

"I want to. Besides, I think nightmare-chasing is another thing very good friends do for one another."

Ethan smiled. "I think you're right."

Jayden found herself gravitating closer to him. He didn't move away, so she stayed there and let her arm brush against his. They sat in silence and watched the remainder of the storm together. Sympathy strong in Jayden's heart, hurt strong in Ethan's.

A dull pang settled below her heart. Was it wrong to sit so close to him? Would Ryan disapprove? No. She was only being Ethan's friend. Besides, Ryan never had to know.

CHAPTER 24

PULLED TOGETHER

Jayden's head fell onto Ethan's shoulder, and he scooted closer so she'd be more comfortable sleeping. She'd been kind to sit with him, though it was completely unnecessary, and it further developed his protective instinct for her.

No one had ever elicited his talent this strongly. Not Tessa. Not his brother Ryan or Ryan's sisters. Not even that other strange woman—Swallow—who had stoked his talent after just one meeting.

At least this time his protectiveness wouldn't get in the way. He was bound to Jayden by a blood oath, and it felt right, like it was his Destiny Path. She could tug on those protective heart strings as much as she wanted, because nothing would stop him from keeping her safe.

The lightning subsided, but the clouds still blocked the sky so not even the moon shone through. Darkness rested heavy tonight.

The skin on the back of Ethan's neck prickled. His stomach seized and heat spread across his chest. The air smelled off, but still calming, which disoriented his feelings.

He focused. The scent was . . . lavender. *Snare me.*

Ethan could see the wolf's silhouette in the fire's dimming light. "Westwind, it's a black lion."

Westwind stood and slipped into the darkness. Moments later Ethan spotted him on the other side of the fire, waking Logan, who rose, knife in hand. Ethan nudged Jayden's arm. She startled, but his face was right next to hers. He pressed his finger against his lips. She nodded and calmed her breathing.

He picked his sword off the ground and pulled it from its scabbard. Jayden raced to her bedroll and grabbed her daggers. Ethan stayed close to her and scanned the tree line. He hoped these black lions weren't as fearsome as legends said. The feeling of danger settling in his gut told him that hope was futile.

Something stirred above him, sounding like a blanket blowing in the wind. Wings.

"It's above us!" Ethan pushed Jayden to the ground and dove on top of her. Pain pulsed through his ribs. Heat hit his neck. Teeth snapped just above his ear. A gust of wind eddied around him as the lion soared back to the sky. That was close. He gritted his teeth and pushed himself up.

Where was Logan? Ethan looked up. Glowing yellow eyes stared back at him. That was all he could see. Great. Just like the legends. The lion screeched. Its looming cloud above them stunted his vision even more than the night alone.

The yellow eyes disappeared.

Quietness covered them as darkness grew deeper. Ethan waited in the silence and braced for anything. Feeling the threat's pulse—alive and biding.

"Watch out!" Logan shouted.

Ethan spun. The creature leapt from cover right at Jayden, and Ethan raced toward it.

The lion hissed.

Ethan could just make out Jayden's figure running toward a crevice in the hillside. He lunged at the cat. It turned and launched itself at him like a released spring. He dove away just in time.

"Keep it distracted!" Logan called.

Ethan crept toward the beast and waved his sword. "Here, kitty."

The beast swirled around and swiped its massive paw at him. He jumped out of its reach. Pale yellow eyes, like twin moons, locked onto Ethan. The lion was huge—bigger than Ethan had expected—the size of a full-grown workhorse. The fur on its wings fluttered in the wind as they spread from its sides and blocked Ethan's view. Blood-red claws extended from black paws. Its tail thrashed back and forth. The creature's hot breath reached him.

Lunging forward, Ethan jabbed his sword at the lion's face. The cat's wings beat and lifted it from the ground to escape the blade.

Logan whisked underneath the lion, but it remained focused on Ethan. It reached down and opened its jaws. Ethan dashed away, but his shirt got caught in the lion's mouth.

It ascended to the sky. Ethan's heart slammed against his chest as his feet left the ground.

The lion faltered. Ethan looked down to see Scout dangling from one of its furry wings. If his dog could get the creature low enough, Ethan could use his sword, but he dared not now, not this high up.

Westwind clamored up the rocky mountainside and leapt up. His jaws grabbed the lion's other wing. It shrieked and lowered.

Ethan sliced at its face.

The lion tossed him to the ground and stabbing pain coursed through his side upon impact.

C'mon, Ethan, get up. He rolled over.

The lion thrust its head upward and attempted to fly. It failed to rise with the canines still clinging to its wings. Ethan followed, staying in the cat's sights, trying to lure it to the ground. Yellow eyes locked onto him. It lurched.

In an instant the creature's massive paws pinned his arms to the ground. Its purr vibrated his whole body. Claws kneaded his shoulders. Pain pricked his skin as the thick claws pushed and the more he struggled, the harder those claws dug into him. If he could just get his arm free—

C'mon, Ethan. You're stronger than this.

Whiskers brushed against his cheeks, and his heart pounded. Still struggling to get his sword hand free, he closed his eyes and braced himself for sharp teeth in his neck.

Maybe he wasn't strong enough after all.

A thunderous roar shook him and his eyes split open. The lion threw back its head. Heavy paws released Ethan's arms. Logan stood beside the beast with a weapon embedded in the creature's heart. The beast crumpled to the ground, writhing and spitting before turning to ash. The scent of burning lavender hung thick in the air above the pile of ash.

The weapon, a wooden dagger, fell to the ground. Dark blood stained its sharp edge.

Logan picked up the dagger. Chest heaving, he offered Ethan a hand. "You okay, kid?"

Jayden raced over with Scout following.

Ethan took hold of Logan's hand and stood. He clenched his teeth. The throbbing in his chest made him want to retch. He hunched over and concentrated on breathing until he could stand. "Kind of handy that you had that weapon lying around, huh?"

Logan wiped the dagger on his shirt, but the blood had stained the wood and didn't come off. "It was a gift from a Whisperer."

"Are you all right?" Jayden's worried eyes scanned them.

Logan motioned toward the wolf. "Westwind's leg is cut."

Westwind growled.

Jayden approached him. "It's not too bad. I can take care of it. What about you, Ethan?"

He focused on taking shallow breaths. "I hope we don't see any more of those."

"I hope—" Logan's voice grew somber. "—we don't see more than one at once."

Jayden drew closer to Ethan and let her arm brush against his. Her breath shook. "Maybe we should get away from here."

Ethan put his right hand on her shoulder. She leaned into his side and slipped her arm across his back. Heavens. That only fanned his desire to protect her, among other things.

"You think the Valley of the Hidden Ones will be any safer?" Logan eyed her. "We'll wait to enter the valley until morning. Why don't the two of you get some rest. You both look like you could use it."

Rest? How could Logan talk about danger and rest in the same breath?

Logan's face remained firm. "Stay close to each other and keep your weapons closer. Westwind and I will take the rest of tonight's watches."

Jayden pulled away and headed toward Westwind with her ointment. Ethan chuckled at the wolf's growl, then moved Jayden's bedroll closer to his.

"Here, boy." Ethan patted his leg. Scout lumbered over with his head down and his ears back. He tilted his head and let out a soft whine. Ethan leaned a hand on Scout's shoulders as he lowered himself to the ground. "You came through tonight."

Scout wagged his tail and a goofy smile spread across his face. Ethan patted the space between his bedroll and Jayden's. The dog turned in three complete circles before he lay between them. He ruffled his dog's ears and let Scout lick his face.

Then he noticed Jayden watching him with round, worried eyes. He smiled at her, and a shy grin grew on her face. She curled up on her bedroll with an arm on Scout, who thumped his tail in return. Ethan wasn't sure why, but with a single smile he could light up her face like a candle ring on a feast day.

He liked it.

○

Ethan pried his eyes open to a warm, gray sky. He attempted to sit up, but the stabbing pain in his chest made him lay back down. This would be a rough day.

"Too much fighting last night?" A pleasant smile splashed across Jayden's face as she leaned over him.

She held out her hand to help him. He thought about waving her away, but reconsidered. She was right—too much fighting.

Logan busied himself with breaking camp. "Sun will be rising soon. I'd like to get to the valley and out before it sets."

Westwind approached them and Ethan noticed the wolf limping. The red gash wrapped around his leg next to his older scars. "Is he okay?"

Westwind chuffed as he nodded for himself.

"I'll put some more salve on it, and he'll be good as new." Jayden inspected Westwind, then gravitated closer to Ethan. Her concerned eyes met his. So blue. "What about you? You okay?"

"I'm fine."

"Of course you are." She shook her head and a small smile formed on her lips. Red tints shone in her dark hair. Did she have any idea how beautiful she was?

She picked up her cloths. He put his hands on her shoulders. When she tugged the cloth tight around him, he bit back a groan. *Breathe.*

"You okay?" she asked when it was over.

"Yes. Thank you." He evened his breathing, and leaned back against the large rock behind him, thankful she'd had the prescience to make him sit in front of it. "You won't think less of me if I sit here a few minutes, though?"

She touched his knee. "I wouldn't think less of you if you sat there a few days."

"Neither would I, kid." Logan walked over and took a seat next to Ethan with his strange map.

Ethan recognized some of the names from an ancient map on display in the Nivek library.

"The valley includes this whole area here." Logan traced the borders with his finger. "Anna said this plant is scarce, so I fear we'll have to split up. Scout, you'll go with Ethan, and Westwind will pair with you, Jayden. That way I'll have a link to you both. No matter what, don't get separated from one another. If you need help, the rest of us will come to you. Got it?"

They both nodded.

"I'll take this area. Jayden, you'll head east. Ethan, you take the west end. You kids ready?"

"Ready," they voiced together.

"Remember, unicorns are dangerous." Ethan cautioned.

Jayden's eyes gleamed. "Do you think we'll see one?"

He had to smile at her excitement. "Maybe you'll bond to one."

Logan glanced at him, his eyes skeptical. "I guess she could."

"Unicorns are fierce creatures. They only trust the pure in heart, their horns are sharp as any sword, and their hooves are stronger than stone. They rely on stealth and speed and ferocity," Jayden said.

"Right." Logan's tone became grave. "They're a match for the creature we fought last night."

Jayden's eyes widened. Scout emitted a soft whine. Westwind lifted his tail and winked. Crazy wolf.

Ethan glanced at Jayden and an ache squeezed his heart. What if something endangered her in the valley and he was too far to sense the threat?

The air cooled the higher they climbed. It carried a glacial taste that sent a thrill through Ethan's blood. How had he stayed away from Nivek and its mountains for so long? The sun warmed his face, and the dry buzz of a dozen or more grasshoppers chattered around them.

Jayden turned to check on him. She'd been doing that all morning. He'd curled his arm around his sore ribs again, so he dropped it back to his side. She'd already, seen though, and her pretty blue eyes rounded. Yes, his ribs hurt, but he wasn't about to be the reason they slowed the pace.

He'd forgotten how nice it felt to have someone care. He smiled, and Jayden's cheeks reddened even deeper than the climb alone had made them. Heavens, she was beautiful.

He shook his head. Thinking things like that would only lead to a torn-up heart. She was supposed to save the Feravolk. And what was he? An orphan from nowhere.

At last they reached the top. The whole world spread out beneath them. Lush vegetation below contrasted with the jagged faces of the steeply rising rock that framed the valley. The sun rose above the mountain peaks and cast its light into the valley. A waterfall, visible from where they stood, cascaded down the mountainside to a sparkling stream below. The crisp, cool air touched his face. A tug in Ethan's heart called to him—a tug from Nivek.

Jayden stood beside him, her eyes wide. "It's amazing."

Ethan smiled at her look of wonder. "It is."

Logan shaded his eyes. "I think I see where the unicorns enter." He pointed.

Ethan spotted the sloping pathway below that led into the valley. "Someone uses it."

"If we do, they'll be alerted to our presence. But I can't see another way in," Logan said.

They descended toward it. The sheer number of hoof tracks that cluttered the gritty path attested to its use.

Logan waved them away from the path. "We can enter here. The brush will hide us."

It sounded like a good idea until a familiar unsettling sensation hit Ethan's stomach and heat burned his chest. "I think we should take the path."

Scout changed direction without hesitation.

Logan stopped. "What's wrong?"

"Jayden said unicorns are fierce beasts who only trust the pure in heart. I think if we enter their land out in the open, we might be left alone. If we enter in secret, they might not take too kindly to that."

"I think Ethan is right." Jayden stepped out of the brush.

Logan conceded with a change of direction. "Still, don't expect a warm welcome."

Ethan tapped his sword hilt. "I'll be ready."

When they reached the valley, no one greeted them. They filled their waterskins from the clear, blue river, and separated. When Jayden walked off with Westwind, Ethan's worry grew, but he didn't let it show.

As she walked out of view, he knew exactly where she was. He closed his eyes. Yes, he could feel her presence—like they were connected somehow. Did this have something to do with his protective talent? Or was it the oath? Whichever it was, he hoped it was strong enough to warn him if she faced any danger.

Scout's cold nose bumped his hand, and he turned toward his dog. "Let's go."

Together, they entered the woods. The trees glittered with silvery leaves Ethan had never seen and peculiar chirps filtered through the valley.

He looked at Scout. "I have a feeling this particular plant is going to be hard to find."

He and Scout searched the ground for the first hour to no avail. When they stepped into a clearing, grasshoppers jumped away from him. The knee-high grass swayed in the breeze with a bluish tint. A few white deer dashed toward the trees when he emerged from the wooded area opposite them.

"This might just be the place." The woods beyond the meadow didn't look inviting.

Scout weaved back and forth in search. Ethan approached the other side of the sunny meadow, closer to the tenebrous tree line, parting the grass as he walked.

Something stopped him. His stomach churned as he parted the grass. On the ground, shorter than the surrounding grass, grew a plant identical to the one he looked for.

He called Scout over to him. The dog bounded up, but came closer more cautiously as he held out his hand for Scout to be careful. He slipped out his sword and pointed it toward the dirt when the sudden sound surrounded him.

It rang deep and mellifluous. He stopped cold. Next to him Scout froze. The fur along his back stood straight up.

Ethan moved his hands toward the plant again. The same resonance swirled around him. It was fierce, rich and trilling, almost like a song, but too deep for any bird to sing. A growl.

He looked up at the dark trees in front of him. The sound's source had come from beyond the threshold of those woods. He could feel it there.

He backed his hands away from the plant, which seemed to be the origin of the unseen creature's anger, and held his sword out in front of him. Scout emitted a low rumble of his own. The answering song from the hidden creature was deafening.

Ethan moved in front of Scout to shield him and his insides

trembled. He tried to hide the fear from his voice. "Come out, whatever you are."

A shadow appeared in the trees and a beast the size of a horse stepped into the meadow.

A unicorn.

CHAPTER 25

HOLD ON

Ryan wanted to pace. Instead he clenched and unclenched his jaw, tapped his fingers against his leg, and stared at the trees outside the open window above the couch where he lay. If only the trees could tell him when Anna would be back with his sisters.

They weren't talking to him.

Apparently they only spoke to Whisperers. But Anna hadn't answered any of his questions, she'd just hurried out of the house, telling him to wait. Not that he was going anywhere.

Had the trees found all three of his sisters? Were they okay? Were they even his sisters?

Oh, right, she'd answered one question. When he'd asked if the girls the trees found had red hair and green eyes, she'd laughed and said, "Trees don't see color the way we do, dear one."

Of course not.

He swallowed the lump in his throat. Surely they knew about Father.

A trickle of heat shot through Ryan's veins. No. His heart beat erratically. His breathing quickened, and he gripped the blanket in his fists, arched his back, and braced for the pain. It flooded through him.

No one was here; he was all alone, so he screamed.

He screamed like he'd never screamed before. Like screaming

would let the fire out of him. Release the pressure building inside. Clear the fog. Stop the pain.

A dark hiss cut through the pain fog and a white lion stepped through. *If you would stop fighting me, this would be over. No more pain.*

No more pain. Sounded good. Sounded great. Sweat trickled over his skin, pink and blood tinged. "Get . . . out . . . of my head." His words were a hoarse whisper.

"It's not your head I want. It's your heart. Just give it to me."

"Never."

"So be it."

Crimson claws extended. Ripped shreds through his chest. He screamed again. Screamed so that the trees outside his window seemed to bow toward him the way Anna had when she tried to help him through the waves of pain. The waves crashed into him more frequently now. More forcefully. And each wave left him feeling weaker than the last. Like he was treading water in his own body. The slow simmer in his blood had become a permanent part of him now.

The fire in his blood never fully died.

Blood gurgled in the back of his throat and he leaned over and threw up into the metal bowl. Black spots started to overtake his vision. Shaking, he lay back against the pillow. If Jayden didn't get back soon, he didn't know how much longer he could hold on.

Wind trickled through the leaves, sending a dry whisper. *Hold on. Hold on. Hold on, dear one.*

Anna was sending him a message. Had she found his sisters?

"Hold on, dear one."

He swore he could hear her actual voice.

Thumps pounded against the steps outside. He did hear her. Footsteps raced across the porch. Someone had found him? The door burst open and a young girl with red hair raced into the room. Kinsey. Her green eyes were wide and red-rimmed. Smeared dirt covered her favorite patchwork dress, and the edges were torn. A piece of her dress bandaged her left arm, and her hair was tangled. She looked tired, hungry, dirty, and perfectly safe. She was alive.

"Kinsey?"

She rushed over to him and dropped to her knees next to the couch. Her arms flung around his neck and she hugged him so tight. "Can I hug you? Am I hurting you?"

She didn't lift her buried face from his neck. She just held him.

"You're not hurting me." He found the strength to hold her with his right arm. And he held her as close as he could. She was so small against him. Her body shook.

"Kinsey, don't cry. I'm—"

"Don't forbid me from crying. You're not Father," she whispered. "I'm sorry."

Her tears dripped onto his shirt. "Father is dead."

His chest tightened and he hugged his sister closer. His breath shook.

"Chloe kept saying you'd come. I didn't believe her anymore. I—I never thought I'd see you again."

He wanted to reassure her that everything would be all right, but he couldn't. Not when it would be a lie.

"Kinsey, get off of him!" The floorboards echoed as someone else entered the house. Chloe practically ripped Kinsey out of his arms. "Anna said he was . . ."

Whatever Anna had said about him died on Chloe's tongue. She sank to her knees behind Kinsey and stared at him. Her green eyes were pinched around the corners. A healing scratch marred her freckled cheek. Her hair was a tangled mass of leaves and burrs, and cuts cracked her knuckles. She stared like a gaping catfish. What was she thinking?

"Are you okay?" he asked.

"Am—" A strangled laugh escaped her throat as if he'd offended and disgusted her at the same time. "Am *I* okay?" She shook her head and backed away from him. Her eyes looked wet. What had Anna said? Was he contagious or something? "You're the one who's lying on a couch looking like a ghost."

"A ghost?" Wren tiptoed into the room.

She had just as many splashes of dirt as freckles on her face, and her red hair was as tangled as his other sisters', but Wren looked unharmed. Her pale green eyes rounded beneath pinched eyebrows. He thought she might cry. Like she might be afraid of him. All he wanted was to wrap his arms around all three of them and promise he'd protect them with every breath he had left.

He reached his arm toward his littlest sister. "Wren, would you let me hug you?"

Her face scrunched up and she ran toward him, arms wide.

"Wren!" Chloe reached to grab her, but she dodged her sister's arms and reached Ryan.

He hugged her tight. "You're all right?"

"I'm fine," she whispered. Warm tears dripped onto his cheek, where she pressed her face against his. "It's you we're worried about. Anna says you're hurt."

She backed away from him and touched his forehead like their mother might. That made him smile.

"I feel better seeing you three."

Kinsey slid close again and he pulled his sister in for another hug. "Good." She gave his hand a squeeze. "We were worried sick."

He looked over their heads at Chloe. She crossed her arms, hugging herself tight. She must be angry with him for leaving. For getting Father killed. She had to be. A tear dripped out of her eye and she wiped it away just as quickly. She tugged the back of Wren's dress. "You need to let him rest."

"It's okay, Chloe," he said.

She glared at him, incredulous.

Anna, who must have been there the whole time, but seemed to appear from the woodwork, squeezed Chloe's shoulder. "Let them hug him. He needs their support right now. And yours."

Chloe walked out of the house.

Anna followed her, and Ryan could tell they'd stopped on the porch.

"How could you?" Chloe's voice carried through the open

window. "He looks like he's about to die! How could you give them hope that they'd see him again and not tell us he was at death's door?"

"I don't think it worthless to hope, and I told you he was ill, dear one."

"He doesn't even look like my brother. Ryan never gets sick. Never! What have you done to him?" Chloe's voice rose steadily in volume as she spoke to Anna, and Ryan couldn't take it any longer.

"Excuse me, girls," he said to his sisters and started to get up.

Kinsey pushed him back. "I'll talk to her. She's scared, Ry."

Ryan sighed and closed his eyes. Why did Chloe have to be so bitter all the time?

Wren whispered, "I think he's asleep."

"Looks that way," Kinsey said.

"Ryan won't leave us, too. Will he?" Wren's voice was so small.

His first impulse was to open his eyes and tug her close, tell her he would never leave her, but he couldn't do that. Truth was, whatever was in his blood was attacking him, every part of him. His mind. His heart. If it left him alive, would he want to be whatever this transformation was turning him into?

Wren's little hand gripped his.

"No, Wren," Kinsey said. "If Ryan has a choice, he would stay with us no matter what." Kinsey's lips pressed against his forehead, and she leaned close to his ear. "Don't leave us, please. I love you too much. I can't lose another brother." She curled into his side, and Wren cuddled close to her, still holding his hand. He touched Kinsey's hair with his other hand, hoping she understood that as his promise to fight this beast inside for as long as he could.

CHAPTER 26

FATED TWICE

The unicorn's white shining fur reflected the sun's rays, and wisps of its white mane blew in the breeze. Large, brown eyes fixed on Ethan. Its tail thrashed to the side and its ears laid flat against its head.

The unicorn strode forward and pointed its glistening horn at Ethan's chest. The animal was close enough to run him through with just a thrust of its head. Spiraled and iridescent, the horn glinted like a sharp blade. Ethan swallowed.

Shaking on the inside, he lowered his sword. "I need this plant."

The growl rumbled again, vibrating the ground.

Ethan looked into the creature's eyes. His words came out in a rush. "I, well, my friend has a friend who was wounded by a poisonous arrow. A Whisperer sent us to get a plant that looks like this one. I need it to save his life."

The unicorn raised its head slightly, but Ethan recognized the gesture, and the feeling of umbrage vanished.

"Scout, did you call Logan?" Without moving his feet, Ethan turned to see his dog's response. As he feared, the golden dog nodded. "You need to go to him. Stop them from coming here. Do you understand?"

Scout stayed put.

"I know Logan gave you orders, but this unicorn won't like it if

Westwind and the others come barging in here ready to fight. You have to trust me, boy. You've trusted me all along."

At this, Scout's gaze softened, and he turned and fled.

Once more Ethan faced the unicorn. "I think you can understand me."

The opalescent creature stared at him, still pointing its horn in his direction.

"May I please take the plant? My dog has gone to try and stop the others from coming. If they see you ready to kill me, they'll fight you. If I can just have this, we'll leave."

The unicorn's eyes narrowed and its head lifted more this time, then its ears rose and its tail stopped thrashing. Ethan bent to the ground again, still eyeing the unicorn, and picked up his sword.

The growl started to resound again in the animal's chest.

"I've got to dig it out."

"Dash can dig it out for you." A feminine voice startled him.

A beautiful young woman stood beside the unicorn with her hand on its shoulder. She hadn't been there a moment ago. Heart pounding, Ethan scanned the area. No more strange people appeared from nowhere. Just her.

Her long blonde hair hung loose around her shoulders, and her eyes were blue—dark blue. Her smile was soft, but there was something impish about the curve of her lips.

She was shorter than Jayden, but her presence was commanding. Ethan wasn't sure if it was the unicorn she stood next to, or if it was something else about her. Her touch seemed to calm the beast. She wore only white, and he noticed her skirts were divided for riding.

Riding what? A unicorn?

"My name is Serena." She held out a delicate hand.

Ethan shook his clouded head. "Pleased to meet you."

He rose, sheathed his sword, and took her hand in his. It surprised him how strong her grip tightened around his fingers when she pushed his hand down to deny his kiss. She smiled instead. Her behavior both confounded and intrigued him.

"What's your name?"

"Ethan."

She smiled. "Dash tells me you're one of the Feravolk."

"No, I'm—"

"Hmmm. You can't deny it. Dash can tell that you are one of them. He says you are of a very strong bloodline." Her blue eyes filled with compassion and she reached toward his neck. "It seems you have seen some rough days."

He backed a step away from her. "A few."

The unicorn whinnied, a normal sound from a horse-like creature. Serena looked in his direction and nodded.

Curiosity overcame Ethan. "Are you bonded to him?"

"Yes, Dash and I are bonded." Serena smiled, then reached out toward his left hand.

Ethan sucked in a breath.

Her dark blue eyes, large and soft, caught his. "It's all right."

Something in her words calmed him, and he accepted her touch. She held his hand in hers and pushed up his sleeve with her other hand. Her fingers slid down across his forearm and stopped at the rope burns. She traced her fingertips along the tender cut on his wrist. Warmth melted through his skin.

Just before it grew too hot, a welcome cooling followed. The sensation leaked to his bones and tingled through his arm. The scabs vanished into normal skin, and not even a trace of scarring remained. His heart thumped faster as she released his left arm and took his right hand. The same sensation filled his right wrist as she healed it.

Serena drew closer, and reached up to place her fingers on the back of his neck. Her small stature made her stand so near to him that, as she rose onto her tiptoes, her forehead touched his chin. He didn't know if he should move, so he stayed still and breathed in the scent of her hair. Flowers.

Her fingers brushed across his neck. Warmth spread over his skin before it cooled and the itch and dull pain left. Serena stepped back and looked at him. Ethan remained motionless.

"Not even a scar. Still, there's something." Her brow furrowed.

She lifted her right hand and held it in front of him, but stopped at the left side of his chest. The throbbing side. "Lift your shirt."

He untucked it. His shirt draped over her arm as she moved her hand up his side, so smooth against his skin, until she found Jayden's bindings. She loosened them and tucked her hand underneath.

The warming sensation filtered through his skin and penetrated deep into his chest. It spread out, wrapped around his side, and pulsed into his every fiber. His body prepared for the burning hot, then the cooling came, and relief rushed though him. At last, the heavy ache disappeared.

She removed her hand and stepped back from him. A small smile drew up the corners of her mouth. "Better?"

Ethan took in a deep breath, deeper than he'd been able to take in weeks. He hadn't realized how awful he felt until he felt normal again. "Much. Thank you. How did you do that?"

"Unicorns are healers. I guess I get that from Dash."

Black specks clouded Ethan's vision. Soft hands gripped him and helped him sit.

"That took quite a bit of energy from both of us. Are you all right?"

He nodded, now able to see clearly again.

Serena rose and returned to Dash's side, her movements smooth like her silk dress. The unicorn dipped his head and cut the ground around the plant with his spiraled horn. Serena bent to scoop the plant and brought it to Ethan.

He took it. "Thank you. For everything."

"You are welcome, Ethan of the Feravolk." She turned to leave.

"Wait, Serena. Wouldn't you be able to heal my friend?"

"Your Whisperer is wise. Take this plant to her. If your friend doesn't get better, you can bring him to me."

"How would I find you? I can't very well walk in here and ask for a beautiful healer with blonde hair."

"You come here, and I will find you." Serena beamed. It was captivating, but not the same as Jayden's blushing smile. Then, almost as an afterthought, she added, "Why, Ethan, you think I'm beautiful?"

Ethan chuckled. He'd been caught in a woman's wit. "Yes, I do. And I'm sure I'm not the first to tell you so."

She twisted her lips and her blue eyes searched his face. "I accept your compliment, but, as you can see, unicorns are beautiful creatures. Perhaps that is something else I get from Dash. Now tell me, are you bonded to unicorns, Ethan?"

He laughed. "Me? Unicorns? I think even Dash is laughing."

The unicorn did flip his head.

"Perhaps I will see you again." Serena grinned. Her eyes seemed to sparkle as she leaned in close to him, and her lips almost touched his ear. "I would like to."

"Perhaps." Ethan found himself unable to move. *I hope so.*

"Good-bye for now, Stone Wolf."

He snapped his gaze to her. "What did you call me?"

She just watched him with an encouraging smile.

"How do you—I mean—*why* do you think I go by that name?"

She touched his shirt collar and moved it aside to reveal the pink Blood Moon birthmark on the right side of his chest. "My birthmark is not on my face."

Of course. Her eyes were the same shade of blue. Her hair the same wavy blonde. "Swallow?"

"It seems we were fated to meet at least twice."

The overwhelming desire to protect her flared in his heart again. "You should—"

"What? Come with you? This time, it is I who must say no."

"When I told you not to come with me—"

"You said I'd be in the way."

"What I meant—"

"You spoke truth."

"Serena, it was for your protection." And someone else's. *Snare me.* Ethan hung his head and hoped she would sense the truth in his words.

"I know. And this time, I'm protecting you. Perhaps our Destiny Paths will cross again. For your sake, I hope the next time I'm not bailing you out of trouble"—she glanced at his chest—"or pain."

"Serena—"

"Trust me, Ethan. If I need you, I'll find you."

He didn't feel a threat for her safety here. With Jayden to take care of, maybe it was best if she didn't come.

Serena put her hand on the unicorn and the two of them disappeared into the trees.

"Bye," he mouthed, sure it was too late for her to hear.

There he sat, alone in the meadow, where the unicorn and the beautiful healer once stood, holding the plant.

The plant. Logan. I'm in so much trouble.

He jumped to his feet. Out of habit he put a protective hand to his chest, but pain no longer throbbed there.

Thank you, Serena. I'll never forget you.

He glanced over his shoulder once more before he ran out the way he had come.

Once in the wooded area, a soft sound slowed him. Scout emerged from behind a bush.

Logan stepped through the trees. "You disobeyed orders, Ethan."

A pang of guilt twisted his stomach. He bowed his head and stood tall, owning his mistake. He hoped it conveyed the remorse he felt. "Yes, sir. I'm sorry."

"Why?" Logan's eyes scanned Ethan's face. He looked more curious than angry.

What was he thinking?

Westwind and Jayden fell in behind Logan. Jayden's eyes focused on the plant in Ethan's hands.

"I feel threats. This unicorn wasn't going to hurt me if I did what it wanted." Now he'd explained his talent for detecting danger. Hopefully he could trust Logan and Jayden to keep it secret.

Before he could ask, Jayden backed away from him, a dagger in each hand. She glared at him. "What kind of magic is this?"

"Jayden?" Ethan took a step back.

Her eyes squinted. "Who are you?"

Logan drew his sword.

"Wait, Jayden, it's me." Ethan put the plant on the ground.

Logan stepped forward, his sword leading. "Raise your hands."
Ethan complied.

"Prove it." Jayden's eyes narrowed to slits.

"I met a healer." He motioned to his shirt. Logan nodded for him to continue. Ethan pulled it up to reveal Jayden's bandages, still there, loosened. "See? I've just been healed."

Jayden exhaled a long breath, then replaced her daggers and ran to him. She wrapped her arms around him and squeezed. "Ethan, it *is* you. I'm sorry." She pulled back too soon.

"You met a healer?" Logan broke their eye contact.

"She gave me the plant." He picked it up to show them.

"A healer?" Jayden's eyes grew hopeful. "Will she be able to heal my friend?"

"I asked her. She said our Whisperer was wise, and the plant should help, but if it didn't, we could bring your friend to her. Then she disappeared."

Jayden's face darkened.

Ethan put his arm around her. "Hey, don't worry. Serena said the plant should work."

She leaned away from him. "Serena?"

"The healer."

"Let's get out of here. Before dark." Logan looked around. He didn't have to say why. The thought of meeting a black lion again wasn't a long forgotten worry, and the sun was setting.

CHAPTER 27

CLOUDED JUDGMENT

The sun dipped lower in the sky. The Valley of the Hidden Ones lay a day behind them. A dark cloud billowing in the west caught Logan's attention. *"See that smoke?"*

Westwind bristled. *"I smell it."*

"It's new."

"A day old, maybe two."

"It's Erivale. I'd like to check it out."

"Do you think that's a good idea?"

"If I can get into one of the cities I may be able to find out some information about where these Feravolk imposters are going next."

"What about Ryan?"

"It won't take long."

"Logan, that kid might not have long."

"I'll still be back before Anna wants us. It's practically on the way."

The plant was packed in the side of Logan's bag like the one Anna made had been, but the last one had started to die, and this one seemed even more delicate. Still, Anna knew how long the journey would take, and he was making it in less time. A stop in Erivale would be just fine.

"So tell me, Ethan." Logan shot a glance over his shoulder at Ethan. "How is it that you claim to be face-to-face with a ferocious, yet beautiful creature and felt no threat?"

Ethan's eyebrows shot up. "The healer?"

"The unicorn." Logan couldn't suppress his laughter, even as Jayden scowled.

Ethan's face bore no smile. He was quiet for a long time. "It's one of my Blood Moon talents, sir."

"And you're just sharing this with me now?"

"Yes, sir."

"You fight in an army, kid?"

"No."

"You're suddenly addressing me as 'sir.' Name's Logan."

Ethan quickened his pace and caught up to Logan. "Wait. Why are you going north?"

Logan pointed to the sky. "Erivale isn't far."

"Fire. That means it's likely the Royal Army was there. It isn't safe."

Jayden sucked in a breath. "Why are we doing this? Shouldn't we get the plant back to Anna first?"

Logan clenched his jaw. "I don't plan to be here long. According to Anna's instructions, we'll still get the plant to her in time to save your friend." He stopped walking and faced them both. "You two stay here." He started toward the city.

Ethan impeded Logan. "You can't—"

"If we catch their trail, we can find out where they're going next." Logan stepped around Ethan, who pushed his hands into Logan's chest.

"The Royal Army might still be there."

"Ethan, you chose to help the Feravolk, right?"

"If we lose Jayden, we lose everything."

"If we keep losing our *people*, we lose everything." Logan's voice rose louder than intended.

Jayden put her hand on Ethan's arm. "He's right."

Logan turned to her. "I have no intention of putting you in danger."

Her hands jammed into her hips. "I have no intention of being left behind, but I won't do anything stupid."

"He will." Ethan shot Logan a glance.

Logan made his stare cold. "Your gut tells you this is dangerous?"

"Yes. If we go there—"

"What if we don't go? Do you sense danger then?"

Ethan's jaw clenched, and he took his time expelling a breath. "It doesn't work that way."

Logan pointed a finger in Ethan's face. "You sacrificed yourself to save a life. I would have sacrificed myself to save the whole town. Understand?"

Ethan's countenance turned to stone and his voice seemed just as hard. "Yes, *sir.*"

Logan's hand balled into a fist. Jayden's fingers curled around his. She pushed his hand down and stood between him and Ethan.

Her eyes softened. "If the Feravolk are my people, then they're all I have now. I'll do what I can to save them."

Logan nodded once. "Good, because your enemy has the same tenacity for destroying us." He didn't wait for a response, just headed closer to town. "You two stay hidden. I'll take care of this."

Both of them remained rooted as he walked away. It wasn't Westwind who followed first; it was Jayden. Ethan close behind.

Logan headed closer to the smell of smoke, but Westwind was reluctant to follow. Much to Logan's dismay, the wolf wanted to side with Ethan. *"I hope you're right, putting her in danger like this."*

"She won't be following me into the city."

"You will embrace this Protector thing, won't you?" Westwind asked.

Logan shot Westwind a glare. *"No."*

Westwind cocked his head and watched Logan with those expressive, amber eyes.

Destiny wasn't something Logan leaned on. Not since . . . well, not since many things. But the pull Jayden elicited wouldn't be ignored. Nor would the memories her face evoked.

Destiny Path, instinct, love—whatever the reason, Logan began to sense that perhaps the Creator did have a hand in all this. But why would the Creator choose him to protect these kids?

Logan closed his eyes; he knew why. He would never forgive

himself if he let someone else take this burden and they failed. And if he failed, he'd be dead.

One question remained: how would he face Rebekah?

"Yes," Logan recanted.

"Then so will I." Westwind nodded.

"Me too," Scout added.

"Thanks, friends. It won't be easy."

"Oh, I know it won't. Especially the way those two look at each other." Westwind pointed his muzzle toward Ethan and Jayden.

"I'll have to set that kid straight."

Scout whined.

"You're opposed to the love story?"

"I don't need his head clouded." Logan's growl was evident in his thoughts. Westwind didn't pursue, but Logan could sense the wolf thinking.

They stopped at the edge of the forest outside of town. A heavy cloud hung above the city, dark and thick. Char coated the jagged and broken wall surrounding the city. The scent of fire choked out anything else. Worse damage than Logan had anticipated.

Jayden pressed hands over her mouth and stared with wide eyes. Ethan's face remained the same emotionless stone as he pulled out his bow and strung it.

A pang pressed against Logan's heart. He didn't want to cause mistrust, but he had to follow his gut. He'd always done what he felt was right. Getting a lead on these wretched Feravolk impostors would save more lives.

"You three wait here. Westwind and I will—"

"Look." Jayden pointed. A carriage rode up to the city gate, a carriage with the sigil of the queen on the door.

Logan's stomach squeezed.

Ethan nocked an arrow and held three others in his hand. "Royal Army or not, you can't take her in there. Anyone the right age will be turned over."

"I don't intend to. Give me an hour."

Ethan nodded tightly.

Jayden chewed her lip.

Ethan gripped Logan's arm and pulled him back. "Wait. We've been spotted."

"We can take them," Westwind said. *"Scout and I both smell six."*

"Snare me." Ethan replaced the arrows into the quiver at his hip, dropped his bow, and drew his sword. "It's too late."

"Look what we have here." A scruffy woman with fire-stained clothes had crept behind them. She smiled, showcasing missing teeth. Five young men with faces resembling hers stood behind her. They all pulled out knives.

Logan put his hand on the hilt of his sword. "We don't want to hurt you."

"No? Then come quietly and help me get my reward money." She pulled a knife of her own from her boot.

"Reward money?" Jayden asked.

"The Feravolk will be back in a few days with reward money for any—" The young man stopped when his mother slapped the back of his head.

"They know," the woman said.

Reward money? It was worse than Logan had thought.

"Logan?" Westwind's voice held a slight tremor.

"Logan," Ethan's voice mirrored Westwind's, "we're in trouble."

"Are you survivors?" A new voice turned Logan's head. A tall man with the queen's sigil on his chest approached them with two other soldiers. "The queen offers you her protection."

"They're with me." The toothless woman stepped closer to them. "I found them. Where's my reward?"

"The queen doesn't pay a reward for—"

"Yes, she does." Jayden pointed her finger at him. "You're masquerading as the Feravolk."

Logan ground his teeth.

"Listen, we can help you." The soldier reached for Jayden.

"We don't need any." She dodged his grasp.

The toothless woman impeded Jayden and went toward the soldier. "You're not going to rob me of my home *and* my money. *I* found these traitors." She threw a knife. It sunk into his leather jerkin. The soldier looked at his chest before he fell.

Logan drew his sword and Westwind let out a low growl.

"He's one of them—one of the Feravolk!" Another soldier alerted more men to their presence.

By the Blood Moon. Logan looked at Ethan, regret strong in his heart. "Run!"

Ethan picked up his bow.

More of the Royal Army infiltrated the woods. Logan spun with his sword.

"No!" Jayden screamed, but Ethan took hold of her arm and Scout grabbed her sleeve.

They ran. Thank the Creator, they ran.

"After them!" a soldier shouted.

"Five," Westwind said. *"Five chase them."*

Logan prayed they'd be okay as he fought to keep any others from getting past him. It was easy enough to knock out toothless and her five sons. The soldiers of the queen were more of a challenge. Pain from a sword blade shot through Logan's arm. It did nothing to take away the pain suffocating his heart. He'd only just decided to be her Protector, and he'd already failed.

The kid was right. *Creator, let them be safe.*

The burn of a threat pulsed through Ethan's chest with every heartbeat as he kept Jayden running toward safety. Didn't look like they were going to lose their pursuers.

Jayden glanced over her shoulder. "Ethan, they're gaining on us."

"Just keep running. Get to Anna's."

"I don't have the plant."

Snare me, Jayden.

"I'll go back for it. Just run!" Ethan pushed her farther up the hill.

She reached the top and stopped. "No."

She was going to get him killed. The five soldiers drew closer, almost to the bottom of the hill. Scout bared his teeth and Ethan said a prayer. He pulled out his bow and three arrows. His slid one arrow shaft above his fingers and breathed in. Remaining calm, he made himself stone.

The first arrow flew. It pierced leather and a soldier dropped dead, tripping the man behind him. He scrambled to his feet and rushed toward the hill.

He readied his next arrow and let it fly. Another man fell, an arrow in his heart. Those behind him stumbled around his body.

Three left. Ethan's heartbeat thumped in his ears and drowned out the cries of the fallen. He let his third arrow go and grabbed the last two. Another soldier toppled back down the hill. A spray of heat hit Ethan's chest. Great. These men weren't the only ones pursuing them. They were decoys.

He pulled back his bowstring and released the fourth arrow, which also found its target and dropped him. He steadied his hand and held his breath. He needed to get his sword out. There was time, if just a moment. A moment was all he needed. He released the fifth arrow and the last man fell.

Ethan dropped his bow, faced the other side of the hill, and drew his sword. The protective instinct in him pulsed through every vein in his body. They would *not* hurt Jayden.

"Why didn't they go for cover?" Her hand touched his shoulder. "Ethan, what are you—"

"Get ready."

Another group of five headed over the crest of the hill.

CHAPTER 28

TRUSTING INSTINCTS

When the first of the five soldiers raced toward him, Ethan called on his speed. He stabbed the man through his chest and yanked his weapon from his limp hand in time to face another soldier. With a sword in each hand, he faced the next attacker. He lunged with his left and the soldier blocked his blow. His right hand swung the blade at his attacker's head and sliced open the man's exposed throat.

Pain shot through his left side as a sword tip cut into his skin. He pivoted and hacked that soldier's arm off with his blade. Blood splattered out and sprayed him in the face. He thrust his sword into the helpless man's chest to finish him quickly. Yanking his blade from the dead man, he spun to face his next attackers.

Metal clashed against metal as he blocked the blow aimed for his sword arm. His other weapon ripped through leather jerkin and flesh.

His speed fueled him. His strength pulsed through every muscle. Not one soldier would make it past him alive. With burning muscles and quivering arms, he faced the final man. Ethan spun out of the way of his enemy's weapon. He lunged and sliced into the man's thigh, and the man lost his balance. Ethan's sword pierced through the man's stomach, and then he slid his sword blade out and watched the soldier fall to the ground near the others.

Ethan shivered. What had come over him? His senses started to clear of the fog of battle that made him only able to focus on one thing: killing to stay alive.

Everything rushed back to him—the color of the forest, the burn of pain in his side, the touch of wind, and the sound of Jayden's frightened breathing. He dreaded turning toward her and instead stared at the carnage in front of him. What would she think of him?

He dropped his enemy's sword and faced her.

She stood next to Scout, clutching her daggers. Her eyes were round with horror.

His throat tightened. "Are you all right?"

She nodded with her mouth open.

He'd seen the bodies behind him strewn along the bloody hillside. She had to think he was a monster. Maybe he was.

She clamped her mouth shut. "How? . . . You just—"

"I had to kill them, or else—"

"I know." Her lips pressed together and she nodded. She looked so scared. Of course she did. He stepped farther away from her and wiped his sword on the dead soldier's clothes. His body shook as the rush of his talents ebbed away.

"We should make sure they're dead." He pointed down the hill at the soldiers his arrows had taken.

"Of course."

He couldn't look at her. "Jayden, I'm—I'm sorry."

"For what? Saving my life?"

"What? No." He faced her. "Never."

"Then there's nothing to be sorry for." She handed him his bow and quiver and walked down the hill.

Jayden crouched behind a tree, daggers in her hands, listening. Bark pressed into her back and she shifted again. "I don't think anyone else is coming."

Ethan didn't respond. He just scanned the trees, bow in hand, no less tense than he'd been since they had stopped here. He hadn't spoken to her, other than to give her an order or tell her they were stopping, since the hilltop.

She stood and stepped closer to him. "I'm sure there's no one—"

His hard glare made her stop. She leaned against a different tree and sank to the ground. Scout padded over, ears back and tail tucked, and sat beside her.

She stroked his head. "Logan was wrong to stop."

Ethan breathed deep. He finally sat down, though his grip on the bow didn't lessen. His brown eyes locked onto Jayden. They had softened. "He should have kept you safe."

His gaze seemed to reach inside her and at once she became acutely aware of her own heartbeat. She looked away from him and tried to catch her breath as she ran her fingers through Scout's soft fur. "For how long? Sooner or later I have to face the queen."

"Not alone."

He would stand with her? Of course, he would. There was no denying his loyalty. Or Logan's for that matter. Logan might be in it to save his people—a noble sacrifice—but Ethan was in this for her—because he'd made an oath.

She ventured a glance into his dark eyes and his gaze caught her. Held hers. That thrumming in her heart intensified, beating like an echo of itself. His heartbeat and hers. There was no denying how he made her feel, as much as she wanted to. But maybe she shouldn't. Ethan's desire to protect her made his decision just as noble. Logan would protect his people, but Ethan would protect those he loved.

So would she.

Today Ethan had been a warrior. She'd never seen a man take on so many soldiers at once. What kind of talents did he possess? Speed was one. Without that talent, no man could move like Ethan had. Yet, whatever had fueled him on that hilltop seemed to be bothering him now. He wouldn't come close to her. Could he not control his talent? Did rage spark it?

When her eyes met his, he looked away. "You no longer trust me?"

So that was the problem. "You *are* dangerous."

Unmoving, he stared at his boots.

Jayden stood and walked closer to him. He watched her askance, but remained still. She sat next to him, not so close as to brush against him this time. "Are you dangerous to me?"

He faced her. "Never."

She touched his arm. "I know. And I trust you. So stop avoiding me."

The lopsided smile she loved tugged the right corner of his mouth, then it vanished. His left hand gripped her wrist and he towed her up while he pushed her behind him. Tree bark bit into her back. Arrow nocked, Ethan stood in front of her.

"It's me, kid." Logan's voice filtered through the trees. Moments later, he stepped into the clearing.

Jayden sighed, but Ethan didn't move. Didn't lower his weapon.

Logan winced. "You kids okay?"

"Nothing a little ointment can't fix." Jayden placed her hand on Ethan's shoulder. His muscles were tense.

"You could have gotten her killed." Ethan's voice was no louder than a whisper.

"It's over now." Jayden tried to push his arm down.

"Is it?" He nudged her hand off. He put down his bow, stepped closer to Logan, and clutched his sword hilt.

Scout shrank away from the men. Westwind lowered his head and stalked closer to Ethan.

Logan clutched his sword hilt. "You're going to protect her from me?"

"If I need to."

"I'd kill you."

"You sure?"

Jayden wasn't.

"What are you two doing?" She raced between them.

"Stay out of this, Jayden." Ethan didn't release Logan from his stare.

She put her hands on both of their chests. Tense, both of them. "Stay out of this? Are you crazy?"

Ethan looked at her. The hardness in his eyes had returned. "Then choose."

Jayden's jaw dropped along with her heart. "You're splitting us up?"

He didn't say anything.

What was he thinking? They needed Logan. They—did friendship mean nothing? "You're cocky, you know that?" She jammed a finger in Ethan's chest. "Who are you anyway? And what makes you think I'd choose you?"

Still nothing but a stone face. What was he doing? And why?

Logan's chest swelled. "Stand aside, Jayden. I'll get an answer out of him."

Ethan's eyebrows shot up. "You know why I trusted you, Logan. But why did you trust me?"

Jayden shrank away from Ethan. Had she been wrong about him?

Logan's hand darted up to his chest. She'd noticed him touch that very spot right before every fight. She tensed, but Westwind stood in front of her, impeding her movement. Was he really going to let them fight it out? Would he join if Logan started losing?

Logan's shoulders sagged and his hand fell to his side. He shook his head. "I don't know, kid."

"You'll need to figure it out if you're going to be an effective Protector."

Logan made hard eye contact with Ethan and stood taller. "Destiny Path."

Ethan's eyes squinted as he searched Logan's face. His hand relaxed its grip on his sword hilt and he nodded once. "That's a start."

Jayden's lungs flooded with air and she breathed out just as fast. She realized she'd gripped the horse charm on her necklace, and she let go.

Logan closed his eyes and released his weapon. "Sorry, kid. I should have listened."

Ethan shook his head. "I should have told you sooner."

"What? That you wield a sword like a man who's fought in the wars?"

Ethan bowed his head. "That I can sense danger."

He could? Then why . . .? Jayden stepped closer to him, but he wouldn't look at her. Was he leaving? What scared him more, what had happened to him on the hilltop, or what Logan had done to jeopardize her safety? "You wanted me to choose Logan. Didn't you?"

Ethan stared at Logan. "I wanted him to choose you."

"What do you mean?" Jayden wouldn't release him from her glare.

Finally, he looked at her. "It means it's good to know he would protect you from anything, even me."

Jayden crossed her arms. "I don't think I *ever* need to see that point proven again. From either of you. Isn't it enough that I trust you both?"

Ethan rubbed the back of his neck and she'd lost his eye contact again. "Your trust in both of us makes you more vulnerable."

Jayden opened her mouth to say something, but she stopped herself. He was right. She stepped away from Ethan and straightened her spine. "I suppose it does."

Logan touched her arm and she stepped away from him too. "Jayden, I'm sorry."

"What's done is done." As soon as Ryan was healed, she would leave these men and face the queen alone. This Destiny Path was hers and hers alone. She forced a smile. "Now are you going to pass out some food? I'm starving."

Ethan watched the pleased smile sprout on Jayden's face as she placed her stick on the ground to complete another square around a stone. She excelled at sticks and stones.

She raised an eyebrow. "So, revenge?"

Ethan bowed his head. "I'm familiar with it."

Her laugh was beautiful. "I'm sure you are."

When her face grew soft like that, he couldn't take it. It was like she was looking straight into his soul. Like she knew what he was thinking. He averted his eyes.

"And who is Ethan's mortal enemy? Whoever it is, doesn't stand a chance."

He granted himself a humorless, dark chuckle, but it didn't seem to scare her off. After what she'd seen him do today—heavens, *he* had done it and it had scared *him*. "The man who killed my parents."

"Oh." Her smile faded. "You would know him if you saw him?"

This time when he looked into her eyes, she shrank back from him. Good girl. Today had reminded him that his heart wasn't safe.

"He has a long purple scar." Ethan touched his left eye and trailed his finger along his cheek down to the corner of his mouth. "His eye is milky white and his left leg is wooden. I'd know his limp anywhere."

Jayden stared at him. All her earlier flirting vanished.

Revenge didn't hold his heart like it used to. Not since One Eye. But that didn't mean he'd be able to control it forever. When he'd taken on those men to keep her safe, it had reminded him of the times his heart called on the old craving for vengeance to fuel him. The feeling this time was different—purer somehow. Revenge hadn't spurred his desire to protect her. His talent had done that.

Still, it scared him. He'd gotten so lost in the need to keep her safe that nothing else had mattered. When revenge controlled him that way, his heart wasn't safe. What if his talent should start to take over the same way? *Snare talents.* If he couldn't trust himself, then she had no business trusting him with her heart, even as much as he wanted it.

Heavens, he wanted it.

His sword she could trust. He would always keep her safe—as long as he wasn't stretched too thin. That wouldn't happen, though. Not unless everyone he loved showed up in one place.

CHAPTER 29

THREE SISTERS

Ethan's legs burned. Logan kept the pace fast, and Jayden had no trouble keeping it this time. Of course she didn't—her friend was dying.

Chatter ceased. Their heads drooped. Worry clung to them like a tired child.

They came to a place where the creek widened.

"It was just around here." Jayden's whisper strained with anticipation. She led them across the stream, toward the reeds. "Right through here."

She started running, but Ethan caught up to her.

A trail appeared, embedded in the grass that surpassed their heads. He stepped onto it. As he did, the path changed, revealing a few footsteps more. What kind of magic was this? Ethan followed close behind Jayden and Logan until the illusion stopped, and a clearing lay ahead.

"Wait." Logan's voice stopped them. "I don't know her."

A red-haired woman stood in the clearing taking clothes off a clothesline. She placed the last article of clothing in the laundry basket resting on her hip, then she turned.

Ethan's heart raced. She looked the same as she did at seventeen. Three years hadn't aged her at all. Chloe.

Wait. Ryan was Jayden's dying friend? His own brother? Ethan's stomach squeezed.

"I know her." Jayden rushed into the clearing and threw her arms around Chloe's neck. "Chloe! How did you get here? Is Ryan all right? What about your family?"

"Jayden." Still gripping the basket, Chloe hugged her back. "My sisters are here. Anna found us. Please, please tell me you have the plant." Tears filled her eyes and Ethan's heart stalled. Chloe never cried.

"We have it right here." Jayden motioned to Logan.

At the sight of Logan, Chloe's eyes widened. Then they flickered to Westwind and opened further before they narrowed.

"You must be Logan." Her sour voice matched her lime green eyes. Typical Chloe.

Scout rushed up to her.

She turned toward him and stopped, still as stone. "Where did you get this dog?"

Jayden motioned toward Ethan.

He stepped around Logan so she could see him. The basket fell from Chloe's arms and laundry jumped out when it hit the ground. She stepped back before straightening her whole body.

"Ethan Branor." She said his name as if it were a curse. That stung. So did the fact that she always had to remind him that he wasn't a Granden. That she'd never accept him as her brother.

"Chloe."

Jayden opened her mouth, but two more red-haired girls spilled out from behind the back of the house.

"Chloe, did you say Jayden was here?"

"Jayden, you made it!"

The three ran toward her, all hugging her at once and towing her toward the house.

They'd grown. Especially Wren. She was seven now. And Kinny—last time he'd seen her, she was twelve. That made her fifteen? She looked so like her mother now. Would she still let him call her Kinny, or would she prefer Kinsey now? Either way he itched to hug her—all of them.

Wren caught his stare and struggled to break free. "Ethan!"

He bent down to catch her as she ran at him. She was still so light.

"Wren, I am so glad to see you." He hugged her close, and Wren wound her arms around him.

"Kinsey said you'd come back!" She snuggled closer.

"Ethan?" Kinny raced to him and flung her arms around him. She whispered, "I knew you'd find us."

"You know each other?" Jayden's voice was soft and a bit dry.

"He's our brother."

"Ethan is *your* brother?" Jayden's wide blue eyes locked onto Ethan's. "You're Ryan's brother?"

"Yes." His voice scraped against his throat.

Her eyelashes fluttered. "How could—these are the sisters you were talking about?"

Ethan wanted to run into the house. "How—how bad is he?"

Jayden swallowed.

Kinny's eyebrows pulled together. "Tell me you got the plant."

Ethan nodded. Why wouldn't anyone answer him?

"Let's get it inside." She grabbed Jayden's hand and towed her toward the house. "Ryan will be happy to see his betrothed."

Betrothed? Ethan's chest tightened. Now that would have been good to know much, much earlier.

"Hurry." Chloe coaxed Wren from Ethan's arms and shooed her toward the house.

Why did he feel so numb? He registered Logan handing Kinny the plant and she raced up the porch steps with it, arm still linked with Jayden's.

Jayden glanced over the shoulder at him, confusion plain on her face. She bit her lip.

Then Chloe's finger blocked his view. "You, he might not be ready to see."

"It seems you weren't."

Chloe stared at him, speechless for a heartbeat. "I never know when I'll see you, do I?"

"Chloe—"

She stifled him with an abrupt turn, and he sighed.

"It doesn't matter." She waved for him to follow her. "You're here now. The Creator knows why."

An old woman stepped onto the porch as Logan and Ethan reached it. Her wrinkled face bloomed with a smile, and her eyes twinkled. "Please, come in." She extended her hand toward Ethan's cheek. For some reason, he let her touch him. She tilted his chin up. "You look much better than when I saw you last."

Ethan stepped away from her. "Do I know you?"

"No, dear. I saw you in the river. The trees showed me. It seems you've met a healer." She looked back at him as if expecting an answer.

Of course. The voices he'd heard from the trees that first night in the forest were a message from the Whisperer. "Yes, ma'am."

"Anna." She turned to Logan, her eyes serious. "We better hurry. The poison is starting to become immune to the poultice I'm using to keep it at bay. I'm not sure how far the poison has spread. Hopefully, I can extract it all."

Ethan's breath hitched.

Anna touched his shoulder. "Come in."

CHAPTER 30

THICK, BLACK POISON

Jayden knelt next to the couch and grabbed Ryan's hand. His face nearly matched Anna's white hair, and his shoulders had lost their bulk. He no longer looked like a blacksmith. Shadows darkened his sunken cheeks and the circles beneath his eyes.

What had she done to him? Tears threatened to escape, but she blinked them away.

His gray eyes penetrated her to the core. "Don't cry."

"I'm not."

His lips curled into a wry smile. "My mistake."

Scout bolted over to him and Ryan's eyes widened. "Where did you—"

Ethan knelt next to Jayden, and he placed his hand on Ryan's shoulder. "Hey."

His heartache squeezed Jayden's chest along with her own. They were brothers. *Brothers.* How could she fall for both of them? She shook the thought from her head. No, she hadn't fallen for Ethan. Had she?

Ryan coughed. "Figures I'd have to be dying to get you to resurface."

Ethan shook his head. "You and your stupid sense of humor."

"I'd punch you if I had any strength left in my arms."

"You get better and I'll give you one free hit."

"Just one?"

Ethan smiled. "Fine. Two."

Ryan's finger beckoned Ethan closer. "I heard you died."

Surprise fluttered through Ethan, along with a hint of panic. "Me?"

Ryan squinted his eyes.

Ethan held out his hands, palms up. "I obviously didn't."

"Right." Ryan turned to Jayden. "He taking care of you?"

She glanced at Ethan, then her gaze darted away. "Yes."

Ryan's eyes grew soft. "Good."

Logan carried a large basket filled with soil and placed it on the floor near Ryan.

"Wren, remember the special cloths I knitted?" Anna touched the young girl's head. "Would you go and get them for me?"

Wren dashed out of the room.

Anna turned and made hard eye contact with everyone in the room. "Some of this is going to be hard to watch. So when I ask one of you to take Wren outside, you will do so without complaint."

Wren returned with the cloths she'd been sent for—bright white and heavy, but otherwise unremarkable.

"Thank you, dear."

Anna turned toward a soil-filled basket, which contained the plant. She hummed a soft, drone, and the plant stirred in the dirt. Its leaves enlarged and spread away from the stem. As it elongated, a bud formed, and a thin, white spiral punctured through the green casing. It unwound and opened into an opalescent flower the shape of a star.

Seeds emerged from the blossom and spilled to the soil, but then the plant started to wither and die. Where the seeds had fallen, small, green wisps protruded through the dirt, some quicker than others. At last, six new specimens littered the soil.

Anna's humming stopped, and she put her hand on Ryan's knee. "We are ready now to finish the healing process. Kinsey, would you mind going outside with Wren? The goats need feeding."

Wren frowned.

Kinsey kissed Ryan's forehead. "You get well soon."

"Don't worry about me."

Chloe shot Ethan a fiery glance. "You're staying? That's not like you."

"Chloe." Ryan frowned.

She just crossed her arms.

Anna touched Chloe's arm. "Can I trust you to stand back and let me work?"

Chloe's arms fell to her sides. She nodded.

"Good."

What was that all about anyway? Chloe was fiery, sure, but she seemed to harbor real bitterness toward Ethan. Jayden resolved to ask him about it later, but when she turned toward him and saw his concern-filled eyes, she decided maybe she'd better stay away from him for a little while. Her feelings for him had not dissipated in Ryan's presence.

Anna looked at Chloe. "You will teach everything you ever learn about healing to Wren when she is ready."

Chloe's eyes widened and she nodded.

Anna showed Jayden and Chloe how to trim and poultice the plant, and which pieces to use for most potency. After preparing it, Anna turned to face Ryan. "You will feel a very warm sensation. It will not physically burn you, but it may get very hot. The poison has been flowing through your veins for days, and it must be extracted. It is a dark, evil poison, from a black lion's venom."

Jayden squeezed Ryan's hand.

"But this plant—white alor is its common name given by the healers—will help fight the venom and expel it from your bloodstream. You won't be conscious for this, though. You may even sleep for a few days as the white alor rejuvenates your blood and body." Anna patted his cheek. "All you have to do is lay back and be still."

Ryan did just that.

Anna gave Chloe the cloths Wren had fetched. "No one can touch the venom. These cloths are woven with unicorn tail hair and will absorb the poison. If any venom touches you, I need to know immediately."

She unlaced Ryan's shirt and removed the wet cloth that covered his wound. Jayden covered her mouth with her hand. The wound had spread into a gaping black hole that distorted part of his Blood Moon birthmark.

"You give me those when I ask for them." Anna pointed to the cloths and Chloe nodded. "Jayden, the poultice."

She handed the dish to Anna, who picked up a handful of the paste and applied it to Ryan's wound. He sucked in a breath and closed his eyes. The paste bubbled into a froth on the wound. Pus, thick and black as pitch, oozed from beneath the foam.

Ryan's eyes rolled back, his eyelids fluttered, and he trembled. Then he shook more violently.

Jayden covered her mouth with her hands.

"He is unconscious now." Anna held her hand out for the cloths.

Chloe handed them over, then squeezed her eyes shut as Ryan thrashed more violently.

"Hey." Ethan touched her arm and tugged her sleeve. She turned her body toward him, buried her face in his chest, and whispered, "Tell me when it's over."

Ethan's other hand went out to Jayden. She gripped back, but didn't tear her eyes from Ryan.

The thick, black liquid expelled faster. As Anna worked to absorb it, the dark poison didn't taint the color of the pure white cloth.

The couch shook under Ryan's convulsing, and Jayden's stomach roiled. She leaned closer to Ethan, who clutched her hand tighter.

Black liquid seeped out from beneath the cloth. Anna removed it from the wound. Uncovered, his dark blood bubbled over the ridges of the hole in his chest. Bile rose in Jayden's throat.

Without any hint of worry, Anna picked up a bowl from the table where she had prepared the poultice and set the cloth in it. Then she took the other cloth that hung over her shoulder and placed it on the wound. It absorbed the dark puddle forming on his pale skin.

Tears streamed down Jayden's cheeks, but she couldn't look away. *Please, Ryan, live.*

Crimson stains seeped into each individual unicorn hair like blood flowing into thousands of tiny veins. In moments, the bottom half of the cloth turned a rich red, and Ryan's convulsions ceased. He lay still and calm, his breathing leveled. Color began to fill his cheeks, and his once pale skin already looked healthier.

"Logan." Anna's voice remained calm. "Hand me the needle and thread."

Logan obliged, and Anna threaded the needle. When Anna removed the blood-soaked cloth, Jayden gasped. Already the hole appeared smaller. No more trace of black.

Anna inserted the needle into his skin.

Jayden watched her fingers, but her eyes saw the memory of that horrible thrashing again. "Will he live?" Her voice shook.

Anna smiled, but she didn't look away from her task. "This one is a fighter. The poison has been drawn out. The worst is finally over."

Ethan whispered in Chloe's ear, and she turned to face her brother. Evidence of her tears remained on Ethan's shirt.

Anna turned to them and a warm smile spread across her face. "Ryan is gaining strength as we speak. The poison took much from him, but the white alor will renew his blood and strength. He will need to rest, and will likely sleep for a week. When he wakes, he will find most of his strength returned to him. The rest will return in time. He is young and strong."

"Anna?" Chloe's voice was quiet. "Thank you so much. I—"

"Dear one." Anna's grandmother eyes twinkled. "You don't need to thank me."

"You were right to send Wren and Kinsey away." Chloe's voice grew stronger. She dabbed her eyes. "Kinsey would have had to be restrained."

"Go fetch your sisters, dear. I am sure they are waiting on a prickly bush."

"Yes, ma'am." Chloe started to leave but stopped and looked at Ethan. "Don't let this go to your head, but I'm glad you're here." Without waiting for a reply, she rushed off.

Anna's face grew sad.

"Is something wrong?" Jayden asked.

Anna shook her head and placed a hand on Jayden's shoulder. "Now we just wait for him to wake up." She walked out of the room, and Logan helped her move the pot back to where it belonged.

Jayden wrapped an arm around herself and looked at Ryan's peaceful face. She expelled a deep breath. At least they'd saved him.

Ethan's presence was unmistakable behind her. She turned to face him. He stood there with his shoulders slumped, and stared at Ryan with wet, dull eyes. Without meaning to, she wrapped her arms around Ethan and pulled him close. He rested his cheek against her head and hugged her tight.

CHAPTER 31

UNANSWERED QUESTIONS

Ethan leaned his shoulder against the archway between the two main rooms in Anna's home. Ryan's chest rose and fell, and more color returned to his face each hour. Heavens, he'd been pale. Ethan closed his eyes, but his brother's writhing form plagued the insides of his eyelids.

It was his fault Ryan lay on a couch, fighting for his life. An urge to slam his fist into the wall twitched the muscles in his arm, but instead he forced his fingers open and rubbed the back of his neck.

If Ethan had stayed with the Grandens, the only real family he had left, he would have seen the danger coming. He could have warned them, and this wouldn't have happened. How could he be so foolish to leave the only family he had?

Not foolish. Selfish. Stupid revenge.

Ethan pressed the heels of his hands into his eyes. Their father would still be alive. A lump threatened to choke him. He wished it would. No wonder Chloe hated him.

Every time he looked at her, she stared daggers at him. But she didn't know what his talents were. Not unless Ryan told her. Chloe? No, he wouldn't have told Chloe.

Then what had gotten into that woman? No one else seemed to harbor the grudge she held against him. But perhaps they were quicker to forgive than the eldest of the Granden clan.

Constant sister-chatter accompanied the clanking of wooden utensils against the table as they set it for supper. If he closed his eyes he could almost believe he was back in their home, warm with belonging. They had been so kind to accept him.

As soon as Ryan had gone back on his vow of secrecy and told his mother that Ethan's parents were dead, Mrs. Granden had pulled Ethan's filthy hide out of their shed and dragged him all the way to the washtub. She had been the one to hold him and tell him he would always have a place to call home as long as she lived. And how had he repaid her?

That stupid lump returned. From now on, if his family needed him to protect them, he'd be there.

Except now he had Jayden to take care of. What was he going to do about her?

Well, what choice did he have? He couldn't leave her. Jayden's pull on his talent to protect was stronger than anyone else he'd ever met. Maybe that's why his heart sped whenever she looked at him as if she could read his thoughts. If that was her talent . . . he stilled a shudder. Best not to think about that possibility since she infiltrated too many of his thoughts.

Surely Chloe didn't sense that? She might have. Women were often aware of things like that.

He slumped against the wall. Why'd he have to fall for his brother's betrothed? Well, Ryan would never have to know. Ethan would just protect her, like he'd promised. Like he needed to. And find a way to protect his family too.

Something soft rested on his shoulder.

"You haven't left this room." Jayden's voice in his ear caused his breath to hitch. "He's going to be okay you know."

He faced her and looked into those pretty blue eyes. Why did she have to stand so close? And touch him all the time? Not that he'd minded—until now. He moved to let her hand slide off of his shoulder. "Someone should keep an eye on him, right?"

Anna approached. "I will make sure your friend is taken good care of. Now, you all deserve a nice meal, so let's sit and eat."

She motioned to the table where all but three chairs were full. One belonged to Anna and the other two were situated next to one another. It would be difficult for him to avoid Jayden if she was constantly next to him, smelling like flowers and rain. Begging to be touched.

What was wrong with him?

Jayden didn't go to the table. She faced him, her fingers worrying the little horse-shaped charm on her necklace.

"One more thing." She spoke so softly, he lowered his head closer to hers. "It will storm tonight, but Ryan and his sisters don't know . . ."

"Your secret is safe with me."

"Thank you." She smiled at him, and he smiled back. but wished he hadn't. Her return blush was so appealing, and her lips so close. If there hadn't been an audience, and if she wasn't Ryan's, he would have kissed her.

"I saved you a seat, Ethan." Wren's voice broke in.

Jayden turned away and took her seat next to Logan. Ethan winked at Wren while he took his seat next to her.

Anna insisted everyone join hands as she thanked the Creator for their meal, their lives, and for Ryan's continued healing. Ethan closed his eyes when Jayden's slim fingers slipped into his palm. Heavens, her skin was soft. Creator forgive him.

Once supper ended, Ethan volunteered to clear the table to make up for not helping set it—and to keep away from Jayden. While he was outside filling the wash basin, Kinny came out with the last of the dishes from the table.

"I can take care of those, Kinny." He put the first wooden plate into the water. "Your mother taught me all about washing dishes."

She beamed. "I thought I'd help you." She grabbed a dish and her smile faded.

"You okay?"

Kinny pushed a dirty bowl in the water. "Chloe says I wouldn't have been able to take it."

Ethan gave her a sympathetic nod. "Chloe was right."

"Isn't she always?"

He'd missed her. All of them. "According to her."

They both laughed. Then Kinny bit her lip. "You're better now. I can see it."

He pulled a bowl from the water and a cool breeze chilled his hands. At least she could see it. His ever-depressing mood had worsened as the idea of revenge became all-consuming. Not now, though. It didn't hold him like that anymore. "I am."

"I know you had to leave. I mean, I didn't understand then, but I do now."

"I came back, you know."

She turned her rueful gaze to his. "Ryan said you'd come back. When you left, some strange soldiers came. It was like you leaving seemed peculiar to them, and they wanted to know where you were. I guess since you were the right age, and left without much trace, it caught their attention. Father decided we should all leave town. He had us move to Tareal.

"Father said it was for Ryan's sake since he isn't a redhead and he's got the birthmark. I'm sure our leaving got their attention more, but you know how Father was—always looking over his shoulder for danger that wasn't there. It turns out he was right though." Kinny paused and sucked in her bottom lip. "Anyway, Chloe needed someone to blame. She was already mad that you left, so you were her target."

"That's why she hates me?"

She smiled. "Hate? I don't know about hate, but she's pretty furious with you, so good luck with that."

Ethan smirked. "You're just glad she's mad at someone other than you for once."

Kinny laughed, then looked at him. "So, what are you doing with this Logan fellow?"

"I'm sworn to protect Jayden and the rest of the deliverers."

Kinny forgot the dishes and stared at him with wide, green eyes. "Really? So that sword you're carrying around isn't just for show?"

He laughed.

Her mouth hung open. "How good are you?"

"I made a living fighting for sport."

Now she just looked like a gaping catfish. "You're serious. Snare me, Ethan. You're serious."

"Watch your language, young lady." He smiled. Kinny had always been herself with him.

She stared at him with squinted eyes, which meant she was hunting for something. "So you lived in Salea? You ever fight Stone Wolf?"

He concentrated on stacking the last of the wet dishes. "No."

"That's probably good. I hear he's as good as Lone Wolf. I mean, that's why they named him Stone Wolf." Her eyebrows shot up as if she was challenging him to disagree.

Ethan watched her study him. He'd never been able to pull off a lie with Kinny.

Her eyes formed slits. "So what about the part where you died?"

"What would make you think—"

"I know you're Stone Wolf, and rumor was that Stone Wolf defeated death."

"Cheated death. The rumor was that he *cheated* death. And I'm not him."

"Cheated, defeated, I don't see a different result when it comes to death. And you're still an awful liar. So, Stone Wolf, what happened?"

"I'm right here, aren't I?"

Her hand went to her mouth and her voice squeaked. "You *are* him."

"You just said—" He sighed. "It's not really a big deal."

"So, what was it, cheated or defeated?"

Ethan settled into the grass. "Does it matter?"

She joined him. "Well, you must be good if you're protecting Jayden."

"I guess."

Kinny jumped up to her knees. "Teach me?"

"Kinny—"

"Ethan, you can see the times we are living in. I need to be able to defend myself. I hear the destruction in Salea wasn't as bad because some heroic young man surrendered, but surely you were there to see the devastation. Surely you understand why I need to be able to defend myself."

The destruction in Salea had been bad enough. He stared at the pond as the fire and smoke poured into his memory again.

Kinny nudged his shoulder. "You surrendered, didn't you?"

He looked at her, unwilling to respond. If she thought him a hero, she had it all wrong.

"Ethan, what a noble—"

"*Noble?*" That lump enlarged in his throat again. "Kinny—"

"Then you know how important it is that I can defend myself, defend Wren?"

He searched her young, innocent face. "I can't promise I'll be the one to teach you."

Kinny squeezed his arm. "But you'll see to it that I learn?"

"I will."

"Thank you, Ethan." She flung her arms around him. Then she backed up, her squinted eyes staring at him again. "You don't look like a hero to me."

Ethan grinned and shook his head.

Kinny's head tilted sideways. "One more question?"

"What?"

"Jayden?"

Ethan hoped she hadn't noticed his heart skip. "Jayden, what? You want some dirt on her? I don't think there is any."

"No." She laughed. Then her face grew serene again, older. "You're in love with her."

It wasn't a question. Still, he panicked inside. How could he lie to her? How could he not?

"You can't be shocked that I know, Ethan."

"I—"

"If you deny it, you're only denying it to yourself."

There was her stubborn side, no winning against that. "Do the others think—"

"My sisters don't know anything, and I won't tell them. But it'll come out sooner or later. Jayden's in love with you too."

"She loves Ryan, Kinny."

"She loves Ryan the way I love Ryan. She loves you . . . differently. I see it. Heavens, I *feel* it."

Ethan leaned forward with his head in his hands. "You don't know that."

"Have I asked her, you mean? Don't worry. I'll keep your secret. But I'll see what I can do."

Ethan groaned. "Kinny, please, if Ryan—"

"Ryan will get over it."

"Right." He rolled his eyes. Clearly she didn't know anything about what brothers *didn't* do to one another.

"I'm going to check on Ryan." Kinny kissed his cheek before she picked up the stack of clean dishes and departed.

Scout's cool nose brushed Ethan's fingertips and he scratched his dog's head. He had to stop thinking about Jayden. That was the only solution.

He gazed at the violet sky. The signs of a storm congregated overhead. Great. More nightmares.

Footsteps padded against the soft grass behind him. Ethan turned toward the sound.

Logan approached. "I need to talk to you and Jayden."

The creaking door caught Ethan's attention. Jayden appeared in the doorway. The inside light behind her silhouetted her curvy shape. Not thinking about her just got harder. He stood and dusted off his pants.

Logan waited for Jayden to join them. "I spoke with Chloe. It seems the Grandens were acclimated Feravolk. They didn't leave the city during the wars, and no one ever questioned their heritage."

Jayden cocked her head. "Acclimated?"

Logan nodded. "Idla looks for those with special qualities. Like—"

Ethan motioned to Westwind. "Like being tailed by a wolf?"

Logan chuckled. "Yes. And any gifts animal bonding might give.

During the wars, some Feravolk chose to try and hide under the queen's nose. They gave up their animal bonds and tried to live like normal city folk. Some of us thought that defeated the purpose. Either way, these kids are hardly to blame for their parents' decisions. Chloe speaks highly of the Feravolk. She says her parents never let them forget their heritage. She asked to come with us."

Ethan tensed. "You can't—"

"I can take them to my camp. They'll be safe there."

"You sure?"

"Not entirely, but I can think of nothing safer. Can you?"

"Can the Feravolk train them to defend themselves?" Maybe Ethan could fulfill his promise to Kinny sooner rather than later. And Logan's plan was good. His family would be safe, and he'd have fewer people to protect. It seemed his Destiny Path would be kind this time.

"Yes, they can be trained there, but if Ryan wishes to come with us, he'll need something more."

Jayden shook her head. "I never know where One Eye is, Logan."

Logan glanced at Ethan. "I was hoping he's still in Primo."

Ethan shrugged. "He was last time I was there. Then again, the false Feravolk burned Primo."

Logan sighed. "We'll have to hope. There's no way I'll let Ryan join us until he's had formal training." He shot a sideways glance at Jayden. "If you don't want him along, I'll make sure he stays with his sisters. Just say the word."

Jayden bit her lip.

Logan smiled, but it didn't touch his eyes. "Think on it." He strode away, Westwind in his wake.

Ethan glanced at Jayden, the one person he didn't want to be alone with right now.

Thunder boomed.

CHAPTER 32

HIDDEN DAGGER

Ethan fondled Scout's ears. His dog never left him during a storm. "I'll be fine, boy. You can go if you want to."

Scout tilted his head back and licked Ethan's fingers with his warm tongue.

Jayden wandered to Ethan's other side, her eyes soft. "You're not sleeping tonight, are you?"

In the night her fair skin looked paler next to her dark hair, but no less beautiful.

"Not yet, anyway."

Lightning flickered. The images of his dead parents, blood pooling from their sliced necks, flashed through his mind.

She rubbed his arm. "Are you okay?"

That just stirred desire he didn't need to feel. He stepped away from her and nearly tripped over Scout. "Yes. Are you?"

After all, the man she loved lay in a deep sleep in the house healing from a wound worsened by the venom of a black lion, of all things.

"I'm a bit overwhelmed." She sighed. "Since you're staying up for a while, do you mind if I join you?"

Ethan remembered Kinny's presumption that Jayden loved him. He felt a bit overwhelmed himself. Besides, time like this with Jayden was nearing its end. "Of course I don't."

She led him to a spot under one of Anna's massive trees, but Ethan stopped. "Jayden, that's not exactly a safe place during a storm."

"It's okay." She motioned for him to join her. "I know where the lightning will strike. It's part of my talent."

"Really?"

She practically beamed. "Yes."

Well, that was good enough for him. They sat against the wide trunk, and Scout curled up at their feet.

The rain began. The branches of the huge spruce were broad enough for shelter. Jayden watched the raindrops as if she wanted them to spill on her.

Ethan rested his elbows on his knees. "So, did you have a name for yourself in Tareal?"

"Name? What do you mean?" Her swift eye contact made him think she wanted to avoid the question.

"Let me guess. Lightning Bolt? Thunder Crash? Something bold, right?"

"Ethan, what are you talking about?"

"You admitted that you and your brothers fought for sport in Tareal. Don't tell me you thought I'd just forget about that. Jayden, the dagger-wielding daughter of an animal doctor. Gutsy." He cocked an eyebrow. "So? Anyone who asks to be paid for a fight has to have a name."

She smiled at least. Maybe she'd entertain his question. "I hoped you'd forget. I'm not sure why it matters. I'm no Lone Wolf or Stone Wolf."

"Stone Wolf?" He nearly choked on his words.

"You haven't heard of him? They liken him to Lone Wolf—the most famous swordsman who ever fought for sport. Surely you've heard of *him*?"

"Oh, I've heard plenty of both names. I'm just surprised you'd heard of Stone Wolf all the way in Tareal."

"*Everyone* has heard of him. Don't be so smug. Saleans think they know everything."

"Do they? Well, I didn't know about your operation."

"Even if you haven't heard of us Jorahs, we held our own well enough to make some extra money when times were hard. My parents didn't know, of course. They would've skinned us if they did. When I found out what my brothers were doing, they trained me rather than risking me ratting them out to my parents. They called me Hidden Dagger. They said no one expected me to be any good. And I was, so I was like the secret weapon." She skirted her eyes from his and clutched her knees close to her chin.

"Hidden Dagger. It suits you."

"Ryan and his sisters don't know about any of that." She fiddled with that white horse charm on her necklace. She seemed to be drawn to it whenever Ryan came up.

Ethan shot her a grin. "I think you'll be indebted to me soon if I have to keep many more things secret about you."

Her brows furrowed. "Secret? I don't mean to keep secrets from Ryan."

"Everyone has them."

She bit her lip. "Not from people they trust."

"Sometimes secrets are needed."

Her eyes grew round. "Would you keep secrets from me?"

His heart sped. What did she want? A confession of love? "Never a secret that could harm you."

She looked at the ground.

He ducked his head closer to her bowed one, trying to regain her eye contact. "Not that we should make a habit out of keeping secrets from one another."

She glanced at him and he smiled. Her return grin was broad. "Good."

"That's a pretty necklace. Ryan give it to you?"

She smiled. "No. My mother did. It's all I—well, I'm glad I was wearing it."

They sat in a comfortable silence until Jayden looked at him again. "So, *Ryan* is your brother?"

"Strange the way the puzzle fits."

She hugged her knees closer. "Do you think he'll come with us?"

"He loves you, doesn't he?"

Her shoulders sagged and she released her knees. "I hope not."

Ethan's heart jumped. "Really?"

Her blue eyes met his. "It wasn't exactly something we discussed."

What was she saying? Even if she didn't return his love, Ryan loved her. "But he's your betrothed."

Her fist curled around the fallen pine needles. "There hasn't been a ceremony. Even if there was, I'd release him. I don't want to put him in more danger. Love makes people take risks they shouldn't."

Yes, it did. "So you'd ask him to stay away? Keep him from protecting you?"

"Yes."

"That's hardly fair."

Her glare was incredulous. "Why would you say that?"

"Do you think he'd be able to forgive himself if something happened to you and he wasn't there to prevent it?"

"Do you think *I'd* be able to forgive myself if he got hurt again— or killed—for me?"

"Love goes both ways, Jayden."

Jayden closed her eyes. "I honestly don't know what to do anymore."

He resisted the urge to cup her face in his hand. "Why don't you let him decide?"

Her blue eyes met his, big and soft and worried. "Like you?"

No. Not like him. Ryan still had a choice. Ethan could never stop protecting her. His talent wouldn't allow for it. If danger threatened her and he was nearby, he'd know. And he'd protect her no matter the cost. Such was the burden of his talent. But if he could choose, he'd protect her anyway. "If you let him choose, it won't be your fault."

"But if I don't let him come?"

"You can't stop him. He'll follow along until we have to accept that he's with us. He grew up with the same parents as Chloe, Kinny, and Wren. Stubbornness is a family trait."

She sighed. "But you—you ran away from your family. To protect them."

More like to rid himself of the distraction of protecting them while he pursued his precious revenge. "Jayden, if you run off, I'll find you. Believe me."

Her blue eyes pierced him. "I know you will."

Did she feel it? The strange connection that seemed to bind them together? Jayden's face was so much nearer than before. Close enough to . . .

Thunder cracked. Ethan pulled himself back.

Jayden had moved back just as quickly and dusted off her boots. "Ethan, do you feel connected to me?"

His heart tripped on a beat. How was he supposed to answer that question?

"What I mean is, something binds me to you and I can't explain it."

"It goes both ways, Jayden." And then some.

"It's more than your oath right? I mean, you feel it too, don't you? Like a pull?" Her eyes searched his face. She looked so vulnerable. "Maybe I'm not describing it right. Or maybe you don't—"

"I feel it."

"You do?" she whispered.

She took his hand in hers and turned it over. The oath scar stared back at her. She traced the mark with her finger, and he exhaled a shaky breath. Her blue eyes met his through her eyelashes. "It scared me at first, you know?"

Did he ever. "It still scares me."

Her return smile was so pure. So enticing. Not good. Why couldn't self-control be one of his talents?

Her gaze locked on to him. "I didn't think you were scared of anything."

Was she closer? Her body heat pressed against him, drawing him in. All he saw were her eyes. And her lips. Her breath warmed his face.

What was he doing? He pulled back and Jayden looked away,

twirling a strand of hair. That was close. He had to get out from under this tree before he did something he'd regret.

Gripping her hand tighter, he got up to his knees. "C'mon, let's get you into the rain before you melt."

"But I like . . . oh. Yes, let's." She giggled as he towed her out into the storm.

The big, fat raindrops fell, fast, fast, and faster still. Jayden let them splash onto her face. They laughed as the downpour drenched them through to their skin in moments.

Even soaked to the bone she was beautiful.

CHAPTER 33

FORGOTTEN ANSWERS

Logan walked around the back of the small house and slid his fingers against its wooden exterior, rough from years of weathering storms, wind, heat, and rain. Westwind loped near as they followed the well-worn trail to the pond.

Anna stood near it, sprinkling seed on the ground while the chickens pecked. "You have finally embraced the bond?"

"What are you talking about?"

Anna's smile sprouted. "Prophecy states that a bond will be forged between the deliverers and their protectors."

Logan drew closer to her and took the basket from her. He knew enough about bonds from experience. "Bonds *can* be passed."

"A dangerous game, that. Messing with this natural order is not recommended."

"How can I bond to a person?"

"Few Feravolk truly know how the bond works." She motioned toward the pond.

Water rippled out in perfect circles from where Westwind had taken a drink. Logan dipped his hand in and disturbed the surface more. Before he brought his hand to his mouth, the water stilled like smooth glass. His reflection faded and the pool showed him something else entirely.

Anna's words reduced to an echo in the corner of his mind as the images played before him. "The bond carries a strong sense of longing with it. Typically, it is the animal or person in need that finds you. They feel you and draw you close."

Tall reeds of grass bent as if being pushed aside. It looked as though he walked through them himself, but a petite hand, distinctly feminine, reached out to move the long blades.

"The animal is usually in trouble, sometimes lost," Anna continued as the watery message consumed him. "It pulls at you, and you subconsciously move toward it."

At last the grass gave way into a clearing and the young girl walked into view. Logan gasped when he saw her. The girl turned, her blue eyes met his, and he held his breath. Could she see him? Surely she hadn't heard him. Her gaze turned away as quickly as it had locked on him—as if she had never noticed him.

She turned to the forest ahead of her and walked toward it. Her golden hair rippled behind her in the wind. So calm, so delicate. She neared the forest edge. Dropping to her knees, she opened her sack and dug out a vegetable. She held out her hand and reached forward. The muzzle of what looked like a shimmering horse peeked out of the trees and ate it. Then she disappeared, and he stared at nothing but a dim reflection of himself.

"Show that again." The demand in his voice shocked him.

"I can't show it again." Anna peered into the pool beside him. "Apparently it was something the trees thought *you* should see."

He searched the quiet waters, willing them to bring back the young woman.

"What did you see?" Westwind's coarse coat brushed against Logan's fingertips, something he did occasionally for Logan's human-driven comfort. Logan pictured the whole scene in his mind for Westwind to see and lingered on the girl's face.

Westwind made meaningful eye contact with him. *"She looks just like Rebekah."*

Logan pointed to the water. "I need to know where she is. The girl from the pond."

Anna stared at him. "She is a healer. They reside in one of three places. Here in the Forest of Legends, in the Forest of Old, or the

Forest of Memories. Close to one of the valleys. She fed the animal a magical plant that no longer grows anywhere but those places."

Anna placed a hand on his shoulder, but Logan couldn't tear his eyes from the still water. Only his reflection stared at him. No more images of his daughter. She'd grown so beautiful, so like her mother. He wished for another look at her and her golden blonde hair, or of her surroundings. A falling leaf rippled the pond, but no pictures displayed.

"You will take the Grandens with you?" Anna's voice pulled him away from the pool.

"Yes."

"Good."

"They are special?"

"I think everyone drawn to you is special. But they are of the true Feravolk bloodline. All of them, Jayden, Ethan, the Grandens—you are right to take them with you. They should be with their people. The Feravolk need to be united if we are to win this war against the queen." She put her hand on his arm and her face bloomed into her wise smile, the one that made him feel like a young boy on his grandmother's knee.

"How long have you been a Whisperer, Anna?"

At Logan's question, her face sprouted more wrinkles as her cheeks nearly overtook her eyes in a deep grin.

"Logan of the Wolves, how long have you been bonded to Westwind? Is he not older than any natural wolf, yet younger in strength and body? Look at the trees. Do you think my bonding gave years to them?" Anna's expression changed, and the corners of her mouth lowered a little.

Logan cocked his head at this new look of sympathy.

Anna took both of his arms in her hands. "The trees are good at remembering if you can point them to the right story. You'll need to find your Whisperer. She may be young when you find her, her talents raw and crude, but with a little guidance she will find her way, grow before your eyes like a well-cared for plant. She can take knowledge from the trees."

"What kind of knowledge?"

"They have seen things the histories have forgotten. They know where the deliverers are. Their memories will need to be awakened so they can point you in the right direction. But your Whisperer can awaken them. Find her."

CHAPTER 34

COLOR OF BLOOD

Jayden stepped outside to get away from the constant Granden chatter. Her brothers had never been quite so talkative. She walked across Anna's back porch and gazed at the full moon.

If Ethan could truly feel the strange connection between them, she'd have to go during the night to gain as much of a head start as possible. Otherwise, he'd be able to find her—and catch up. She only hoped she could get far enough away from him that the connection would break.

She tapped her fingers on the handrail. She was almost ready. Her bag was always packed. Every time she helped Anna prepare meals, she'd stolen something from the cellar. After Ryan woke, she'd leave to go after the queen. The "how" part of the plan was still fuzzy, but she had time to sort it out. If only he'd hurry up about getting better. She wasn't sure how many more times she could lie to his sisters with a smile.

A breeze tousled her hair and the cool scent of pine and leather hit her. She closed her eyes and breathed in.

"They say the moon was full the night of the Blood Moon."

Ethan leaned on the railing next to her. His voice shouldn't send shivers across her skin, but it did.

Scout nuzzled her legs, and she gratefully let the dog take some of her attention. "And the color of blood."

A small smile creased the corners of his eyes. "Well, that goes without saying."

"You took off after supper in a hurry. What were you doing out here all by yourself?"

He held up his bow. "Target practice."

"Isn't it a little dark for that?"

"Then stargazing."

"You like the stars?"

He smirked. "That okay?"

"Of course it is." Jayden's eyes drifted to the sword propped up against the cabin wall behind him. "So, how did you get to be so good with that thing in such a short amount of time?"

"Short? I've had a bow in my hand since I was strong enough to pull the string back."

"Hmmm. I meant your sword."

Ethan shrugged. "I guess I'm just talented."

"I imagine the ability to detect danger makes you an excellent swordsman."

His eyes darted away. "It helps."

"Are there other talents that aid your exceptional ability?" Jayden poked the right side of his chest where she remembered the replica of the moon to be.

Ethan's breath caught. "You expect me to tell you?"

She looked right into his eyes. His dark eyes. Her talent picked up a little trepidation rippling through him, though she hadn't tried to read his emotions. They were still trickling into her unbidden. Children tended to keep their talents secret, but some told people they trusted. Did he trust her?

Jayden had never shared her ability to read people's emotions with anyone. "Yes."

He stepped just out of reach and set his bow next to his sword, then shot her a dubious glance. "So, you're going to share all your talents with me?"

"Well, you already know one of my talents."

"Predicting weather?"

"Just storms."

"Right."

"So you tell me another of your talents and I'll tell you another of mine."

Ethan crossed his arms. "Is that how it works?"

"Yes." A giddy feeling fluttered in Jayden's chest. He would tell her—if she prodded just right. Not too fast.

He cocked an eyebrow. "And how do you know I have more than one talent?"

"Because you assumed I have more than one."

He straightened his spine and crossed his arms. His smile bordered on a smirk. "All right."

There were talents people could see, easy ones that hid the deeper, more upsetting ones. If a village knew a Child could run fast, there was no need for them to fear, but if that Child could also call up a dust storm, then they would fear. Those talents were the kind that made villagers stare at Children when their backs were turned. Who knew what kind of secret thoughts they held?

Jayden wanted to know what talents Ethan hid from the world. "I already know you're fast."

His eyebrows shot up. "How do you figure?"

"It's one of my talents too, and you're faster than me."

"If you already know, why press me to share my talent with you?"

"I think you have more talents than two."

Interest shone clear on his face. "And you have more?"

Jayden smiled. "Yes."

"How fortunate you are. Or how very unlucky." Though he smiled, his tone betrayed his sadness.

"Children are supposed to think of their talents as blessings."

He scoffed. "Don't you have a talent you wish you could turn off sometimes?"

Like sensing emotions? Jayden recalled how he'd fought those men on the hill. Did something make him lose control of his talents too? "I see what you mean."

"You do?"

"You killed ten men, Ethan. Ten came at us and you killed them all. You were like a rabid wolf."

He backed away. "It's not like I want to kill people."

She winced and wished her whiplash tongue had been slower. She eased closer to him and hoped she could fix what she'd done. Maybe too close, but he didn't back away. "Whatever talents you possess, I'm glad for them. They've saved my life more than once, haven't they?"

He just stared at her.

"Ethan, I'm sorry. I—"

"I'm gifted with strength." One of those melancholy smiles tugged at his mouth.

"Strong, fast, and able to predict danger? That would be useful in a fight."

"I can't predict danger. I feel threats to . . . certain people."

"People you've given an oath to protect?"

"You're the first, so I'm not sure." Unease washed over him like a tidal wave and crashed into her. She wasn't using her talent. Why were his emotions slamming into her? Why couldn't she turn it off?

He was still keeping secrets from her, but she'd stick to the bargain. "Well, I can sense people's weaknesses—only if they threaten me, though."

His boyish smile returned. "Now *that* would be useful in a fight."

She shot him a sly smirk. "I think I'd need it going up against someone like you. Still, there's more to you than you've shared."

"I could say the same of you."

"I think I'll keep my last talent to myself."

Ethan's surprise filtered into her, though he didn't show it.

She couldn't help it, she had to know. "How many more talents do you have?"

"Three."

"Six in all? I've never heard of someone with so many."

His gaze darted to the ground and his chest heaved. "So even among Children, I'm a freak."

"You're not a freak."

Jayden recalled the time her father raced out in the middle of a storm to bring her inside. Lightning had struck the lone tree in the neighbor's field while she watched. Such power had congregated in the heavens before the strike, and she'd felt all of it ripple through her, like it was building inside of her. It was amazing.

When father carried her inside, telling her not to go out during storms because he feared she'd be hit by lightning, she'd realized how different she truly was. Lightning hit her? How absurd. She knew where it would strike.

She turned back to Ethan and his soulful eyes. "Even if you were, I'm glad to have you."

Hope filled him, followed by regret. "As your protector?"

"Yes."

"Jayden, I . . ." His shoulders drooped and he shook his head.

"You what?"

He licked his lips and stared right into her eyes. "I would be honored to die for you."

How could he even say that? "Ethan, that's not—I didn't mean that. I—"

"Well, it's true."

"I don't want you to have to die for me."

"I'm not saying I plan to, just that I would be honored."

She turned away from him. How he talked so casually about being willing to throw his life away for her was infuriating. His hand touched her shoulder, but she wouldn't budge.

His cheek nearly touched her ear. His warmth radiated against her back. "Jayden, you remember what we said about very good friends being worth dying for?"

She whirled to face him. "You're *my* very good friend too."

He frowned. "*You* are the important one."

"That doesn't mean I want to lose everyone I—" Love? She breathed in, thankful she stopped that sentence in time. "Everyone I'm close to."

He just stared at her.

"Ethan, how many very good friends do you have?"

"Seven."

"And you would die for all of them?"

He stifled one of those shocked laughs. "I only have one life." Then his face grew serious. "Five of my very good friends are here, right now. So you better believe I'm going to make sure you're all as safe as I can make you."

"And this talent of yours? This detecting threats?"

"It works for those I'd give my life for."

Fear gripped Jayden's heart. She wished he could turn off his talent too. But even if he could, he wouldn't, would he? No. Not Ethan. Not with his very good friends involved.

He smiled. "Hey, I'm strong and fast. Who's a match for that?"

"Don't forget cocky." She swung at his shoulder, but he caught her hand.

"That too."

"Well, don't get yourself killed on my account. Please."

His eyes softened and his thumb brushed back and forth against her hand. "I'll do anything to keep you safe. Anything."

Her heart flipped. Of course he would. But she'd never survive the guilt of losing him. The very thought of it made her throat ache.

"Well, suit yourself. I still think it's silly what you did—promising to protect me—even if keeping me safe is necessary for the survival of the Feravolk. Which may or may not be true." She whirled away from him, tearing her hand from his grasp.

"It's necessary for my survival," he whispered.

She froze, her heart hammering against her chest. She couldn't risk a glimpse of his dark eyes. Just the thought of feeling his emotions right now had her hands shaking. "What do you mean?"

His crisp scent surrounded her. It shouldn't make her knees turn to water.

His cheek brushed her ear. "Well, all Children are Feravolk."

Heart pounding, she turned to face him. He was entirely too close, his eyes far too expressive.

"Ethan? Promise me you won't die for me."

He shook his head. "I can't promise that."

"Why not?"

He held his hand out next to her, palm up. A long pink scar stared back at her. "You know why."

Jayden slid her hand beneath his, cradling it. He didn't resist. His skin was dry, rough, callused where the cross guard of his sword rubbed against his knuckle. She placed two fingers in his palm, one on either side of the scar. Gliding them over his skin, she traced the mark of his promise.

He trembled.

She tore her gaze from the evidence of his oath and looked at his face.

His eyes met hers. So dark. Intense. Yet soft. Something electric, like a building storm, hummed between them. For the first time, Jayden opened her talent and deliberately searched his mood. Instead of the unbidden trickle she'd been feeling, his emotions flooded her. So intense, they felt like a part of her. Not something she'd have to filter into herself. They were already hers. His heart hammered so fast, she thought it might explode. Anger, desire, hatred, regret all flickered alongside one another, like flashes of lightning battling with one another.

Like a lightning storm, his emotions stilled. The electric current between them pulsed as if beckoning her to kiss him. She leaned closer. His heartbeat picked up again, thundered through her core like an echo of her own. Desire shot through him like an arrow.

Her heart tripped on a beat and slammed into her chest.

A squeal shattered the moment, and Kinsey popped her head out the door. "Ryan's waking up!"

CHAPTER 35

A NEW BEGINNING

Ryan's eyelids fluttered. He squinted as the light coming in from the window blinded him. Slowly, he let a slit of brightness through, then more as his eyes adjusted.

The colors of the room popped out at him like paintings on a canvas. The orange tint in the wooded walls, the dark blue blanket wrapped around him, the yellows and deep browns on the rocking chairs opposite him, and his sisters' rich, red hair.

The scents of spiced pie and rabbit stew were so strong, he thought someone had put a plate under his chin. But there was no food there.

Someone called his name.

His eyes focused, and he recognized the faces in front of him. Filling his lungs with new air, he put his hands on the soft cushions at his sides and sat up. His muscles jumped to life as if they had been waiting for that very moment. A sharp pain stabbed the left side of his chest, right next to his birthmark, where the arrow had sunk in. The sting dulled until it remained just a soft ache.

An image of a white lion flashed in his mind. A shudder rippled his body as the beast's yellow-moon eyes locked onto him. *"I will claim you."*

Ryan gasped. Had the taint reached his heart? No. Anna would tell him.

The face of the creature turned black as night and it roared.

"Are you all right?" Kinsey's wavering voice cut through his vision. Calmed him.

It was just a dream. Hopefully the last.

Kinsey sat near him, perched on knees and toes. The rest of his sisters, plus Jayden and Ethan, clustered around her. Ryan looked at their familiar faces as if seeing them with new eyes, eyes not used to filtering out detail. The worry each of his sisters wore reminded him of his mother's face.

"I'm fine—better than that. I feel like I could run a race." The rasp in his voice did nothing to change the concern in any of the faces staring at him. He cleared his throat. "I'm fine, really."

His legs itched to move. He swung them down on the side of the couch, ignoring the soft pleas of his sisters to stay put. Okay, Chloe's plea was none too soft. His injured leg felt almost as good as new.

Wren wrapped her arms around his neck. "You're better now?"

Her eyes glistened with tears. He had almost died in front of his sisters. The ultimate helplessness. Hadn't his father always told him to take care of them? He squeezed Wren close to him.

"Yes, I'm better," he whispered in her ear, but for all to hear.

The weight that crushed his chest had been lifted. The pain that had pulsed through his whole body was gone. The thoughts of rage had vanished. His blood no longer boiled in his veins like fire. He shuddered as he remembered the fire and the lion's yellow-moon eyes.

He'd thought he'd never see Jayden again, never make it back to retrieve his sisters. He had believed he was going to die. That's why he'd called out to Ethan. Somehow his brother had heard.

Anna's face sported a huge smile. "C'mon, boy. On your feet. I've got a hot meal waiting for you."

As if on cue, Ryan's stomach let out a growl big enough to cause Scout's ears to swivel. Wren climbed off his lap and his siblings extended arms to him, but he clasped Ethan's. He rose to his feet with more ease than he'd anticipated. He swayed once, but Ethan held him steady.

"How long have I been—" Ryan stopped, unsure how to finish his question.

"You've been asleep for seven days." Jayden strode over to his other side.

Her radiant smile was more beautiful than he'd remembered. She linked her arm in his and offered subtle support. Ryan let go of Ethan's arm, but squeezed a thank you before he did. He didn't have to lean too much on Jayden as he made his way the short distance to the table.

Anna's warm smile met him at the dining table as she handed him the biggest bowl of stew he had ever seen. "Your strength will return, but you have to eat."

No problem there. After a seven-day fast, he was famished. He stared at her, wanting to ask if she'd felt the taint in him, but he couldn't. He glanced at Logan instead. The man stood in the corner of the room, watching. Ryan swallowed.

Once he finished eating, all he wanted to do was go outside. It had been so long since the sun had warmed his face. It had been so long for a lot of things.

Anna needed help with her evening chores, which Ryan gladly volunteered for, but everyone—even Scout, who placed his paw on Ryan's knee and whined—denied his offer. Anna told him to sit on the porch and heal. His sisters hung laundry on the line, while Logan and the canines headed out to find some rabbits to replace the food Anna had made them, and Jayden and Ethan proceeded to feed Anna's goats and chickens. Together. While he sat and watched.

This was a new kind of torture.

Sitting around was bound to be the death of him. Of his pride anyway. Jayden and Ethan looked awfully comfortable around one another.

Jayden threw a handful of seed at Ethan who waved it away and made to chase her. She tripped, but Ethan caught her hand just before she could topple into the pond. He pulled her close. A little too close. Then he let her go and picked up a feed basket again. Jayden stood there blushing after him.

Ryan ground his teeth. A fortnight lying on Anna's couch was apparently a long time.

"Ryan?" Three identical voices brought him out of his jealous stupor.

His sisters joined him on the porch.

"Logan says we will go with him to live with the Feravolk," Wren said. "If we want to. I want to."

"He did, did he?" He arched an eyebrow.

His sisters' return glances mocked his doubt.

"You do plan on going with Jayden, right?" Chloe asked.

"If she wants me to." After all, Ethan could take care of her.

"Of course she does. She's leaving the decision up to you because it's so dangerous."

"I'd like to go for a walk." Ryan stood.

Black spots overtook his vision. He wavered. Someone touched his shoulder softly. Relieved, he waited for his vision to clear. Kinsey still stood next to him, her subtle support on his arm. She winked.

Chloe crossed her arms. "He can hardly stand."

Ryan rolled his eyes. "I'm fine."

Kinsey dismissed Chloe's comment with a wave. "Let him. Anna said it would be good for him to get a little exercise."

"You will go with Logan, won't you?" Kinsey whispered in his ear. "He'll have you trained to fight so you can go with them on their journey. Take the training, brother. As for Jayden, well, you'll do as your heart tells you."

Ryan looked over his shoulder at Kinsey. She stood on the porch and he on the ground, a step below, making her eyes level with his. "You think I should go, Kinny?"

"What do you think?"

He smiled. Kinsey was never interested in bossing him around.

"I'll follow Jayden. I will be trained, if that is what Logan has planned for me. And I will protect you and our sisters."

"You're a good brother." Kinsey squeezed his shoulder and let him leave.

The soil gave under his brown boots, so different from the smooth wooden floors in Anna's home. Every uneven patch of ground that pressed against his soles threatened to trip him. As he went farther, the sensation dwindled into perfunctory walking.

He wondered how much his body had forgotten in those seven days of sleep and the other blurred and painful days before. Echoes of his own screams still rang in his ears. He shivered when he remembered that lion, the one that was stealing his blood and trying to consume him from the inside. Those yellow moon eyes would haunt him forever. Best to not think about it.

"Ryan, how do you feel?" Jayden raced over to him. Her smile was beautiful, but more borrowed than before.

"I feel amazing." He touched her flushed cheek with the tips of his fingers. The softness of her skin was another of those sensations his body rushed to remember. Every ridge of his fingertips brushed against her smooth skin. It lasted for a moment before touch returned to what he remembered. Jayden sank to the ground and Ryan joined her. "So, tell me what I've missed."

Her eyes darkened and her face reddened. "Thank you for—for saving my life."

"No, no. Don't do that." He put a finger under her chin and raised her head to look into his eyes.

"I want to say this."

"Consider it said."

One tear escaped and she wiped it away. Then her smile blossomed again, not borrowed anymore. This time it was his, all his.

"I'm glad your sisters made it." Jayden looked at him, then at the ground.

"I'm sorry about your family." He couldn't imagine the guilt she must feel. Wait—his father knew. He'd told Ryan to protect Jayden at all costs. How had he known? "Anna says you're one of the deliverers?"

She slipped a dagger out of her boot to show him.

Ryan took the weapon. A real work of art. And light too. The blacksmith in him hoped to someday make weapons of this beauty and strength.

"Anna's husband made it. He was a Wielder."

That explained it. Wielders could mold metal in ways no one else could, and they were usually magical. Or so legend said. As he examined the dagger's detailed etching, its sapphires glinted in the sunlight.

"Lightning? It's like he knew you'd have a fascination with storms. I wonder if there's some kind of magic linked to it." He returned the dagger to her.

She offered him a sideways smile. "You believe they use magic?"

Such a dreamer. He took the dagger from her again. "You're kidding, right? Don't you remember anything from history class? Caden, a deliverer from the first century, shot fire out of the tip of his arrow. The tip was made by a Wielder and a carving of a flame was on the stone."

"Of course I remember. And I've felt the magic. The stones glowed when I first picked up the daggers." Her eyes sparkled.

"That's all? There's got to be more. Maybe it shoots lightning." Ryan pretended to throw the dagger at a tree and stopped short.

"Stop it." Jayden pried the weapon from his grip. Her smile betrayed the angry look she was trying to give him as she replaced the dagger in its sheath.

He stood and offered her his hand. "Walk with me?"

Pink colored her cheeks as her fingers slipped into his palm. Maybe he hadn't lost her yet. He led her into the wooded area behind Anna's house, and they strolled in the shade of the trees from morning into afternoon, feeling the summer breeze, and listening to the sound of leaves rustling as she shared with him her adventure.

Ethan came up often, and every time, her cheeks flushed and her eyes sparkled. That stung. Still, Ryan encouraged her to talk about him. It was worth it to see her smile after all she'd been through. But it seemed his hold on her heart was slipping. Maybe he still had a chance—if she'd let him go with her.

"Look." Jayden stopped in front of a bush. She plucked a handful of the blueberries and held one between her thumb and finger. Her eyes glistened. "Just like home."

Ryan's chest ached, not from his injury—from loss.

Jayden's eyebrows pulled together, and she stepped closer to him. "Are you okay? You want to head back?"

He shook his head and sat down near the bush with a tree at his back.

Jayden sat with him, those worried eyes tracking his every move.

He couldn't help but chuckle. "I'm not going to drop dead."

"Not funny, Ry."

If he didn't joke, he had to face reality. "Too soon?"

Berries pelted his shirt.

He held up his hands, palms out. "I'm sorry. I am."

She sighed. "I know. You lost everything too."

More reality he wasn't ready to face. "You think old Norm Grotter survived?"

Jayden laughed. "That old man survives everything. What was your favorite story? How he clung to a cliff's ledge for a half day? Or the shipwreck?"

"Which one?"

Jayden giggled. She picked a few more berries and popped them in her mouth. Her chewing slowed. "Have you ever wondered why you don't have Blood Moon talents?"

Ryan couldn't contain his laughter. "What makes you think I don't have any?"

She stared at him, her eyes wide. "I was right there when you told Norm you didn't."

So that's what she'd heard? He always wondered how his talent affected others. "That's not what happened. Norm said anyone with a Blood Moon talent would be wise to hide it."

"And you told him you had nothing to hide."

"Right."

Jayden rolled her eyes. "That's the same thing, Ry."

"Not really."

Her eyes searched his face. "Were you going to tell me your talents at the betrothal ceremony?"

"Of course."

She twirled a loose strand of her dark hair. The tips of her fingers were stained purple. "So, what are they?"

Ryan shook his head. "Oh no. We're not having this conversation now."

"I'll tell you mine."

So willing. Why? The way she chewed her bottom lip could only mean she felt guilty for something. What? That he'd almost died for her? Didn't she see? There was no need for her to feel that way. He'd do it again if he had to.

He pushed off the tree and leaned closer. "You don't have to tell me anything. And if you never told me, I'd marry you anyway."

Her eyelashes fluttered. "You would jump in, not knowing whether or not I could—I don't know, read your mind, or tell where you've been, or know if you were lying?"

Ryan bowed his head. Deception, such a noble, honorable talent. More like a tempting curse. How would he describe to her what he could do when he wasn't even sure he knew how his talent worked, let alone how it affected others? All he knew for certain was that it was unpredictable, which was why he'd stopped using it. He'd never gotten away with a blatant lie—in fact his talent didn't seem to work at all when he lied outright. But he'd certainly been able to make others believe things that weren't necessarily true. The day he tricked Chloe into believing a gryphon ate her bread was the day he thought he understood. Unfortunately, it wasn't the day he'd stopped using his talent.

His memory replayed the scene. A young Chloe had sat next to him on the outside picnic table. Her eyes narrowed when she looked at her bread. Half of it was clearly missing. She glared at him. "You ate my bread?"

Ryan opened his talent. "No."

"Don't you lie to me, Ryan Granden. I see crumbs on your tunic."

Well, that hadn't worked. He wiped the evidence from his shirt. Maybe if he tried a different tactic. "Something else could have eaten it."

She crossed her arms. "You're the only person here."

Ryan grinned. "Yeah, but I'm not the only living thing. I mean a bird could have swooped down and eaten it. Or a squirrel. They're thrifty. For all I know, a gryphon could have stolen it."

"Gryphons are extinct." Was that doubt in her voice? Chloe had always been fascinated with the winged creatures.

He leaned closer to his sister. "That's just what people think. But that's because they only believe in what they can see. You know gryphons can make themselves invisible."

Chloe still scowled at him. "They can't make themselves invisible. They're masters of hiding."

"Near enough, then."

Her lips twisted. "Did you see the gryphon?"

"Of course not."

"You think a gryphon ate my bread?"

Ryan swallowed. If he said "yes" she wouldn't believe him, but . . . "I think it could have happened."

Her eyelids fluttered—that was a good sign that his talent was working—then she looked right at him, her eyes as big as a bull-frog's. "I have to tell mom that gryphons are real." She held up her bread. "And I have proof!"

Ryan shook the memory from his head. The same unsettling feeling that had squeezed his stomach then came back as he looked into Jayden's expectant eyes. Wouldn't that just be a great conversation? *Why, yes, Jayden, I can make you believe half-truths, as long as I am very careful with my words. But don't worry. I never use my talent.*

He breathed deep. "Yes, I would still marry you, because either you've been using your talents against me all this time or you haven't. If you haven't, you'll be honest with me, and if you have, you'll keep using your talents without my knowledge. Knowing, not knowing—it wouldn't change a thing."

"So no one knows your talents?"

"Careful. I didn't say that."

She rolled her eyes. "You're always so literal."

Ryan smiled. A soft blush colored her cheeks, but her gaze darted to the ground. What was she hiding from him? "Thanks for saving me."

Her forehead wrinkled. "I can't believe you thought I'd leave you."

He reached for her hands and she let him take them. "I never thought you'd leave me, but you should've."

"How can you say that?"

"I know we didn't make the betrothal ceremony, Jayden, but—"

"Don't." Eyes wide, she slid her hands from his grip.

A pang hit his heart. "Don't?"

Twigs snapped under her knees as she closed the distance between them. She knelt in front of him, hands resting on her thighs. Tears welled in her eyes. "I'm sorry. I'm sorry because that path would have been perfect. I would have been so very happy. I would have tried my best to make you happy, but—"

"Jayden—"

"Let me finish. The moment we turned off that path, we forfeited that future."

Why was his throat so thick? "Are you saying we can never be together?"

"I'm saying right now is not the time for those decisions. Right now everything is different. I have to walk this new path first. Maybe, when this is over, we can start fresh, but until this is over, I—I can't." Her voice strained.

"I'll wait, then."

Her hand reached to touch his chest where the arrow had sunk in, but her fingers curled up and her arm fell to her lap. "You've already put your life on the line for me. If your path branches away from mine, I'll understand."

"It takes more than a bad shot to put me down."

The setting sun's light reflected off her eyes. "Don't you see? I can't let you do that again. Your sisters would have no one. You— I can't risk your life."

Ryan sucked in a breath. How did he not see what she was saying before? "You don't plan to come back. That's what this is about, isn't it? You're letting me go because you don't think you'll survive."

Her face scrunched up, and he pulled her close, held her while her shoulders shook. She could set him free all she wanted. As long as he lived, he'd see to it that she got out of this alive.

"Jayden, how about this? You stop worrying about tomorrow. We'll take this new path one step at a time, together. As friends. Like always."

Her tear-streaked face tipped up and a smile formed on her mouth. "Ryan, you're the best friend a girl could have."

He brushed away the stray tears. "Took you long enough to notice."

She slipped out of his arms and chuckled.

Her smile, although tearful, was genuine.

He settled back against the tree and propped his left arm on his bent knee. A twinge shot through the healing wound. Something was wrong. He shouldn't be feeling such a deep ache still. Not that he'd ever been shot with an arrow before, but the time the jagged tree branch impaled his leg seemed a good enough comparison, and he'd healed from that quicker. Quick enough that Jayden didn't notice how bad it was.

Maybe Anna's little potion for keeping his self-healing talent at bay was still in effect. He rolled his shoulder, testing it out. A deeper pain flared, burned.

He froze. His chest tightened. Not burning. No more burning.

"Are you okay?" Jayden's soft voice pulled him out of his panic.

His throat tightened. "Yeah."

She squinted and tilted her head. "You sure? Because you looked a little scared just now."

Ever-perceptive Jayden. "Didn't I just tell you not to worry?"

"About tomorrow, not about you."

He stood and offered her his hand. "Now who's being literal?"

She took his hand and he pulled her up. The burn shot through him again, this time so strong he bent over and groaned.

"You can't run." That deep, purring voice shot through his mind.

"Ryan?" Jayden's hand touched his back.

He focused on her touch. That was real. The white lion was just a remnant of the fever dream. He breathed deep and straightened. "I'm fine."

Jayden's eyes scanned his face. "You're not fine. There's something you're not telling me."

Didn't she already have enough burdens to bear? Whatever was wrong with him, he'd figure out. There was no need to add to her worry.

The throb that pulsed in his heart dulled as he looked into her eyes to do something he'd never done to her. Something he hadn't done to anyone in years—he'd make the truth a lie.

As the power of his talent flared in his chest, the burning ache receded. "It's all right, Jayden. You shouldn't have to worry about me."

There was no telling how literally she'd respond to what he'd said. She may just assume he didn't want her to worry about his recent injury, or she may never worry about him again, but it was a risk he was willing to take to keep her whole, to give her a chance to make it out of this alive.

Her eyelashes fluttered and she shook her head. His talent had taken hold. When her blue eyes focused on his face again, she smiled. "I think I was going to tell you something, but I forgot."

He offered her his arm. "Should we head back?"

She nodded and linked her arm through his. "I remember. I wanted to thank you for protecting me."

A lump rose in his throat, but the burn in his chest disappeared. If his ability to deceive eased the burning ache, did that mean some of the black lion's venom still pulsed in his veins? More importantly, were there other side effects?

A deep purr echoed in his head.

CHAPTER 36

A FITTING
DEPARTURE

In the dark, Jayden crept down the stairs from the loft. She'd spent the last week memorizing which stairs were the creakiest and which spots to avoid altogether.

Her satchel waited for her by the back door. She picked it up and headed outside. The moon was waning again, but still was big and bright. It also seemed the slightest shade of red. Fitting, perhaps. She risked one last glance at Anna's warm home, then headed to the barn to retrieve Aureolin.

Her breathing came easier, now that she was out of the house, but blood still thundered in her ears, and her heart beat against her ribs. She stopped in front of the barn. The left door was far squeakier than the right. She set down her pack and lifted the wooden beam across the doors.

"Where are you off to?"

Jayden's heart jumped into her throat. She froze, except for her shaking limbs.

Footsteps crushed the thick summer grass as Ryan drew closer.

She whirled to face him. He was so close she could touch him. Thinking up a lie wasn't part of her plan. Not that she could speak if she tried. Her throat had constricted.

She backed against the rough wood of the barn door. "H-how did you—I mean—"

"Come on. You're not that hard to figure out." He leaned his forearms on the barn doors, one on either side of her head, and cupped his hands together above her.

Every breath smelled like embers and hot steel. Heat radiated from him. Consumed her. Calmed her jumping heart. Everything about him was so comforting and familiar, and reminded her of home. If she stood here any longer, she'd never want to leave.

He smirked. "You've been looking over your shoulder and sneaking off to hide things all day. I've been waiting for my invitation."

"Ryan, you can't. I have to go alone."

"That brings me back to 'where.'"

"If I'm a deliverer, I have to face the queen. And that means—"

"Alone? Whoa, Jayden—" He pushed his elbows off the doors.

She grabbed his shirt and pulled him back. "Let me finish."

He settled back into that protective stance, but this time, his jaw was tight.

"I won't go alone. I just can't let anyone else I care about get hurt."

Ryan inhaled a deep breath. Even in the dark, she could see his eyes had softened. She might be in the snare, but this hunter looked like he had a mind to let her go.

"What happened to your family is not your fault."

She looked at trees as they fluttered in the wind. "It sure feels that way."

"So you won't let me protect you?"

She ducked beneath his arms and walked away from that comforting warmth. "I won't let you do stupid things to keep me safe."

He faced her, but didn't follow. Instead he crossed his arms. "So I'm supposed to let you do the stupid things?"

"Yes."

"I can't."

"You don't have a choice. I'm leaving. You won't abandon your sisters, will you?"

"Not fair."

"Life isn't."

He tore his gaze from her and the muscle in his jaw twitched. His arms dropped to his sides and he walked over to her. "I can't make your decisions for you. I've known that for a long time."

"Thank you."

"Oh, I'm not letting you go alone." His finger lifted her chin until she looked into his gray eyes. "Because you can't make my decisions for me either."

She fell into his chest and hugged him tight. That was exactly why she had to get as far away from him as she could. She had to protect those she loved, just like they wanted to protect her. The difference was, facing the queen was her destiny, not theirs.

A harsh bark interrupted the night's silence.

Jayden turned away from Ryan. "Scout?"

The dog spun in circles, barking. He'd alert everyone to her departure.

She waved a hand at him. "Go."

He grabbed Ryan's pant leg and pulled.

"What's wrong with him?"

Jayden saw her chance. "I think he wants us to follow."

"All right, all right." Ryan crouched next to the crazed canine. "What, boy?"

Scout dashed away a few paces then turned. Another bark.

Ryan followed.

Jayden picked up her satchel and ran the other way. She rounded the barn, then glanced over her shoulder. No one followed. She might make it after all.

Her body slammed into something. Hard. A hand closed around her wrist and kept her from falling.

"Really, Jayden?" Ethan did not look pleased.

She yanked her arm, but his grip on her wrist didn't lessen. "You're going to drag me back?"

"If I have to."

Every muscle in her body tensed. He had some nerve. Some cocky nerve. "Fine."

"Fine?"

"I'm not going anywhere. Just let go of me."

"As you wish." He dropped her arm.

They stared at each other in a very uncomfortable silence.

"I just didn't want anyone else to get hurt," Jayden said, but her words overlapped Ethan's. "What did you say?"

"I told you I can find you."

"That's not what you said." She'd clearly heard the word, "feel."

He cleared his throat. "Anna's dead."

That wasn't what he'd said either, but her knees buckled just the same. "What? How?"

Ethan shook his head. "She left a note. Apparently when Whisperers die, the trees carry away the body. She's completely gone. We can't stay here anymore. It's not safe, but she left us some things. You coming?"

She slipped her fingers into his palm. "I guess I have no choice since I can't get away from you."

"Hopefully, you've learned your lesson then." That harsh voice wasn't Ethan's.

Jayden cringed, dropped Ethan's hand, and turned to face Ryan who stood with his arms crossed.

The intensity of his glare made her heart race, but when he glanced at Ethan, Ryan's eyes narrowed farther.

"Ryan—" Jayden touched Ryan's arm and flinched—he burned so hot. She pulled back.

He sighed. His face softened as he extended his hand. "Better get you back."

Her fingers threaded through his, and his skin was no warmer than normal. Perhaps she'd imagined it.

As Ryan tugged her forward, she glanced over her shoulder. Ethan followed close behind, of course. He mouthed the words, "I'll find you."

That was why she'd have to be more careful with her next escape attempt.

CHAPTER 37

THE CREATOR'S SONG

The moon disappeared behind dark clouds, making it harder for Ryan to see Jayden's expression. He walked in step with her back to Anna's house—Ethan only a stride behind—but she wouldn't look at him no matter how many times he glanced her way.

Had she felt the heat radiating off his skin?

He had.

It wasn't the same as the burning sensation of the venom in his blood, but seeing Ethan and Jayden in such close proximity had shot heat through his veins. And the way Jayden had flinched to his touch made him wonder. It wasn't like he could just ask her.

They reached Anna's home, and Jayden practically ran up the steps, but Ryan paused. Ethan stopped with him and glanced over with his eyebrows raised, asking if Ryan was okay.

Ryan nodded. Ethan clasped Ryan's shoulder and gave a quick squeeze before following Jayden inside.

Ryan entered the house. A few lit candles sat in the center of her oak table surrounded by a bunch of bundles that resembled bedrolls tied with twine. Were those clothes rolled up between layers of blankets?

A note and a red funeral sash sat atop each bundle. A pang hit Ryan's heart. "She's really . . ."

Logan fingered the sash. "She's gone. We have to pack up and get on the road before midmorning. We will honor Anna's memory before we go."

Ethan stood next to Ryan and leaned close. "Anna left one for everyone."

So Anna knew she was going to die, and she took time to prepare this for each of them? Perhaps that kind of prescience came with living to be a thousand.

Logan assigned Chloe the task of sorting out the bundles. Ryan opened the note first and read the Whisperer's words.

Ryan,

I know you and your sisters came here with little but the clothes on your back. I didn't give Wren a knife, but Chloe and Kinsey each have one. The blankets and clothes are a gift from me, too. I knew you were all coming one day. I just didn't know when, or how fond of you I'd become.

You're a fighter, Ryan. I know you worry about your sisters, about Jayden, about what your purpose is in all of this. I think you'll find it. Listen carefully to your heart. It will guide you.

I say listen carefully because, as I feared, the black lion venom did taint you. It's not much—not like what happened to my friend. But it's still there. A small piece of you will always be at war with the bigger part. I have faith that you will overcome it, dear one.

You are strong enough. The Creator placed you here for a purpose. Hold onto that truth. Don't let the taint obtain a stronger hold. Keep true to who you are. Your friends will help you. Of this I am sure.

> *Creator's blessings, dear one.*
> *Love, Anna*

Ryan gripped the note in his hand so tight the paper crinkled in his fingers. So the taint *had* reached him. His chest tightened. What exactly did that mean? Would it get worse? Could he stop it? Anna seemed to think he could keep it at bay. He breathed deep. If she thought he could, then that would have to be enough. He would overcome it.

The house felt strange with Anna gone, like the warmth had left with her. The trees seemed to droop and a steady rain dripped off their leaves. Fitting.

Logan sent Ryan and Ethan to collect any food they could bring. Ethan opened Anna's cellar door and cool air rushed out toward them. Bread, cheese, nuts, dried fruit, and meat were arranged inside.

Ryan began to pack some. "I wasn't sure you'd hear me."

Ethan paused for a moment, but there was no question on his face. Ryan was certain Ethan knew what Ryan referred to: the night he'd called out mentally to Ethan to come and protect Jayden and their sisters. The night Ryan had thought was his last.

Ethan turned his attention to packing the provisions. "I didn't know it was you tugging on my talent. I just knew someone close to me needed help."

"I'm sorry I dragged you into this."

"You know I would do anything for you and our sisters, right?" Ethan placed his hand on Ryan's shoulder.

"I do."

"Then don't be sorry. I'm glad you reached out to me." Ethan squeezed Ryan's shoulder and then got back to packing. "How are you feeling?"

Ryan shrugged one shoulder. "You know, at least I got a decent scar out of it."

Ethan cracked some semblance of a smile.

"I got you back." Ryan playfully punched his brother's arm.

Ethan grinned. "That's one of your two free hits."

Ryan laughed. "I'll be sure to make the next one harder."

"I wouldn't doubt it."

"Admit it. You're glad to be back."

Ethan chuckled and glanced at the ground. "Of course I am. It looks like Chloe will never forgive me for leaving, but it's nice to know you have."

"Give her some time. Though not too much or she'll start to remember all those pranks you pulled."

"*I* pulled?" Ethan pointed to himself. "It's more like *we* pulled."

At least Ryan had gotten him smiling. "You missed me more than you thought you would."

Ethan froze for a heartbeat. "Of course I did."

"That's not what I meant, Ethan. I know you had to go."

He rubbed the back of his neck. "I shouldn't have."

"No, I should have made sure you knew how to find us." Ryan bowed his head. "I told Rose. I was always surprised she didn't go with you—her father had just asked our father about the possibility of betrothal. She took it pretty hard when you left."

Ethan paused for a heartbeat. "I did ask her. She made her choice. Apparently she loved other things more than she loved me. Besides, it wasn't your fault; I could have tried harder to find you."

Ryan breathed deep. "It must have looked like we were abandoning you. I hope—"

"Ryan, we all made mistakes. What's important is that we're together now."

"It's good to have you back." A hole been refilled. He looked out at his sisters helping Logan load the goats into the back of the wagon. Chloe muscling them. Wren feeding them so they would stay close. Kinsey scaring half of them . . . and Jayden. She calmed each of them and led them onto the wagon. Bringing Ethan back was something he wouldn't change. But he still felt a pang in his heart. It hurt on more than one level. First, how Ethan looked at Jayden. Second, that Ryan had handed his brother to the throes of danger. And he didn't regret it. He didn't want to be alone in this. "You're not going to bolt again are you?"

Ethan chuckled and then his face turned serious. "Never again." He walked out of the cellar, his bag full of food.

Ryan stood there for a moment. The late summer sun broke through the rain just as Ethan reached Jayden. She smiled at him, warm as the sunshine, and something in Ryan's heart heated. Just one corner, like a sliver.

He shivered. If that was the tainted part, he'd have to make sure jealousy didn't get a hold of him. He couldn't risk becoming a monster.

Once Aureolin was bridled and hitched to the wagon, and the goats and chickens loaded, Logan led them back inside to the oak table where eight red strips of cloth lay. The funeral sashes.

Logan picked up his and handed it to Jayden who stood nearest him. He held out his arm, and quiet hung over the whole company as they watched Jayden tie the red sash just above his right elbow. She then picked up her sash and her eyes darted in Ethan's direction first. Ryan glanced at the wood grain pattern in the floor, but it was to him that she handed her sash. He tied it onto her arm. Maybe he hadn't lost her yet. She was worth hanging on to. Worth fighting for.

By the time the ceremony had completed, every eye glistened and sniffling was the only sound.

Logan led the whole party outside. They formed a circle around one of the flowering trees in Anna's yard. The tree had already lost its blooms, but there was no body to stand around, so Logan said he felt this tree would be appropriate.

Each head bowed. Chloe stroked Wren's hair.

Logan kissed his fingers and lifted them to the sky. "In memory of Anna."

The others repeated the gesture and words, then they all knelt around the tree. Westwind and Scout lay down with them. Ryan had sung the Creator's song enough times that old emotions raced into him with the words, but he wasn't just singing for Anna today. He also sang for his father.

Tears fought to be released, but his father wouldn't have wanted him to cry, so he didn't. Someone rubbed his arm and he turned, expecting to see Kinsey coming for comfort, but he saw Chloe instead. She wrapped her arm around him and pulled him close. And they sang.

The Creator sang
at the dawn of time
That His creation
should never die.
But the heart of creation
was fragile and soft,
Able to harden,
Able to lie.

The hearts of the forests
remained pure and strong.
They told of love
forgotten,
not gone.
Of the Creator and His song.
Still hearts grew hard,
but some stayed true
To remain one with the hearts
of the forests,
of the few.
Who would remember the heart
of the Creator
Who knew.
The hearts of the forests
remained pure and strong.
They told of love
forgotten,
not gone.
Of the Creator and His song.
When evil grew
and tainted the pure,
the Creator gave hope
to the hearts
of the sure.
So sing your song
tonight, my friend,
with the Creator
the beginning
in the end.
The hearts of the forests
remained pure and strong.
They told of love
forgotten,
not gone.
Of the Creator and His song.

Silence followed. The birds, the animals, the trees—everything remained quiet.

"Look." Wren's soft, innocent voice brought everyone's attention to the tree they encircled.

The thick branches above them bore buds. Soft white and pink petals opened from every tip of every twig on the tree and began to fall like a warm, summer snow. New flowers unfolded in their places until they covered the ground in a blanket of pink and white. The scent of the fragrant blossoms filled the air around them. Petals littered everyone's hair and rested in the folds of their clothes.

Wren's small voice broke the silence. "The Creator sent Anna flowers?"

Jayden smiled at her. "I think so."

"All right." Logan motioned toward the house. "It's time to say good-bye. According to Anna's note, the trees will only uphold their protective shroud here for a few more hours." He headed toward the wagon.

The others followed, but Chloe stopped in front of Ryan. She stared at the ground. "I was afraid . . . to lose you."

"I know." He touched her shoulder and nudged her in for another hug.

She wrapped her arms around him. "I'm sorry I was awful to you."

He chuckled.

She stepped back and eyed him. "What's so funny?"

"It's just you've never apologized for being awful before."

She laughed and smacked his arm. "And I never will again."

At least she had some hope back in her eyes. She picked up her satchel and followed the others. Ryan swallowed as he watched how closely Jayden walked to Ethan. If he could protect her just fine, perhaps Ryan should let Ethan take over.

"He's stealing what's yours."

He sucked in a breath as his heart hammered. That voice sounded so like the white lion. He shook his head. Anna had said to fight the taint. He would. Even if it meant letting Jayden go. Anna also said he'd find his purpose in all of this. He swung his satchel over his shoulders and made sure his bow and quiver were secure. Then he glanced at Anna's house one last time. Hopefully the voice in his head would stay here as he left.

"You okay, Ryan?" Jayden rubbed his arm and snapped him out of his thoughts.

He nodded, but her blue eyes searched his face. "You seem scared."

Terrified. "I'm just . . . worried. Where are we going?"

"We should make it to Acaitha by nightfall," Logan said.

Ethan's eyes narrowed. "You're taking us to a city?"

"I'd take the woods the whole way, but it will add two days' travel. It's not exactly free of the queen's false Feravolk army. Besides, I've got friends in Acaitha. It'll be safe. Unless . . . do you sense danger?"

Ethan rubbed the back of his neck. "It doesn't exactly work that way. But if something threatens them, I'll know."

Ryan glanced at his sisters. Ethan could protect them. That was his purpose. Ryan clenched his jaw. It would be his purpose too.

CHAPTER 38

CASUALTIES OF REVENGE

When the orange sun hung low in the sky, Westwind and Scout left to stay in the comfort of the forest. Logan led everyone forward, the sense of worry gnawing away at his stomach. He had a lot more to protect now, which was why getting to Moon Over Water as soon as possible was his best option. As the sun dipped lower on the horizon, they reached the small town of Acaitha.

The smell of ash and smoke lingered over the town.

Logan clenched his fists. The queen had struck here too? He stilled the urge to kick something. It was too late now to set up camp. He couldn't risk a run-in with village survivors in the woods this close to town.

He turned to the worry-worn travelers. "Ryan, Ethan, Jayden, hide in the wagon. The rest of you, up here." Logan patted the seat.

They did so without complaint. He stuffed his Feravolk cloak in his sack. Then he led them toward the town gate.

Two gatekeepers eyed Logan. "You're not welcome here, stranger."

"Am I such a stranger?" Logan held out his arms, palms up. "A man made a widower who comes to aid family? My cousin sent word she had lost her husband. I came to comfort her and her children. You would deny me entrance to my cousin's home?"

"What's your cousin's name?" the guard asked, his gruff voice harsher this time.

"Her husband was a Lindon."

"Lindon? I don't know a Lindon."

"Come now. You know every person in town? Abby Lindon—brown hair, green eyes, pretty teeth, and a shy smile?"

"Oh, right. Pretty girl with three little ones already?"

"Yes, that's her," Logan lied.

"Go right in, sir."

"Thank you kindly." Logan smiled and inclined his head, and the Grandens mimicked him. Ethan, Jayden, and Ryan remained hidden in the back of the wagon under hay and goat hooves.

Soot littered the town. A thick fog of smoke still hung in the air, and the smell of burnt homes and shops lingered everywhere. Ash covered the ground and swirled under horses and carts. The people scurrying around bore dark circles under their eyes.

The majority of the damage surrounded the entrance of the town and stopped spreading past the town square. Who had surrendered here?

He walked farther into town and rounded a corner. The White Rose still stood at the end of the street. If his luck held, Lady Tevisa still ran the inn. Logan urged Aureolin forward.

When they reached the tavern, he handed the reins to Chloe. "Give me a moment inside. I think I can get us a place to sleep tonight."

Inside the tavern, disheveled townspeople sat around full tables. It smelled of rabbit stew and smoke. Not smoke from a pipe, but from fire-stained clothes.

The serving girls still carried full trays of food, but unlike the normal smiling, laughing, joking, gambling, and back-slapping that filled the White Rose on any given evening, tonight somber faces, the sound of slurping soups, and low murmurs filled this place. Not even music played on the hearth.

"Sir, you'll have to find a seat if you wish to be served." A woman about Logan's age with dark circles under her eyes stared at him.

"I'd like two rooms for the night."

She sighed. "We are packed full for the night."

"I can pay you."

"Money isn't buying much around here, now is it?"

"I have a wagon full of chickens and a few female goats."

A glimmer showed in her dark eyes. "I think I can get you your rooms. Just for tonight?"

"Two rooms, hot meals for all of us. And we would like to keep our presence quiet. Just for the night."

"You in some kind of trouble?"

"No, I just want some privacy for me and my family."

"You and everyone else."

He pulled a wooden chip out of his pocket, one with the engraving of a rose on it, and handed it to her. "Is Lady Tevisa here? You can tell her an old friend has come to call."

She examined the token and handed it back to him. "I'll get your rooms ready and have meals sent up to you. I'm sure Lady Tevisa will want to talk to you. She always wants to make sure her friends aren't being impersonated."

After the woman walked away, Logan stepped out of the tavern. Kinsey held Wren's head in her lap, and Chloe watched the door with a hawk-like gaze. They all straightened when they saw him. He took Aureolin's reins and led them toward the stables.

In the stable, an older, but distinguished-looking, woman with fiery red hair glided toward them.

"Logan, your visits, as always, are a surprise." Her voice was low for a woman's. She extended a hand for him to kiss and eyed the Granden girls. "And a pleasure. Jenna tells me you need your presence to be kept quiet?"

He tapped the wagon. "C'mon out."

Three straw-covered heads rose. Ryan, Jayden, and Ethan dusted themselves off.

Lady Tevisa nodded her head once. "I see. You will have your two rooms, you will have your hot meals, and you will have your secrecy. I don't need to tell you to be careful traveling with fugitives, Logan. I also know you well enough to recall that my warnings won't do any good. The Lon—"

She stopped short and with a petite smile as Logan pressed his finger to his lips. He didn't need these kids learning that he was the Lone Wolf. The reputation he'd earned as the swordsman didn't exactly incite trust.

"Well, I know you will always help the innocent. In the morning, I will arrange for you to exit the town with a little gold and no extra attention."

Lady Tevisa returned Logan's smile before she swept aside her skirts in a turn and walked back inside.

Logan helped the others climb out of the wagon and dispersed their belongings.

"We'll need the horse ready in the morning. Everything else belongs to Lady Tevisa," Logan told the stable boy.

A little girl with features resembling the stable boy's approached Aureolin. "She's so beautiful." The girl stroked the horse's shoulder. Aureolin lowered her head for the little girl to touch her nose. She smiled at Logan. "I'll take good care of her."

Jayden crouched next to the girl. "I'll bet you will. Her name is Aureolin, and she loves sugar."

"I have a few lumps of sugar." The girl's eyes sparkled.

Logan led them toward the tavern entrance. Lady Tevisa waited inside with Jenna, the woman he'd spoken with earlier, who led them to their adjacent rooms. There were three beds in each, a window, a washstand and a mirror, one chest with three drawers, and two chairs. The wooden floors showed years of wear. The place smelled exceptionally clean, though the bedding was mismatched.

"Your meals will be up soon," Jenna said before she curtsied and left.

Logan ushered the girls into their room. They were exhausted from a day of packing and traveling. He suspected they would fall asleep after eating. He hoped for it too, because he had his own work to do.

All taverns had a distinct odor with alcohol and sweat at the root. Logan propped his legs on the bench across from him and leaned against the wall. He had often melted into the dark corners of taverns like this one.

He didn't excel at gambling or getting others to strike up a conversation, but he had long since mastered listening and observing. Besides, every tavern had a mysterious man who took his drink seriously—he played the part well.

The queen's soldiers sat at a table near the east wall. They didn't wear the crest of the queen here, but he'd pegged them when they strode into the room with hands hovering over the swords at their hips. To his wolf-like sense of smell, they reeked of arrogance.

The tavern door swung open. Logan shifted his eyes to the newcomer and his heart sped. He was a good deal older than the last time Logan had seen him, but the man's dark hair was still cropped close to his head, graying at the temples. The same white scar ran from his left temple to his jaw.

Balton.

His shoulders appeared broader, if possible, probably from all the torture sessions he still implemented. Logan couldn't see the general giving up his favorite hobby. Logan's ribs hurt just thinking about the general's heavy boots thudding into his chest.

Logan fought for sanity. His teeth ground together. Snare alcohol. Focus. Revenge right now wouldn't happen. And revenge was nothing more than uninhibited rage.

One Eye's voice rang clear in his memory: Revenge is a killer. It starts with your heart, ends with your soul, and makes you rationalize the casualties in between. You want to be a killer, Logan?

No, but he wanted Balton dead.

CHAPTER 39

SECRET THINGS

Logan watched Balton take a seat at the table of soldiers and stilled his hand from touching the familiar scar on his chest.

Jenna, the shifty barmaid who had almost denied Logan a room, sauntered toward them. She leaned over the table and exchanged half-full beer mugs for full ones and let her bosom brush against the general's arm. She looked over her shoulder, eyes scanning the room. A promising look—she had a secret.

Logan tuned his wolf's hearing onto their conversation.

"The queen's pigeon has arrived, General." She handed him a scroll with a red wax seal.

Every muscle in Logan's body tensed. Was it the next target? If he could get that information, then he could send it to Alistair. They'd finally be a step ahead. Better yet, maybe the pigeon was still here.

Balton wrapped a hand around Jenna's waist and pulled her atop his lap. She laughed and swatted his shoulder. When she stepped away from him, Balton pinched her bottom.

Pig.

Logan flagged down a different barmaid and ordered another drink.

One of the soldiers leaned forward. "Well?"

Balton unrolled the parchment. His lips curved into a smile before he held the message over the candle on his table. Balton turned to his men and Logan watched his lips form the words, "We head to Lancia."

Lancia? Logan chuckled as he brought his brandy glass to his lips. *"Westwind?"*

"Yes?"

He set his glass on the table with a clank. *"Send Alistair a message for me—a message from Balton."*

Westwind's pleased growl echoed in Logan's thoughts. *"Gladly."*

Logan sat on his bed and stared at the dark sky out his window. A storm raged soon after black clouds blanketed the moon. Not following Balton ate at his insides, but he had kids to keep safe. Duty first.

He scoffed. He was supposed to be giving up his protector duty.

"Patience. You need the pack to pull down prey of that size." Westwind's tone exuded pent-up energy.

Logan dragged the tip of his knife beneath his fingernails. If it weren't for the young girls, Logan would have left the tavern already. Too much worry to sleep. Too many soldiers in close quarters. He wore his boots, and his bag rested next to the bedpost already packed.

Ryan had taken the same precaution and slept in his boots.

Ethan didn't sleep. He stared out the window, motionless.

A flash of lightning rent the sky, and moments later, thunder boomed.

Hopefully the message would reach Alistair soon enough. They had to get on the trail of these false Feravolk before all of Soleden forgot what an important role the Feravolk played.

The people suffered because of the queen's selfishness. Idla had to be stopped before Soleden died.

Ethan turned away from the window. "Someone knows there are Children here, and plans to take us."

Logan's knife pricked his finger. "Do you know who?"

"I just felt the warning, so someone who found out recently. I can't—"

"You did well." Logan stood and grabbed his cloak. "Wait here." He headed down the corridor. *Westwind?*

"Yes?"

"We've got trouble."

Westwind bristled. *"I'm awaiting your orders, friend."*

"Me too," Scout said.

Logan smiled. He liked that dog.

He crept down the hall and sniffed. Lady Tevisa always smelled of roses, the white kind. The red were slightly sweeter. Though the fire stunted much of what Logan could distinguish, he caught the faint whiff of her perfume. Edging toward it, he heard her unmistakable voice coming from her room around the corner.

Logan crept closer, careful not to upset the floorboards. Another voice from the room stopped him. A tingle spread across his skin like a wildfire. He'd know that voice anywhere. Balton was in the room with her. Was it any wonder the inn survived the fire?

Logan's heart pounded. The scars on his chest and around his neck burned like fresh wounds. Perhaps he'd have his chance to kill Balton, but the inkling of fear that returned with the general's presence wasn't something Logan had expected.

He pressed as close as he dared to the door, and peered through the keyhole that allowed a bit of candlelight to flicker through. His wolf-given night vision helped. Lady Tevisa stood straight-backed, her cloak pulled tightly around her shoulders.

"I've been told you have a secret." The general's smooth voice glided out the keyhole.

"I know lots of things that don't concern you, General. Let's not pretend vagueness is becoming." Lady Tevisa's deep voice did not waver.

Balton laughed and drew nearer to Lady Tevisa. "We'll get to the other secrets later. For now, I have been told that three Children of the Blood Moon are hiding within these walls. I just need to know which rooms—or I can lift my hand of protection at any time."

"You don't have to make threats. I know what you're capable of."

"Do you?"

A new sound tickled Logan's ears. Shoes pounded against the steps. A candle's glow came up the stairs.

He moved around the corner and held his breath as he peered around the edge of the wall. Jenna. She looked around before tapping on Lady Tevisa's door. Just as she raised her hand to knock again, the door opened.

"What is it?" Lady Tevisa asked.

"There is a supply cart from the queen. The driver will only speak to you."

"Thank you. I will see to it right away. Tell him."

Jenna scurried off.

Logan waited. The door didn't close.

"I'll come with you," General Balton's slick voice said.

"Suit yourself, but the supply cart comes from the queen weekly," Lady Tevisa said.

"I know, but I want to see to it your stowaways are warned of nothing before we meet them in their rooms tonight."

The door shut. The lock clicked. Footsteps echoed in the hall. Logan peered around the corner to see Balton walk away. Hate flared in his chest. He could kill Balton now. He could sneak up and slash the man's throat open, and—

"And whoever else knows about Jayden will still be after her."

Westwind's thoughts broke Logan's rage. His fingers uncurled from his sword's hilt. He stood and fled back to his room.

Outside the storm still raged.

Ethan stood as soon as Logan entered the room.

"Go get the girls," Logan said. "I'll take Ryan. Meet us outside the stable. Don't let anyone see you. There is a supply cart leaving soon. We will be on it."

Ethan nodded and left without a word.

Logan woke Ryan, and the kid followed him. As silently as they could, they descended the creaking stairs, rounded the corner, walked through the empty kitchens, and out to the barn. A covered wagon sat out front, and the golden gleam of candlelight leaked around the side of the building. Someone must be standing at the doorway of the building.

A low conversation between a man and a woman came from around the corner of the barn. Logan recognized Lady Tevisa's voice. That meant Balton was there too.

The grass was soft, and the rain still fell, both of which would mask the sounds of Logan and Ryan stepping outside so near to the speakers.

It wasn't long before Ethan led the rest of the disheveled lot out to the wagon. Logan lifted Wren into the back. Chloe and Kinsey climbed in.

"We have to change plans," Logan whispered to Jayden. "Aureolin—"

"Aureolin will be fine here. I left sugar cubes in my room." Jayden's eyes were as wet as the ground.

Logan patted her shoulder before he helped her into the wagon. Ethan and Ryan climbed aboard, and Logan behind. He made sure everyone was hidden behind crates and barrels. Wren clutched Ryan's shirt, and Logan's stomach squeezed tighter when he looked at her face.

They waited with the constant tapping of raindrops above them. The wagon shifted as the driver got on board. Wheels jolted free of their ruts in the soft ground.

They would be free if they could just keep unnoticed until they reached the woods.

The rain fell in a steady rhythm on the canvas above them for most of the night. Silence accompanied them, but none slept.

When morning broke, the inside of the wagon lightened, and hope with it. Logan peered out to see where they were. Strong fingers curled around his arm. Logan turned.

Ethan whispered, "They're going to check the wagon."

CHAPTER 40

ALMOST TOO QUIET

Ethan released his grip on Logan's arm and grabbed his sword hilt. The burn in his chest pulled his protective instinct five different ways. How would he know which pull to listen to? He stared at the canvas across the back of the wagon. A tiny slit let light in. No threat would make it past the edge of the wagon if he could help it.

Logan and he were closest to the door, hunched behind crates of apples. The crates of other fruits and vegetables behind them hid everyone else. Jayden and Ryan were behind Ethan, while the girls huddled behind Logan.

With a quick glance at Jayden and then Ryan, Ethan mouthed a silent message, "Stay down."

Ryan nodded and readied his bow.

Ethan faced the back of the wagon, muscles tense. He gripped his sword hilt tighter, feeling the leather against his palm. Every fold and crease pressed against his skin. His fingers slid into the leather's comfortable indentations. Soon he wouldn't feel it anymore—it would become part of him, an extension. His means of protecting those he loved.

A zap of energy seemed to flood through his veins—his talent at work, urging him to protect. Fear of death became a distant memory. He would kill if he had to, and die if it came to that. No one would hurt his loved ones.

The wagon stopped. Wheels settled into mud. Even if one of

them could make it to the reins, getting the horses going would take time.

"Make way for the carriage of the general!" a loud voice boomed outside.

Horses whinnied, chain mail clinked, footsteps shuffled. How many men were out there?

"You don't own the road. What happened to common courtesy?" The driver snapped the reins.

"What are you carrying?" a strong, liquid voice asked.

Beside Ethan, Logan clenched his jaw and rubbed two fingers against his chest. "General Balton," he whispered.

Ethan recognized the flash of heat in Logan's eyes. The man wanted revenge. That would make him more reckless. Ethan turned his hand over for Logan to see and ran his finger along his oath scar. Logan nodded, his stern stony expression returning.

The driver sputtered. "I—I, uh, goods and supplies to the townspeople devastated by the Feravolk, by orders of the Queen of Soleden."

"Then you won't mind if we have a look?"

"A look? Of course, General."

"Some escaped Children of the Blood Moon ran this morning from Acaitha. You wouldn't know anything about that, would you?"

"No, but what does the queen hold against the Children? I thought she was helping them."

Balton laughed, deep and frightful.

The ground squished under a good number of hooves as the horses drew closer to the rear of the wagon. Then silence. Eerie quiet tempted them to move. One shift, one sneeze, and everything would unravel. Ethan held tight to his weapon and prayed that his sisters would be able to stay silent.

Ethan held his breath. The back flap of the wagon peeled open. The small, white-haired wagon driver peered inside. Outside light filtered into the darkened area and threatened to expose their hiding places. The threat pulsed like a hunting dog waiting to be released.

"See there, Soldier? Nothing hidden here."

"What's this?" The soldier pushed him aside and slid a crate over, exposing Logan's hiding place.

Ethan's pulse quickened, but Logan didn't even glance his way, just put his hands up and stood slowly. If everyone else remained quiet, they still had a chance to remain undiscovered.

"Well, sir, my eyes are old, but it don't look like he's young enough—" The man's voice stilled and he crumpled to the ground, and the soldier stood there with a bloody knife.

A stifled scream gave away the hiding place for his sisters, and the threat exploded like a fire in Ethan's chest.

"General, we found them."

Logan drew his sword. "Jayden, drive! Ryan, cover her!"

Boots thumped against the floor of the wagon as Jayden and Ryan scrambled to the front. Ethan sprang to his feet and jumped over the crate of apples, sword drawn. No one would make it past him alive.

Soldiers climbed into the back of the wagon. Ethan stood next to Logan and they swung. Ethan's sword sliced through chain mail, and a soldier fell off the wagon. The threat in his chest burned. Jayden was in danger, but he couldn't get to her. He should have gone with her to the front.

No. Ryan had this. He was amazing with a bow.

Ethan sliced open one man's neck. The wagon jolted forward, and he nearly lost his balance. Someone grabbed his ankle and tried to climb aboard. He sliced the man's hand clean off.

The wagon started to pick up speed.

"Catch them!" Balton's voice boomed. "No arrows! I want them alive!"

Another soldier climbed around the side of the wagon and slashed his weapon toward Ethan's arm. He dodged just in time and stabbed the man clean through.

A threat ignited. For Wren. Ethan raced to the back of the wagon. The sound of canvas ripping brought his attention to a blade slitting the fabric. Ethan pushed Wren back from the canvas with his right hand and stabbed his sword through the material with his left. He pierced flesh.

The fabric ripped as the soldier tried to hang on but fell.

Wind whirled inside the wagon.

Chloe screamed.

Ethan turned to his sisters. "You all right?"

They stared at him, eyes bulging.

"That could have been Ryan coming in. Y-you didn't even look." Chloe's voice shook.

Ethan's heart hitched. "It wasn't."

Logan still had the back covered, so Ethan checked to see if he could spot any other men clinging to the sides. Two. And they were headed for the new opening.

He braced himself and faced the hole. "Get back."

Both men sprang through at once. Ethan swung at the first. Metal met metal and sent a shock through his arm. His calf bumped into a crate—no moving backward. He leaned forward, and the tip of the other man's sword met his side, slicing through his shirt and into skin. He spun, kicked the first attacker, then lunged forward. His blade met flesh and bit in hard.

The burn across his chest warning him of a threat intensified. Ethan whirled around to face his attacker, but a knife embedded into the man's chest. He rocked back and fell off the wagon.

Ethan spun around to see Chloe standing right behind him. She wrapped her arm around her middle. "There goes my hunting knife."

"Thank you." He touched her shoulder and headed back to help Logan.

Logan kicked the man he was fighting hard, and the soldier fell into the cloud of dust behind them. Horses veered to avoid him, but couldn't, and trampled over him. Balton's men had nearly caught up with the wagon.

"Is that all of them?" Logan asked between breaths.

"They're still gaining." Ethan motioned to the soldiers behind them.

"We could push the food out," Chloe said. "Maybe it'll trip up a few of them."

"Good idea." Logan moved toward one of the crates.

The threat still pulsed in Ethan's chest. Something else was wrong. The wagon shifted to a slower speed.

"Why are we stopping?" Chloe's voice was wild.

Hooves thundered against the ground outside. Ethan headed to the front of the wagon and peered out in time to see Ryan shoot his last arrow.

His gaze met Ethan's. "I'm out."

A score of soldiers blocked the road in front of them.

Jayden yanked back on the reins. "Tell Logan we've got company."

Ethan scanned the road. There was nowhere to go. They'd have to abandon the wagon and run into the woods.

"Come out, and we will spare your lives." General Balton's voice boomed from behind.

Ethan tugged Jayden's sleeve and made eye contact with his brother. "Get inside."

They jumped into the back of the wagon. Jayden handed Ryan one of her long daggers. "Remember what my brothers taught you."

Ethan tried to focus on his talent, but it just told him what he already knew: danger surrounded them.

A chorus of growls resonated around them. Loud neighing surrounded the wagon. Horses reared. Heads low, two dozen canines stalked out of the woods.

As one unit, they lunged and snapped. In a cloud of dust, horses bolted. The wolves gave chase.

"Ethan!" Logan thrust his sword through the wagon's cover and ripped it open. Westwind and Scout still stood there. "Get them out of here! Follow Westwind."

One by one, they jumped out of the wagon and raced for the trees. Soldiers met them outside and Ethan barreled toward the mass of them. "Run!"

His sword met two at once. He called on his speed and his strength, and they fueled him like a bonfire. A sword sliced into his skin, but he barely felt it. One soldier dropped to his blade. Another. He lost track of how many men he'd sliced open.

A scream pierced the air and he stilled.

Chloe.

General Balton stood flanked by two other soldiers. Balton's arm curled around Chloe, and his knife pressed against her throat. A circle of soldiers at least two men thick surrounded all of them.

Ethan threw his sword to the ground.

Logan did the same.

Ryan and Jayden were both being held from behind, weapons ripped from their grasps.

Three soldiers surrounded Ethan and wrenched his arms behind him.

"I thought we could be reasonable," Balton said. "If you cooperate, I'll be happy to let your friend go."

Wren and Kinsey were missing. So were Westwind and Scout. At least they had gotten away. He glanced at Jayden, and his heart squeezed.

Ahead, horses drew a prison carriage up the road.

A cord wrapped around Ethan's wrists, biting into his skin. Strong arms muscled him toward the carriage. It would do no good to fight back, not with Balton holding the rest of them.

"Make sure they have no hidden weapons on them, and bind their ankles." General Balton approached the carriage and looked them over.

Whimpers rose from Chloe's throat.

"That'll teach you to run from the queen." The corners of the general's mouth curled up. He chuckled and tossed a bound Chloe into the carriage.

Balton locked eyes with Logan. "You are too old to be a Child. They'll probably kill you, but I wouldn't want to deny you a good torture first, so you'll come with us."

When the general turned away, Logan spoke. "Felix Balton?"

Balton swung around to face him. "Do I know you?"

"You should." Logan sneered without breaking eye contact, without submitting.

Balton's fist connected with his cheek.

Logan slumped against the floor of the carriage, and Balton nodded at the soldiers to shut the door. Reins slapped, and the wagon rocked along the road.

"Will he be okay?" Chloe asked, staring at Logan's still form.

"I think so," Jayden said. She glanced at Ethan and her eyes rounded.

He leaned toward her. "Are you okay?"

She nodded.

"This is hardly okay." Ryan looked at Ethan. "Tell me you're working on something."

Ethan smiled. "Always." He just wished he had thought of something already.

Ryan leaned toward the edge of the wagon, closer to a soldier. "So where are we going?"

The soldier grunted.

"Not feeling talkative?"

"Ryan, stop." Chloe nudged her knee against his.

"You're going to Galea. The queen has special accommodations for Children," a soldier answered. All the soldiers shared a chuckle.

Ethan swallowed. If the burning in his chest would stop for a moment, maybe he could figure out what his talent wanted him to do.

The city wall of Galea became visible a mile down the dirt road— tall and thick and made of stone. As they drew closer, it was clear to see this city hadn't been hit by fire. No haze hung over the city, just blue sky and sunshine. Eight soldiers guarded the front gate. Ethan caught movement in the watchtower as well. Escaping from inside the city was going to be hard.

No one stopped the wagon. They went right into the city. People had gathered to gawk as the wagon made its way down the city center. Jeers and shouts met them, as did curses to the Feravolk and curses to Children of the Blood Moon.

Idla owns this city.

The carriage halted in front of a large stone building with heavy, wooden doors. More soldiers stood outside the doors. They carried swords and spears. A meadow stretched behind the building and ended at a line of trees. That suggested that this prison sat on the outskirts of the city. Perhaps the city wall lay beyond the wooded area. They might be able to make it out that way. If they could get out of this mess.

"Anything yet?" Ryan whispered.

"Don't worry." Ethan shot his brother a smile he couldn't back up with confidence.

"Who's worried?" Ryan shrugged.

Jayden's gaze darted between both of them and landed on Ethan. He opened his mouth, but couldn't think of a thing to say.

A soldier opened the carriage door and grabbed Logan's arms. Logan jolted from sleep. In one fluid movement, he bashed his head into the soldier's nose.

Three soldiers dragged Logan to the ground and one swung his mace toward Logan's stomach.

"Stop!" Chloe and Jayden screamed.

Balton's hand curled around the soldier's wrist

"Stand down," Balton said. "This one is mine." He motioned for the soldiers to bring the rest of them out.

The people congregated to watch the spectacle as the soldiers lined their prisoners up in front of the stone building.

Ethan glanced at Ryan, warning him not to do anything stupid.

Ryan looked at Chloe and Jayden, and then nodded once.

A hard-looking man—a captain by the look of his insignia— limped toward them followed by a dozen soldiers. Their chain mail clinked as they formed ranks behind him. The captain's red hair spilled out from beneath the helmet he wore. "What did you bring me, General?"

"Captain Rarek." Balton clasped the man's shoulder. "I'm glad you could be here for the delivery. I found a few runaway Children. The queen collects tomorrow, doesn't she?"

"First, we have to make sure we're actually sending Children to the queen." Rarek nodded toward a soldier who dipped his head and hurried away.

Balton's gaze snapped to his prisoners. "I'll have them stripped down."

Beside Ethan, Jayden sucked in a breath.

Rarek held up his hand. "No need. The governor has his own ways of finding out." With squinted eyes he looked at Logan. "What's he here for?"

Balton's lips curved up. "Answers."

"Tyrone," Rarek said.

A burly man with at least six inches on Logan stepped forward.

Rarek motioned to Logan. "The general needs some information out of this prisoner."

Tyrone cracked a smile as he slammed his fist into his palm. "What do you want out of him?"

"How he got to be traveling with four Children of the Blood Moon, who his informant in Acaitha is, and how he knows my name."

Logan chuckled.

"Don't think you'll break?" Balton's fist connected with Logan's cheek, snapping his head to the side. Slowly, Logan faced the general and spat. Red flecks peppered Balton's face.

Ethan sucked in a deep breath. Could he count on Logan to put his thirst for revenge aside and help them escape? Ethan knew all too well how consuming revenge was.

CHAPTER 41

A BRAVE FACE

Jayden's stomach pressed into a ball as the soldiers muscled Logan toward the stone building. The general would make sure he suffered. This was all her fault. She should have run sooner. Now Logan would be tortured, and the rest of them shipped to the queen.

The queen. What would that woman do when she got her hands on them? Jayden's stomach squeezed harder. How would she defeat a sorceress? She couldn't even get out of this mess.

Rarek's men lined up behind the prisoners. One thrust the butt of his spear into her back. "No trouble, you hear?"

She swallowed hard.

The gathered crowd parted down the middle, announcing the entrance of six armed soldiers who surrounded a frail-looking man. Jayden inched closer to Chloe.

"I have been told we have new prisoners." The frail man spoke in a monotone with a permanent whine that reminded Jayden of her town teacher. "Queen Idla has declared war on the Feravolk. That includes Children. Any Children we find are to be handed over to her to be executed on the grounds of treason."

The crowd bellowed, "Death to the Feravolk! Death to the Children!"

Jayden's heart stalled. *Treason?*

The frail man cocked a white, bushy eyebrow at Chloe. "I shall test you first." He held out a pasty arm and curled bony fingers. "The dust."

A soldier produced a pouch from his pocket and handed it over. The frail man sprinkled purple sand into his palm, where it collected into a mound, then he brought his hand to his pale lips and blew the violet dust at Chloe. It turned into a green cloud around her face. Some wafted in front of Jayden and turned a brilliant red.

"She isn't one of them, governor," a soldier said to the frail man as he motioned to Chloe.

"I can see that." His nasal voice snapped. The governor turned to Ethan and Ryan. The purple dust cloud turned bright red in front of them also.

The skeletal man rocked back on his heels. "The one who isn't a Child is free to go. Escort her out of the city, and make sure she doesn't come back."

The soldiers advanced, separating Chloe from the rest of them.

Panic crossed Chloe's face. "They've done nothing wrong!"

"Chloe, please," Ryan said, his eyes pleading with her. "Just go."

Tears wet her eyes. "You—promise me you'll—" She broke off and her face scrunched up.

Ethan leaned around the man separating him from his sister. "Hey, Chloe, look at me."

Her glistening eyes met his.

"I'll make sure he's okay."

Tears dripped down her cheeks.

As the guards pushed them closer to the stone building, Jayden searched Chloe's emotions. Sorrow and fear weakened her knees. She'd find a way out of this somehow. Some way, Creator willing.

The large, wooden double doors creaked open, and the scents of blood and urine, feces, and sweat wafted out. Jayden heaved.

Six cells flanked the east and west walls—three on each side— and an aisle big enough for three burly men to walk shoulder to shoulder ran down the center. Rust-colored bars made up the cell doors. One chair sat against the back wall, bathed in sunlight from the open doors behind Jayden. No one sat in it now, but she assumed one of the guards pushing her into this putrid place would take up that post.

Were there any windows?

There—a small, circular one on the wall above the chair. Too high for anyone to reach. And too small to crawl through, unless she was a rat.

The ground in the aisle was dirt packed hard and tight. No digging out anytime soon, especially with a guard watching.

The only way in or out was the door on the southern wall.

Two prisoners already sat in a cell—women, both of them. They didn't seem that interested in the presence of new prisoners. One had reddish-blonde shoulder-length hair, the other had waist-length hair like corn silk. Both had piercing eyes and identical shifty gazes.

The soldiers unbound Jayden and pushed her into their cell. Hay lined a small portion of the packed-dirt floor. She peered through the rusted cross-hatched bars of her prison door to see Ryan and Ethan in a cell across from hers. They rubbed their raw wrists.

The two other prisoners in her cell were also Children. Both of them bore the birthmark, one on the back of her left hand, and the other on the back of her right. One wore a blue dress, the other a red one. Their wrinkled clothes and gnarled hair showed at least one night had been spent on the dingy hay.

All but the largest soldier exited. Instead he took his seat at the chair in the back. It groaned as he sat on it.

Silence hung in the prison. Jayden heard every sniffle. She welcomed each noise, pretending the sounds could distract her from Ethan's emotions. They lapped over her with every beat of her heart, and she could do nothing to turn them off.

He paced in his cell, wearing that face of stone, but fear and protectiveness pulsed through him with such force, she almost believed they were her feelings. Of course he would feel the danger threatening them, his very good friends. Whenever his brown eyes met hers, the fear in him exploded.

Jayden's stomach clenched. If he did something stupid to try and save them and got killed for it, she'd never forgive him. Or herself.

"The guard is asleep, you know."

Jayden spun around to see which of her cellmates had spoken. She wore a deep red dress, slender like her. Her eyes were a greenish blue. She seemed . . . bitter. It was the only word Jayden could think of to describe her sneer.

"You can't be sure." Ryan shot her a dubious glance.

"Oh, he's asleep," the other woman said from her spot on the floor. Her eyes matched her blue dress.

This woman didn't seem the trustworthy type. A knot formed in Jayden's stomach. *Stop feeling sorry for yourself. Do something about this.*

For some reason, she recalled the words written to her in Anna's last message:

Have faith, Child. The Creator always chooses the right Child. Your talents were given to you for a reason. They serve you well much of the time. Other times they overwhelm you—especially the ability to know what others are feeling. Do not be afraid to use your talents, dear one. Fear is a suffocating thing. Just remember the one thing that is stronger than fear: love.

Okay. Then it was time to stop being afraid of her talent and start using it. Jayden reached out with her talent into the heart of the woman in blue. She seemed relaxed, unafraid.

"We've been here for days. You'll all be lucky. The wagon comes tomorrow to take us to the queen." Red Dress laughed.

Ethan neared the bars of his cell. "What will the queen do with us?"

Jayden shuddered, because for the moment Ethan matched the calm woman's mood—relaxed, confident, and intrigued. Heavens, he was cocky.

Both women shrugged, but the one in red answered, "I can only imagine. There have been rumors that she tests you to see if you are the deliverers. Some say she tortures you, kills you, befriends you, makes you part of her army. The possibilities are endless."

"I'm sure we'll be able to make friends with the queen—if we play nice." Ryan winked.

"You're quite the charmer." The woman in red faced him.

Ryan flashed a smile as he leaned his elbows against the bars of his prison.

Jayden dropped her jaw. What was he doing?

"Kara. This is my sister, Thea." The blonde in red introduced herself and her cellmate.

Thea sprouted a seductive smile. The two might not look identical, but they certainly had similar facial expressions. "Your friend seems shy. Doesn't he like a pretty lady?"

Ethan glanced at the women. No, he looked them over. "I don't like being caged."

"Don't mind him." Ryan's lips slid into a lopsided smile. "He's a bit esoteric."

"Well, we have two things in common, then," Kara said. "But I'm guessing the similarities stop there."

Ethan cocked an eyebrow.

Kara's lips curved in the corners. "Underneath that tough exterior you're a sweet thing aren't you?"

"Hardly."

"Ooh, you're feisty. A soldier? Seen any battles?"

Ethan grabbed the bars of his cell.

"Got any scars?" Kara's eyes wandered over his whole body.

Heat hit Jayden's cheeks and coursed through every vein.

Ethan just chuckled.

"Yep. Too soft for me," Kara said. "But I noticed your sword belt. You know how to wield a sword? Or do you just keep it in the scabbard to avoid being cut?"

One side of Ethan's mouth curved up and he locked gazes with Kara. What were those boys up to?

The double doors swung wide and the setting sun's light poured inside. Jayden clasped her hand over her mouth as two soldiers dragged Logan in. Blood dripped from his face and saturated his stained shirt. A cut under his eye looked like it needed stitches, his nose was likely broken—the bruises around his eyes made that much clear—and one of his eyes had swollen shut.

The soldiers tossed him into his cell, and he groaned as he

slumped against the back wall, clutching his side. Were his ribs broken? Jayden's knees weakened. They would kill Logan here.

Tyrone, the huge bald man, slammed Logan's cell door closed. "Don't worry, my friend. The carriage comes from the queen in the morning. I'll send for more persuading equipment. Then we'll talk like old pals. Your precious cargo will be on its way to the palace, so you'll have no one else to talk to anyway."

Tyrone dusted his hands before he strode out. The soldiers opened the doors for him and followed on his heels.

Jayden moved as close to Logan as her prison bars would allow. "Are you okay?"

"Don't worry about me, Jayden. I'll be fine." Logan waved her off. His voice rasped. Of course it did. He'd probably been screaming.

Every eye turned to the snoring prison guard as he snorted, scratched his stomach, and settled back into his groaning chair.

"I've got a plan," Thea said.

Jayden wanted to slap the seductive smile off of her face, and then Kara's too, just because she could.

"Care to share?" Ethan's whisper grew harsh.

Thea laughed and motioned to the sleeping guard. "Not in front of him."

Jayden pressed her palms into her eyes. The emotional tension in the room suffocated her thoughts.

The sisters settled on the ground with their backs pressed against the cell bars. Kara picked up a twig. Dusting the hay aside, she revealed the dirt floor underneath. The stick pushed into the dirt as she began to write.

Jayden stared at the letters on the ground: *You feeling guilty about something, Deliverer?*

What? Jayden was sure they could hear her pounding heart.

Kara passed the stick to her sister. Thea's handwriting nearly matched her sister's: *I can tell you're one of the deliverers. It's my little secret.* She tapped the Blood Moon birthmark on her left hand.

Jayden held out her hand for the stick. Gripping it tight, she sat next to Kara and wrote: *So what?*

Thea's face lit up as she asked for the stick back: *We want to defeat the queen.*

Kara took the stick from her sister and smoothed the dirt over so she had room to write: *You in?*

Jayden's heart thumped. This could be it. This was the alliance she needed. Her hands shook when she grabbed the stick. *What's the plan?*

The sisters exchanged smiles. It was Thea who wrote: *We break out of here and get you to the palace. Only a deliverer can defeat her, but we can get you very close.*

With every word she read, Jayden's heart beat faster. Her fingers curled around the thin wood. *How will you get us out of here?*

Kara slipped the stick from Jayden. *That part is easy. We're assassins.* With a cocked eyebrow, she pulled a thin tube out from her bodice and a sharp, wooden dart from her pocket. She slipped the items away and then wrote: *Ever heard of tangle flower?*

Jayden's eyes grew wide. Of course she had. Every wise woman knew about it, and *only* the wise women knew about it. If ingested or put into the bloodstream, just a dab of tangle flower would put a grown man to sleep for hours.

Kara chuckled.

Jayden took the stick Kara dangled in front of her. The tip pressed into the packed dirt, and she wrote: *As long as my friends aren't a part of this, I'm in.*

Kara pulled the stick from Jayden's hand. *Don't worry about them. We'll make sure they get out of this. They'll have no idea you're headed to the palace to kill the queen.*

Jayden scarcely read the words before Kara's boot rubbed the dirt smooth. Three little words were burned into her mind: *kill the queen.* She was going to do it. The problem was, she had no idea how.

Thea slipped her hand up her sleeve and pulled out a small knife.

Jayden gaped. Before she could ask how the woman smuggled that in, Thea's finger touched her lips. She slid the blade over her palm. Blood trickled out of the new cut. She passed the weapon to Kara.

Kara cut her palm and passed the knife to Jayden.

Jayden cheated a glance over her shoulder at the guys and made sure to hide what she held.

Ryan's eyebrows shot up; Ethan's pulled together.

She squeezed closer to Kara to further block their view and slid the blade across her hand. A twinge shot through her before the blood started to pool in her palm.

Two warm, wet hands shook hers. Salt stung the wound, sealing the promise. She handed the knife back to Thea.

The assassin smiled. "Keep it."

With renewed hope, Jayden cleaned it off and stashed it up her sleeve. She was going to face Idla with two assassins. Hopefully she'd picked the right allies.

CHAPTER 42

UNEXPECTED CONSEQUENCES

Sunlight spilled through the one window in the room. Logan lifted his head. He'd fallen asleep, sitting with his back against the stone wall of the prison. Shifting his weight reminded him of his recent beating. At least he could see out of his right eye again. He pressed his back harder into the wall and let the dull ache in his bruised sides intensify. The pain was deserved. Some protector he'd turned out to be.

He glanced to the other cells. Everyone still slept except Jayden's two cellmates. What had Jayden called them? Right. Thea and Kara. Whatever their names were, he didn't trust them.

Hooves thumped against the ground outside. The heavy man who had kept the night's watch rose from his chair and stretched, then walked over to the door and opened it. The burst of sunlight called the prisoners to stand.

Soldiers filtered in and lined up down the center of the narrow walkway between the cells. The pale, bony governor from last night nestled himself between them again. General Balton strode in behind him, his helmet polished.

Heat coursed through Logan's blood and he balled his hands into fists.

"The prisoners are to be taken to the queen, who will punish them for treason," the governor said in his wispy voice. "The iron carriage awaits."

Balton neared Logan's cell and raised Logan's sword into the sunlight.

"Have you ever seen a weapon of such quality? The Feravolk are known to make such well-crafted swords. I keep weapons from men I've killed, and I'll relish using this one, but today isn't the day you die. The queen wished me home, and she wants you to come along." He leaned closer to Logan's cell. "You should have told me you and Queen Idla were such old friends. I could have been more accommodating."

Logan didn't flinch, but a wolfish growl rose in his throat.

"Oh, I think we'll be getting to know one another well." Balton laughed.

Logan wanted to kill Balton. Grab him and throw a rope around his neck. Stomp on his chest. Watch him scream just like Balton had done to him.

Balton leaned against Logan's prison. "Isn't your wife one of the queen's advisors? She is beautiful. Her hair smells like roses."

Red ones.

"I know her well. Perhaps as well as you do."

Hot, jealous rage filled Logan, but he kept his voice even. Somehow he kept it even. "Be careful. You don't know the spider has bitten until your arm swells."

"Your wife is hardly a spider."

"Tell me, does she whisper my name when you kiss her?"

Balton raised his hand to strike, and Logan turned his face and closed his eyes.

Balton's deep laugh sent a chill through his core. What a fool Logan had been. Of course Balton couldn't reach him in his cell. Too late. He'd already shown weakness.

Logan opened his eyes to find Balton's face close to the cell bars. His fingers curled into a fist and he threw a punch at the general's face. Balton moved fast and Logan's elbow knocked into the cell bars as he retracted his arm. Balton lunged forward and thrust the tip of

Logan's sword into the cell. Logan backed away from the blade and looked into the general's eyes.

Balton's eyes narrowed. "It seems I have more unfinished business with you than I thought. Now, let's see how you like the iron cage. You'll have to tell me about the ride later, since I'll be in something a bit more comfortable."

Balton chuckled before he and his shiny helmet disappeared through the door.

The iron cage backed into the opening of Galea's prison and blocked the exit. Logan scanned the setup for a weakness, but found only one: a small opening under the carriage by the back wheels looked large enough for them to slip under. Not that it would do them any good—there was no time to wiggle through the opening with so many soldiers.

His stomach squeezed. He'd failed.

"Load up the prisoners," said the governor.

One by one, the cell doors unlatched and soldiers with swords advanced inside with rope. Logan held his hands forward. The weight of what he'd done crashed down around him, and his hands shook.

"I found Chloe. Don't worry, I'll get help," Westwind called to him.

"You won't make it in time."

"But I'll be trying. Don't quit."

Logan breathed. *Creator, help me.* Before the rope fastened on Logan's wrists, the soldier tying his hands together fell.

Another fell.

Logan looked around. Above the growing commotion, he heard a soft sound like a forced breath. Thea caught his eye. He watched her mouth open slightly. Her lips pressed into a tiny circle. She raised a small tube to her mouth. Her cheeks puffed out and a barb flew. Another soldier fell, clasping a hand to his neck.

The bony, white-haired governor crumpled to the floor.

"What in the name—" That soldier silenced.

Ethan grabbed a sword from the fallen man in front of him. Logan ripped the ropes from his wrists and stole a sword.

In moments, all of them were armed. The iron cage still blocked the door. As soon as Balton found out what was going on in the prison, he would scramble to get it moved. For now, the small opening under the carriage was the only way out.

Logan pointed to it. "Run! Ethan, get out there and cover them. The rest of you, go!"

Ethan hurried out, sliding along his belly. Logan sent the others after him and prayed they'd make it to the woods behind the prison.

When they'd all made it out, Logan dove to the ground. Dust sprayed his face as he slid beneath the carriage.

"Move the carriage!"

Someone had spotted them. Logan could only hope those kids had run. The wheel moved. Logan rolled his body out of the way and sprang up. Soldiers of the queen raced toward the prison from their stately carriage. There were too many to handle alone. But he wasn't alone. Kara and Thea stood on his left, weapons ready. Ethan flanked his right.

Logan pushed the kid's shoulder. "I told you to take over if I fail."

"You haven't failed yet."

"Ethan, who will she have if we both die?"

"Then go. She needs you more than me."

Logan wasn't sure.

"If you two are going to argue like a married couple, can it wait? We're busy here." Kara shot them a sneer.

"We should all run," Thea said.

Kara stared at her sister. "What?"

"They're going to get by us anyway. If we split up, we'll split them up."

Kara nodded, and she and Thea sprinted off.

Logan pushed Ethan toward the trees. "She's right."

The kid glared back at him.

"Run, Ethan. Standing here is killing me."

Ethan swore, then he ran. Logan followed him. Ethan almost made it to the trees before he turned. A look of panic crossed his face and he pointed, then crumpled to the ground.

"Ethan?" Logan's legs pumped harder. He scanned the direction Ethan had motioned. Thea's dark blue eyes stared back at him from the trees.

Something pricked his skin. His hand flew up to his neck, and touched the tiny shaft of a dart before he fell.

CHAPTER 43

SHARP TONGUE

Ropes burned Jayden's skin as she tried to loosen the bindings around her wrists. A wall of trees rose up on either side of them as they followed the road through the woods. They were headed right to the palace, no doubt.

Logan still lay sleeping on the floor of the iron carriage while Ethan and Ryan sat on either side of Jayden—also asleep thanks to Kara's and Thea's darts coated in tangle flower.

Some allies they'd turned out to be. Anger burned in Jayden's chest. She'd trusted them, and for what? And why would they lead her on anyway?

One of the iron carriage's wheels hit a rock and it bounced. Ryan groaned.

Jayden scooted closer to him as his eyelids fluttered open.

He shook his head. "What happened?"

"Those girls." Ethan's voice was bitter. He sat up and shook his head.

"We ended up in this bloody contraption anyway." Ryan tried sawing his bindings against the iron bars.

"You'd better quit that, boy!" the driver of the carriage behind them shouted.

"Or what?" Ryan sawed harder.

A whip cracked against the iron bars, and Ryan moved his hands just in time to avoid being injured. The soldier holding the weapon shot him a smile.

Jayden's heart jumped. She leaned close to Ethan and whispered, "There's a knife up my sleeve."

His eyebrows shot up.

Ryan's did too. He eyed the soldiers on the carriage behind them. "I'll keep watch," he whispered. Then he neared the back of the carriage, careful not to step on Logan.

Jayden put her back to Ethan so he could reach her sleeve. His fingers inched up her sleeve and fumbled to find the knife. At last he slid the weapon free.

Ryan placed his bound hands against the carriage bars again, catching the attention of the soldier with the whip. "So, how long till we reach the palace?"

The soldier with the whip cocked his head, likely trying to figure out Ryan's game.

"Not talkative? Or has the general cut out your tongue? Is he still doing that? My father knew a guy who got his tongue cut out by the general."

Jayden couldn't help but smile. Ryan could converse with anyone. Hopefully it would be enough of distraction. She glanced at Ethan. His jaw was tight as he worked to saw through his bindings.

"It's barbaric, really. I mean a guy's tongue? How do you eat without a tongue? Do you taste anything? There's a bright side, though. You'd have good luck choosing a bride. I mean, you've got first pick of all the pretty ones who can't cook."

The soldier whipped his arm back and forth, and the black, snake-like weapon snapped against the bars near Ryan's hands. "Shut up."

"He *does* speak!" Ryan glanced at Jayden. Then his eyes grew wide and he whispered, "You guys about done, 'cause I think we're there."

Jayden turned around. The tree line surrounding them ended and opened up to a meadow. The dirt road cut the green grass in half and led straight up to the massive castle on a hill. Its black spires towered into the sky. The queen's flags, white with a red silhouette of a muzzled dragon, rippled in the wind. The wall surrounding the palace was massive, not made of crude, crumbling stone or weak sticks. This stone was cut into squares and the wooden drawbridge looked sturdy, strong. Impossible to escape. Jayden's mouth went dry.

"Here." Ethan's elbow nudged Jayden's arm. He pressed the knife hilt into her hands.

They were so shaky she was sure she'd nick herself. Flipping the weapon over, she laid the blade's sharp edge on the ropes and started cutting.

Logan sucked in a breath and sat up. He winced, likely still sore from his session with Tyrone. His eyes widened, and Jayden could only assume he saw the palace.

The carriage lurched to a stop. A drawbridge lowered in front of them.

Jayden's bindings loosened. Perhaps she could squeeze one hand out. Yes. Her heart pounded. She locked eyes with Ethan.

He nodded and got onto his knees. "You okay, Logan?"

She couldn't see the look he shot the others, but Logan and Ryan both got on their knees in line with Ethan and faced the carriage behind theirs. Their bodies gave her a perfect wall. She could remove their bindings if there was enough time. She snuck behind Logan and sawed through his ropes.

Horse hooves clopped against the wooden drawbridge. They'd be in the outer court in moments. With sweaty palms, she cut through Ryan's bindings.

"Hey, where's the girl? You three move." The whip flew in between the metal bars and smacked against the floor in front of Logan's knee.

Jayden sawed harder. At last, Ryan's ropes fell to the floor. Jayden kicked them over the side of the carriage, then slipped the knife back up her sleeve.

Ryan moved so the soldiers could see her. "Honestly, where did you think she was going?"

The soldier's lips formed a thin line. The whip connected with Ryan's thigh and he flinched. "Didn't I tell you to shut up?"

The carriage lurched to a halt. They were now in the outer court, surrounded by merchant stands full of fresh produce. Tomatoes so plump and red they made the ones her family grew look like shriveled plums. Only the best for the queen. Must be nice to be able to control the rain.

A dozen fresh soldiers raced over to the carriage. The one with the crescent-moon shaped scar on his cheek eyed Ethan and smiled like a child with a forbidden box of expensive chocolates. His chuckle made Jayden step back. "Looks like my *dog* has returned to his master. You won't get away this time."

Dog? She leaned near Ethan. "You know him?"

Ethan just stared at the soldier, hate burning in his eyes. He glanced at Logan who nodded once.

Logan looked at her. "You let us protect you. Do you understand?" Without waiting for an answer, he turned to Ryan. "Take Jayden and run."

The door to the iron cage squealed open.

Ethan blocked the exit, unwilling to move. The soldier who'd called him a dog reached for Ethan's shirt collar. Ethan stepped forward, grabbed the soldier's sword and bashed the man's nose with his forehead. Blood streamed from the soldier's face, and he toppled off the carriage steps.

"He's free! Grab him!" a commanding voice yelled.

Soldiers scrambled closer to the carriage as Ethan—sword in hand—jumped out. Logan followed and motioned for Ryan to take Jayden back toward the horses.

Ryan waved for Jayden to follow, and she ducked between the carriages.

Balton barked orders. "Take them alive!"

The sound of metal against metal rang in the courtyard. Ryan tugged her sleeve. Her eyes met his for a heartbeat. Her chest ached. She couldn't leave the others to rot in the palace. She had to get them out of there somehow.

Soldiers scurried around the carriages. The thumping of their boots matched her heart. The drawbridge was closed, the horses bound to the carriages. Townsfolk grabbed their children and ducked behind their vendor carts. She had to get out from between these carriages. The vendor area looked like the best place to blend in. Ryan's hand closed around her wrist. He pointed to an apple cart not far from them, then he shoved her.

She bolted, but he didn't follow. Jayden ducked behind the apple cart and scanned for him. People running everywhere blocked her view. She crawled to the other side of the apple cart and peered around it. Two soldiers brought Ryan into her view. Her heart leapt into her throat. Ethan and Logan were also being held by several soldiers.

"You'll pay for what you did!" The man whose face Ethan had bashed in stood in front of him. His fist shot forward and connected with Ethan's temple. Again and again he punched Ethan's ear until blood dripped out. The soldier would kill him.

Jayden raced toward them. "No!"

She flew in between Ethan and the man's fist. Pressing against Ethan's body, she squeezed her eyes shut and braced for the punch.

"Stop!" Balton's voice rose above everything.

Her body trembled as she waited, but no fist slammed against her. Ethan's chest heaved against her back.

Jayden cracked an eye open to see the general standing in front of her.

"Isn't this an interesting development?" His eyes narrowed in what looked like pleasure. She would not search his emotions. He leaned closer. "Take them to the queen."

CHAPTER 44

EYE OF
THE BEHOLDER

Rebekah clasped the necklace together and let the sapphire fall into the dip of her collarbone. Another thin golden chain hung around her neck and disappeared beneath her dress. That chain held her marriage stone, but it was hidden enough that Idla had stopped complaining about it.

The sapphire was a gift, and Rebekah had been instructed to wear it tonight. She was dressed in the brilliant blue gown, which reminded her of glacial runoff, and ready for Oswell to escort her to the throne room.

Her reflection in the mirror above her dresser showed an emotionless woman—at least she hoped that was how she looked. Idla never summoned her to the throne room unless she intended to make some sort of example. Sometimes of Rebekah, sometimes of someone else.

Rebekah's hands trembled as she opened her drawer. Thea's gift—the crushed tangle flower seed—was still hidden beneath her clothes, undisturbed. That didn't mean the assassin hadn't double-crossed her, though. Rebekah had been certain Thea and Kara were trying to help her escape for their own reasons, but she had wanted to go along with it. Hopefully she hadn't missed her window of opportunity.

Those two were still possible allies in her own plan. She might make enemies out of them in the process, but Connor was the one who mattered. And Thea had been right about one thing. It was time to focus on her Destiny Path, not just survival.

A knock told her Connor stood outside.

She closed the drawer. "Come."

He entered, glancing over his shoulder first. When his eyes met hers, he straightened his back. "You look lovely." The look on his face told more of his suspicion than an actual compliment. "I've never seen that dress. What's going on?"

She smiled. "The queen has summoned me to the throne room."

"Wearing that? Does she plan to marry you off?"

"I hope not. I'm already married."

He winced. "I've been summoned for a hunting trip and sparring lesson *off* castle grounds."

Coupled with Rebekah's summons, that could not be good news.

"I thought it seemed suspicious." Connor grabbed a pear from the fruit bowl and bit in. "Now I know it is."

"Tell me you're not going to remain here for my sake."

"I'm not going to tell you anything." He smiled, bright and convincing. "That way there's no reason for Belladonna to spot a lie."

"You have to stop trying to protect me."

His eyebrows pinched together. "Trying? I thought I was doing a decent job." He picked up an apple then froze for a heartbeat, tilting his head toward the door. "Are you expecting Oswell?"

"Yes."

"He's on his way."

"Then you'd better leave if you're already supposed to be gone."

"No time."

"Connor."

He dismissed her worry with a wave of his hand. "I got this. I'll see you . . . well, tomorrow. Stay safe." He slipped the apple into his pocket and opened the door to reveal Oswell on the other side, one hand extended as if he was getting ready to knock, the other balanced a tea tray.

Connor squeezed out the tiny space between Oswell and the doorframe, causing Oswell to step back and nearly lose the tray. He steadied it and shot Connor a pinched look—the closest thing to a glare Rebekah had ever seen on his face. "Connor, I thought you would be headed out."

"Only just." Connor held up his half-eaten pear. "Can't hunt on an empty stomach."

"I suppose not."

Connor leaned over to inspect the tray, which Oswell tucked slightly closer to his chest. Connor slipped a payn puff off the tray and held it between his teeth, then took another. His muffled "thank you" followed him down the hallway.

Oswell watched Connor leave for much longer than Rebekah thought necessary.

Now there was no way Connor would leave, not when everyone seemed to have an agenda that involved splitting the two of them up for the evening.

Oswell turned back to Rebekah. "Well, it seems your dessert pastries have absconded."

"Please." Rebekah couldn't help but laugh as she ushered Oswell into the room.

He set the tray on the table and proceeded to pour her some tea.

Rebekah stared at the steaming tea.

"Is something the matter?" he asked.

Her fingers curled around the table. Oswell could not detect lies like Belladonna could, but the question still set her on edge. She composed herself and put on a soft smile. "I was expecting to be summoned to the throne room. Has something delayed the meeting?"

Postponed it indefinitely would be more wonderful, but this was Oswell, not some general servant sent to bring her tea. Oswell, who never had a hair out of place or a smudge on his shoe. Oswell, who took orders from the queen directly.

Oswell, who knew far more than any servant should.

"No." He answered her without glancing up. "Honey or cream?"

"None. Thank you." Rebekah sat, back straight, and Oswell placed the cup in front of her.

"Her Majesty wants you to come very soon. She believes you should have some tea to—how did she put it—calm your nerves."

Poison.

Rebekah's heart beat so fast she was sure Oswell could see the pulse jumping in her neck. She smoothed her features. No emotion. "I must drink it, then?"

"It would behoove you to. Don't worry. Queen Idla needs you alive."

"For what purpose."

Oswell's smile grew wicked and he looked down his long, hooked nose at her. "Drink, and I'll tell you."

She shook her head. Oswell would be easy to overpower. Slowly, she stood. She could kick him and knock him out, but where would that leave Connor when she didn't show up to the throne room with Oswell leading?

"Connor is with five of my trained soldiers. One wrong move, and I'll arrange an accident. Of course, I'll have to keep him alive, since we can't kill a deliverer before Idla uses them for her purposes."

"I simply stood to fetch my napkin. You neglected to give it to me."

He handed it to her without taking his gaze from her face.

Rebekah sat, spread the napkin across her lap, picked up the cup, and downed the tea. It poured over her tongue, bitter and hot, and burned the back of her throat.

"There. See? No harm." Oswell poured the rest out the window. "Though your free will belongs to Idla for a while. She'll need to make sure you don't recognize anyone tonight—just in case it would cause her to lose your loyalty. Little does she know, you're not loyal to her at all, are you?"

Rebekah's heart sped. But her thoughts seemed so clouded.

Oswell smiled. "Don't worry. We all have secrets. Agendas. Plans to usurp the throne. Your secret is safe with me. You're a pawn I'd like to have stay in the game for as long as possible." He stood and held out his arm for her to link elbows with him. "Now. Shall we?"

Rebekah stood and a cloud seemed to cover her vision.

"Oswell?" Her voice seemed distant. As if it wasn't hers. As if she were hearing someone else speaking while she bordered the edge of a dream. Not fully awake nor asleep. "Why tell me these things?"

"There's no harm. You won't remember anyway."

She linked her arm in his, and, though she didn't want to, she followed him out of her room and down the hall toward the throne room.

"Wait here until I come for you." He motioned for her to sit on a golden chair with a red velvet cushion.

Rebekah complied. Her thoughts seemed prisoners in her mind. Whatever was going to happen on the other side of that door, she wouldn't be able to stop.

Harsh hands gripped Jayden's shoulders and held her steady. Her knees wouldn't stop trembling.

"Hold still." The gruff soldier gave her shoulders a shake.

With her ankles bound, she couldn't compensate for her loss of balance. Coarse rope bit into her wrists as she stumbled.

The soldier grabbed a fistful of her hair and yanked her head back.

"You'll get your chance to kneel." His chuckle was deep.

Shoes scuffed the marble floor as Ethan struggled against his soldiers, and Ryan glared at the man behind Jayden. She cringed. They needed to stop trying to protect her.

"There's no reason to be rough with her." Ryan's voice hovered just above a whisper.

One of the soldiers guarding Ryan smacked his head, but Jayden's soldier loosened his grip on her. "Quiet."

She glanced at Ryan, and he gave her an encouraging smile. Leave it to Ryan to think there was a silver lining. He'd probably chastised the soldier as much for her as for Ethan. Every time someone thrust a spear butt into her back, Ethan lunged at them. He now had four soldiers assigned to keep him "compliant," as Balton called it.

Ethan's lip was already split, a purple bruise formed beneath his right eye, and dried blood caked his left ear, but he hadn't said a word since they left the iron carriage. He just watched everything like a caged gryphon.

The soldier who'd called Ethan his dog sported a pair of black eyes and a swollen nose thanks to Ethan's head, and he paced in front of Ethan, glaring, as if he wanted more payback.

And Logan—his face was worse than Ethan's. It was a wonder General Balton had kept him alive, though he probably had some vengeful plan in mind too.

Footsteps echoed down the hall. Each tap reverberated off the towering stone walls. Jayden shivered, but not because the palace was cold. Idla was coming.

Cool air wafted in as the crimson double doors opened. Jayden's stomach twisted, forcing out a small whine.

A woman with dark, reddish-brown hair strode into the room. She wore a golden crown encrusted with emeralds and diamonds. Her dress, a deep green, enhanced her icy blue eyes.

Jayden gaped. She recognized the woman from the drawings she'd seen, but Idla was far more beautiful than any sketch artist's rendering.

A handsome young man with similar piercing blue eyes walked on her right. He must be Franco, her son, but Jayden couldn't place the seductive woman in black on the queen's left. Her skin was pale, like she never saw the sun, and her lips redder than any natural skin tone would make them. Her long, dark hair was pulled into a tight ponytail and her eyes—almost black—met Jayden's gaze. She smiled like a cat with a crippled mouse.

A score of soldiers followed them.

A thin man with a long, hooked nose stepped forward. "Kneel before the queen."

"She's not my queen." Logan's voice echoed in the high-ceilinged throne room.

Balton twirled a mace in his gloved hand. He swung the mace at the backs of Logan's legs and his knees slammed into the marble floor. Jayden's stomach squeezed tighter.

The soldier with the black eyes smirked, and mimicked Balton's action with his mace. Ethan's knees hit the floor and he winced, but he kept his back straight and his shoulders squared.

Balton blocked Jayden's view and his eyes locked onto her. "Anyone else need a reminder?"

A chuckle rumbled in Ryan's chest, and Jayden shot him a worried look. He wouldn't dare say anything stupid here. Would he?

He clicked his tongue. "You know, I completely forgot what I was supposed to be doing."

Balton's mace hit the back of Ryan's knees. He went down and he buckled over. The metal sculpture on the end of Balton's weapon pressed under Ryan's jaw. Balton pushed, forcing Ryan's head up. "I will relish making you into one of my soldiers. They don't talk back."

Ryan swallowed several times before Balton released him. The general whirled around and swung his weapon again. A stinging thwack hit Jayden's legs and forced her knees to bend. Pain shot through them as they slammed into the floor. She curled over.

As she straightened, she caught sight of Ryan's concerned expression. His silver-lining smile was gone.

The queen sank onto her throne, and her icy eyes scanned each of them. Jayden's blood turned cold.

Idla's fingers tapped against her armrests. "They cannot all be deliverers, Logan, since two are young men and, as you know, I already have your son."

Logan met her eyes. "You forget who you are dealing—"

She waved her hand. "It is almost painful to watch you threaten me now. Do not worry. If you didn't bring me the deliverers in this batch, you will have time to make it up to me. After you are broken, you will help me find anything."

"I'd die first."

"My healers will make sure that doesn't happen." She leaned forward and gripped the edge of her armrests.

Jayden shot Logan a glance. Could she really use healers to keep people alive for torture?

Idla's lips slid into a terrible smile. "I have a nice place for you in my dungeon, Logan. I thought you might like to reunite with your wife first. Oswell, fetch Rebekah."

The thin man who had announced the queen scurried to the crimson doors. When he opened them, a beautiful woman with long, blonde hair stood on the other side. She kept her back straight and her gaze forward as she walked up to the queen.

"Your Majesty." She curtseyed low.

"Rebekah, say hello to Logan." Idla prompted with a smile.

Rebekah looked at him askance, her eyes seemed clouded and her face held no hint of recognition. "Hello, enemy of the queen."

How could she be so cold?

Logan's gaze fell to the ground, and Jayden's heart ached for him. That was his *wife*. How could she betray him like that?

Idla's smile grew. "Take him away."

"Yes, Your Majesty." Balton gave another humble bow. "But will you let me dispose of him once your torture is done?"

"My, General, I do love your enthusiasm. It piques my curiosity to know what this man has done to offend you, but I want him alive. He is the father of two of the deliverers, and it is said in the Old Custom that the parents will always draw the deliverers close. I think I will keep him around for a time. Then, perhaps, I will let you have your way."

"Thank you, Your Majesty."

Soldiers lifted Logan to his feet and marched him toward the crimson doors.

Jayden's breath caught. She was powerless. Hopeless. Just like when her family was killed. Just like the prison at Galea. She was no warrior to defeat this sorceress. She was nothing. A dagger-wielding daughter of an animal doctor. Anna was wrong.

"Now to find out if any of you are the deliverers I so dearly want to get to know." Idla's cold stare rested on Jayden. "Certainly you are."

Fear, cold and hard, settled into Jayden's stomach. Ethan's fear. She glanced at him and he shook his head. Of course she had to lie or Idla would take her. "No, I'm not."

The queen turned to the woman in black on her left, who wore a satisfied smile as she shook her head.

Idla's eyes lit up like lanterns. "Belladonna says you're lying to me."

What? That woman was too old to be a Child. How could she detect a lie? Jayden's throat closed. The queen knew. She would know everything.

Idla stood. Her emerald green cloak rippled as she walked away from her throne and down the three steps. Her blue eyes searched Jayden's face.

"Lying to me is a dangerous business. You will learn not to keep secrets from me." White hands with red, lacquered nails reached forward, and Idla's long fingers gripped Jayden's chin. "You belong to me now. Let's see if your friends will suffer the same fate."

Her fingers slid from Jayden's skin and a chill skittered over Jayden's body. She had to get them out of here.

Idla turned to Ryan. "Ah, the boy with the sharp tongue. It won't help you here. Now you have seen what Belladonna can do, you know lying is futile. So tell me, are you one of my deliverers?"

A smooth grin curved Ryan's lips. "Lying is never futile."

Jayden swallowed. *Oh, Ryan, don't be stupid.*

Idla's eyes narrowed. "So, you wish to try my patience?"

"I don't wish to, no."

"You want to please me?"

"Who wouldn't?"

"Are you a deliverer?"

"I could be."

Idla glanced at Belladonna, and the woman simply glared daggers at Ryan. Jayden nearly giggled. He was fooling the lie detector?

The queen seemed unruffled. "You are clever, but your running in circles is starting to make Belladonna dizzy. Would you answer a question straight for me?" Her tone dripped honey.

"Absolutely."

"Good. Are you one of the deliverers?"

"If it means I get my knees off this hard-as-rock floor, yes."

Idla looked at Belladonna, and the healer gave her one of those open-mouthed helpless shrugs. She clenched her fists and stared Ryan down. He just shot her a cocky grin.

Idla's hard gaze turned back to Ryan. "Are you admitting to being one of the deliverers?"

"Your Majesty, I don't want any trouble."

"Enough. I can play games too." Idla's eyelid twitched. She calmed her exterior and turned toward Ethan. She glanced at Jayden and a wicked smile spread her lips. "The general tells me you like this one."

No. A shudder ratcheted through her body.

Idla pointed a long finger at Jayden. "Here's how the game works. I ask a simple question, and you will answer, or things will get uncomfortable for him." She nodded and one of the soldiers wrenched Ethan's arms back. He locked one in a tight grip and turned Ethan's arm so it bent the wrong way. Ethan folded over, a grimace plain on his face.

Jayden looked at Ethan, her gaze pleading. His brown eyes glanced in her direction, but his jaw was set. She wasn't to interfere.

Let us protect you, Logan had said. *Do you understand?*

No, she didn't understand this madness. Her heart ached. She couldn't sit by and let them torture Ethan.

Idla's heels clicked against the marble floor. "Is he one of the deliverers?"

The soldier wrenched Ethan's arm slowly.

Ethan cringed.

"Stop!" Jayden shouted. "Stop. They aren't deliverers. They're just protecting me. Let them go!"

Ryan's incredulous stare stabbed her. Ethan wouldn't even look at her.

"I knew we could be reasonable." Idla snapped her fingers and the soldier holding Ethan's arm released him. "Take these three to their cells. We'll have a double execution at sundown." Her blue eyes bored into Jayden. "And you can watch."

Execution? Jayden's insides knotted. "No. Let them go, please."

Idla's right eye twitched. "You do not make decisions here."

Jayden's chest ached. How could she be so foolish? Of course the queen wouldn't just let them go. She'd sentenced them to death.

Soldiers muscled Jayden to her feet, but she kept watch over her shoulder until Ethan finally looked at her. His emotions flooded her. Mostly fear, but his ever stubborn protectiveness matched it. And something else—heartache?

Someone grabbed her chin and forced her to face the queen. Idla stood in front of her with her arms folded.

"Love." The vile woman put her red fingernail under Jayden's chin and tilted her head back too far. She sneered. "Love, affection, devotion, friendship—they are nothing but weaknesses. You never would have made a good queen."

Jayden let out a shaky breath. If she gave up on love, this is what she'd become? Another Idla?

All along Logan and Ethan and even Ryan had been trying to show her that love was important. Love for her family, her friends, and her people would convict her to do things, because she wanted to. Not because of someone else's mistakes or wishes, but because it was her choice. Her friends weren't here with her because it was her fault. Logan had chosen to be her protector. Ethan had chosen to take the oath. And Ryan—he'd made it pretty clear that she couldn't make choices for him. She didn't have to be alone. They were all here, because they'd made a choice to be here. For her. For the Feravolk. For love.

And that's why she was here, too.

She wouldn't fail them.

She ripped her chin from the queen's grip, not caring about the stinging slice Idla's fingernail left on her skin. "I pity the person who has no one's strength to stand on but her own."

The queen shook her head. "See what I mean? You are weak because of love."

Jayden shuddered. How had she almost made herself a monster like this loveless woman? "No. I persevere because of it."

"We shall see how you persevere in my torture chamber."

CHAPTER 45

THE WEIGHT
OF A SWORD

A padded footfall touched the floor. Soft breaths cut through the silence. Someone approached.

Logan waited in the dark. His arms, spread out at his sides and chained to the wall, offered no protection. He stood vulnerable. Even so, his instinct screamed at him to protect himself.

The sound faded. At first he thought the movement must have stopped, then he wondered if he'd imagined it.

"I thought I might find you here." A feminine voice penetrated the emptiness. "Perhaps you remember me from the prison in Galea?"

"The girl who shot me with a sleeping dart?"

"That's right. Thea. Remember?"

"I remember you're not fond of using people's real names."

"That's more my sister's game, but sometimes I play along. It is fun. She didn't call you anything, but I'd be inclined to call you a lone wolf."

"What do you want?" Even if she came to taunt him, he'd at least get some news before he rotted away, or died by someone else's hand. In truth he hoped to die sooner, but he deserved nothing more than to sit in his own filth, slime, and misery. He'd earned the promised torture. He had failed everyone.

"That's complicated."

Her footsteps became clearer. She was close. Her presence was palpable next to him. Logan suddenly ached for the warmth of another human.

She settled next to him. "I have something I think you'll need."

Her lean body pressed up against his side and she nestled her head on his arm. She snuggled closer and put her hand on his chest. He wanted to put his arm around her. Hold her there so she couldn't escape. Ask her where the others were and make her pay for tricking him into trusting her.

Her breath kissed his ear. "I may be the queen's assassin, but she isn't my only employer."

Logan's heart quickened, and Thea chuckled.

"I thought you might like that." Her voice sounded soft and enticing. "See, your job isn't done. I need you to find the deliverers. Idla plans to keep you alive, because they are drawn to you, but I think her reasoning is flawed."

"Oh?"

She moved away from him. Cold air swirled against his side.

Her wicked giggle returned. "Yes. Are you going to ask me how?"

"Sure, I'll play."

"Good. I love games. See, Rebekah doesn't draw any deliverers to her. So I think you need to be free in order to lure them in with your fancy powers."

Logan would have interrupted her with a denial if he didn't taste freedom so close. Still, danger tainted the freedom she offered. It didn't matter this time—he had nothing to lose.

"But I can't free you."

"Then how will you finish your job?" He kept his voice even somehow.

Thea placed her face so close to his, her breath touched his lips. The sound of metal clanking against the stone floor jolted Logan's heart to skip a beat. A key. She gave him a key?

"Oops. How careless of me. Well, I must run. Your torture session starts soon. If I were you, I would leave through the Assassin's Gate. It's the only way out." Her body heat receded. "If you have even one ounce of trust for me, Logan, you will put it in this warning: if you take any other route, you won't make it out alive. Take the Assassin's Gate."

"Where is the Assassin's Gate?"

Nothing but silence. He couldn't even hear her footsteps. She'd left him alone.

Logan pressed his legs against his bindings and slid his feet across the floor as far as the chains allowed. Where was that key? The sound of metal scraping against stone stopped his breath. He'd pushed it out of reach.

His boots hit something. Carefully he picked up his feet and stretched, setting them against the floor. The tip of the key nestled under the edge of his shoe. Logan stilled. He could sense something else. Warmth. He wasn't alone. Another trick.

"Who's there?" he asked into the darkness. "I know you're there." It couldn't just be his imagination. He trusted his instincts again.

"I think you can hear me."

"You're a wolf?"

"Yes, Speaker to the wolves."

"Can you help me?"

"I can."

Now that he knew what to listen for, it was as if deaf ears had been opened. He noticed the quiet padding of a wolf. The key scraped against the floor as the wolf picked it up. Metal touched his palm, and the cool, wet, leathery nose of a wolf.

"Flip it around, and I can release the shackle."

This wolf spoke too much like a human not to be bonded. But to whom? "How did you get here?"

The key's tines pressed into Logan's palm. The key was on a ring, and it wasn't the only one.

"Do you hear that?" the wolf asked.

Voices echoed outside the door.

"Soon you won't be alone. This key won't turn. Here, let's try the other."

Logan fumbled it in his hand and held the handle out for the wolf to grab. The wolf slid it into the lock and turned it, and the shackle slipped off. The wolf handed him the key, and Logan clicked the other lock open. He groped around in the dark to unlock the cuffs binding his ankles.

Freedom pounded in his heart, but so did the ache of fear. The footsteps and voices came closer.

"Your sword is here," the wolf said.

Logan touched the animal's coarse coat and found where the wolf pointed. His fingers curled around the familiar hilt of his weapon and slipped into the worn indentations. He nearly tossed the cloth his sword had been wrapped in, but the feel of the fabric was so familiar—his cloak. How had Thea gotten them?

The wolf nudged him. *"Follow me. I can take you to the Assassin's Gate."*

"The others—I'm not leaving without them." And his son. He was so close to finding his son. How could he leave him with Rebekah?

"Of course. I will help you while I can."

"Who are you?"

"A friend. That is all you need know. Brace yourself."

The door grated open. Light spilled in, and Logan shielded his face from its harshness.

"He's missing," the man said.

Another pointed toward Logan. "There."

Logan pocketed the keys and lifted his sword. Next to him the wolf lowered his head and ducked into the shadows.

The two men rushed at Logan, and he sliced through the first. The second man was skilled, but unaccustomed to the dark. The pommel of Logan's sword connected between the man's eyes, and he fell to the ground.

The wolf shot out of the dungeon. Logan followed him down the dank, torch-lit hallways to a small opening in the stone walls.

"We are underground." The wolf's amber eyes glowed in the torchlight. *"Your young ones are two stories up. I cannot help you there. My presence must be a secret. I will meet you here when you have rescued them, if you do it quickly."*

Logan caught a glimpse of the creature helping him. He was tall and lankier than Westwind, but his coat was all brown. It seemed a peculiar coloring for a wolf, more like that of a dog, but this animal held no trace of dog in its gaze.

"Rebekah has a son. Do you know where he is?"

The wolf's eyes softened, and the fur on his head wrinkled. *"I know of whom you speak. Trust me when I tell you, you won't be able to rescue him. He would never go with you."*

Logan's heart squeezed. His nose burned. "Tell me where he is?"

"He was sent away, and isn't expected home until twilight."

Perhaps there was hope then. Maybe Logan could find him if he ever made it out of the palace. Turning to where the wolf pointed, he found a staircase. It looked forgotten, at least at this level.

He'd be alone up there. No matter, he'd gotten his sword. He'd use it until all his strength was gone. Hopefully it would be enough.

CHAPTER 46

MISTAKES

Ethan sat on the floor of his cell and tried to ignore the pounding in his head, the ringing in his ear, and the prickles of heat on his chest. He didn't need his talent to tell him they were in danger. They'd been escorted up two flights of stairs. If he was right, Logan had been taken down—to the dungeon. That made getting him out just as impossible as getting out of here.

Ryan shared the cell with him, and Jayden sat in the one across from them. Iron bars and stone walls and floor. They were in here pretty tight.

Ryan glanced at Ethan and shrugged. "At least this place smells better."

The door opened, and Ethan caught at least three guards standing outside the door. Probably more. Two were still in here. Things were looking worse.

A serving girl entered through the open door. Her cheek bore a birthmark just like the one on his chest. She carried a water bucket. The serving girl walked over to Jayden's cell and gave her a drink.

Jayden sucked the water down. She looked at the girl as if asking for more.

"I'm sorry, miss. If I give you more, they can't have any." The girl's voice shook as she motioned to Ryan and Ethan.

"Let her have mine," they said together.

The girl stared at them with wide eyes.

"No." Jayden waved her away. "They need water too."

The serving girl approached their cell with her eyes lowered. She handed a ladle of water to Ryan and he drank. Then she tipped the bucket to put the last of the liquid into the ladle and beckoned Ethan to come closer.

He stood, still dizzy from Scarface's blows to his head. He leaned against the cell bars for support. The serving girl stepped closer to him. She tripped. Water spilled to the ground.

Her scared, brown eyes met Ethan's. She sank to the floor in front of him, trembling. "I—I can't get you more or she'll kill me."

Creator in heaven. "Hey, don't worry about it."

"No—you three are kind. I know you're not the enemy."

"What's your name?"

"Nora."

"Nora, she's forcing you to treat us like this. It's not your fault. You don't have a choice."

Her eyes brightened. "There's always a choice. I'll be right back."

Ethan watched her go. Something in his gut told him no matter her intention, she wouldn't be back. "We've got to get out of here."

Ryan planted his head against the stone wall. "I'm not seeing much we can do."

"If we don't come up with something, then Jayden belongs to the queen, and we'll be dead."

"All right, give me—"

A muffled laugh interrupted Ryan.

Ethan remembered that laugh. He had no desire to deal with her. "Kara."

She emerged from the shadows. "Soldier, I didn't know you were so attuned to my voice. How's your head?"

He glared at her. "What do you want?"

"I don't express my deepest desires with those I'm not intimate." She approached his cell. Ethan refused to back away. "But I don't express my deepest desires to those I'm intimate with either," she whispered.

"Then why are you here?" Jayden's voice rasped.

Kara spun on her heel and faced Jayden's cell, leaning her shoulder in front of Ethan. "To help you escape, of course."

Her air of confidence prickled Ethan's guard. "No thanks."

"He didn't mean that." Ryan was quick to leap toward the sultry woman. Quick to give Ethan a look too.

"You can't trust her." Ethan jabbed Kara's shoulder.

At least he felt no urge to protect this one.

"No one said anything about trust, did they, Kara?" Ryan gave her his smoothest smile.

Ethan rolled his eyes.

"No, Charmer, they didn't. I like your style."

Ethan looked at Jayden. Her hands were balled into fists and her face turned red.

"But you want something in return?" Ryan leaned closer to Kara.

"Of course I do."

"What?" Ethan realized his rough voice broke Ryan's and Kara's lingering eye contact.

Kara's eyes brightened. "I want to come with you to Logan's camp."

"No." Jayden came out of her jealous stupor. "You betrayed me once."

"Betrayed? I'm here aren't I?"

Ryan furrowed his brows. "If we take her offer to help, we have a chance."

"I'll let you three argue about it for a moment, but the queen is sending her soldiers up here to have Miss Softheart brought to the torture chamber very soon." She nodded toward Jayden. She slid her dart blower out of her sleeve and said in a sing-song voice, "The two of you will be executed at sundown, which is in an hour. Here come the soldiers now."

Ethan stilled his hand from rubbing his neck.

"Ethan, please." Jayden's eyes pleaded with him.

"Jayden, I told you—"

"I know what you said." Tears welled in her eyes.

"I'll get Ryan safe too." He had to. His protective instinct for his brother flared nearly as strong as it did for Jayden.

"I'll make the bargain with you, Kara," Ryan said.

"Done." Kara slipped into the shadows.

Ethan dropped his head into the cell bars. Kara was not trustworthy. And Idla's threats weren't idle. She intended to kill him and Ryan and torture Jayden. They were both people he needed to protect with his life. He only had one life to give, so he had to make it count. For both of them. If only standing didn't make him want to retch.

"Ryan."

Ryan stared at Jayden, his eyes wide with what Ethan could only describe as horror.

He bumped Ryan's shoulder, afraid to raise his voice any louder. "Ryan."

Glossy gray eyes met Ethan's.

"Listen, Ryan. As soon as we're free, you'll take Jayden's arm and get her out of here."

"What about you?"

"I'll be right behind you."

Ryan's eyes trailed to door. "Have you seen all their shiny weapons?"

"Trust me."

Ryan winced, but he nodded. Thank the Creator, he nodded.

The heavy clops of soldiers approaching resounded from the hall. Moments later, the massive door opened.

Six soldiers strode in, carrying shackles.

Ethan's protective instinct throbbed through his bones. Being unable to stop the threat was painful, but he had to find a way. There wasn't a choice.

He looked to the shadows of an empty cell and caught sight of Kara. She placed her blow tube in her mouth.

One of the soldiers clasped his hand to his neck before he fell. The powder worked quickly. Ethan remembered. The slight sting of pain preceded warmth running through every vein. Terror followed when muscles no longer obeyed.

"What—" That soldier fell next.

The noise of another dart being shot whipped past Ethan's ear. She missed. The target had moved to check one of the fallen soldiers. Kara cursed.

"What is going on?" That soldier fell.

Logan appeared in the doorway with a sword in his hands. How he had managed to escape was nothing short of miraculous.

Logan lunged at the remaining soldiers. After he dispatched the last of them, Kara stepped out of the unlocked cell. She met his eyes in a moment of tension, but the sound of approaching reinforcements spurred them into action. Logan tossed Kara the keys.

She hurried to Jayden's cell. She unlocked the door and unfolded a blanket, then handed Jayden her confiscated daggers, a dart shooter, the cell keys, and a small pouch of something.

"It's tangle flower seed." Kara's whisper barely raised over the footsteps in the hallway. "Remember, if only a pinch is ingested, it'll put a full grown man to sleep for hours."

Jayden unlocked Ethan and Ryan's cell as Kara picked up their swords.

Logan moved to the hall. The sound of a swordfight echoed from the hallway.

"I hope you can use this, Charmer." Kara handed Ryan a sword. He grabbed it and Jayden's arm and ran.

Kara turned to Ethan. "This is the shabbiest sword I've ever—"

Ethan snatched his weapon and raced to join Logan in the hall. A large soldier barreled toward him and pushed him back into the prison room. Ethan held up his sword, ready to strike.

The man's hand flew to his neck, and Ethan saw the tiny dart before the man tumbled forward, flailing. His beefy arm knocked Ethan down and pinned him to the ground.

Pain pulsed through Ethan's head and the room shook. Those blows to his ear had affected him more than he'd thought. He closed his eyes, feeling as though he spun in circles. *C'mon, Ethan! You're stronger than this!*

Kara's laugh sounded above him, and he opened his eyes in time to see her satisfied smile as she stepped over the bodies in the doorway and out into the fray.

Ethan pushed the unconscious man off and rolled out from underneath. A small, thin piece of wood lay on the ground. A dusting of fine powder covered its pointy end. Kara's dart—the one that had missed.

He pulled his arm free and plucked it off the floor, then pocketed it and stood.

Sword ready, he raced into the hall. He counted three soldiers headed his way. Logan, Ryan, and Jayden were gone.

A soldier raced toward Ethan and swung his sword. Ethan blocked the blow. Another chop jolted into Ethan's weapon and sent a shock down his arms. He pushed back.

The soldier probably thought he'd be stronger, but he wasn't. Ethan pushed against him, let up, and pushed again. This time the soldier stumbled, but still managed to swing his blade at Ethan, who dodged it and sliced the soldier's neck open. He fell, and his blood drained onto the marble floor.

Another attacker raced toward him. Ethan shifted his stance and his foot slipped a bit, thanks to the first soldier's blood. Great.

The second soldier's weapon crashed into Ethan's sword and the blow knocked him off balance. His foot slid on the floor and he fell in the red puddle. His head knocked the ground, causing the room to spin.

The soldier towered above him, blurring into three men, with his blade high and falling. Ethan's heart hammered against his chest as he tried to get up.

He raised his own weapon to hopefully block the coming blow, but the soldier thudded against the ground. The clank of his sword against the marble echoed through the corridor.

Kara stood behind the fallen man.

Ethan sucked in a breath. He was alive, thanks to an assassin. An assassin who remained a threat to Jayden and Ryan if she found the location of the Feravolk camp.

Kara held her hand out to help him up. He grabbed it and she pulled him up.

She tapped her knuckles against his temple. "You should really get that looked at."

He pulled away from her.

"Here." She held out her fisted hand.

Ethan eyed it.

She wiggled her fist. "*Here.*"

He put out his hand and she dropped a couple of dried leaves into his palm.

"Chew them. They'll help with the dizziness."

He gave her an incredulous glance.

She chuckled. "What? Don't you trust me?"

"No."

She nudged his shoulder and he stumbled. He braced himself against the cool stone wall and shot her a glare.

She shrugged. "Your choice."

Ethan pocketed the leaves—just in case.

Kara motioned toward a door. It wouldn't have looked like a door, except it stood ajar. "Looks like your friends took the Assassin's Gate. Not many people know about this exit. Come on, before reinforcements see us."

Ethan grabbed her arm. "Thanks for helping me."

She glanced over her shoulder at him. A sly smile graced her lips. "I wouldn't call it helping *you.*"

He cocked an eyebrow. "I'm just a means to an end?"

"I'm not the first assassin you've met, am I?"

He leaned in closer. His cheek touched her hair.

She chuckled. "You like how I wield daggers?"

"Very much."

Kara turned to face him. Her fingers curled around his shirt collar and she pulled him close. Her whole body pressed against his. "You're not really my type, Soldier."

"No?"

His hands shook. He focused on her green-blue eyes and calmed his breathing. He'd been told he could still his emotions like a stone. He wasn't so sure himself, but he did what he'd done many times before to guard his emotions.

Kara didn't seem to detect his nerves as he slid his hand up her back.

She pressed harder against him, her whisper breathy. "I like a more dangerous type. You're too protective."

She didn't know the half of it.

Ethan's heart pounded. He touched her hair and brushed it away from her neck.

She looked at his lips and licked hers. As Kara moved closer, he thrust the dart into her neck. Wide eyes stared back at him.

He caught her falling form.

"I underestimated you, Soldier." She glared up at him. "But I don't make mistakes twice."

Ethan eased her to the ground and slipped her knife from her belt. "I'll bet you don't."

CHAPTER 47

POWER IN PAIN

Ethan fled through the door and pulled it tight behind him. Torches lit the way down a circular stone staircase. No bannister. Just looking down them made the room spin. Great.

He leaned against the cold, stone wall, pulled Kara's leaves out of his pocket, and stuck them in his mouth. The earthy taste of dirt spread over his tongue and they crunched as he chewed. They were probably useless. He resolved to spit them out, but stopped.

His dizziness subsided. That was unexpected. It didn't do anything for the persistent ringing in his left ear, but at least now he could stand without his stomach churning. Kara would have his head if she ever found him again.

"We have to go back for Ethan." Jayden's voice echoed up the stairs.

Heavens, why did she have to care so much? He headed down the stairs. "Careful, Jayden. I can hear you."

"Ethan?" Her voice sounded entirely too relieved. Once he turned the corner, he saw them.

"Get down here, kid." Logan stood there with Ryan, Jayden, and a brown wolf and waved at him.

"Where's Kara?" Ryan asked.

Ethan winced. "She won't be coming."

Jayden's mouth fell open. "She's dead?"

Ethan shook his head. "If we run now, she can't follow. Don't worry. I'm sure she'll be her chipper self in a few hours."

Logan followed the wolf down the hidden staircase. The moldy smell and damp walls told him they were headed underground. Once they hit the bottom of the staircase, Logan realized it was dirt beneath him. The wall seemed to be carved rock, as did the ceiling.

The other three kept quiet behind him, but Logan thought his pounding heart noisy enough for all of them. The torches spread farther apart, but there was still enough light. A moving light source up ahead infiltrated the corridor.

The wolf slunk to the ground.

"You three stay back." Logan sucked in a breath. Perhaps this wolf was bonded to an enemy. How could he be so foolish? He looked over his shoulder. "If I tell you to run, don't hesitate."

Footsteps came closer, the roving light with them. The sweat of fear broke out on Logan's face. Whoever it was could turn toward the staircase and find them, or worse, away—using their escape route. The footsteps were light and deliberate. This person knew where they were.

"Connor?" A voice called.

Logan stopped breathing. He knew that voice. He feared that voice.

Rebekah.

"Are you here?" she called again.

"She's coming this way," Ryan whispered. "Should we run? We could beat her."

Logan wanted to make certain she'd come alone before he sent those kids off running without him. Rebekah was formidable enough. "Wait for my word."

Descending the final stair, he turned toward the corridor and peered around the wall's edge.

The wolf blocked him, bristling. *"What are you doing?"*

"I'm getting them to safety."

"All of you run. I'll hold her back."

"I don't trust you, wolf. I know to what this woman bonds."

The wolf backed closer to the tunnel. *"Of course you do. If—"*

"There you are, Connor. Who are you talking to?" Rebekah asked.

Logan drew his sword. He didn't want to face Rebekah. There would be no way to defeat her without hurting her, and he wasn't sure he could. But he was a protector now. These kids had to make it out alive. "Run!"

The wolf whirled to face Logan with his teeth bared. *"You will not hurt her."*

Jayden, Ethan, and Ryan raced down the corridor, and Logan impeded the wolf from following them.

"What is going on?" Rebekah looked into Logan's eyes. "Logan? You are the queen's prisoner. You shouldn't be here."

"I will fight you, Rebekah." He had to.

Her face sprouted a smirk, and she drew a dagger from a sheath on her belt. She waved the torch in her other hand. "You don't know what I am capable of."

Had she overcome the few weaknesses he knew so well under Balton's training? "I know exactly what you're capable of."

Her chuckle was darker than he wanted to hear. "Then I'm surprised you're not running."

"We are nearing the palace." Westwind's voice echoed in his mind, distant.

"Come for the three."

"Where are you?" Westwind sounded worried.

Logan did nothing more than visualize what he saw. Bekah, dagger in her hand, flanked by a wolf, facing him.

Westwind skidded to a halt and his voice trembled. *"You're facing her?"*

Aurora saw the image too and howled. He could hear her. He could hear her! She was close. Westwind had reached her?

"Westwind, the kids are coming. Find them." He had no time to say anything else to his wolf friend.

Rebekah raised her weapons. "Idla will be very displeased if you leave. But she would also be displeased if I killed you."

A pang shot through his heart. She had become the monster he hoped she hadn't. What little hope remained for her salvation vanished. Angry for even having any, he stepped toward her.

Maybe she wouldn't sense his fear. "It won't stop me from killing you."

"I will." The wolf growled.

"No." Rebekah pushed the wolf back. She said to Logan, "Don't hurt him."

Her eyes pleaded. Eyes he remembered. An emotion he wished dead squeezed his stomach. *Snare you, Rebekah.* He turned and ran down the corridor.

"Stop."

He didn't.

A growl resounded. Something sliced the side of his neck, and her dagger clanked to the floor at his feet. He turned. She had the guts he'd hoped she didn't.

"You can't get away from me that easily." She held another dagger.

Logan pointed his sword at her, but he couldn't stomach using it against her.

The brown wolf jumped in between them.

She pushed it. "Leave me."

Logan looked into her eyes. *Creator in heaven.* He loved her. He still loved her. Ached to hold her. He dropped his sword and held out his hands, palms up. "I won't hurt your wolf, Bekah. Just let me go."

"Go?" She laughed, but something in her face changed—softened. Her eyelids fluttered. "Bekah?"

"Run." The wolf jumped into Rebekah and drove his shoulder into her arm. Her dagger fell to the ground, and then he toppled her sideways. He took a protective stance in front of her fallen form and stared at Logan with his teeth bared. *"I'm protecting you both. Go."*

Logan couldn't believe what was happening. "You—"

"Run, you fool!" Westwind shouted in his head.

"Run!" The brown wolf howled.

Logan sheathed his sword and ran. He ran from Rebekah. He'd left her alive when he could have killed her. No one could ever know that.

Outside the horns sounded. Idla knew they had escaped.

CHAPTER 48

VERY GOOD FRIENDS

Ethan skidded to a halt where the tunnel ended at a split. North or south? No torches. He pulled one off the wall and handed it to Ryan. "Which way?"

Ryan scanned both ways. "They look the same to me."

Jayden pointed north. "That way feels right."

"Feels?" Ryan cocked an eyebrow.

Heat spread across Ethan's chest. No. Not now. He glanced south. A light headed down the passage—and a threat.

"She's right. North." Ethan grabbed Ryan's arm. "Listen to me. Take Jayden and run."

Jayden's fingers gripped Ethan's shoulder. "Ethan, no!"

"Run. Please." It was the only way to keep both of them safe. And she'd forgive him, eventually.

A tear spilled over the brim of her eye.

Ryan's eyes widened, his gaze fixed on the south passage. "Let me fight with you."

He pushed Ryan and Jayden farther down the north passage until the walls narrowed around all three of them. He'd at least have a fighting chance if he limited the number of men that could reach him at once.

"Someone has to get Jayden to safety," he pleaded.

Ryan's eyes filled with tears. "No, Ethan, I won't let—"

"Well, well, well. Planning a little escape?"

Idla.

Ethan stared at Ryan, imploring him to take Jayden and run. His brother's jaw was set, and pain filled his eyes. Ethan's heart clutched, but Ryan and Jayden could be happy together. Only if they made it out alive. He touched his brother's shoulder. "Ryan, please. I'm okay with this. Don't make my sacrifice worthless."

"Sacri—Ethan? I'm not worth this. Please. I can fight." Jayden's nails dug into his arm.

Ryan's face scrunched up as he held back tears, but he nodded.

Ethan exhaled. Good. He'd take her and run. He locked eyes with Jayden. "Very good friends are worth dying for."

Her eyes widened as Ryan's arms hooked around her waist. Her scream echoed through the tunnel as Ryan carried her away.

Idla's threat dominated Ethan's attention. He held his sword up and faced her.

Idla stopped in front of him. "You can't win. You might as well surrender."

"Never."

"I have the power to let you live a little while. You could join my services. With your fighting talents, you could be a captain in my army. A pretty face like yours and money in your pocket would attract women. You could have a life worth living."

"I've already had that."

"Really?" She stepped closer to him. Her soldiers clustered around her as the walls narrowed. "Because what I see is the short, insignificant life of a peasant boy."

"You die today."

"I die?" Idla laughed. "*I* die? Look around, boy. There are twelve highly trained men here. You cannot be resilient enough to get through all of them. You would have to be uncannily fast to even get two steps toward me before you lay on the ground in a heap of your own blood."

Oh, I am.

"Tell me, boy, is a slice in my direction really worth dying for?"

Yes. He slipped his hand behind him and gripped the hilt of

Kara's knife, still tucked in his belt at the small of his back, allowing its weight to settle in his palm.

A smile spread across Idla's face. "Even your friends have abandoned you."

He stepped back two paces. The soldiers raised their weapons. In one fluid movement, he let the knife fly.

It sunk deep into her chest. Idla staggered. Red stained the white of her gown around the weapon. Her mouth dropped open. Her blue eyes bulged. She fell to the ground with her fingers curled around the hilt. It was done. Now he just had to buy Ryan and Jayden some time.

Two soldiers advanced. Ethan lunged, and his blade pierced through the first. He ripped it free in time to block a blow from the next soldier. A third took the place of the one he'd killed, his sword high and crashing down. Ethan dodged his enemy's blade and stabbed the man's stomach. Then he kicked, sending the man into the wall where he thudded and fell.

He turned to face the other soldier, but his blade had already lowered, slicing deep into Ethan's sword arm and chipped into bone.

Crying out, Ethan grabbed his arm. His grip on his weapon loosened, and his enemy's blade headed for him again. He switched his sword to his left hand, then ducked, spun, and slashed his opponent's thigh.

Calling on his talents, Ethan lunged forward. Strength fueled him as he hacked off the next soldier's arm. Speed rippled through all of his muscles. His sense of danger heightened like he'd never experienced before. A threat loomed on his other side and Ethan turned. His sword stabbed a soldier clean through the stomach.

His arm burned, his muscles quivered. Blood sprayed his face as he slashed open a man's throat, and a fresh soldier advanced.

Four to go.

Weariness gripped Ethan. A blade ripped deep into his side and drove a shock of pain through him. His knees weakened and he stumbled. Three left, but he had little to give. At least Ryan and Jayden had gotten out.

He pushed another body off of his blade. Heavens, his shoulders ached. Ethan turned to face the final two soldiers, fresh and waiting their turn, but he was tired.

Together they charged at him. The first one ran at him. Ethan's blade clipped the soldier's hand and the soldier's sword skittered across the stone floor. Disarmed, he raced to recover his weapon as the second soldier advanced. Ethan's blade clashed against his enemy's. He kicked the soldier's gut and sent him slamming into the tunnel. Stunned, the soldier slumped to the ground.

Footsteps crunched against the rocky ground and Ethan spun to face his other attacker. Sword high, the soldier advanced. Speed flooded through Ethan, and he pierced the soldier's gut, but the soldier slammed Ethan against the tunnel wall and his head hit rock. Dizziness overtook him. The tunnel quivered, and he fell.

Cold stone pressed against his cheek. With his hands against the cool floor, he pushed, but his right arm shook under the weight. He thudded back to the ground. Black spots flooded his vision. The throb of a threat warned him to move, but he couldn't. Kara's leaves no longer helped. He couldn't stand.

He opened his eyes. Idla's dead body lay on the ground across from him. At least he'd stopped her. Jayden and Ryan would be safe now. Idla's lifeless eyes stared into his. Dull and brown.

Brown? Didn't the queen have blue eyes? Why were they changing? Then a birthmark appeared on her cheek, and her face changed.

Nora. The serving girl.

Blood pounded in Ethan's ears. He'd killed Nora? Idla still lived. She still threatened Jayden, and his bones ached to protect her.

C'mon, Ethan. Get. Up.

His talent pulled him—he had to protect her. It masked his dizziness. A new surge of strength flooded into him. Ethan pushed himself up. His stomach churned. His balance wavered, but he stood.

The threat was upon him. Not only did he sense it, but also the way to stop it. He lunged. His sword deflected the blade that would have run him through and pierced into flesh and bone. The final soldier gasped, then slid off of Ethan's blade, dead.

He dropped his sword, gripped his injured arm in one hand and his throbbing head in the other, and sank to his knees, exhausted and alone. Blood from the gash in his arm trickled between his fingers. If he could just stand . . . The rush of his talents ebbed away and dizziness overtook him.

Okay, just a quick rest.

A horn blast resounded in the distance. Footsteps echoed down the tunnel toward him. Ethan cracked open his eyes as a burn pulsed across his chest. General Balton stood over him, a sneer on his face. His sword plummeted toward Ethan.

Creator help him, he had nothing left.

CHAPTER 49

YELLOW MOON

Ryan raced down the tunnel until nothing but darkness surrounded them. Jayden pounded against his back and wriggled against his grasp. If she kept this up, she'd break open the healing hole in his chest. A stab of pain shot through it.

"You let him die, Ryan! You sentenced your brother to death!"

Didn't he know it. Different pain gripped him. Crippling pain— sadness. Snare Ethan for making him choose like that. No, snare himself for putting his brother in this mess.

He should be the one facing Idla right now, not Ethan. He'd asked Ethan to protect Jayden. Just because Ethan had the sword-fighting skills, Ethan was back there giving his life. All Ryan was good at was pounding things with a blacksmith's hammer.

Ryan's throat tightened. He'd never be that weak again. No one else would fight his battles for him. If Logan didn't make it out of this alive, Ryan would find this One Eye and get the training he needed to protect Jayden and his sisters.

He stopped and placed Jayden against the wall, holding her there as she shook with sobs. Her hair clung to the tears on her face. He pushed the strands away to look into her eyes. "Jayden, listen to me. Ethan wants you safe. I'm doing as he asked. He made me choose. I chose you. I'll always choose you."

She grabbed his shirt in her fists. "Why?"

The ache in his throat spread to his chest. She loved Ethan.

Would she have been happier with him? "Ethan would kill me if I didn't."

Her eyes widened, her gaze stuck on his shirt. "Ryan."

He looked down. A huge red mark stained his clothes above the healing wound. Strange. He picked up the fabric. "At least it isn't black."

She pushed him. "How can you make jokes right now?"

He gripped her arms. "Jayden, look at me. I am going back to help Ethan, if I can trust you to run."

"I couldn't bear it if either of you died for me."

"You are supposed to save all of the Feravolk. If you die now, all is lost."

Her face scrunched up.

Can you hear me? A hiss echoed in his mind and a shock of pain ripped through Ryan's chest.

No, no, no. Not again. Not now.

The loud rumble of stone grating against stone filled the corridor. Ryan stood in front of Jayden and pulled out his sword. Torchlight spilled through the new opening. Footsteps echoed down another tunnel. Fire pulsed in his wound.

A low growl crept closer. *Can you hear me?*

The queen's son stepped out of the corridor, followed by ten soldiers, and looked into Ryan's eyes. "Belladonna told me you might just like the gift I have for you."

Franco motioned for about twenty more soldiers who came forward holding chains. The massive body of a black lion filled the mouth of the tunnel.

Yellow moon eyes locked onto Ryan. A tremor shot through his whole body as he recognized the creature from his fever dream. Only this was no dream. This one was real. And calling his blood. His knees buckled as the burning singed his heart.

The black lion licked its lips.

"No!" Jayden screamed.

Why was he so hot? Ryan clutched his sword tighter and fell to his knees. *Ethan, I'm sorry.*

Jayden watched Ryan hunch forward. His sword clanked to the ground beside him, and he pressed a hand over his open wound as crimson spread across his shirt. Memories of the arrow in his chest stabbed her.

She raced in front of him and met Franco's eyes. "Let him go."

A wicked smirk curled Franco's lips, and his eyes roamed the length of her body. "And you'll come with me?"

She gripped her daggers. Behind her, Ryan screamed. Jayden turned. He knelt on the ground and blood oozed out of his chest. "Please. Stop hurting him."

"I'm not hurting him."

The lion crouched low.

"Let him go. Let him go, and I'll come with you."

Franco scanned her face with hard eyes. He motioned down the corridor. "Very well. After you."

"Let him go first."

"Jayden . . . don't do this." Ryan's voice was so weak.

Franco turned to his soldiers. "Grab her. Release the lion."

"What? No." Jayden spun.

Her dagger slashed one soldier's arm from elbow to shoulder. Another soldier lunged at her and she hacked into his side, but the chain mail was too strong for her to sink her blade in. They had her surrounded now. Her heart beat like a thousand galloping horses in her chest, but she remained in control of her talent.

She lowered into a crouch before she sprang at the nearest soldier. Her heel met his face, and his neck snapped back. As she landed, she swung, and her blade clashed against a second soldier's sword.

A strong grip wrapped around her left arm and shook her weapon from her hand. She whirled toward her captor with her fist clenched, but another soldier grabbed her right arm and squeezed. She struggled to stomp on his foot, but the other man wrenched her arm behind her. A scream rose from her throat as her other dagger fell from her grasp. Without the weapon, the skin behind her ears tingled. No. This couldn't happen now. She had to save Ryan before the soldier's emotions took control of her. She pushed them away, but the fear in her rose. Suffocated her.

Chains clanked against the ground. Wind whooshed over her head. She looked up to see the black lion's sleek form sail above her. Massive paws smacked into Ryan's chest and knocked him to the ground.

Jayden pulled against her captors. "Please. Let him go."

Franco's men pushed her into the tunnel and shut the door.

"Ryan!" She screamed against the stone walls surrounding her.

Torchlight distorted Franco's face as he leaned closer to her. "Sorry about your friends."

Jayden bit her lip to keep from crying.

He reached out a hand and touched Jayden's face. His fingers were smooth. No calluses. He was no fighter.

Jayden pulled away from his soft fingers, and her gaze fell on her daggers, which lay against the wall. She turned back toward the prince.

Franco nodded and the soldiers released Jayden's arms. They formed a tight circle around her and cut off her access to her weapons. "My mother believes love is weakness. I believe it's the path to power. Let me show you."

Love? What did he know of love? "Where are you taking me?"

"My chambers. I want to be civil. My mother would torture you to make you behave. I . . . well, I will love you." He took her hand and tugged her along.

Jayden followed, each step away from her weapons harder. The wild look in Franco's eye made her heart race. What was he going to do to her? She pulled against his grip, but his hand tightened around her arm, cutting off circulation. He slammed her against the tunnel wall with strength no normal man could possess. Her head hit stone and a throb of pain shot through her. His hand gripped her throat and pressed her against the wall. Her feet no longer touched the ground. She strained to suck in air. She kicked off the wall, but his hand around her neck held her in place. She clawed at his arm.

Strained, pushed. Her lungs screamed for air. How was he doing this?

Franco leered closer. "Do not think me weak, Princess."

Princess?

One eyebrow quirked. "Yes. Get used to the title." He released his hold and she slid down the wall, gasping for air. She clasped her neck.

His iron grip tightened around her left wrist, and he pulled her to stand. He was too strong. She'd have to outwit him.

The tunnel split and they walked left, up a steady incline. A door opened and daylight spilled in through huge windows in a massive room. The scent of citrus consumed Jayden—too strong—and she shied away momentarily from the bright light.

"Soldiers, please man the doors."

The soldiers walked through the room and opened the doors to the hall, then closed the doors behind them. Jayden was alone with the prince.

She glanced behind her. He'd left the secret exit unmanned? Probably counting on his strength to keep her here.

Franco led her in. "Do you like it, Princess?"

Exotic animal furs with spots and stripes covered the floors. Lion hides draped over four crimson chairs near the fireplace. A round table sat behind them with golden candlesticks, bowls of fresh fruit, and a bejeweled goblet. But Franco led her toward the largest piece of furniture in the room.

His bed.

Jayden's throat tightened. *No. Creator, please. No.*

CHAPTER 50

UNEVEN GROUND

The tunnel split. Logan looked south then north. Dead bodies littered the whole north passage. A frozen lump settled in his stomach. Logan grabbed a torch and searched for faces he knew. His chest tightened. He found one. Ethan.

He dropped to his knees next to Ethan. "Kid?"

His hands trembled as he slapped Ethan's face. No response.

"Maybe you shouldn't have left them alone." A deep voice caught Logan's attention—a voice he knew. Balton. So much for a secret exit. It seemed everyone knew about it.

A tremor shot through Logan's body as he turned around. The general wasn't alone. A dozen soldiers flanked him.

Heat filled Logan's chest and a wolfish growl rumbled in his throat. "You killed him?"

Balton shrugged and held up his bloodied weapon. "He didn't even put up a fight."

Sword high, Logan raced toward his enemy, but the coward hid behind his men in the narrow tunnel.

The first man held his sword too high, and Logan ran him through, leaving his left arm exposed. Another soldier's blade sank into his skin. Logan spun and his sword slashed that man's neck open. His blade hacked into the next soldier's sword arm. As that man fell and clutched his useless arm, Logan swung his blade at the man behind the fallen soldier. Chain mail stopped Logan's blade from delivering a fatal blow. He lunged and nicked the man's cheek with his sword tip. Then he thrust his blade into that soldier's chest.

Sweat beaded on Logan's forehead. The number of men separating him from Balton dwindled. Two more fell to Logan's sword. Balton would not get away this time. Three more men stood between Logan and the general.

A soldier lunged at his side, and Logan dropped to his knees and rolled. Pain shot through his bruised ribs.

When he stood, paces away from the remaining three men, he caught a glimpse of Balton's wide eyes. All the pain ebbed away, merely an echo in the back of his mind. Revenge was close. The taste of it tingled on his tongue.

Logan held his hands out to his sides and exposed his chest. "Face me, coward. Or are you afraid of the Lone Wolf?"

"Stand down." Balton's voice was almost a whisper, but the remaining three soldiers stopped advancing. "Go and tell Captain Tevont where to send his men."

The three soldiers shared incredulous glances, but they put away their weapons. One pushed the wall and a door in the stone slid open long enough for them to pass through.

Balton took a step forward. "I fear no one, *Lone Wolf.* You're supposed to be this legend, and yet this meeting seems the highlight of *your* life. A little anticlimactic, don't you think?"

Logan tipped his head back, revealing the scar from the leash the general had placed on him all those years ago.

Balton shrugged. "I've left that mark on hundreds of nameless, faceless prisoners, and so have my men. It's nothing personal."

Logan pulled down on his shirt and revealed the scar on the right side of his chest. The letters Balton's knife had carved into his skin—the general's initials. "You still sign all of your handiwork?"

Balton's chuckle reverberated off the dank, stone walls. "Ah, yes. I remember you. Peasant boy who claimed I killed your parents. You were right. I tortured them first. Oh, how your mother screamed."

Logan lunged. Balton's steel crashed against his blade. Burning rage fueled every desire, and one thought pulsed through Logan's brain: Balton had to die.

Again and again his sword reached for the general only to hit steel. Balton advanced and pushed Logan out to the open mouth of the tunnel. Dead bodies threatened to trip him. He was losing ground. All the pain from yesterday's torture flooded back into him.

No. Balton would not win this. Could not win this. If Logan was going to die in the palace walls, he'd take the general down with him.

A blade nicked his finger. Balton lunged and Logan batted his blade away. He would lose this fight if he didn't concentrate.

Shouts and heavy footsteps thundered down the long tunnel. Logan risked a look over his shoulder. A stream of torches headed toward them. Reinforcements. Heart pounding, he faced the general and his cocky sneer.

Balton chuckled. "Nervous?"

One Eye's voice rang in Logan's head. *Always remember your training. Revenge will try to strip you of sanity. If you let it, it'll also strip you of your life.*

If not for revenge, then why was he fighting?

Balton's sword clashed against Logan's, and he pushed. Logan's arms quivered under the pressure.

Balton's eyes locked onto him. "I'll kill you, too. And everyone you hold dear. That's why I marked you."

Life. He'd fight for life. Not his own, but of those who still lived—for the deliverers he was meant to protect.

He swung his sword at the general's head.

Balton blocked the blow and a shock shuddered up Logan's arms. Steel screeched against steel. Logan pushed harder and Balton stumbled back. Logan's heel connected with the general's exposed knee.

Groaning, Balton shifted sideways. A slight limp hindered his movement as he scurried away.

Logan advanced. Metal clashed against metal. Logan pushed the general closer and closer to the wall. There would be no escape for him. Balton would die.

Logan's blade crashed down on Balton's sword arm. Glancing off the metal bracer, the tip of Logan's sword sunk into Balton's hand. How easily it sliced through flesh and bone. Balton's sword clanked against the floor, his thumb with it. The general cried out. Blood poured from Balton's wounded hand as he groped along the wall.

Logan lifted his sword again. Balton was his, helpless, unarmed. He thrust his sword toward the general's exposed chest.

A loud crack shook the tunnel. Logan shielded his face as bright light blinded him.

When it faded, Balton was gone. Stone scraped against stone as the revolving door in the tunnel wall sealed shut.

No!

Logan nearly slammed his fist against the stone, but he had to get out of the tunnel. The advancing soldiers were almost on top of him.

Leaving Ethan's body here tore at his heart, but there was no time. "Forgive me, Ethan. I would have given you a hero's burial."

Tears stung his eyes as Logan raced down the north passage.

Again the tunnel walls shook, and a scream that didn't sound human echoed off the stone. Rocks rained down around him. Logan covered his head as the walls crumbled behind him. Hopefully Jayden and Ryan made it out. And hopefully whatever creature had made that noise wasn't waiting for them.

CHAPTER 51

TAINTED

A hot spray hit Ryan's face and the creature's hiss echoed in his ear. His blood answered, coursing out of his chest. The lion pressed its crimson claws into his flesh and sniffed. *"You aren't mine as I thought. But you smell tainted. How did you overcome my poison?"*

Overcome? Blood leaked out of his wound as if it was being summoned. How was that overcoming anything? A faint burn surged through his veins, but it reminded him of the pain. He shook.

"You fear me. Perhaps I can finish the process."

"What do you mean, finish?"

"Don't you want to become like me? Venomous and powerful?"

"You mean evil?"

Acrid wind hit Ryan's face as the beast roared. Black saliva dripped from its fangs. *"If that's what you want to call it, but let me in and you'll never be weak again."*

Never? "H-how—what happens if I let you in?"

The cat closed its mouth, but a smile revealed the tips of its long fangs. *"Your blood reaches out to me already. Deep in your heart the scar is opening."*

Was that right? So the price he'd pay would be too steep. He had to get this stupid thing off his chest. "Quit stalling and kill me. Or would you rather play chase? I'll be the mouse."

The lion's claws pressed harder and pierced deeper into his flesh. *"I will enjoy watching you writhe."*

"You know, I'm rethinking your offer."

"I won't make it easy. You want my power? You'll have to kill me."

"Yes. Kill the black beast," A different voice whispered.

Ryan's heart stuttered.

Lavender breath heated the side of his face. He turned his head to see the same yellow-moon eyes, but a different creature.

The white lion.

It tilted its head. *"You do hear me?"*

Its voice matched the one from his dream—the one that plagued his thoughts after Anna had healed him. Was this one real too? "What do you want?"

"You." It stepped forward, its legs red as blood. Then the vision winked out.

Cold sweat broke out on Ryan's face. Oh good. Now he was seeing things. Heart hammering, he reached for the sword again, straining against the black cat's weight. Something cool and sharp bumped his hand—he could just reach the blade. His sweating fingers grasped it, inched it closer.

The black lion laid down on him. Its eyes, the only things he could see, narrowed in what looked like pleasure. *"Little mouse, you shouldn't be so stupid."*

The beast's thick, muscular tail rammed into Ryan's hand, and the blade sliced his palm. The sword ripped from his grasp and clanked into the stone wall. Now he had nothing.

Hadn't he already been in this position? Dying under taunting yellow eyes? He gasped for air.

"What are you really?"

"An agent of the Mistress of Shadows. We've escaped from guarding the Afterworld, and I've had more fun playing with living things. I'm going to kill you now."

Ryan spat in its face. "I'd like to see you try."

The lion stood. Hind legs pressed into Ryan's thighs, forelegs held down his arms. Its deafening roar flooded out every other sound.

Fire exploded in Ryan's veins, and he arched his back, not sure if he was screaming.

Pain filled him, burning pain, worse than before. Something in his heart throbbed, like a scar trying to burst open. His fingertips scraped against the rocky floor as he tried to claw away from the creature. He needed . . . he needed to save Jayden.

No one else would know she'd been taken down the secret tunnel. He had to go after her.

His hands grew hot. Burning hot. Straining against the lion's weight on his biceps, he bent his arms and wrapped his hands around the beast's forelegs. Heat shot from his palms.

The black lion glowed. Orange light pulsed from within the creature like a hot ember being fanned. Ryan tightened his grip. The pain in his chest ebbed away. The cat screeched. Flames shot out from the beast's ears and mouth. Fire licked at the black fur, burning it away. Hissing and screaming, it shrank back.

A deep, feminine chuckle echoed off the walls. He knew the voice now. The white lion. Was it here?

Panicked, Ryan scrambled free of its weight and crawled toward the sword. The black beast burst into white hot flame and shrieked. Ryan dove for the weapon and grabbed it.

Bright light burst forth and Ryan closed his eyes. The tunnel floor shook and rock rained down.

Then the screeching stopped.

He opened his eyes. No lion. Just a pile of ash and a wall of lit torches.

Ryan looked at his hand. The cut was healed, but a spot of black char remained on his palm. Both of his hands were black. He rubbed them against his breeches. Perhaps he had another Blood Moon talent—one that no one could know about.

He rubbed his chest. The fabric of his shirt was wet, but he was healed. Why? He stared at his hands again, willing the heat to come, but he didn't even know how to call it.

That female chuckle drummed in his mind again. *"Quite power-ful, aren't you, Tainted One?"*

Tainted. Ryan shook his head. "Who's there?"

Bright light appeared in the tunnel again. The white lion stepped out of the glare. Red blood stained its chest and belly.

Ryan swallowed. His sweaty palms gripped the hilt of the sword tighter. "You don't own me."

"We shall see."

He lunged and swung the blade. It sliced through the lion's neck and severed the white light, but touched nothing. The lion disappeared.

Ryan's chest heaved. It wasn't real. None of it was real. Maybe he could block out the voice in his head if he just remembered that.

He dropped his weapon and sunk to his knees. Hadn't the black lion said it was a creature of the Mistress of Shadows? It had played him, showed him the things he feared.

Still, he *had* killed the black lion. Did that mean . . .? If his new-found power was from the lion, he never wanted to use it again.

Not unless he had to.

He shook the thoughts away, picked up his sword, and groped along the stone wall to find the door. His fingers found an indentation. He pressed it. A door opened on the other side of the wall. These stupid revolving doors were everywhere. He searched again. Jayden didn't have much time.

○

Franco stepped closer to the bed. Jayden resisted his pull to no avail. Her boot caught on the rug and she slipped right into him. He wrapped his arms around her. "Now that you are weaponless, I think I will find you more accommodating, no?"

Jayden's body tensed. Everything was a weapon. But could she fight him? Her fingernails hadn't even left a scratch on his arms. "I think you mistake what love is, Prince."

"Do I?" He shrugged. "What does it matter? You believe it is weakness."

He pushed her onto the bed. She sank into the mattress and his body pinned her down, pressing against her, suffocating her. He held her arms down, above her head, with one hand. She pushed back and he chuckled. Tears burned against her eyes. Fear crushed her.

"I made you a potion. It's a drink. I think you'll like it. It's sweet—like you—and smooth." His finger trailed from her neck to her collarbone. "Very much like you, and secret. We'll both drink. It will make you love me—forever."

Her stomach squeezed. She could still feel where his finger had touched her, like a greasy stain on her skin. Just thinking about what else he was going to do to her shot a tremor through her body. What would the potion do? Could it really make her love him? What would she become? A sob choked her.

His awful fingers caressed her cheek. "Don't cry, my love."

Her chin quivered.

"Here, this will help you relax." He reached for the glass.

His grip on her hands loosened. His body lifted as he rose to his knees. Jayden tucked her right knee to her chest, bringing it between his legs. Then she kicked him hard in the groin. He toppled off the bed. She jumped up. Her heels sunk into the soft mattress, and she scanned the floor. Where was the lunatic prince? She vaulted off the bed and headed to the secret door.

Something caught her shirt. She kept going, the ripping of her clothes loud in her ear. Franco pulled her back and pinned her against the wall. Not again. She clawed his forearm, leaving no scratches in his thick skin. Fear flooded her.

His eyes burned. "My mother never loved me. She told me love was a weakness, and I'd be stronger if I grew up without it."

Jayden trembled. Wasn't that the lie she'd been feeding herself this whole time, when in truth, the love of her family had made her who she was? Given her courage? Fueled her hope? Yes. The fear began to melt. She gripped his arm and pulled herself up. Air filled her lungs. "She was wrong."

"Was she?" His grip loosened and Jayden's feet touched the ground, but he still pinned her to the wall.

"When you love someone, you protect them. Who protects you,

Franco? Your soldiers? Do they love you? Could their love withstand a bribe?" Her head slammed against the wall and her cheek stung.

He lowered his hand. "I could have been gentle with you. Who protects you now? Your friends are dead, thanks to me."

Jayden remembered Anna's note. The Whisperer had said the only thing stronger than fear was love. "Their love will always protect me. They gave me what I needed to survive. To persevere. How will you survive, oh, unloved prince?"

"I see a woman before me, powerless. Would love make you stronger? Not stronger than me."

She couldn't give up. Physically, he had her beaten, but she still had . . . tangle flower seed. It was still in her pocket. Jayden evened her breathing and carefully slid her fingers inside her pocket until she found the opening of the tiny bag.

"Because of love . . ." Fine powder clung to her fingers. "I will never give up."

She gripped Franco's shirt collar in one hand, and with the other, rubbed the tangle flower seed into his eyes, mouth, and nose. He recoiled, his face painted white like a clown. Gasping, he fell to the floor.

Jayden knelt next to him as his eyes struggled to stay open. "I pity you, because no one loves you."

She ran to the wall and groped for anything that would release the secret passageway. A stone moved, and she pushed it. The passage back to the tunnel opened, and she fled.

In the dark, dank dungeon, she wiped the tangle flower residue from her hand. Tears streamed down her face. She had lost everyone now, but she couldn't give up. She would never give up.

Ryan had said he loved her perseverance. Well, she wouldn't fail him now. She wouldn't make Ethan's sacrifice worthless.

She froze.

She had to go back.

If it was her Destiny Path to face Idla, she had to end this, even if she didn't make it out alive. She wouldn't let everyone else die so she could run away. No more running.

Jayden balled her hands into fists and marched down the descending floor of the tunnel toward her daggers. She'd get them, then she'd seek out the queen. And kill her.

If only she could see. Her hands groped along the rocky tunnel wall. Where was that door?

"You almost made it."

Ice crystallized in Jayden's blood. She knew that voice.

Idla.

Jayden turned to face the queen. "I was just coming to see you."

CHAPTER 52

WEAKNESS

The queen stood there, alone. She clapped her hands together, and flames burst on every torch. Shadows and golden light flickered over Idla's face. "The game is over."

Jayden's gaze fell on something that glinted near the tunnel wall. Her daggers. Her heart thumped. If she lunged she could reach the weapons, then one good toss and it would all be over.

She crept along the wall closer to her precious daggers. "You won't take me back there."

Idla's gaze trailed Jayden's movement. She stepped closer.

Jayden froze.

The queen's laugh echoed off the walls. "Who will rescue you? Your friend with the sword is dead."

Idla held up a shiny, silver mirror, and firelight reflected off the ornate jewels encrusting its edges. Jayden's face stared back at her, dirty, disheveled, but no longer scared. She'd embraced her role now. She was a deliverer.

The reflection clouded. As the fog cleared, the mirror showed a new image. Dead bodies lay on a torch-lit floor. Tunnel walls surrounded them. One face caught her attention. Ethan lay motionless in a pool of blood.

Jayden's lungs emptied. Tingles spread through her whole body and her knees weakened. Her fingers dug into the rocky wall to stabilize herself. "You—you're lying!"

"Mirrors don't lie. No one can make a mirror show what isn't."
Jayden stared at his face. *Breathe, Ethan.*

Idla released the mirror. It shattered and shards skittered across
the floor. "What do you have to live for now? Or . . . do you love the
other one too?"

Jayden lunged. Uneven ground bit into her skin as she dove across
the floor. Her fingers curled around the hilt of her dagger, and she
picked it up. In one fluid motion she jumped to her feet and let the
dagger fly. It aimed true, right for the queen's heart.

The dagger froze, inches short of Idla's body, and stayed there.
Idla poked the tip with her finger, and the weapon clattered to
the floor. A green pod, like the casing over a flower bud, solidi-
fied around the queen's body. It withered and peeled away from the
queen and, just as quickly, a new one formed in its place. Then the
bud faded from view. An invisible shield?

Idla's icy blue eyes met Jayden's. "Foolish girl. You think I am
that easy to kill?"

Numbness settled into Jayden's body. This was the woman she
was supposed to defeat? An untouchable sorceress? How?

Idla's arm extended and a thin, black vine snaked across the floor
toward Jayden fast. It shifted with her movement and slithered up
her leg. The vine grew thicker, longer, and crept up the wall on both
sides of her. It constricted around her arms and legs and lifted her
from the ground, pressing her against the tunnel wall in moments.
Thorns pricked her skin, biting deeper as the vine squeezed. Its skin
looked like tanned leather, except it was black.

Panic surged through her as a black tentacle curled around her
neck. Powerless to pry it away, she strained against the bindings.

The queen walked closer as Jayden hung there, helpless, her
backbone grinding into the stone wall. Again. Idla's fingers curled,
and the vine tightened around Jayden's neck, pressed against her
windpipe.

"Just . . . kill . . . me." She choked out the words.

"Now why would I do that when I've fought so hard to get you
here?"

The suffocating hold loosened and Jayden sucked in air. "What do you want . . . with me?"

"Your power."

"My—"

Idla laughed. "When you give me your allegiance, which you will, you will give me your key to unlocking the Creator's power for myself. Four deliverers, four keys. Then I will have the Creator's full power. I will be unstoppable."

Jayden writhed, trying to break the vine's hold. "I will *never* give you what you want."

"You say that now, but you haven't visited my torture chambers yet." Idla lowered her arm.

Jayden slid down the wall, and her back scraped against the rock. The choking hold around her neck released, and her feet hit the ground. She lunged forward, but the vine kept her from moving.

Idla's chuckle reverberated. "You will give me what I want."

She held up her hand. With a sneer, she curled her fingers into a fist and jerked her hand back. The vine slithered beneath Jayden's necklace. The cord pressed against the back of her neck, digging in until it snapped. The horse charm her mother had given her flew into the air before it clattered against the ground.

Jayden's heart forgot to beat. What else was this woman capable of?

Idla's lips curved into a smile. "You understand now? You are no match for me, and no one is left to help you."

"I'll die before I give you anything."

"You won't. I've been lent healer's powers for tonight's torture session, so I will make sure of that."

Tears flooded Jayden's eyes. She'd failed everyone. They all died for her, and she couldn't even hold up her end. The queen would win. Anna was wrong. The Creator had picked the wrong deliverer.

Something electric skittered over Jayden's skin. It felt like—like a storm was coming. The storm filled her. Poured into her like a welcome chill. The electricity warmed her. This storm was angry, unnatural—Idla's. Jayden's throat constricted.

Idla's hands lifted the air and a cloud billowed above her fingers. "Don't worry. This will only make you writhe until I heal you."

Electricity built up in Idla's fingers, and Jayden knew the lightning would hit her right shoulder, but she couldn't move.

Wait. Weakness. She sensed the queen's weakness.

When Idla used her power, the vine would lose strength—so would the invisible pod. Jayden would be able to move, but she'd seen how fast the vine had bound her. The queen would have her tied up again in a heartbeat. She'd only have one shot at this. But she'd have to get free and toss her dagger all in that same moment of weakness.

Bracing herself against the wall, Jayden glanced at her dagger. Idla couldn't know what she was about to do, or she would be trapped under the queen's torture until she gave in. Jayden's heart clutched. The thought of lightning striking her sent a tremor through her body. She had to think, had to be ready.

Idla locked eyes with her and smiled. "This is my favorite game." Her fingers crackled with greenish light.

Jayden trembled. If she didn't get the dagger in time, all would be lost.

Lightning sparked. Warped flashes sped toward Jayden. The tension in the vine loosened. Jayden yanked her right hand up. The vine still clung to her arm, but it was too weak to hold her against the wall. With her eyes squeezed shut, she focused on the feel of the lightning. Its presence pulsed though her every fiber. She placed the snakelike body of the plant in the lightning's path.

A jolt shuddered through Jayden's body and jerked her arm as the bolt blasted into the vine instead. The plant's hold withered and Jayden burst free. Eyes open, she dove toward her dagger.

The lightning left a black, gaping hole and the remains of a charred vine. She clutched her dagger. Its familiar hilt rested in her palm like an extension of her hand.

She looked up at her target and the skin behind her ears burned. Hatred flooded her—hatred so intense it made Jayden's chest burn—Idla's. No! What was happening? Why weren't the daggers helping her control her talent? She didn't want to act in hatred. She didn't want to become a monster like Idla. She couldn't do this. As she tried to push away Idla's emotions, fear choked her.

There is one thing stronger than fear: love.

Of course. A new emotion flared in Jayden's chest. Love. Love for everyone who had made a sacrifice so she could live. It grew hot, like a blue flame. Yes. She understood. Love fueled a righteous anger. It was not the same as Idla's. The queen's rage was thick black—like tar on Jayden's heart.

Idla sneered. "Oh, you'll wish you were dead, now."

Jayden embraced her own emotions and gripped her daggers tighter. The fog from Idla's hate cleared, leaving Jayden's senses sharp. She felt the lightning pulse.

Idla shot another bolt toward Jayden.

From her spot on the ground, she launched her arm forward, but her fingers tightened around the dagger instead of releasing. No! These weapons usually obeyed her flawlessly, as if they always knew what she was thinking, but now—they chose to stay in her hand?

She sensed the lightning build. It would strike the dagger. She would be killed. Wait. The dagger? Maybe that was why they'd stayed in her hand. Maybe Ryan was right about the magic. Jayden braced for the pain and prayed Ryan was right. She held the dagger in the path of the lightning bolt and willed her own lightning to strike the queen.

Nothing. No storm answered her summons.

A shock jolted Jayden's arm. She clutched the dagger hilt tighter. Every bolt of electricity struck the dagger's blade. Blue light shone from the sapphire in the hilt until it overpowered the soft yellow of the torches. Then all went quiet.

The dagger hummed in her hand. Jayden kept it aimed at the queen. Filled with the charge of electricity, lightning poured out of the blade and skittered around the queen as over the queen's protective shield in a blue light. A deafening boom shook the tunnel. The bud opened and withered away from the queen, leaving her exposed.

It had to be now. Jayden whipped her arm back, then forward. The dagger left her hand and sailed through the air.

The blade sunk deep into the queen's heart. Light shot through Idla as the dagger pulsed one more bolt of electricity. Her mouth opened in a scream. Blue light shot out of her open mouth and eyes. A spasm ratcheted her body, then the light died, and she dropped to the floor.

The storm subsided. Everything grew quiet.

Jayden crawled over to the queen's body. Blood trickled from Idla's ears. Her eyes were nothing but black holes. The stench of death rose from her charred body. Jayden yanked her dagger free, turned away from disfigured queen, and heaved.

Queen Idla was dead. Gone.

A grating sound echoed, and sweet, summer air wafted in through the tunnel and fluttered Jayden's hair. Outside air.

Footsteps padded against the ground and a thick, raspy whisper came from the darkness. "Jayden?"

She shivered. Was Ethan alive? Hope filled her. She could just make out the tall form headed toward her.

Ryan. He'd made it. Tears of joy prickled her eyes.

He wasn't limping or acting wounded, but dark blood stained the whole front of his shirt.

"Ryan? I thought you—"

"So did I." His arms enveloped her.

The scent of smoke rolled off his clothes, embers tinged with blood. She touched his shirt. The fabric was wet. "Are you okay?"

"I'm fine. Let's get out of here."

"Fine? How can you be—"

"Trust me. I'll tell you later."

Jayden nodded. "What about Logan?" Her throat tightened. "Ethan?"

Ryan opened his mouth, but no words came out. Then he finally spoke. "They'd want us to get out."

Jayden choked back tears as she picked up her daggers and stashed them in her belt and boots, and then she grabbed Ryan's outstretched hand.

His fingers squeezed around her hand and, sword leading, he led her farther down the tunnel, closer to the clean scent of air. A ray of light shone through. Outside. They were almost free. The sounds of their shoes scraping against the rough floor reverberated off the walls.

"Here." Ryan stopped. "There's a door. Hopefully it's the right one. They're everywhere."

A bright outline shone in the wall ahead of them. Beside Ryan, Jayden placed her hands on the cold stone and pushed. It gave way with a loud scrape, but light spilled in. Jayden shielded herself from the brightness with her hand, but plunged through the door.

Sunshine warmed her. Knee-high grass brushed against her clothes. A breeze tugged her hair, and dry grass blades rubbed against one another, sending a quiet hiss through the air.

She was free. The tunnel had led them almost to the forest, a bowshot from the palace. The gray wall outside the castle towered behind them, no longer their prison.

Ryan touched her arm. His gray eyes searched her face. He reached up, and his finger slid gently over her neck. "Are you okay? Did—did he hurt you?"

"No. I'm okay. You?" She touched his shirt, now stiff from the drying blood.

Unshed tears glistened in his eyes and he cupped the back of her head in his hand. "I'm fine."

Her chest ached. "I—I'm so sorry."

"This wasn't your fault."

The tears she'd been holding in rushed forward. Yes, it was. How did no one see that? Idla wanted *her*. Ethan was only standing in the way, and it had gotten him killed. Her strength left her and she buckled over.

Ryan caught her, held her.

"He's dead." She sucked in air, but her throat clenched and her voice came out as a whisper. "Ethan's dead."

S.D. GRIMM

Her legs would no longer support her. Ryan pulled her close and sank to the ground with her. "That's not your fault. He wanted to protect you. It was his choice."

Jayden looked up into Ryan's tearful eyes.

He cupped her cheek in his palm. "Don't blame yourself. Please."

"You're not planning on throwing your life away for me, are you? Because I can't lose anyone else."

One side of his lips pulled up in a half-smile, but the look in his eyes grew intense. The rough skin on his thumb brushed against her cheek. "You know I'm not that great at planning ahead."

Just his joking made her smile, but a pang still pierced deep inside her chest. "Ryan?"

"You would do the same for me. You know it, and I know it. Asking me not to protect you isn't fair, but I don't plan on dying anytime soon."

That was all she could ask for. She wrapped her arms around him, and he hugged her back. Tight. His embrace was so familiar, comforting.

It was over. Idla was dead and the Children would be safe. The Feravolk would be free of her. Jayden wouldn't return to Tareal, but she had Ryan—a small piece of home.

He helped her stand. "Let's get farther away. This place isn't on my list for second encounters."

Jayden brushed the loose twigs and dirt from her clothes. When she straightened, Ryan gripped her wrist and pushed her behind him.

A man stood in front of them with a loaded crossbow trained on Ryan's chest. His Feravolk cloak, draped around him, camouflaged his movements as he stalked closer.

Ryan let go of her. "Run, Jayden."

CHAPTER 53

NO MORE

Jayden stared at the arrow. Not Ryan too. Everyone was being taken from her. She raced in front of Ryan. "Let him go!"

"Jayden!" Ryan grabbed her shoulders.

A growl resounded from somewhere near, but she saw nothing. What was it? More magic? Was Idla rising from the dead?

The man lowered his weapon. "Westwind seems to think you're a friend."

Westwind? A surge of relief flooded her veins. Two wolves stood, the grass no longer hiding them from view. Westwind raced over to her and flipped her hand over his head with his cool nose. She fell to her knees and hugged his neck. His soft coat brushed away her tears.

"I'm so sorry," she whispered into his fur. "Logan's dead."

Westwind pulled away from her. The fur between his ears wrinkled and he shook his head.

"He—he's alive?" At his nod, joy welled up in her heart.

The Feravolk man put out a hand to help Jayden up. "Come on. We've got to get you out of here."

"You're Logan's friend?"

"Name's Gavin." He motioned to the other wolf. "Follow Aurora to the trees. My wife Melanie will take you to our camp. Some redheads will be happy to see you, I'm sure."

"But we—"

"Come on, Jayden." Ryan towed her up, but Westwind growled and nipped Ryan's leg.

"Westwind, they need to leave," Gavin said.

"Look." Jayden pointed to the secret exit.

Logan emerged. Jayden's heart tripped on a beat. Blood covered his shirt in more than one place and soaked through a bandage around his left arm, but he was alive.

When he saw her, he sighed. She raced to him and wrapped an arm around his waist. "I'm all right, Jayden." He hugged her close. "You?"

She nodded once, tears collecting in her eyes.

Together they followed the wolves into the forest.

Ryan stumbled often. Jayden walked near him and clutched his arm. He had to be just as exhausted as she.

Just when Jayden thought she'd collapse, Aurora stopped. She realized at once how much she needed water, and how much her legs had been relying on emotion to keep her running. They felt like wilting celery now.

"Logan?" Ryan's voice cracked.

Heart pounding, Jayden whirled around. Ryan never sounded panicked.

Icy water spread through every one of her veins. Standing ten paces away was a huge, tawny mountain lion. A long, pink tongue swept over the cat's whiskered cheek.

The cat paced closer.

Jayden let go of Ryan's arm and slipped her hand inside her boot. Her fingers curled around the familiar handle of her assassin's dagger. Yellow eyes locked onto her as if the cat knew what she was doing.

"*Wait.* Callie's with me. She won't hurt you if you don't do anything stupid." A petite blonde-haired woman stepped out from the trees and lowered the hood of her Feravolk cloak.

"Melanie." Logan seemed relieved.

"You don't look very good, Logan." She walked toward him, but glanced toward Gavin and her eyebrows shot up. "You were going to let her hurt Callie?"

"Me? You could've come out sooner." His smile deepened the wrinkles around his eyes.

Melanie reached Logan and inspected his arm with a wince. "You need stitches."

"Thank you for coming."

She smiled. "We found your red-headed tagalongs, and a dog?" She eyed him. "They're just through here, setting up camp." She led them past a cluster of trees, and Jayden blinked. She was apparently exhausted, because she would have walked right by Ryan's sisters and Scout had Melanie not led her right to them.

Tail tucked, Scout wandered over. His brown eyes looked large and sad as he curled up beside Jayden's leg. So he knew about Ethan. Jayden hugged his neck.

Three red-haired girls rushed forward. Chloe stopped in front of Ryan, her green eyes wide as she reached toward the red stain on his shirt.

"I'm fine, Chloe."

Tears formed in the corners of her eyes, and she flung her arms around him. His other two sisters joined the hug.

Ryan chuckled. "Careful. I'm not made of steel."

"Ethan?" Chloe whispered.

"I—I'm sorry," Ryan whispered.

Jayden swallowed the lump in her throat. If Ryan had died too . . . The lump choked her again, and she squeezed Scout tighter.

"You could all use a good rest. Some of your wounds need tending to," Melanie said. She nodded toward Ryan. "You first."

Ryan backed away. "I'm fine."

Melanie cocked an eyebrow.

He touched the dried blood on his shirt. "I just pulled—"

In one swift motion, Melanie lifted his shirt, and Jayden gawked at the sight. Ryan's stitches were pulled, all right. Pulled clean out. Gone. Only a huge scar remained—healed. The uneven edge encroached on his birthmark like a dagger piercing it.

Above the scar were four small marks in the shape of a crescent moon—also healed—where the black lion's claws had dug into his skin.

Ryan swallowed. "I heal fast."

"That you do." Melanie let his shirt fall. Her brown eyes searched his face.

Logan's hand thudded on Ryan's shoulder. "Why don't you kids get some rest?

Ryan nodded, but avoided Jayden's questioning eyes. He headed to grab a bedroll.

Oh no, he wasn't going to just walk away without an explanation. Jayden followed him, and towed him farther away from the others. "What happened in there?"

His eyes met hers and his emotion slammed into her. Fear. Sorrow. Hurt. Why were they hitting her so freely? As quick as they'd come, every feeling winked out like he'd blocked them from her. His chest heaved. "You first."

Jayden closed her eyes and bowed her head as the pain gripped her insides. It was unfair to make him tell her what happened so soon. This was Ryan. He would tell her when he was ready. "I shouldn't have pushed you. I'm sorry. And I'm sorry about Ethan."

His finger grazed her arm. "I told you not to blame yourself. I'm the reason he was in this mess."

She looked up. "What do you mean?"

"I asked him to take care of you."

"What?" Her fingernails dug into her palms. How could he do that? Didn't he know about Ethan's sacrificial tendencies when it came to protecting his very good friends?

"When I was dying, I sent him a message. I don't know how, but I did. And I asked him to take care of you."

Now it all made sense. The connection, Ethan's commitment—he was just following his brother's wishes. Dying wishes.

Jayden's heart clutched. She leaned against Ryan. With her eyes closed, the scent of her mother's honeysuckle swelled in her memory. She could almost feel the warm summer sun and hear the cowbells clanking. He'd taken her back home, a place she could never go again. He would always remind her of home.

Ryan tucked a strand of hair behind her ear. "Do you believe what the queen said? About love being a weakness?"

She hugged him tighter, and his arms—his strong blacksmith's arms—gripped her back. "No. But I believe using any strength has its risks."

"But you're willing to take that risk now and let love protect you?" His breath heated her hair. "Like what your family did? Like what Ethan did, and I will continue to do?"

"Yes." And her love would protect him back. Always. "Exactly like that."

Dry twigs crunched. Jayden looked up from Ryan's chest to see Logan approach.

He handed her water and the satchel her mother had given her, and gave her a weak smile. "Chloe went back to the wagon for our belongings."

She clutched the satchel close. Idla had broken her necklace. This was the only thing she had left from her family.

Logan placed a warm hand on her shoulder. "We should put more distance between us and the palace. Idla might be dead, but she's not our only enemy. My camp is three days from here. I'll feel a lot safer when I get you kids home."

Home. Something warmed the numbness in Jayden's chest. That felt right. She may have lost so much now, but Ryan was right. She would persevere. Her mother had told her to survive; Ethan had given his life for her. She wouldn't waste their precious gifts. Anna had made her Destiny Path clear, even if she didn't want to believe it at the time.

She strapped her satchel to her back, grabbed Ryan's hand, and fell in line behind Logan. The love of everyone who had ever protected her would fuel her perseverance. She would save the Feravolk, no matter the cost. They were her family now.

Thunder rumbled in the distance. The next storm broke.

EPILOGUE

Connor's paws padded against the tunnel floor. The stench of blood and death hung thick in the air. A score of soldiers' bodies littered the ground, but he was only searching for one: Captain Tevont.

He crept closer to the carnage and his stomach tightened. Dead faces—faces he knew—stared back at him. It was more awful than he'd imagined. His mother might have sheltered him from battle, but he'd have to face it sooner or later. The deliverers were born for a time of war.

Sticky blood clung to his paw pads as he weaved his way through the bodies. Their milky-white faces and lifeless eyes made Connor's fur stand on end. He tried not to let his gaze linger on anyone.

A familiar form lay facedown in a dark puddle. More drying blood caked to Connor's paws as he stepped closer. After all this, the stone had better be in the captain's possession.

It looked as if no one else had disturbed the body. Anticipation pulsed in Connor's veins. He pressed his nose against the man's cheek and pushed. The cold, stiff flesh made Connor squirm. It wasn't natural for a human to be devoid of heat.

The dead man's head resisted his push. Connor thrust harder and forced the man's head to move. Clouded eyes stared back at him. A shiver raised all the hairs on Connor's body. It was the captain all right. Now where would he keep his untraceable seeing stone?

Connor nosed inside the man's pocket. His teeth gripped the edge of a handkerchief and he yanked it out. The white cloth was rolled tight around something. This had to be it. He lifted the corner of the handkerchief and shook his head slightly. The fabric unfurled. A *clink* resounded and something skittered across the surface of the floor. An object, small and hard, bumped into Connor's paw. The stone.

He scooped it up. It was dangerous to leave a seeing stone uncovered. Anyone watching through it could see him. But they wouldn't know where he was. That was the beauty of an untraceable one.

He placed it in the center of the handkerchief and pinched one corner of the fabric between his teeth. He draped it over the stone and gripped the next corner. After he'd folded the cloth around his prize, he picked the bundle up and headed back to find Rebekah.

A sound slowed his movement.

His ears swiveled. Footsteps—quiet and calculating—headed toward him. His heart hammered. No one could know he was here.

He headed back where he'd come from. There was no place to hide, not even among the dead. He glanced right at the pile of rubble from the tunnel's crumbled walls. The pile was dark—nearly black. He could hide there.

Jagged rocks shifted under his weight as he climbed. He balanced on them to keep any loose rocks from falling. Once he was high enough, he crouched low and pressed as close as he could to the debris. Then he watched.

The footsteps tapped closer. What if it was someone coming to find the stone? Would they see his paw prints? He should have been more careful.

A slender figure came into view. Thea? What was she up to?

Her eyes scanned the tunnel. He stopped breathing as her gaze traveled over his hiding place. She headed toward the wall. Was there another exit? Her palm pushed against the rock and a thick stone door grated against the floor as it opened. Evening light filtered in, but the soft yellow rays didn't touch Connor.

After one more look over her shoulder, Thea slipped into a Feravolk cloak, pulled the hood over her head, and headed outside.

Connor fought the urge to growl. Of course. She planned to follow the deliverer.

When she was out of view, he loped to the doorway. Anger burned in his chest. He itched to follow her, but a tug on his hind leg told him that if he stepped outside, he'd trigger the trace spell. Someone would know and hunt him down.

With Idla dead, there was no telling who would be alerted to his disappearance. His next task would be to find out who held the other end of his leash. Then he'd find a way to break it. No more being bound to the castle and sheltered from the world.

The door slid shut.

Connor bit down hard on the handkerchief and turned back. Maybe the stone would tell him where Thea headed. She also carried one.

His paw slipped on something wet. Stupid blood. A shiver rippled through him and he froze. All the other blood coating the floor was sticky. Could one of these soldiers still be alive? His heart pounded. No one could know he'd been here.

He set down the stone and sniffed. The blood trail led him close to the wall where another body lay. He recognized the face and his heart sank. This was one of the men who had protected the deliverer. There was no way he was alive—Connor just couldn't see Logan leaving his friend to die. Still, Connor dipped his head low and leaned closer to the body. He cringed, ready to feel the cold, stiff flesh of another dead man. His nose pressed against the young man's neck. The skin was . . . warm.

ACKNOWLEDGMENTS

Scarlet Moon would not be the story it is today without the encouragement and expertise of a number of amazing people, and I am eternally grateful to each of them.

I thank my God, who gave me the desire, talent, and creativity to make this story happen. Without Him, I would have a blank page.

To my wonderful husband for everything, including believing in me when I didn't believe in myself, when I did believe in myself, and all the in-between stages—thank you.

I thank my family: my dad, who read the very first version of this novel and told me to pursue writing because I have talent; my mom, who loves my characters as if they were her own ink and blood; my best friend, sister, and heart twin, who reads everything I write and helps me visualize my characters.

I also want to thank my amazing beta readers and critique partners, who helped me see what was working in those early stages and refine the story in the later stages (Dudie, Cilia, Evie, Cathy, NOF, Phil, Char, Dana, Avily, Lindsay, Todd, Kate, Tony, Jenn, Azalea, Terri, Katie, Kathrese, Loraine, Scott, Sarah, Karen, Amy, Cara, and Karin). Y'all rock so much!

Because people do judge books by their covers, I want to thank Kirk DouPonce—the cover is perfect.

To my awesome agent, Julie Gwinn, for all her behind-the-scenes help and encouragement—thank you.

I can't thank Steve Laube enough for believing in this book and bringing it to Enclave. The day he sent me a contract, dreams came true. And I might have cried.

And last, but never least, I want to thank my editors: the fabulous Ramona Richards, who really understood my characters and story and helped me uncover this final polished stage, and the amazing Ben Wolf, who took my unrefined story and helped me see the good, bad, and ugly so I could make it into something that turned the right heads.

Without all of you, *Scarlet Moon* might still be sitting on my computer as an unrealized dream. Thank you all so very much.

MEET THE AUTHOR ONLINE!

Website:	*sdgrimm.com*
Blog:	*sdgrimm.com/blog*
Facebook:	*www.facebook.com/SDGrimm*
Twitter:	*@SDGrimmAuthor*
Pinterest:	*@SDGrimmAuthor*

Look for Book Two: AMBER EYES
COMING SOON